LOST IN THE SUN

Lost in the Sun

Copyright © 2025 by Jared Glenn

Cover Design: Heather Nicole
ISBN: 979-8-218-76221-6 (paperback)

First Edition: September 2025

LOST IN THE SUN

JARED GLENN

For every love story that ended before it was over...

1

Five million dollars gave Chris the freedom to go anywhere, and yet he was going backwards. It was a lot of money, especially for a severance package, but not enough to ease the burden of his life's unmet expectations. Being squeezed into the middle seat of a cross-country flight was the tip of the discomfort iceberg. Chris Mitchell preferred movement, rarely sitting still for extended periods unless work called for it. But he'd been paid a fortune to clear out his office. And on a redeye from San Francisco to New York City, the harsh new reality ricocheted against every corner of his mind.

He was no stranger to the trip, nor the sense of restriction that accompanied it. He'd only done it so often to avoid further indignation from his mother. Going back home every weekend wouldn't have been enough to appease her, so they'd reached a compromise. He'd endure the trek for Mother's Day, Thanksgiving, Christmas, and her birthday. A typical visit involved landing on day one, spending time with the family on day two, and being on a return flight by dawn of day three. But none of those milestones fell in April. This was an involuntary one-way trip.

Chris was fleeing the city that had rejected him for the city he'd rejected. Like leaving a spouse for someone else, then coming back and being unsure how to confess he'd rather still be with his mistress. Such a domestic dilemma would've been preferable. But he had neither a wife nor a mistress. He was a forty-year-old man with as few connections as possible.

Without a better way to pass the time, he returned to an activity that had occupied him for weeks. He'd already filled out half of a crossword puzzle, read one chapter of a book, and watched the second act of a movie he still didn't know the name of. The flimsy tray table shook as he opened his laptop and typed his name into the search bar. There was nothing new to discover since he'd last done it at the departure gate, but the headline was as jarring as the first hundred times he'd read it: *Christopher Mitchell Ousted as CEO of Once-Promising Dating App.*

Various versions of the same headline couldn't affect him any more than sitting through the contentious board vote that had spurred them. He'd convinced himself he was numb to them. It didn't have to be true; he just needed to believe it.

"Sir, would you like a beverage?" asked a well-meaning flight attendant, interrupting his conciliatory process.

"Vodka cranberry," he said loudly enough to be heard over the heavy white noise in the cabin, without disturbing the reading woman to his right and the sleeping man to his left.

"Coming right up."

As the attendant handed over a plastic cup filled with more ice than drink, an elbow nudged him. The young woman's attention was now on him instead of her book.

"I'm sorry, did I hit you?" he asked.

She shook her head and pointed at his laptop. "That's you."

Chris returned to the screen as though unaware of what she was referring to. A three-year old headshot was prominently displayed beneath the headline. The photo featured a suit and a smile, of which were genuine at the time, and a stark contrast from the joggers and hooded sweatshirt he was currently wearing. "That's me."

Chris distracted himself with the first sip and wished ordering a bottle was an option if he'd be forced to stick around for wherever this interaction was headed.

"I go to Stanford Business," she said. He nodded without looking away from the plastic cup. "You spoke at my school," she continued, "you might not remember it."

He remembered it, but only because he hadn't done enough keynotes for them to be forgettable. The same headshot, currently attached to an article chronicling his downfall, had been on a posterboard outside of the venue, above a very different headline: 'I Don't Care' Isn't a Four-Letter Word.' In the brief silence, he tried to recite the opening salvo in his head. After a few lines, he'd wished his memory wasn't so clear.

"When you said, 'telling someone you don't care is a form of self-preservation,' it blew my mind. I wrote it down immediately. And I remember thinking 'that's such an odd thing to hear from a guy who started a dating app.' But you made it make sense."

"Thanks," he replied through a manufactured smile.

"Plus 'why lie now when you'll have to live with the truth later anyway' right?" The woman seemed pleased with her ability to recite the speech to its source. "I met my boyfriend on your app."

If she was waiting for Chris to be happy for her, it was going to be a while. "Good luck with that."

It didn't take much skill to monetize selfishness. Making people care less about each other was the American way. He'd aspired to a level of success that could rebrand self-centeredness as blind ambition. And now, he was returning to the suburban classroom that taught him why caring was complicated.

"Such a simple idea, I'm amazed no one else had ever thought of it before."

"So was I." It was likely the most genuine thing he'd say no matter how long the chat continued. Honesty on a dating app shouldn't have been a novel idea, but an app encouraging it in such a unique way had been a breath of fresh air. "People lie all the time about who they are, but not as much about the shows they like."

"Parks and Rec was the one that connected us." The woman latched on to his words before Chris could undo the mistake of fueling the conversation. He would've rather discussed anything else. And while no stranger to being rude, midway through a cross-country flight wasn't the best time to prioritize his own comfort. "And having our first date without either of us having to get dressed up or leave our apartments… chef's kiss." She said the words but held up the 'OK' symbol, puzzling Chris.

It was a good opening to close the discussion. "Happy to help."

"Never would've thought I'd see you in the back of economy. Shouldn't you be up front?" It had the cadence of a joke.

Chris tapped the screen with his forefinger, drawing her attention to the headline. "Probably not."

The gesture was enough to accomplish the mission. She smiled politely and returned to her book. It was hard to be dismissive and kill a conversation at the same time, but Chris had pulled it off — a justifiable homicide that made the weak cocktail taste a little bit better. After three more, he managed to nod off. It took the jolt of tires touching the tarmac to wake him.

Three suitcases kept Chris company as he watched the sunrise from the arrival terminal. A recognizable Ford Explorer pulled to the curb just as Chris had grown impatient with sitting again.

Greg slid out of the SUV, either too proud or too tired to care that he was, essentially, wearing pajamas. A rotund physique was wrapped in red flannel pants and a T-shirt that matched his Crocs.

"You look like shit," Greg snarked as he opened the trunk. His former business partner and college roommate was good at keeping him humble. They'd remained close despite only one of them taking a trip across the country when the app gained traction.

"Good morning to you too," Chris replied groggily in a raspy tone as they heaved his luggage into the trunk.

"Hey, you're the psychopath who decided to take an overnight flight. If you want me to pick you up this early, you're getting honesty."

"That's fair," Chris smirked. "For what it's worth, I do appreciate it."

"It'll be worth more after you treat me to some coffee. Get in the car."

For the thirty-minute ride, Chris got lost in the scenery, watching the congestion on the westbound side of the Southern State Parkway to his left and Long Island's dense greenery to his right. It was a ride he'd been on countless times, but it hit differently knowing it was more than just a visit. Greg stayed mostly quiet, a departure from his usual disposition. Maybe it was fatigue or being unsure what to say, two feelings the friends would've had in common. Neither man needed to rush to figure it out.

After relegating his corporate self to the dungeons of his mind, Chris worried about people anticipating a version of him that was long gone. He'd been willing to put on a show for brief visits, to appease his mother and avoid follow-up questions. But he could only hide for so long before the genuine Chris would make more than a cameo. The thought was enough to generate a sigh that Chris didn't expect to be so audible.

"I know it's not easy to see right now, but things will turn around for you. I know it. And I know I'm supposed to say that, being your friend and all. But this time, I mean it."

"You didn't mean it before?" Chris jested in an overt attempt to lighten the weight of Greg's words.

"I'm serious," he said as he stopped at a red light. "I know how badly you wanted to get outta here. But being back doesn't have to be a step backward."

"I wanna believe you. It's just —"

"Too soon?"

Chris nodded right away and slowly. "Yup."

"Well, don't let those west coast suits define you. Especially the kind of people who wear dress shoes without socks. You're better than that." Greg bumped Chris's shoulder twice with a heavy fist. "Take your time. Then dust yourself off and figure out your next move."

It was the right message. And Chris needed to hear it. But he wasn't ready to be mature about it. Not yet. After how hard he'd worked to build a company from nothing to something worth millions, just for a board he'd compiled to tell him he wasn't fit to lead it, it would take more than a timely credo to repair his state of mind. Being escorted from the premises, having his office belongings mailed to him, even the revocation of his parking pass — it all drove home the point that his keynote subject wasn't original. Selfishness was an acceptable form of currency in some circles. A lucrative separation package was a Band-Aid on a bullet wound; enough to allow time to chart the next leg of his life without feeling hurried to do so. But a life preserver is harder to feel good about when it's thrown by the people who'd tossed you overboard.

Bitterness temporarily shrouded Chris until they reached the upper-middle class suburb of Rockville Centre. The relationship with his hometown was complex. It never did anything bad to him. Worse, it never did anything at all. It was safe in every way, good and bad. It had a vibrant business district in the south of town, but was quiet enough at night that you could walk through any of its small local parks without seeing another soul. One could enjoy a fine dining experience or fast food, a movie or live music, all without leaving the radius of a few blocks. On its own, the place was perfect. But that didn't mean Chris belonged there.

As they turned onto Avildsen Avenue, Chris braced for the sight of the modest two-story structure he'd called home for the first twenty-nine years of his life. Every detail tethered him as soon as Greg pulled to the curb. The red of its bricks wasn't as red anymore. The black paint of the window panels had been chipped in the same places for years. The slate stone walkway stopped at two short steps, leading to a heavy black door with a simple gold knocker that was purely decorative. But one aspect was as vibrant as always. Chris wasn't sure how his mother still had the energy to do it, but the yard was pristine. Tall hedges flanked the porch, pastel hydrangeas and sunflowers sat in front of them, leading to thick, green grass that extended from a bed of red mulch to the sidewalk. It was one of two areas lush with color, the other located on the side of the house, where her more precious plants resided, and she could care for them in relative privacy.

Chris stepped out of the vehicle, careful to keep his attention on only his suitcases and the front door. There was more to see, but he wasn't prepared to look. The time would come for the two-story white colonial tucked in the corner of his eye.

Half-expecting his mother to be waiting, Chris was surprised he had enough time to fiddle with his keys before assuming, correctly, that the door was unlocked. No one on the short block ever locked their door unless they were on vacation.

After bringing two suitcases into the foyer, Chris peered around the corner leading to the kitchen, certain his mother would be there, elbow deep in one of the countless amazing recipes at her disposal. Ever since his father had passed away seven years prior, Barbara consistently pursued reasons to cook large meals. Chris couldn't fathom how much leftover food got thrown out every week.

"Mom! You home?!" Chris droned.

Behind him, Greg lumbered in with the last suitcase. "You need any help getting settled?"

"No, I got it."

"Good, because I didn't have time to help anyway. Gotta hit the gym before work."

"The gym?" Chris chuckled. "Is that a new bar in town?"

"Laugh all you want." Greg patted his midsection with both palms. "There's a six-pack in here somewhere. And I'm gonna find it. Not that your mom is any help."

"Excuse me?" Chris shot back.

"Well, someone has to eat all the extra food, Christopher," Barbara gleamed as she descended the nearby stairs. Despite her diminutive frame, her presence loomed over any room she entered. "You know I have no idea how to cook for one." Barbara wrapped her short arms around Chris before he could turn to hug her back. By the time she'd let him breathe again, joyous tears stained his sweatshirt.

"I'm back," he said into the bun of grey hair atop her head.

"What took you so long?" Barbara asked rhetorically as she pointed a stern finger at him.

Chris could do without making more of the moment than necessary. He didn't want to be coddled or watched over like some social experiment of anguish and acrimony.

"I wasn't flying the plane, Mom."

"You could've gotten here a week ago."

"I got back as soon as I could," he countered.

"You're not back." She cupped his face with both hands. "You're *home*," she emphasized with a kiss on each cheek. "Get yourself settled while I make breakfast. How's pancakes sound? Or a western omelet? Ooh, or maybe French toast?" She tied a floral-print apron around her waist, already preparing for her favorite activity.

Chris waited until she couldn't see him, then scoffed at the idea of a meal. He hurried one suitcase toward the base of the stairs to avoid facing more of her smothering attention. To decline food was to decline her love.

"All of those sound delicious, Mrs. Mitchell," Greg appeased. "But I'll have to take a raincheck this morning. I have to go to the gym."

"There's no need for lies, Gregory," she prodded, always taking on a motherly tone with her most frequent visitors.

"Good to know two of my favorite people on the planet believe in me," he said with a grin. "I've gotta run." He hugged Barbara then pointed at Chris in an overstated fashion. "I'll be back to check on you."

Chris nodded dismissively at the well-meaning comment, waiting until he heard the door shut behind him before rolling his eyes. His mother's attention would be enough to deal with. The last thing he needed was additional hovering eyes. His mother's vigilance was heavier than the first suitcase he'd begun hauling up the steps. Chris couldn't find a way to ask her to ignore him for a little while. Such a request would've been futile anyway. His mom, like any mom, would try to protect him even when they both knew she couldn't.

Chris wiped a bead of sweat as he reached the top of the stairs and turned left. The wheels of the grey Samsonite rattled along the creaking grooves of the aged hardwood floor. Upon opening his bedroom door, a familiar foreignness struck him. It smelled new and sterile, like his mother had taken enough bleach and orange-scented cleaner to every surface to render him unconscious if the door wasn't left open for a little while. He parked the suitcase in the doorway and sat on the edge of the full-sized bed. Its wooden frame still succumbed to his weight the way it had in high school, not helped by the nearly forty pounds he'd gained since being a scrawny teenager.

The long mirror on the closet door pulled his attention toward his reflection. It had been days since he could stand to look at himself. His face was drawn and dehydrated. His dark brown hair was messy and in need of a trim. A five o'clock shadow veered closer to a midnight silhouette and his skin needed more than just a shower to remove life's filth. He stood abruptly and roamed the room to escape his reflection.

Every wall held a story from a past he'd hoped to forget. The room hadn't changed as much as he'd needed it to, but he only had himself to blame. He'd spent so much of his twenties outside and in pursuit of a dream. Whereas inside, the bedroom remained a time capsule of his adolescent years, wrought with reminders of who he wasn't anymore. Magazine pages of celebrities he'd once admired had been turned into makeshift posters — the cover of the Marshall Mathers LP, a posed photograph of Neve Campbell, a page of Allen Iverson and Kobe Bryant smiling beside one another at an NBA All-Star Game. He cringed at how painfully typical of a kid he'd been.

The computer desk was a relic of its time, complete with an elevated corner for a monitor the size of a small TV set, and a rolling tray meant for a keyboard, back when you had to be home to be on the Internet. Above it, a corkboard with thumbtacks that once kept treasured photographs in place. Chris could, if he wanted to, remember every picture and why each one wasn't there anymore. The thought of a few once-forgotten images drove him toward the lone window near the foot of the bed.

Chris parted the white linen curtains and succumbed to the view. The spring weather was reviving every lawn, and each yard displayed its own personality. He worked his way from one house to the next, remembering what each had looked like while he was a teenager. Some neighbors had changed their siding, or added vinyl fencing, or rows of shrubs, or repaved their driveway. But one house, the last house before he couldn't see any farther, remained unchanged.

Chris had plenty of reasons to avoid his hometown, but none managed to hold as much influence as that house. The cliché of such a hangup made his skin crawl enough for him to swiftly close the curtains and return to the bed. He didn't enjoy being back in this house because, in addition to the litany of other reasons, it meant he could see her house. And he didn't want to see her house.

He didn't want to think about her.

2

Senada stopped pretending she hadn't been waiting for Chris's arrival. There was no one to impress with a convoluted display of resistance. With one hand parting the Venetian blinds of her bedroom window, and the other tapping through one song after another on a shuffled playlist, she endured the strained nostalgia keeping her attention across the street and three houses down.

She allowed it to ruin her morning routine, distracting her from the most basic tasks as she prepared for the day. The hazelnut coffee wouldn't be consumed until at least two stints through the microwave. Her shower had been twice as long as usual. Getting dressed had been delayed. But, as she looked out on Chris entering his residence, there was no song to scratch such an itch. She watched until he disappeared, then wondered how long it would take before he'd be willing to look out of his bedroom window and risk seeing her.

Silence was better, she realized. The playlist was turned off and the phone tossed onto the cotton sheets of her queen-sized bed. She moved her damp dark ash blonde tresses over one shoulder and returned to her open closet. The towel wrapped around her still-dripping-wet torso was the only protection against a gentle breeze flowing through the deep red curtains.

Senada could read his window like it was a language only she was fluent in. It was one of many ways they'd learned to communicate throughout an adolescence spent at each other's hip. Before they were old enough for long talks in his car, before they were allowed their own landlines, before AIM away status messages, they spoke through the lights of their bedroom windows. The houses were too far apart for audible conversation, but distance hadn't stopped them.

Early in their bond, dusk signaled the dawn of their most vital discussions. All she had to do was flicker the lamp and wait for him to respond in kind. It was all the signal she needed to sprint across the street and through his side door, often after an alcohol-induced tirade from a mother who resented her existence. Yet, nearly twelve years after their last conversation, she worried he may have forgotten their shared language. The man who'd just entered the Mitchell home may as well have been a stranger. There was no way to know if, beneath a reasonable amount of armor, the boy she'd once known was still in there somewhere.

Senada pulled her mind back to the present. Her closet had more jeans than dresses, more sneakers than high heels, and lots of vintage T-shirts. It was her luck that she could wear the same things to work as she would if she'd ever decided to have a life outside of her business. But working with dirt was more comforting than any occupation requiring a more professional dress code.

Resistant to anything that could be construed as typical, Senada chose an unconventional path whenever possible. There was something about how things were 'supposed' to go that made her want nothing to do with conformity. She'd had plenty of reasons, and she was surrounded by the memories of most of them. Her inherited home was the layover on her mother's guilt trip to whatever afterlife she might've believed in. It was the literal least Carrie Williams could do, especially after treating Senada like an interloper for thirty-one of the forty years since her birth.

Senada pretended not to see the messy pile of envelopes on her small, circular kitchen table while she waited for the microwave to reheat her coffee. When you've seen one 'past due' notice, you've seen them all. She didn't have to guess whether it was from the gas or electric companies, or the landlord demanding the rent for the space that housed her flower shop. She was late on all of them.

The hanging baskets and window boxes around the kitchen and adjoining living room were beautiful distractions from her concerns. They soaked up every beam of light that made its way through the windows, feeding the colorful blooms and green leaves.

A sudden tinge of discomfort stabbed her in the abdomen, making her flinch and prompting a droplet of coffee to spill from the travel mug and onto her shirt. The sensations, unlike her stress, were unpredictable. It was probably worth getting checked out, but she couldn't afford it in more ways than one. Senada hurried toward the beat-up Ford Econoline van waiting for her in the driveway, shaking off concern about the role a coffee stain might play in some hypothetical confrontation with her new neighbor.

The van barely had what it needed to run, but it was Senada's only hope of sustaining a livelihood. A turn of the key had a 50/50 chance of being followed by silence. It had become a not-so-fun game of its own. Senada would rest her head on the steering wheel in prayerful submission to the automotive triumvirate: the starter, the alternator, and the holy battery. Each time, it prompted a smirky smile, a subtle reminder of the day Chris taught her those terms. He'd taught her more than the words, but most of it hadn't been retained. When she was ready to be disappointed, she put the key in the ignition and turned. The van roared to life, ensuring at least one more ride.

With so many things on the brink, such small wins were momentous. She wouldn't often allow herself to get too high or too low, knowing something was always around the corner, waiting to pull her back to the mean. As if on cue, her phone buzzed its way off the dashboard and onto the floor of the passenger side. There was no hurry to retrieve it. She knew what the notification was. It usually arrived after a night with someone who didn't understand that when Senada said she wanted to share a connection, the 'temporary' was silent. A morning-after text was unnecessary, but like most gentlemen, he didn't get the memo, no matter how quickly she'd hurried him out of the house. Better to end the night before they caught their breath and realized at least one of them had made a mistake.

Senada never developed a strategy for how to handle the aftermath. She used to hope they would get the hint when her responses shrank by one word at a time. But most men could barely listen when she was speaking. She didn't have much faith in their ability to catch her hints.

As she drove past Chris's house, she stared straight ahead, irrationally aware of the possibility that he might catch her customary glance at the Mitchells' front door. With one hand on the wheel and the other inexplicably clutching her thigh, she pressed the gas harder and commenced the short drive to the shop. Breathing couldn't resume until she knew she was out of sight.

At a red light, the van's reflection in a bagel store window caught Senada's eye. The logo of her business, painted on the smoothest section of the white surface, was in dire need of a touch-up. The three pink flowers were still legible, even if no one could tell they were lilies. But she could no longer trust a passerby to make out 'Symbol of Symphony Floral Shop' in faded black calligraphy beneath them. The words would have to wait. It didn't matter what the side of the van said if it couldn't reliably run. And she couldn't make the money to fix the van without the van, especially since it doubled as her personal vehicle. It was the 'snake-eating-its-own-tail' kind of problem that defined her existence. She couldn't heal without hurting.

Senada parked in the alley behind the shop, already praying the engine would have the will to get her home at the end of the day. Silence welcomed her on the other side of the back door, along with the scents of treated water from automatic pump sprayers and freshly cut stems. Lex, the shop's only other employee, was most likely sitting at the front counter. But Senada wasn't ready to put on the required face for morning chitchat.

The shop' s showroom was modest yet vibrant, full of various flowering plants most people didn't acknowledge beyond their aesthetic. Senada was compelled by the meaning of every species in the store, but she was left catering to patrons who often did not share her enthusiasm. The customer area was decorated with what they'd expect, but she kept the more mean-ingful blossoms for herself, near the workspace in the rear of the shop. Her favorite flowers — dahlias, gardenias, morning glories — required more time and attention, like any other worthwhile thing.

Senada plopped onto the short wooden stool set before a permanently stained white cutting board at her makeshift desk. After a few deep breaths, she pulled a potted daffodil closer to her nose. It wasn't her favorite flower, but it stayed within arm's reach — a symbol of the grace she'd often forget to give herself. While deeply admiring its fragile yellow petals, Senada hadn't noticed she'd gained an audience.

"Hey!" Lex exclaimed too loudly for the early hour, startling Senada. "I heard someone come in and just wanted to make sure it was you."

"It's okay, don't worry about it." Senada's vision slowly sharpened on the white Post-It between Lex's fingers. She reached for it without a word.

"Two dozen roses, long stem. He was hoping they'd be ready by five. Wants the note to say 'Happy Anniversary' and his name."

"What, is he worried she'll be confused about which husband waited until the last minute to get her flowers?" Senada lamented sarcastically. "Thanks. Anything else?"

"Not yet. I told him we'd call when they were ready."

Lex stayed in the doorway, eyeing Senada with a demeanor far removed from the Alexandra she'd been when first arriving for her job interview a year earlier. To Senada, it was a badge of honor for a new hire to become comfortable so quickly. Lex moved a lock of curly hair out of her face. It was jet black, save for the dyed streak that was purple but would probably be different in a day or two. Lex's contrarian approach might seem forced on most adults, but Lex pulled it off in a style Senada admired.

"Are you alright? You seem a little… I don't know," asked Lex.

"That's exactly how I feel right now," Senada murmured as she rubbed both palms along her cheeks before pulling her still-wet hair into a taut ponytail. "Any other orders for today?"

"Uh, yeah." Lex hurried back to the counter before returning with another order slip. "I got a call from the wholesaler about six bags of high-end soil and two full trays of Impatiens, but the delivery address might be wrong. It's got your street but the wrong house number. I told them I'd check with you first."

Senada looked at the slip and handed it back just as quickly. "The address is correct. The delivery isn't going to my house."

"Gotcha. Sorry about that. I'll call them back right now." Lex hurried back to the counter.

It shouldn't have taken so long for Senada to realize how inevitable it would be to encounter Chris. While she'd spent days wondering when and how they might run into each other, she'd lost sight of the most obvious opportunity: she'd been largely responsible for maintaining his mother's garden.

"Lex, when did they say the delivery would arrive?!" Senada shouted toward the front of the shop, grateful for her angst being invisible from the counter.

"A week! Give or take a day!" Senada couldn't decide which would be better, but at least there was an idea of how long she had to prepare for a moment that was already overdue.

She was going to need more daffodils.

3

It took waking up for Chris to realize he'd fallen asleep. An unexpected midday nap ended up lasting longer than he'd slept in months. It wasn't spurred by typical fatigue. It was the kind of sleep that followed days without it. He was beyond familiar with the signs of depression.

Sitting up in bed, he struggled to see through the dry contact lenses he hadn't cared enough to remove. A delicious aroma crept through the half-closed door. After a few seconds of blinking, he recognized the time of day and the source of the smell: the sun was setting, and beef stew was on the stove.

The hallway floor creaked beneath his socks as he followed the familiar scent. It sounded the same as it had during his sleepless nights in high school. It was another on a growing list of ways the house had stayed the same. The framed photographs on the walls charted his adolescence from birth through college graduation. There were too many reminders of how far he'd gone while still ending up back where he started. He wasn't prepared to cope with such a realization, but the house doubled as a form of exposure therapy.

The stairs required a measured pace, mostly because he needed to find his existential bearings. One foot could no longer be trusted to end up in front of the other. When he reached the last step, a forgotten moment from a memorable night made him wish he'd moved faster. The last frame crushed his chest with the force of a sledgehammer. It hadn't been there during his two-day visit in December. Chris would've noticed before covertly taking it to the middle of nowhere, setting it on fire, and burying the ashes.

More treacherous than the photo's presence was the reminiscence it brought with it. It portrayed one of the best days of Chris's life, and Senada had been a vital part of it. She'd been a part of most of his days, for much of his life. Even while he'd been gone. Especially while he'd been gone.

Every memory shard reassembled in his mind, like a puzzle slowly coming to life. Two adults posed on the front lawn, smiling like they're preparing to go to a formal dance. Considering how awful their actual senior prom experiences had been, such a pose should've been an omen for how things turned out. He could remember Senada's laugh, the novelty of seeing her in a dress and high heels, and the way his tuxedo vest turned into a vise around his diaphragm as soon as he saw her.

Back when Chris was still hustling to get any investor to take his app idea seriously, he'd seized every networking opportunity he could find. A black-tie gala at Manhattan's Union League Club was the biggest chance he'd ever gotten. It was the kind of party worth crashing, yet he'd managed to be on the guest list. He hadn't given a second thought to who deserved to be on his arm for the occasion. Part of him was grateful for the work-life imbalance that had kept him chronically single. Taking Senada to such an event would've been hard to explain to a significant other.

Their younger selves looked back at him like they'd just been introduced. Her cheek gently pressed against his. His arm wrapped around the narrowest part of her waist. The fabric of her dress and the subtlety of her chamomile perfume still tinged his senses. It was the last photograph before their last shared mistake. Like most devastating decisions, its impact took time to set in. He'd wanted to get out of town for years, but by the end of the night, Senada had fooled him into reconsidering. Fond memories of their bond had been as difficult to bear as the way it ended.

"I thought I heard your footsteps," Barbara said, wiping her hands with a paper towel on her way toward him. "Ahh, you found my most recent discovery. Such a wonderful day. You looked so happy. Both of you. Two twenty-somethings still wearing that teenage joy."

"I remember, Mom." He didn't know how to appeal for silence or a subject change without sounding like an asshole, so he fled the scene and walked into the kitchen.

"I made your favorite," Barbara said as she followed close behind.

A large bowl of steaming goodness awaited him on the kitchen island. Barbara's homemade beef stew — chopped tenderloin, diced potatoes, carrots, and peas soaked in a mixture of broth and water — was not an innovative combination. But it was consistent and enjoyable, two traits all but extinct from the rest of his life.

Chris slid onto one of the four wooden barstools along one side of the island and peppered the stew's surface with soft, futile breaths. Barbara's cooking was worth rushing into. As he huffed through the first spoonful, he noticed he was eating alone.

"You aren't going to have any?" he asked quizzically, knowing she loved the stew almost as much as he did.

"I haven't had much of an appetite lately," she sighed as she hopped onto the stool beside him. "Plus, my doctor thinks I need to cut back on the red meat, the salt, pretty much everything in the stew that isn't a vegetable." She let out a single chuckle as though it were a coping mechanism for discomfort.

Chris took a stern tack. "What's going on that made the doc say that?"

"Nothing for you to be concerned about, hun. You have enough on your mind."

"Oh, that'll definitely make me stop thinking about it." He put the spoon down. "What's going on with you?"

Barbara placed a comforting hand on his forearm, enough to convey there was no path forward, so he may as well drop it. There was never any doubt where his stubbornness came from. "Eat, Christopher."

Chris powered through a few more steaming spoonfuls while she watched with a satisfied expression. He ate in silence for a few minutes before realizing she was watching him even more attentively than he'd grown accustomed to.

"What is it?" he asked through a mouthful.

"Sometimes you look so much like your father." She looked away, like there was something beyond Chris. "I always miss him. But sometimes, somehow… I find a way to miss him more than usual."

"I know," Chris replied in a way probably more comforting to his ear than in reality.

"What about you?" she wondered.

"What about me?" Chris girded himself against where the thread might lead.

"I just want you to know… you don't have to treat this like the worst thing that's ever happened to you."

"But it *is* the worst thing that's ever happened to me. What else could it be?!" His volume increased until it startled her, then he moderated his tone and kept his eyes on the stew. "I'm sorry… can we not do this right now? I knew this conversation was coming. But I just got back, and—"

"I'm just saying that maybe this is the best place for you right now," eased Barbara.

"How could this possibly be the best place for me?" Chris's volume went right back up as he put the spoon down and gestured around the room. "If it was so great, it wouldn't have taken my life blowing up to get me back here for longer than two days at a time."

"Your life hasn't blown up, Christopher," she cut in with tangible hope in her voice. "You lost your job. It happens. It even happened to your father. Some of the greatest—"

"I don't care who else it happened to, Mom. I care that it happened to me. I didn't get laid off from some factory. I lost the business I built from nothing. I lost the only thing that still mattered to me."

Barbara withdrew. "That's a hurtful thing to say."

"Don't do that. Don't make this about you. You know what I mean."

"That doesn't make it hurt any less," she said, barely above a whisper. "I thought I taught you to dream bigger than that."

"I started a multi-million-dollar company! It doesn't get much bigger than that!" he shouted, then reined himself in. "And then I got fired from that company. It doesn't get much lower than that."

"Alright, alright," she eased off.

Barbara stood and moved around the island, occupying herself with wiping surfaces that already looked spotless. "I just want to say one thing."

Chris resisted an eye roll by stirring the stew. "Go ahead."

"It may take some time for you to adjust to being back in a place you don't want to be, but that doesn't mean this place doesn't want you. Give it a chance to welcome you back."

Before Chris could rebut, he realized Barbara had a point, and that's why he couldn't agree with her. He'd always moved at full speed, making it easy to lose sight of the world around him and the people in it. But that was part of the reason he'd moved so fast for so long. Now, there was nothing left to distract him from the void that had pursued him for years. Everything he'd eluded was waiting for his return. He wanted to fight back, but there were too many opponents to choose from. The decision, unfortunately for Chris, didn't feel like it was only his to make.

"How is she?" The words sliced through his throat on their way out.

"How is who?" She offered a knowing stare.

"Mom."

"Don't 'Mom' me. You're a grown man. You want to know how she is? Go ask her. It's not a long trip."

Chris knew the answer but asked anyway. "You haven't spoken to her?"

"Of course I've spoken to her."

"But you can't just tell me how she's doing," he bemoaned.

"I can. But I won't. That's not fair to her."

"But I'm your son," he jabbed.

"It's not fair to you either," she replied as if expecting his rebuttal. "If you want to know how she's doing, but you aren't ready to talk to her… then you're not ready to know."

Barbara wasn't always so obvious about it, but she had a way of taking whatever you were most confident in, turning it inside out, then giving it back to you for a new perspective. Chris knew what she really meant, and he knew he wasn't ready. Pride might be the death of him, but a feeble version of it was all he had left.

"Go relax, Mom," he pivoted. "I'll clean this up."

Barbara removed her apron and hung it on a nearby hook. She kissed him on the cheek before making her way to the steps. Chris noticed her shuffling steps had gone silent, and he peeked over. She was taking another look at the photograph.

"Chris," she said as she turned toward him. "As far as I know, she's okay. But if she weren't, you're probably the only person she'd tell."

4

The crisp air of a spring night bathed Senada as she drove home with both windows down. The breeze would normally waft the lingering odor of the day's deliveries, but it had been a slow day. Instead, the van held the freshly grilled smell emanating from a boxed-up diner cheeseburger she'd been looking forward to since closing the shop. The six-pack of Stellas in another bag would pair with it perfectly. As stressed as she'd been all day, the night's coda would have to be the highlight.

At the final turn, Senada eased off the accelerator, drawn to the possibility of movement in the familiar bedroom window. Fond memories of the Mitchell residence made it hard to ignore in the morning. If the man beyond the window would be on her mind anyway, she figured, it made little sense to resist. Before a long night that would inevitably contain more of such thoughts, a little nostalgia was an apt appetizer for the entrée that awaited her.

The short stone steps of the front porch always caught her eye first, where many conversations were had on nights of similar serenity. They'd always felt like the most meaningful chats in the world, but every problem felt colossal when your world was limited to high school and home. The upstairs bedroom window pulled her in next, where a glow resided that hadn't been seen in a long time. It was her first confirmation that some things could still feel the way they once had. Behind those thin curtains was a bedroom she knew well enough to walk through blindfolded. Knowing he was on the other side of those curtains, beneath that glow and far away from her, only made the thought more difficult.

There was a time when that glow was all the green light she'd needed to sprint down the street, through the front door, up the stairs, and into that bedroom. Such freedom was hard to explain to any guy she'd tried to date in high school, but Senada had always brushed off such concerns. No matter how things played out with any potential boyfriend, Senada had been confident Chris would be around for longer than any of them.

Senada ran a firm palm along her forehead as she imagined some new woman walking up those steps, through that door, and up those stairs. One thing had changed — that confidence was long gone. The shudder of doubt consumed her until she pulled to a stop in the driveway.

As she exited the van, the final and favorite thing she couldn't ignore was calling out to her. All the way up the Mitchell driveway was a carport that lorded over a classic car beneath a plastic cover. Chris would roll his eyes nearly out of his skull if he knew she couldn't remember the model, but she knew it was a Chevy and filled with nuanced regrets. But she remembered the car more fondly, for its role in getting them around town from their junior year of high school until they'd graduated from their respective local colleges.

Senada ascended the steps, careful to ease through her front door. She really needed to sleep, but there was no chance of that happening if she didn't take time to relax first. And the path toward tranquility was littered with every bill she'd ignored in the morning.

It took over a year for Senada's home to become a reflection of her personality, and not a haven of bad memories and a worse mother. She was thankful to inherit it, and proud when she managed to keep the bank at bay after discovering it wasn't paid off yet. Her mother's idea of protecting Senada was pretending everything was fine until cirrhosis absolved her from owning the mistakes she'd made. Senada found out she was a homeowner on the same afternoon she'd learned there was another $140,000 to be paid.

The only act of resistance she could salvage was to change the way she'd related to the house, scrubbing it of any trace that another person had ever lived there. The space evolved into a vibrant home for Senada's creativity, depth, and emotion. The only areas that weren't adorned with oil paintings and landscape photography were decorated with various green plants. The new age exterior was camouflage for her appreciation of old-fashioned accessories. The long, brown leather couch was purchased at a Levittown garage sale, and her refurbished coffee table was pirated from a curb in East Rockaway. Her most modern possession was a 70-inch flatscreen TV that she couldn't be happier to have on the wall whenever exhaustion had won the day. Television had been a welcome refuge from the sound of her mother's drunken tirades and one of the things she'd bonded with Chris over. The pairing of such opposed experiences was not a coincidence to Senada.

For a brief stretch of the late nineties, Senada had a lot in common with many American teenage girls. She would imagine living 'down the creek' with Joey Potter and sneaking across the street to hop through the window of her Dawson. Luckily, she didn't need a ladder. Chris's parents had become so welcoming of her frequent presence, she could walk through the front door at any hour of the day or night without much fanfare.

Senada kicked off her Crocs, cracked open the beer on the table's edge, and curled up cross-legged in front of the aluminum container that held her dinner. As soon as her back touched the leather of the couch, so began the deceleration of her nervous system. She sifted through the waiting envelopes, deciding who would be paid and who would be left waiting for another month. After telepathically paying the bills that she couldn't actually afford, she decided not to wallow through an uneventful evening.

The first sip of beer paired well with the first bite of burger. It was rare and satisfying when a craving met expectations. In that regard, food was more reliable than people. And even if someone met expectations, it opened her up to disappointment. Whether it was the latest tryst or the next one, Senada wasn't interested in giving anyone else the chance to hurt her. She didn't need anyone's help to do that. All it took was sitting with her thoughts for a little while.

Any battle against her own psyche was exhausting. She could blame her state of mind on finances, but it was only the most convenient excuse. The lonely life she'd created was a reminder of how it felt to share an experience. Between her business and her bills, there wasn't much room for herself. Chris's return was a memento of what she'd forgotten she wanted, and worse, a reminder of how she'd lost it.

Since first realizing Chris had left town, Senada had googled him almost every day. Every high and low was on display in front of the digital world and, in her own way, she'd experienced them, too. She'd wanted him to succeed in every way he'd always hoped, in every way he'd shared during countless sleepless nights contemplating their futures: going IPO, a Fortune 500 listing, and retiring by fifty. All born from an epiphany he'd had about how much they loved watching TV.

Hurting Chris was never a part of those plans. It just happened along the way. For years, Senada had talked herself into and out of calling him. Despite desperately wanting to explain, she knew the more she tried, the more it would hurt him. The words hadn't done him in — it was the speaker.

Her only solace came from knowing she didn't have to wrestle with the decision anymore. Their paths were bound to cross, sooner or later. Neither of them could avoid it forever, though she wondered if that was what he'd prefer. She couldn't control that. All she could do was be prepared for when the moment arrived.

As impatient as she was to rip off the band-aid, a refractory period was probably needed. Given how things had turned out for Chris, he might be even less inclined to see her, let alone engage in an honest conversation about where things stood. He epitomized so much good to her, yet she likely represented the opposite for him.

Senada already had enough regrets to last a lifetime. Getting too close to her best friend was the kind of thing that shouldn't be possible, but she'd found a way. If she could get back any of what they'd once shared, she would jump at the chance. It was worth the risk.

Senada was doing the opposite of relaxing, unintentionally working herself up instead of winding down. She turned on the TV, not sure what to watch and with little desire to find out. After ten seconds of watching the home screen, she turned it off.

Music was her natural next step. She cued up one of her many playlists and sipped beer as she scrolled through her choices. A viola-cello duet deserved her attention. A symphony played, reverberating through her consciousness. Senada took a long swig as she closed her eyes and allowed the music to have its way with her. Her head and shoulders swayed with the subtle rhythm, as the walls of her emotional fortress came tumbling down.

By the time she'd realized she could use a good cry, the tears were already falling. They flowed so freely, yet she couldn't pin down exactly what she was grieving. The vagueness pulled her from the couch and spurred frantic movement in hopes of combatting the waterworks. Just because the tears needed to fall didn't mean she had to let them. She switched back to consuming sustenance, finishing the burger in a whirlwind and immediately regretting she hadn't bought two.

Snacking had always been a reliable outlet for her nervous energy. Her mother credited some form of dark magic for Senada's ability to eat constantly and never gain a pound. But Senada didn't feel so lucky as the deep pain from the morning slowly returned. Given Senada's diet, it wasn't alarming. Nothing a Zantac couldn't fix, but not worth venturing back outside to buy some.

Once her eyelids got heavier, she made her way upstairs. The bedroom door and Senada groaned in unison as she noticed the lamp she'd left on all day. The oversight could be chalked up to a morning of distraction. The light illuminated the vanity, prompting more thoughts of a long-lost friend.

The tall mirror's cherrywood frame was lined with three-by-five photos, a sight most modern teenagers wouldn't recognize. It was a relic of a time when memories required a lot more effort to hold on to. The pictures were as vibrant as they'd been when she'd retrieved them from the Kodak kiosk at the local pharmacy.

Each image encapsulated a core memory. Chris wasn't in all of them, but he was in the best ones. Their bond didn't thrive at the homecoming parades or the Saturday night parties that followed football games. One photo captured the day they'd spent walking on a beach in the Hamptons after speeding through the night to catch the rising sun. They weren't selfies back then — just Chris extending an arm and hoping their faces were in the frame when he pressed the button. Another photo was just her exuberant face, half-covered in ice cream; a mundane snapshot to anyone who didn't know it was the day they'd celebrated their respective college acceptances. Chris could've known a week earlier, but he'd waited until hers arrived, even going so far as to hide his letter from his parents.

Senada reached for a slightly hidden shot on the bottom right corner of the frame, pulling it closer as she rubbed dried tears from her cheeks. She shimmered while remembering the night depicted: Chris and Senada, posed together outside the Union League Club. An eager usher had taken it with her cellphone. After Chris left, Senada went the extra mile to have it printed. It was still a night worth commemorating. Neither of them could've known it would be the last photo of who and what they used to be.

5

There was something about depression-induced sleep that was worse than staying awake. Chris had grown tired of being fooled into thinking he was resting, only to wake up in the middle of the night, more fatigued than before. Finding out depression could be hereditary didn't make things any easier, but it made them make sense. After years of blue-collar work, James Mitchell hadn't possessed any valuables to bequeath to his son. As a teenager, Chris could tell their modest life was a weight on his father's shoulders. James did the best he could to pass down what he knew. Coincidentally, the most vital thing he'd taught his son was how to hide pain from the world.

Chris snuck down to the kitchen, hoping to avoid waking his mother and, with her, a slew of questions about why he wasn't asleep. He'd chased a handful of salt and vinegar chips with a mealy apple before settling on a stout beer. The longer he went without sleeping, the more worried he became about not sleeping, then the more nervous he became that he wouldn't get any sleep — a vicious cycle he'd identified, but it still managed to frustrate him.

Chris lingered on beams of blue moonlight and the way they glided through the windows. It made sense to turn on a light, but the brightness would kill any slim remaining chance of going back to sleep before the sun came up.

As he approached the window for a better look at the full moon, a relic of his adolescence caught his eye: his high school pet project, parked beneath the carport and cloaked by a beige plastic cover. Chris knew more than he'd ever need to know about cars, and he learned most of it from his father, using a 1979 Chevy Nova as a classroom. Chris would bring home good grades and get a pat on the back. But if he'd ever really wanted to make a good impression, it would happen under the hood of the Nova. Restoring a car required qualities that Chris had taken for granted until it was too late to thank his dad. Both men knew how to set a difficult goal and see it through.

The day before his junior year of high school had begun, after restoring it from a hapless junker, Chris had finally completed the revival of the symbol of automotive ingenuity. He'd never seen a wider smile on his dad's face. The car represented more than a mode of travel. Leaving it behind was a decision Chris had wrestled with for a long time. If the Nova could've handled a cross-country road trip, Chris surely would've driven it to California. But despite the renowned ego he had at that time, he wasn't *that* optimistic about his handiwork.

The vehicle demanded closer attention. Chris pondered how much time, effort, and money it might take to return the Nova to its former glory; he had more than enough of two out of the three. But getting it running again wasn't a given, even with his skill.

Muscle memory propelled him toward a hook near the side door. He retrieved the key and stepped outside in a single smooth motion, but was unsure what to do once he stood beside the car. Hearing the engine rumble to life again might work miracles for his spirits. But it was a lot to ask of a vehicle that was older than its owner. And in its heyday, a turn of the ignition risked waking up the entire block.

He removed the cover at a measured pace, taking in the deep burgundy paint job one foot at a time. The exterior was still in good condition, due in no small part to Jim's maintenance over the years. When Chris left, he didn't need to ask his dad to keep an eye on the car. The recently retired patriarch was bound to be in search of ways to occupy his time. It would've been easy for James Mitchell to sell it to one of the countless car collectors along the South Shore of the island. Maybe he kept it as an insurance policy, in case his entrepreneurial failure of a son ever came back for it.

There hadn't been much need to acknowledge the Nova during his previous visits. The trips had been too short for detours down memory lane. Nostalgia wasn't just an emotion Chris couldn't afford to have; it was an attachment he didn't want. The longer he'd stay, the more things, places, and people, he'd be forced to remember. And if he'd sold the car, the remaining void would've been even more prominent.

The door lock welcomed the key like a forgotten friend. It took both arms and plenty of strength to open the door before the odor of untouched leather and stale air roared back at him. He descended into the stiff driver's seat and soaked in the perspective from behind the wheel. The car was a suburban tank, constructed to prioritize housing an enormous amount of power beneath its hood.

The steering wheel was worn from years of his tight grip, and his hands still managed to fit in the grooves. The leather was cracked and creased. The floor mats had seen better days. The dome light didn't turn on. But every flaw fueled an intrigue around what could be resurrected. For a few minutes, a car succeeded where every other distraction had failed. He forgot why he was back home, because he'd forgotten he ever left.

Finally, Chris wasn't being pulled one way or another. There wasn't a right or wrong direction. He had nowhere else to be and indulged in the freedom that came with such circumstances. He leaned as far back as the seat allowed and consumed the cold beverage in measured sips. If it were possible to recall the last time beer tasted so satisfying, Chris wasn't going to waste the moment trying to remember.

The empty passenger seat silently called out, like it was hoping to conjure its most frequent occupant. But Chris declined the call. To acknowledge the empty space, meant to look in the direction of her house again. He wanted to believe in 'out of sight, out of mind' but, like most idioms, it was as sterile as it was catchy. Sometimes, the harder you tried to force a memory out, the deeper it buried itself.

Senada was inescapably linked to the Nova. She was more than its most frequent passenger. It was as much a part of their friendship as either of them. He would drive the forty yards from his driveway to hers as if it were across town. Senada would occasionally top off the comedic commute by handing him a dime for gas money. Whether it was to pick her up for school or a late-night diner jaunt or a movie at the Farmingdale Multiplex, the Nova got them to and through anything worthwhile. He thought of how many nights they'd laid a thick blanket across the car's hood and watched the stars. Deep conversations had been their favorite pastime, and they usually occurred on the hood. Regardless of the occasion — something to celebrate or something to complain about — by the end, one of them was talking the other out of packing the car and speeding out of town. Senada had almost convinced him once, on a night when her mother found a way to be more horrible than usual. They'd gotten all the way to the Verrazano Bridge before Senada stopped crying long enough to ask Chris to turn the car around. They had so much to run from, but only he had escaped. She'd always been stronger than him. It was one of the many qualities he loved about her, but he never figured out how to assure Senada that, with him, she didn't need to prove it.

Such a conscious insight would've been more useful during their last conversation, when she shattered any hope they had of finding out what could've been. No matter how many people assumed they were dating, including his parents, they'd always been just friends. Senada was his closest confidante, his lighthouse amid the storms life would bring. He knew she loved him, just not in the way he loved her. Until that final night, they'd never said it out loud. They'd never really needed to acknowledge it at all. Falling for her was an accident, and Chris learned a valuable lesson from the mistake: implied love wasn't the same as explicit love. When the word traveled from one's mouth to another's ears, things changed. They had to, no matter how much he'd tried to prevent it. He thought there was no way he could stumble, but he ended up flat on his face.

Chris took a long sip as if the cold beer could ease the burning sensation in his chest. The wound proved to be deeper than he knew. It was as exasperating as it was painful. If moving across the country didn't fix it, what the hell could? Chris did every single thing he'd read on the Internet about how to get past someone. From meditation to social media blackouts, to cutting visits short just to resist the urge to 'run into' her. Living with it was the only thing he hadn't tried.

Once a haven for his hopes, the car transformed into a tomb for the pieces of himself that he'd never get back. Senada had changed more than their friendship. She'd changed his relationship with love itself. Connecting with anyone beyond a cursory level had become a wasted hope, discarded by the person he'd trusted most with his heart. No one should hold so much power, but Senada knew she had it and hurt him anyway. It was the only time she'd ever made him regret being honest with her. A juvenile side of Chris wanted to walk down the street, bang on her door, and wake her up just so he could lie to her. Maybe it would make him feel better, but any gratification wouldn't last long enough to make such a sacrifice worth his remaining dignity.

The same mistake he'd been lamenting for a half-hour had just repeated itself: he'd made an impulsive decision without thinking of the consequences. Checking out an old, beat-up car from his childhood wasn't worth the emotions that came along for the ride. He departed the vehicle, slammed the door behind him and poured the rest of the beer onto an empty patch of dirt. More awake than before, Chris surrendered to sleeplessness and went back inside. Staring at the ceiling for a few hours had to be better than looking backwards for another second.

40

6

A surge of business relieved more than Senada's bottom line; it provided some peace of mind. It wasn't enough to get her ahead of the bills, but she wouldn't fall further behind either. May's turn toward warm weather invited local residents to repopulate their home gardens, celebrate their mothers, and plan for the upcoming wedding season. Though, Senada's favorite spring pastime was providing floral arrangements and corsages for the Spring Dance at her old high school. Roses and carnations of every color imaginable were flying out of the shop and onto the lapels and wrists of teenagers eager for the preamble to the prom.

Of Lex's many appreciable qualities, Senada was most grateful for her shared interest in the symbolism and meaning attributed to every flower. They weren't just rushing around the shop in every direction putting together bouquets for the sake of making money. Few things had such an immediate and transformative effect as unexpected flowers. Though even when they were expected, the act lifted the spirits of the giver and the receiver.

Lex blared a Paramore playlist from the Bluetooth speaker at the front counter while they ping-ponged around the store and each other. The floor of the work area was littered with snipped stems and errant petals. Senada found brief fulfillment while putting the finishing touches on the last of twenty long and low arrangements. She couldn't wait to see the faces of the South Side High School prom committee when they picked up the table centerpieces in a few hours.

"Stunning as usual," Lex exclaimed as she stopped to take a load off. "My feet are killing me. How do you manage to do this without keeling over from exhaustion?"

"Practice," Senada winked.

"I guess the better question is how you managed to do all this with a smile on your face the entire time."

Senada eased onto a stool and admired the fruit of hours of labor.

"I don't know. This kinda work, it's why I opened the shop, ya know?" Senada ran a finger across a lilac, appreciating its delicacy. "It makes me miss a time when this was all we had to worry about. No bills, no drama, no bullshit. When the world was so small a problem didn't have to potentially ruin your life for it to be the biggest thing in the world. But with every corsage I box up, or every flower I put in some ecstatic girl's hair, I'm reminded of how special that time can be. A time before the world could touch us."

Her voice tapered to silence at the acknowledgment of the ways the world had gotten to her. While Senada often wished she could, it was hard to separate her passion for flowers from her upbringing. When Senada's mother wasn't tearing her down or drinking heavily, she was caring for plants. No matter how hard Senada tried to blossom into something worthy of her love, the affection was rarely delivered. Years later, Senada was still searching for the love she didn't think she was meant to have. It was easier to pretend not to want it at all.

"If we let ourselves forget, we won't have those memories when we need them most," she added, buckling under the weight of the words.

"If you say so," Lex chortled.

"You didn't enjoy high school?"

"I had a great time in high school, but none of that great time involved anything that called for tuxedos, evening gowns or, well… flowers. So those 90s movies about high school were like documentaries to you, huh? 'She's All That'… 'Can't Hardly Wait'… that one with the cheerleading, uh —"

"Alright, now you've gone too far. I wouldn't've been caught dead in a cheerleader outfit." Senada barely got the words out before both women doubled over with laughter.

The hanging bells at the front door chimed, yanking them back to alertness. "Of course," griped Lex, "just when I'm catching my breath."

"I can handle it if you want to chill out for a minute," Senada offered.

"Nah, I've got it. You probably need a minute or two while you swoon over Freddie Prinze, Jr. or something."

"Couldn't be any further from my type! *Way* off!" Senada shouted as Lex retreated to the front. "And whatever they want is probably gonna take a while. We're swamped."

Alone with her thoughts, Senada exhaled months of stress into the air above her. A strange contentment flowed with it. Not quite happiness, but better than whatever she'd been lately. While it might've been fleeting, that didn't make it any less enjoyable. Some things are special because they're temporary. Senada shifted her weight and winced as another stabbing sensation slalomed across her midsection. The pain's return heightened her concern because she hadn't eaten anything yet. She brushed it off as a later problem, not a now problem. Senada didn't have the time to worry about something as arbitrary as her physical well-being.

When Lex turned down the music, Senada could hear the customer speaking. The voice was gentle, light, and familiar. Senada walked toward it without deciding to.

"There she is," Mrs. Mitchell said with faux surprise as Senada stepped around the counter and hugged her, careful to keep her soiled apron from touching Barbara's bright orange sundress.

"What are you doing here? Was something wrong with the delivery?"

"Actually, there was. Something was missing." Barbara wore a grin that betrayed a deeper meaning. "I would've said something sooner, but I figured I'd give it a week to show up."

Senada's expression swung from curious to somber while she folded her arms and tried to decide which foot could best carry her weight. "I've been really busy."

"You've never been any good at lying." Mrs. Mitchell pinched the flesh of Senada's forearm as if it were her ten-year-old cheek.

"I just… I'm not sure it's a good idea for me to plant your flower bed this year," Senada confessed.

"Sounds like a good idea to me." There wasn't a hint of doubt in Barbara's voice. "Look at me. Do you expect me to get on the ground and do it myself?"

"No," Senada chuckled before switching to an uncharacteristic timidness. "I thought you might already have some help."

"Ah, I see."

Senada was suspended in the air of silence, feeling a spotlight on her.

"If my garden ran on gasoline, he'd be great help. But you know his thumbs aren't green. They're grey." Laughter was pulled out of Senada, leaving Barbara with a glint of accomplishment on her face.

"I really don't think it's a good —"

"Listen." Barbara became more direct. "I don't want to pretend you aren't an important part of my life, too. And you don't have to pretend either."

Senada nodded slowly, unsure if she agreed but unwilling to admit uncertainty.

"Do me a favor, hun." Barbara wrapped a hand around each of Senada's shoulders. "At least, think about it. Worst case scenario, I don't have a flower bed this year."

"High stakes," Senada snickered, happy to elicit a smile from Barbara. "Alright, I'll think about it."

"Thank you," Barbara beamed as she turned to leave. "And when you make up your mind, remember to bring some Miracle-Gro soil."

The chimes were a little louder on her way out the door. Senada turned to the sight of Lex's quizzical stare.

"You never mentioned Chris was back," said Lex. "Like, *back* back."

"I have a hard enough time thinking about it, let alone talking about it."

"If not talking about it makes you give our best customer the cold shoulder, I am happy to be all ears," Lex ranted. "Because we can't afford for you to be avoidant. We need to find you a different coping mechanism."

"It's not a… I just don't think there's a right way to handle it," Senada couldn't decide which word most deserved to be in air quotes. "I've been a little messed up about it."

"It's understandable to be messed up over a situation like that. Especially with a close friend."

"It's been years since I could call us close. Or friends," Senada said with palpable resignation.

She walked past Lex and both women returned to their workstations. Lex turned the music back up and Senada turned it off just as quickly. Lex filled the silence anyway.

"Have you thought about reaching out? Talking to him?"

"What the hell kinda question is that? Of course I've thought about it." Senada was as shocked by her sudden snippiness as Lex appeared to be. "I'm sorry, it's just… there's a lot to the story and it does something to me every time I tell it out loud."

"I've heard the story a hundred times by now." Lex slowed her approach. "But if you need to talk, I'm fine with hearing it again. Even if the nineties already overdid the unrequited-feelings-between-aloof-friends trope," she winked.

"The feelings were very much requited."

Lex spun around instantly. "Plot twist! You never mentioned that part before."

"Yes, I did." Senada portrayed confidence, but inside, she questioned if she'd subconsciously held back the detail.

"I would remember hearing that. You told me about growing up together, about the party, about what went down in the limo, and —"

"Lex... please."

"Right right, sorry," Lex regretted. "So... he loved you. I've got that part right?"

"Yeah."

"And you loved him?"

"Yes," Senada breathed.

"And *that* ended your friendship?" Lex attempted to do the math. "That's where you lost me."

Senada turned her attention back to the flowers on her station. "Me too."

7

If Chris possessed a special skill, it was an ability to recognize a pattern. It's what made him innovative enough to revamp the way lots of people approached dating. Something was missing and he could usually tell what it was. And as they sped along Sunrise Highway, Chris knew, at any stoplight between Rockville Centre and Merrick, Greg was bound to fill the silence with something. That was his pattern.

"I'm gonna go ahead and assume there's a direct relationship between how early you asked me for a ride and how much better you look than the last time I saw you."

Greg had used the wrong equation to reach the right answer. Chris was still either sleeping like shit or not at all, but he'd grown tired of having nothing to do. Work had consumed much of his life for years, and the void needed a new occupant. Either he could find a new job — unlikely, given how uninterested he was in working for someone other than himself — or he could find a new hobby. Since he'd been struggling with looking backwards, it made the most sense to transform his past's most prominent symbol.

"I'm tired of sitting around the house. I need something to do," said Chris.

"And of the all the options at your disposal, you're going with this one?" Greg's retort was timed perfectly with their arrival at Colvin Motor Parts, a staple for classic automotive enthusiasts throughout much of Long Island. "Why can't you act like most millionaires and pay someone to do this for you?"

"I'm not a millionaire."

"The Internet says otherwise. And if it's on there, you know it's true," Greg jeered. "I wish I could get paid a few million dollars to stop working."

"That's not exactly how it went down."

"For that kinda money, it can go down however it wants."

The banter was enough to coax a giggle out of Chris as the car came to a stop in a parking space near the entrance.

Colvin Motors was a reliable and trustworthy place for classic car parts. Housed in a red brick building with a rickety, hand-painted sign, the shop was archaically simple. Every employee specialized in a particular area, from paint to transmissions to tires to interiors, and they loved cars as much as anyone Chris had ever met. It was customary for to at least one car to be parked outside as a beacon of what could be accomplished. A cherry red 1957 Corvette sat two spaces away, too perfect for either man to dare approach for a closer look. They admired it from afar as Chris led the way inside.

An electronic bell chimed as soon as they entered. It was probably the most modern amenity in the store. The place smelled like old paint and metal shavings, with a consistent film of dust on every surface. The aisles of wooden shelves held various small parts for general use, inside of cardboard boxes with their tops sliced open to reveal the contents. A steel grate acted as a cage, behind which was every aerosol one could possibly need, from battery cleaner to compressed air. Behind the counter, several silver-haired gentlemen tended to customers. Chris stepped in line behind three other men, knowing it might be an eternity before he reached the counter. With every purchase, a long conversation was often included. It was a personal touch that made Colvin such a heralded institution in the tight-knit fraternity of restoration specialists.

"Alright, man," started Greg, "there's something I've been dying to ask you. And you've been back for long enough that I'm not worried about pissing you off."

Chris sighed and groaned at the same time.

Greg shifted his weight as if preparing for an attack. "Why did you come back here?"

"What do you mean?"

"Don't get me wrong. I'm glad you're back, even though you haven't made much time for your old college pal yet. Plus, your mom's cooking goes up a notch whenever you're home." Greg cleared his throat as they moved one step closer to the counter. "Look, I deal with wealthy people all the time. I know how they think. And now that you're one of them —"

"I'm not weal—"

"You are, but that's not the point. Let me finish." Greg placed a firm hand on Chris's shoulder. "Shouldn't you be shacked on the Amalfi Coast with some Swedish supermodel who's a head taller than you? Or at least still on the west coast? You got five million dollars and then left the best place to have five million dollars!"

Chris pressed a finger to his own pursed lips, prompting Greg to remember their surroundings. On the surface, Greg had asked a reasonable question, and Chris had thoughts of embracing the midlife-crisis energy of it all. But it would've amounted to covering the same wounds with fancier bandages.

"I didn't hit the lottery, Greg. I lost my fuckin' job. There's nothing to celebrate."

"Fair, but there are better ways to stem the bleeding than starting a greasy restoration with summer right around the corner."

"Can I get my feet under me again before you start telling me how to spend my time?" Chris sensed rising defensiveness in himself and wanted to blunt its harshness. "I'm not one of your wealthy clients, man. I'm the same guy you've always known, with a little more money in my bank account."

"Does that mean you'll lend me a few dollars for old time's sake?" Greg sneered. "It'll be just like undergrad."

"In undergrad, you were working at Foot Locker, not in private equity," Chris jabbed back, reminded of what life used to be.

"I'll take the next customer over here!" a gravelly voice bellowed.

Chris turned toward the sound and left Greg behind to approach the counter. The man's gaunt face and long, grey beard caught Chris's attention right away.

"What can I do for ya, son?" the man grunted with an off-white smile.

Chris pulled a folded sheet of paper from his pocket. "I've got a list of parts here. Everything is for a '79 Nova."

The gentleman pulled hanging spectacles to his nose, and scanned the list, occasionally humming in the process. Chris looked beyond the employee to watch a few young apprentices dash around the warehouse area, likely in search of whatever an elder expert had requested.

"We've got most of this in-house," the man interrupted. "Some of these'll have to be ordered. We can send 'em to your home or we can let ya know when they come in and you can pick 'em up." He looked up from the paper and squinted at Chris. "Have we met before?"

Chris suddenly felt foolish for believing he'd get in and out of Colvin without someone recognizing him. Car enthusiasts had elephantine memories for more than just the proper oil filter for an 80s Dodge Daytona or the best spark plug for a 350Z. There hadn't been enough time for Chris to be forgotten.

"I used to come here a lot with my dad," begrudged Chris.

The man kept spinning his wheels until his face lit up. "Jimmy Mitchell! You're Jimmy Mitchell's boy, aren't you?!"

Chris nodded tensely as he plotted an escape.

"Russ, get a look at this! Jimmy Mitchell's boy is at the counter!"

In seconds, a slightly younger man with a shorter beard and a long pony-tail of brown hair with traces of grey, emerged from the storage area. "Whadja say, Lonnie?"

"This is Jimmy Mitchell's kid! Remember Jimmy?"

Chris waited uncomfortably while the new entrant processed the image and combed his memory banks. Russ's face then matched Lonnie's. "I'll be Goddamned. It's good to see ya, kid!"

"Thanks." Chris was drowning in a mixture of unwanted attention and embarrassment. "Can you have someone bring the stuff out to the car?"

"Yeah, yeah, sure, of course," Lonnie brushed it off in a way that made Chris wonder if his request was actually being filled, or if they'd gotten lost down a nostalgic rabbit hole. "Russ, remember Jimmy used to come in here all the time with this kid years ago. Teachin' the brat the ropes of being a grease monkey. Ended up becoming a big-time businessman. How bout that, huh?"

"Yeah, and then he kept comin' back for wax and touch-up paint. Always goin' on and on about how proud he was of ya," added Russ. "How long ya been back?"

"A few weeks or so," Chris replied. "Just wanna get some stuff for the Nova and be on my way if you don't min–"

"Damn is that the same Nova Jimmy was goin' on about twenty years ago?" Russ reflected. "One thing about Jimmy, he was sentimental. I tried to take it off his hands when you left, but he wouldn't even hear my offer."

"Mine neither," Lonnie chimed in. "You plannin' on bringin' the ole girl back to life?"

"That's the plan, if I can get the stuff on this list sometime." Chris didn't enjoy having to move things along, but they'd forced his hand.

"Oh, yeah, yeah, we'll take care of ya," Lonnie replied, aloof to Chris's frustration with their nostalgic detour. "Russ, have one of the kids fill this and bring it out front."

Chris pulled out his bank card, hoping to expedite the process rather than leave room for another delay. After typing into what appeared to be an antique computer, Lonnie came back with a verdict.

"That'll be $4,345.87, altogether," he said as if disclosing a secret. "How do you wanna handle it?"

Chris silently handed him a credit card, aware of Greg glaring at the balance.

To most, it was a lot of money, and it was still a significant amount to Chris, but the hefty receipt wouldn't plague his mind as much as the reminder of times spent with his dad. And both gentlemen were right about Jimmy Mitchell — he was sentimental. It reminded Chris of one more thing he'd reluctantly inherited from his father.

The drive home was a lot quieter, the car weighed down by a lot more than a couple hundred pounds of auto parts. The wind was warmer, the traffic was louder, and Chris had even less to say. His father wasn't doting with verbal praise. Chris didn't take it personally; it just wasn't something Jimmy Mitchell was comfortable with. To hear how willingly he showered such devotion on the guys behind the counter was equal parts heartwarming and infuriating.

Jimmy's advice had usually been pretty predictable, but Chris had no idea what his dad would tell him now. It was reasonable to assume he'd tell his son to do exactly what he'd been trying to do — keep his head down, keep himself busy, and don't make another move until he was sure of the next step. Even if that were true, Chris wished he didn't have to guess.

As Greg backed into the driveway and parked, Chris's mind decided it was time to slow down too.

"I needed a reset," Chris said as he opened the door and stepped out.

"What's that?" Greg replied while hurrying toward the trunk.

Chris carried two heavy boxes and rested them under the carport while Greg seemed to pine for clarity.

"The reason I came back. Everything that went down... it messed me up. I needed to get away from it and figure out what to do next."

Greg wiped a layer of sweat from his brow as both men alternated short trips from the trunk to the carport.

"The French Riviera would be a much better reset than here," Greg gibed.

"You really need a vacation, don't you?" Chris asked through unexpectedly hearty laughs.

"I really do." Something caught Greg's attention. "When's the last time you laughed that hard?"

"Good question." Chris slowed down as if it would help him find the answer. "I can't remember."

The last of the boxes were unloaded, and both men leaned against their respective vehicles. Chris still hadn't thought of the last time he'd laughed so hard. Instead, he thought of a moment when he hadn't.

"Did you know?" Chris wondered.

"Stop talkin' to me in riddles man, I'm not an expert Chris-reader yet."

"Did you know I wasn't cut out to lead my company? Is that why you didn't come with me after we got that first round of funding?"

"That doesn't make any sense. You led that company for a helluva ride. Don't let a bunch of brown-nosing board members make you question yourself."

"Being back here makes me question a lot of things." Chris protested. "That one might be the easiest to deal with."

"I have an answer for your question, but you might not like it." Greg took a deep breath. "I knew exactly what kind of leader you'd be. And that's why I stayed behind."

"So… I was right?"

"You were wrong. Spectacularly wrong," Greg declared. "You were so locked in, so driven, incapable of stopping to smell the roses for even a second. I couldn't match that. I didn't love it enough. I loved it, loved you, what we built, all that. Just not enough. I couldn't let the work define me like you did."

Chris sulked at the grating truth. "You managed to compliment me and insult me at the same time."

Greg shrugged. "Probably because I never know which one I'm doing. Maybe neither. Maybe both. But I don't make that call. It's all about how you take it."

"I let the work define me. And look where it got me."

"Rich?"

"Here." Chris held up both arms, imploring Greg to look at how far he hadn't gone from where his journey had started. Chris stayed on Senada's house for a second longer than necessary as he tried to find a solution to an internal struggle. It was easier to let things define him. Then he wouldn't have to figure it out for himself.

The side door kicked open and Barbara emerged holding two glasses. "You boys look like you could use a beverage. I made iced tea."

"Long Islands?" winked Greg.

"Only if you give me your car keys," she winked back.

"Thank a lot, Mrs. Mitchell." Greg pretended to be sarcastic.

"Thanks Mom," Chris added as he took the first sip.

"Can I take this for the road, Mrs. Mitchell? I gotta run."

"Sure, honey, just bring the glass next time you're around."

Greg waved once more at them before starting the car and pulling away. Barbara looked around the scene. "Well… this takes me back. Colvin?"

Chris nodded. "They remember Dad."

"They better. All the money he spent in there," she jested while shaking her head.

"I didn't know they tried to buy the Nova."

Barbara scoffed without an ounce of hesitation. "Waste of their time, if you ask me. There was no amount of money that was gonna make your father sell that car."

"I don't know why not. I was gone."

"Not as long as that car was here." Barbara leaned against the car beside her son and rested her head against his shoulder. "Can I say something without upsetting you?"

"Sure." Chris wondered how walking on eggshells had become the common theme of the day.

"I'm glad you're home," she sighed. "Not just for the obvious reasons. But I do believe this could be good for you."

"It doesn't feel like it."

"That sounds like the first time I had to give you penicillin for strep," she recalled. "You wiggled your whole body whenever you tried to swallow. Then you took one sip of the medicine and acted like it was worse than the strep throat."

Chris stared ahead for a few seconds, unable to join her on memory lane. "I don't remember any of that."

"Really?" she said while looking up at him. "You weren't *that* young."

Chris shrugged his shoulders helplessly/

"Hmm. That's funny," she said without an ounce of humor.

Barbara returned her head to his shoulder as Chris wondered what could possibly be funny about that. But he wasn't going to ask. He'd had enough sage advice for one day.

❈

Where others heard noise, Senada heard music. The clamor of the Hicks plant nursery composed a ballad made specially for her soul. The occasional spurt of handheld sprayers, muffled chatter about plant care, and squeaky wheels on old shopping carts were pleasant to the ear. But some tones were only audible to Senada, the unspoken words of every plant she passed in the aisles.

Every imaginable hue pulled her away from the anguish of monthly restocking visits. There was an unfortunate void between the flowers she wanted to see around her shop, and the products people would buy before they withered in the showroom. Flowers in the nursery appeared even more delicate, one step away from where they'd grown from seedlings into blossoms, and one step closer to becoming a product for profit.

Senada traveled from one section to the next, giving each plant rack most of her attention while waiting to find out the van had been loaded with the shop's usual allotment of flowers and soils. The practice had become so routine, there was no need to bring a list anymore. She lingered beneath a trellis covered in coral honeysuckle, admiring their tubular red blooms while resisting the urge to taint them with her touch.

"Senada, you're all set," a young man in a green apron said, snatching Senada back to Earth. "Your van is loaded. Steph needs you to check in with her before you leave."

"Thank you." Senada pretended to be nonchalant, but her blood pressure rose. The music stopped and she could only hear the soles of her Chucks slapping against the damp paved floor on her way to the front of the nursery. A burly, middle-aged woman with a slick and tight ponytail awaited her, leaning forward and resting her thick forearms on the counter.

"We gotta talk, Senada." Stephanie's bluntness was accompanied by a firm finger pointed at the computer monitor beside her. "We go back a long way, so I don't wanna be the villain here."

Senada held a slim hope she was being summoned for a different purpose, but it wasn't worth feigning surprise. "What's my tab at now?"

"You still owe for March and April, so add May to that." Stephanie spun the monitor for Senada to take a closer look at the remaining balance. "I'm trying to give you the benefit of the doubt. If you were anyone else, I wouldn't have let them load your van. But I need something in return for the amount of leeway I'm giving here."

Senada ran the numbers in her head, accustomed to calculating how much she could handle without drowning. It had become standard practice with every expense from meals to utilities. "I can handle March right now."

Stephanie scowled back, likely recognizing the rerun she'd watched of the same show Senada put on last month before paying February's bill.

"And a little bit of April…" Senada lilted with uncertainty.

"How little a bit are we talkin'?"

Senada dug the wallet from the tote bag on her shoulder and began counting bills as if she didn't know exactly how much money she had, down to the cent. "Half?"

A thick tension settled between them as Senada contemplated her next move, in case her plea fell on deaf ears.

"Fine," groaned Stephanie.

"I really appreciate this, Steph. Seriously." Senada was gracious considering the settlement would require skipping a meal every day until the end of the month and living on ramen and tuna for a few dinners. She handed over the money without betraying the immense reluctance lying beneath a veil of politeness.

Senada couldn't get back to the van fast enough, as if escaping from a place that normally represented sanctuary. Hyperventilated breathing overwhelmed her while the steering wheel acted as an unforgiving pillow. The tension in her abdomen worsened as another stabbing pain shot through it. Whatever the cause, the distress had finally become too great to ignore, even if she couldn't afford such luxuries as taking care of her health.

"Please have a little mercy on me today, okay?" Senada whispered into whatever part of the vehicle might be able to hear her plea. Once the engine answered her prayer, the absurdity of allowing a car to swing her day in either direction began to set in.

Senada had constantly been evading surrender, but wondered if it was time to slow down and let it catch her. Running from it was becoming too exhausting to bear. Senada was willing to give up if it meant she could have a break, a day where the worries were worth the amount of life they'd been consuming.

8

It was blasphemous to be back on Long Island for nearly a month without enjoying a bagel, but Chris had given himself a pass. He'd barely left the house except for the occasional middle-of-the-night walk to cope with insomnia. But last night's sleepless trek rolled through sunrise. Seeing the neighborhood as it slowly came to life was an entirely different experience. It allowed him to take stock of how much had changed, and how much he hadn't.

The morning stroll took him into the small market district that covered about six short blocks near the southern border of town. There was no rush. He had nowhere to be. And while slowing down was akin to death, it helped him see how alive things had become.

The movie theatre was still there, though under a different name. The coffee shop across the street was exactly as it had always been. The pizza joint was still a few storefronts down the block, though it was too early to enjoy the delicious aroma that normally emanated from it by lunch hour. Chris was only a few stores away from his destination, still waiting for something completely new to show itself. As he reached for the door handle of the bagel shop, a reflection in the glass made him turn around. Across the street, a narrow sushi establishment occupied the space formerly owned by a Mexican restaurant that held a special significance to him and the woman he'd hoped to avoid. Chris and Senada had spent countless summer evenings there, enjoying birria tacos and fruit-flavored sodas. The outdoor dining area looked the same, like the tables and chairs had been sold to the new owner on the way out of town.

A pedestrian interrupted, more interested in getting around Chris and inside the bagel shop than allowing a chance for his mind to wander. He was thankful, unsure how much further the nostalgia was about to take him and still kicking himself for feeling so much.

Chris got out of his head long enough to purchase a dozen egg everything bagels and a tub of cream cheese. The entire walk home was an exercise in reassessment. He didn't need any more thoughts of what could've been. He was ready to focus on what could be. And none of those possibilities involved her or this town. It was time for the beginning of a new approach to life. And a vital first step was to bring his mother's favorite bagels home, a small penance for how needlessly petulant he'd been since arriving.

When Chris wasn't holed up in his bedroom, wrapped in resentment and resisting the urge to call every board member and tell them what he'd really thought of them, he moped around like an angsty teenager. If he'd heard another 'you can talk to me about anything,' he'd have done exactly that, and it wouldn't have ended well. Barbara had never given him a reason to question her good intentions, but the incessant optimism had become exhausting.

Silence greeted him when he arrived back at the house. On any other morning, his mother would be wiping every surface before dust had a chance to accumulate, or dancing alone to Bobby Womack, all while coffee brewed and breakfast scones baked. But as he placed the bagels on the kitchen island, Barbara's cackling laughter could be heard just outside, near the modest garden. He couldn't see anything from the window, so he crept to the side door and looked through the mesh screen.

Before he saw his mother, he saw the back of a familiar body kneeling on a folded mat in the dirt. Neither woman had noticed Chris yet, giving him a moment to survey the scene. Senada was only fifteen feet away, but it was the closest they'd been since being closer than they ever should've been. His heart raced toward her and back to the west coast at the same time, as if it could cover both distances in the blink of an eye. Senada turned slightly toward Barbara, revealing her profile and the corner of her smile as she tucked errant strands of hair behind her ear. Her effortless beauty snatched his breath as if he no longer needed it to live.

"Now I know you're the expert on this stuff, but trust me, those Impatiens are too far apart," Barbara lectured as she sat in a tailgate chair, doing the best version of helping that she could while being in her seventies with two arthritic knees.

"I understand why you'd feel that way, Mrs. Mitchell. But trust me, we need to leave some space. They tend to grow out, not up." Gestures accompanied the explanation. Senada never could resist talking with her hands. "Remember we talked about this last year too?"

Barbara rubbed her forehead in confusion before noticing their observer. "Christopher! Good morning," she glowed. "Were we too loud?"

In a single motion, Senada stood and spun around before Barbara could finish the question. She wiped dirt from the distressed thighs of her light denim jeans. Chris couldn't tell if she was being excessively humble or covertly terrified. The sight of her pained expression softened him, and he hated it. He didn't want to care about hurting her feelings.

The silence lasted too long for Barbara's liking. "Chris," she interjected.

"I got bagels." The words seeped through his lips, barely audible over the tension.

"Oh thanks, hun. But I'm not very hungry, I might have one later." Barbara then seized an opportunity to do what she probably knew her son wouldn't. "Senada, you should go in and get one. You must be hungry after all this."

Barbara opened her arms, bringing Chris's attention to the rows of colorful, newly planted flowers in perfect symmetry.

Senada looked up at Chris as if he'd made the offer. "Sure, I could use a break." She walked past him as closely as she could without touching him. Chris's ego told him it was a purposeful action, until realizing he was blocking most of the doorway.

Instead of letting his eyes follow her, he turned his attention to his nefarious mother. "Seriously?!" he whispered aggressively.

"Oh, don't start," she jabbed. "Would you rather they get stale than for her to have one?"

Chris got close enough to Barbara to ensure Senada couldn't hear him. "I don't care about the bagels, Mom! What the fu—," Chris fumed before catching the expletive on its way out of his mouth. "What is she doing here?"

"She's been helping me with the garden. Well really, at this point, she does all the work while I occasionally interrupt."

"And you didn't think that might be worth mentioning to me?"

"If you'd come home more often, I wouldn't have forgotten to mention it," she shrugged.

"What the hell does that have to do with anything?!"

"You know how much she—"

"Mom, don't gimme more of that 'she's a daughter to me' crap. You're not her mother. You're *my* mother."

"And you're not my father, Chris," she intoned with a finger pointed at his chest. "I don't live my life around your comfort anymore. *You* came back to *my* home, not the other way around. So if you want to be angry at someone, there are mirrors all over the house. At least Senada doesn't punish me over some grudge she has with you."

Chris got a glimpse of Barbara he hadn't seen since she'd caught him smoking in high school. It was enough to be the first and last time he'd ever held a cigarette. Without a viable rebuttal, Chris turned and stormed back inside the house.

Chris walked in on Senada covering the last of her bagel's empty space with cream cheese. His ego had taken enough of a hit, and he wasn't willing to cede any more ground. Telling her to leave would've been morbidly satisfying, but his mother would never forgive him for it. He could hide in his room but didn't want her to think she still carried such weight.

Chris occupied himself with a peek inside the refrigerator and settled on a carton of orange juice, pouring a glass and taking a sip before wincing immediately.

"Pulp?" Senada asked with a rhetorical shrewdness.

It was an unwelcome reminder of how well she knew his thoughts on just about everything, including his stance on drinking fruit and eating it at the same time. Chris poured the remaining liquid down the drain as he caught a faint smile on Senada's face from the corner of his eye. He wondered if she was hiding it from him. Then he scolded himself for caring.

Knowing someone was one thing, but growing up beside them — watching them become who they're destined to be — was like someone possessing the blueprint for how to hurt you. And no matter how often she'd said it wasn't done on purpose, it didn't hurt any less.

"I tried to talk her out of it, but… you know your mom," Senada muttered.

Chris hardened before showing his entire face. "What?"

"Me, uh, ya know, popping up like this. I told her it wasn't a good idea, but she insisted, and I didn't want to upset her. And I'm sure neither of us want her to try and do the gard—"

"You don't have the slightest clue what I want," Chris cut in, putting an end to her rambling. "Look, if you want to be gardening buddies with my mom, have at it. I really don't care."

The air between them was plagued with hostility.

"It doesn't have to be this way between us," she pleaded.

"What way? There's no way between us. Because there is no between us. Because there's no us."

For so long, anger and regret had dictated his every thought of Senada. He didn't owe her a disingenuous attempt at politeness. If she wanted to advance their interactions, then she was going to have to live with an outcome she could neither predict nor control. It was only fair; she'd made him pay for the same mistake.

To his satisfaction, there was a sign his shots had hit the intended target. Senada kept her eyes on the bagel, picking away small pieces and putting each one in her mouth in rapid succession. Senada's penchant for snacking was a running gag that had followed them into adulthood. She wasn't much of a cook, but she loved to eat. It was the easiest way to lift her spirits. It was also the surest sign of nervousness. Chris stared at the behavior, hoping she'd notice being caught in the act.

"I'm going to, uh, get back out there. Thanks for the bagel," she said before awkwardly finding her way out the door.

For their first real exchange in years, Chris was content with how he'd handled it. He hadn't told the entire truth, but he also hadn't lied. And after pretending to be okay with so many recent changes to his life, he was proud to stand firm on something, no matter who might get hurt by it.

9

In the days since the embarrassment of her encounter with Chris, Senada wanted to blame someone for being forced to endure his vitriol. She'd ticked through the list over and over again — from Chris to Mrs. Mitchell to non-human options like the invention of domestic flower beds and bagels — but she really only blamed herself. Against her better judgment, Senada had agreed to being in proximity to his attitude. Sure, she could've fought back with some of the sarcasm and fury she'd inherited from her mother, but it would've been unfair to Chris. Hurting him had been hard enough. It didn't feel right to tell him how he was allowed to show it.

There were probably better ways to pass the time than staring at the ceiling of recessed lighting, but Senada couldn't think of any. The cleanliness of a medical office made her uncomfortable. Everything seemed sterile, untouched, and lacking life. After the debacle in the Mitchell kitchen, the sense of feeling out of place was more pronounced. While steeling herself against most emotions, Senada was glad to be reminded she could feel anything so deeply without it being the stress of bills and business. Chris, being one of the few people who could pierce her armor, may have done her a favor.

An eternity had passed since the intake nurse left the examination room. Senada hoped she'd get a reprieve from the excessive air conditioning by receiving prompt results instead of the slow torture she was being put through.

"Sorry for the wait," Dr. Lawson said as she entered. "It's been quite the day. How're you feeling?"

"Good enough," Senada riffed without hesitation.

"Okay, we can work with that." Dr. Lawson seemed caught by surprise, but she stayed composed. "What brings you in today?"

"Check-up, I guess. I think the IUD has been giving me some problems."

"What kinds of problems?"

"Soreness. A little pain further up." Senada pointed to a particular spot on her lower left abdomen.

"Alright let's have a look at you." Dr. Lawson put on latex gloves as if preparing for a stage cue. "I'm going to start with a pelvic exam, and then we'll take an STI test and see if that tells us anything."

"Sounds good," Senada said while tentatively lifting her shirt and exposing her belly's skin to the frigid air.

Dr. Lawson pressed and prodded with her fingertips, while Senada looked everywhere else to avoid eye contact. It was taking longer than usual, but the doctor was silent and expressionless.

"Shit!" A sharp sensation rattled Senada's foundation. Her eyes sprang wide, and she nearly leapt off the table. "What the hell was that?!"

"Alright, take a few deep breaths for me," said Dr. Lawson, unfazed. "I was just about to ask what kind of pain you've been experiencing."

"Nothing like whatever I just felt." Senada preferred eye contact now, glaring angrily at the doctor as if she'd caused the pain.

"Good to know," the doctor said. "What else have you been feeling?"

"I don't know. Just a sharp pain every now and then, but it's not like it was slowing me down or anything."

"Have you been particularly stressed?"

"Who isn't?" Senada chuckled to blunt how depressingly the words came out.

"Any breast tenderness? Pain during sex?"

"No sex pain. My breasts always get tender around this time in my cycle though."

"Has your period been irregular at all? Whether it's timing or flow? Pain? Anything?"

"Nothing out of the ordinary, uh, the usual amount of pain I guess." Senada was fed up with the interrogation. "Can you just tell me what's going on?"

"I don't want to alarm you, but I'd like to do an abdominal ultrasound and see if we can pin down the source of the pain."

"I know the source of my pain right now. You. Thirty seconds ago."

Unmoved by the attempt at humor, Dr. Lawson placed her fingers in the same spot, pressing gently enough to remind Senada how bad it felt. "Better to find out now than let an issue wait until it becomes worse."

Senada exhaled with her entire body. "Fine."

It wasn't her first time enduring an ultrasound, but it only took one instance to know it warranted the keenest of coping mechanisms. Something about even watching one on television was agonizing. The moment the gel touched her stomach, she tuned out, content to look away from the monitor. After however long it took, Dr. Lawson wiped the cool substance from Senada's stomach and lowered her shirt.

Dr. Lawson slid her stool closer to the table and put on a face that more closely resembled a psychiatrist than a gynecologist. "I want to send you out for more tests. An MRI, more specifically. But... I am concerned there may be multiple cysts on your ovaries. And at least one on a Fallopian tube."

Dr. Lawson kept talking, and Senada listened through rising walls of resistance. Senada had an idea of what a woman was supposed to feel upon hearing such words, and she was intent on feeling absolutely none of those emotions. The doctor's voice might as well have been traveling through water.

Senada waited for a break in the monologue to ask the only question on her mind. "What does this mean? Is it like cancer or something? Will I need surgery? What happens now?"

"Cancer is a possibility, but very rare. If the presence of cysts is confirmed, surgery is one of your potential treatment options."

Senada nodded and rested her head on the table. The recessed lighting had become worth staring at again.

"And, depending on the severity and location of the cysts, it can cause fertility issues."

"Issues like what, like I can't have kids?"

Dr. Lawson paused as if there was a medical school standard for silence before delivering tough news. "That is a remote possibility. But you really shouldn't get ahead of yourself. We don't know anything more than… there's something worth looking into. Our first step is to remove your IUD. So if you intend on being sexually active, you'll need another form of birth control. Then I'm going to refer you to a radiologist, and we can take it from there."

Senada didn't know how to respond to the news, or to the onslaught of anxiety slamming into her. While she'd never considered becoming a mother, something about being told it might not be a possibility was upsetting. She'd never thought of herself as particularly gentle, caring, or soothing — all traits she'd presumed were necessary for motherhood. Such a premise was hard to trust, given it was based on the qualities she'd never seen in her own mother. And she was living evidence of what could go wrong when an unqualified person took on such a role. Between being in debt, being alone, and feeling helpless against the tides of life, Senada was already more like her mother than she'd ever wanted to be. At least now, Senada might avoid adding a neglected and resented child to the list. And

Senada preferred to be a good mother in theory over a bad mother in reality.

An ounce of pride made her curious if she could've been better at it. She might've shown her mother how it was supposed to be done. But Senada's mother was long gone. Even if it were possible to watch Senada from above or below, her mother wouldn't be in the audience. She was too selfish to hold much interest in her daughter's life before. There was no way she'd spend the afterlife paying attention to Senada's ups and downs.

"Are you okay?" asked Dr. Lawson.

Senada had gone so deep down a rabbit hole, she'd forgotten the doctor was still beside her. "I just want to know nothing is… wrong… with me." Senada realized she was talking about more than a medical outcome. "Have you ever felt like you were… broken? Like you're a bunch of parts and pieces, but not quite a whole person? Like something that's supposed to be there is missing?"

"I know it might not feel like it right now, but lots of people feel that way. And so much weight is put on a woman's ability and desire to bear children, I think you're wrestling with things that are way more common than the world is ready to acknowledge."

Her rational knew the doctor was right. She wasn't alone and it should've provided some ease. But in her core, Senada didn't really care how many other women she could relate to.

"It's easy to beat yourself up," Dr. Lawson continued. "You're the easiest one to reach, and you know all your weaknesses. But you're not broken. Nothing is, quote-unquote, wrong with you."

Senada was grateful for Dr. Lawson's incredibly limited perspective. Most people didn't know enough about Senada for her to worry about their acceptance. And while she appreciated the doctor's reassurance, it brought a pivotal realization. She missed Chris more than she thought. He used to be who she'd run to when life gave her things she couldn't make sense of. And he was frustratingly effective at getting Senada out of her head in order to see the bigger picture. Even when she knew exactly what he'd say, it was still soothing to hear him say it. Days ago, in the kitchen, she'd taken for granted how cathartic it was to hear him say anything to her again.

In a blur between the doctor's office and the parking lot, Senada made it back inside the van and sank into the driver's seat. She counted her breaths, holding each one for a few seconds before releasing it through a small opening in her mouth. The engine was already running when Senada realized she'd inadvertently skipped the prayer ritual.

Her body was begging for rest, but Senada had to go back to the shop. With Mother's Day fast approaching, she couldn't afford to shrug off potential profits. Lex, with all her abilities, wasn't quite ready to take on that much work by herself.

On her way back, Senada barely accelerated, in no rush to beat red lights. At the second to last one, she caught a glimpse of a movie poster outside the theatre on the passenger's side. She knew every inch of that place — she was willing to bet any sum of money that she could find seat C7 in any of its theatres with her eyes closed.

Senada had lost count of how many movies she and Chris had seen together. Ever since they were allowed to leave the block without parental supervision, every major release had been consumed there. Chris used to check the showtimes in the newspaper every Sunday, and they would plan their viewing. Once aware of Chris's weekly routine, Senada started to do it too. She enjoyed the anticipation of his phone call to find out if she was free for a screening.

Her inundated mind retreated to the end of their junior year of high school, when his was the only muscle car in the parking lot on the night The Fast and The Furious was released. Invigorated teenagers came out two hours later, motivated to take on all challengers in their mother's minivan or their dad's Oldsmobile. Senada would smile in the passenger seat as the mere rumble of the Chevy's engine had been enough to remind everyone in the parking lot of the difference between movie magic and reality. Chris unwittingly reminded her of why she'd enjoyed his company. No matter how much others tried to goad and pressure him, he wouldn't race. There was no fear in him, but he had nothing to prove. She missed that version of Chris. Senada missed every version of him.

A car horn blared, returning her attention toward the now-green light in front of her. She tingled like she'd been in a deep trance, a feeling that lingered until she'd parked the van. Relaxation had become so foreign that her body assessed calmness as a threat.

Lex looked up from a freshly wrapped bouquet of roses and tulips. "You're back… and you're smiling. I take it the appointment went okay?"

Senada couldn't tell what her own face was doing. "It was fine."

"Must've been better than fine."

Senada could've told her what a smile might be masking. But a hint of guilt poisoned any possibility of an explanation. Her wounds were too fresh to trust where her words would come from. And whenever she'd felt that way, Chris was the most trustworthy audience. Talking to him used to be the safest option imaginable. While living in their present was no walk in the park, living in their past was dangerous. Some feelings refuse to stay where we put them because they aren't where they belong.

10

First contact hadn't gone as badly as Chris worried it would. He hadn't crumbled under the weight of Senada's presence, a big step towards the internal peace he craved. After countless hours doubting how he'd handle being in the same room with her, he was proud of himself. It wasn't ideal to view their interactions through a competitive lens, but he looked back on the brief interaction as a triumph. His next conquest was Mother's Day breakfast, but the odds weren't in his favor.

Chris ping-ponged from one part of the kitchen to the next as he balanced frying bacon, scrambling eggs, and making sure the biscuits didn't burn in the oven. More ambitiously, he tried to pull it off without waking his mother. But the smoke alarm had other ideas. Chris didn't spend enough time in the kitchen to know where to find a rag or towel that might help abate the vapor and silence the blaring alarm. He became more scrambled than the eggs, opting to remove his T-shirt and wave it in front of the sensor until the beeping stopped. Chris was willing to accept the silence as another victory under his belt until steady giggling interrupted.

Barbara looked on from the base of the stairs, sporting a wide smile slightly covered by a palm. The faint giggling eventually gave way to full-blown laughter. Chris willingly claimed defeat at the hands of two AA batteries for the sight of his mother's joyous expression.

"If you're looking for ways to fill your days, might I suggest… anything else imaginable?" Barbara spoke through continued guffawing.

"You're hilarious, Mom," he replied in half-faux frustration as he watched Barbara step in and turn off the burner beneath the eggs.

"Hard to scramble eggs while doing a bunch of other stuff." Barbara put on two thick mitts like a surgeon and removed the nearly smoldering biscuits from the oven. The remaining sizzling pan awaited her judgment. "Well, at least the bacon looks good. But I can't have any."

"Why not?"

"Fried strips of heavily salted fat? Not a good idea for me."

Chris raised an eyebrow. "This is the same thing you've made just about every morning since I've been back."

"For you," smirked Barbara. "I quit bacon when the cardiologist made your father stop eating it."

Chris was in Barbara's way and stepped aside so she could commandeer the kitchen. He sat on the other side of the island, dejected. "Ya know, the plan was for you *not* to have to do anything today."

"Does that mean you have to do something you'd never do otherwise?" she quipped. "When's the last time you made a full breakfast? Hell, when's the last time you made something that couldn't be served in a bowl and eaten with a spoon?"

Chris avoided her gaze. "You don't have to gloat, Mom."

"That's exactly what this day is all about." Barbara finished securing the kitchen and turned to face her son. "Why didn't you just order in?"

"That doesn't take much effort."

"Burning the house down takes effort, but that doesn't make it a good Mother's Day present."

"Fair point," he conceded. "Okay, I'll do what I should've done days ago and just ask. What would you like to do for Mother's Day?"

Barbara pondered for a moment while Chris tried to predict where her hopes might take them. Past celebrations involved anything from Broadway shows to fancy dinners. Money was an easy crutch, in lieu of thoughtful planning.

"You know what? I think I have an idea." Barbara reached into a cabinet and slid a small package across the island.

"You want popcorn?" asked a befuddled Chris.

"I want to watch a movie like we used to. As a family," she answered before pointing at the package in his hands. "*That's* the one thing I trust you to make."

Chris could only muster a shrug of acceptance. "What do you wanna watch?"

Barbara looked toward the ceiling once more, then lowered her eyes back to Chris. She didn't answer. She didn't need to.

❁

If Senada had her way, it would've been just another Sunday. Her biological mother wasn't worth commemorating, and her de facto mother was out of bounds. No amount of Mrs. Mitchell's doting adoration could fill the void left behind by everything Carrie had stolen from Senada.

The remnants of cutting insults and scornful resentment were distracting enough without abdominal pain becoming more frequent. In light of Dr. Lawson's distressing news, Senada wondered how it might feel to be worthy of such celebration by a child of her own. Senada wasn't carrying the same level of resentment and self-loathing, but maybe Carrie hadn't planned on carrying those things either. The idea of passing those feelings on to an innocent child was too much to bear.

Senada preferred spending her least favorite day in the shop, surrounded by the sights and symbols of everything Carrie should've been — caring, tender, and receptive. It didn't matter that the shop was closed on Sundays; it was a chance to have peace with her thoughts. She sat at her clean workstation, reminded of how the place sounded when music wasn't playing.

A childhood that was absent of a mother's affection and love made Senada unwilling to trust its presence in others. She didn't possess much of a capacity for love. Most people learned from experience, but she had none. The only worthwhile lesson, as she'd been taught, was to resist falling for the fantasy. Love wasn't something you said or did. It was something you either believed in or didn't. The Mitchell family stood alone as an emblem of love's reality.

But this year, the annual applause for matriarchs opened Senada's eyes to how much she really wanted to say to Chris. By allowing him the space to dominate their short conversation, she'd left a lot of things unspoken, betraying everything she wanted to tell him, and everything she should've told him a long time ago. Most mistakes were easy to let go of, but any misstep with Chris reverberated against every other one. She was tired of fucking up, and even more tired of worrying about making another mistake.

Senada had navigated around his life for long enough, sacrificing what little love she could receive just so her presence wouldn't bother him. There'd been more Mother's Day Monday dinners than she wanted to count, always careful to make sure Chris was already on a flight before she'd escape purgatory and celebrate Mrs. Mitchell too.

While he'd been gone for most of every year, whenever Barbara needed a hand with something, Senada was at the top of the call sheet. There wasn't a legitimate reason to feel bad about helping Barbara with her garden. There was even less of an excuse for relegating herself to the shop to mourn in silence while there was someone worth celebrating.

Senada rose from the stool, turned on the music, and hit shuffle. Any sound would be enough to motivate her as she entered the showroom and scouted her stock of flowers and plants. Many things caught her eye, but only a few deserved to be a part of the idea milling in her mind. Senada pulled three of every worthy option: red carnations, white lilies, purple tulips, and pink roses. She brought the collection to the station and laid them out.

Midway through clipping, trimming, and tweezing them to perfection, she noticed an absence. The bouquet-in-progress was abundant with color and beauty, but lacked a foundation; a contrasting flower that could separate it from something any mother was going to receive. Senada jogged back to the refrigerator and spotted the perfect target: blue primrose. It balanced the love and affection of the other flowers, while representing the protection and kindness that Mrs. Mitchell had selflessly provided for decades. Senada was all smiles as she wrapped the stems together and bound them in white wrapping paper, complete with a linen tie.

Senada admired her handiwork and enjoyed her calling. This came naturally to her. But getting the flowers to their intended recipient would require a foreign style of courage.

❀

Barbara had given birth to him, but their innate connection didn't make her any easier for Chris to understand. If she wanted to spend the morning watching a movie, he didn't have the capacity to fight it. His mother loathed burnt popcorn as much as he did, so he hit the stop button a little earlier than was probably necessary. Intermittent beeping from the living room indicated Barbara still hadn't figured out which streaming service had the movie she was looking for.

"Try YouTube, Mom!" he shouted midway through carefully removing the scalding bag by its corners and dropping it on the counter.

"I don't know how to do that!" she replied.

Chris filled the biggest bowl he could find, then hurried to join the search.

Chris handed Barbara the bowl and took the remote. "Enjoy, Mom." He smiled in a way she mirrored immediately upon sight of the popcorn. A few button presses later, the big screen television, once a Father's Day present for his dad, displayed a black-and-white Henry Fonda above '12 Angry Men' in bold red lettering.

Barbara lit up. "How'd you know it would be there?"

"Because this movie is from 1957," he snickered. "Not exactly gonna be prime placement on any other service."

"If these tech guys were so smart, they'd appreciate the classics a little more."

"Don't get me started on the intelligence of the tech industry, Mom." He plopped beside her on the couch while she was already a handful deep into the bowl. Pressing play triggered a long-held curiosity. "I feel like an idiot for asking this because I should've already known, but… why was this movie such a big deal for you and Dad?"

"He never told you?" she asked with rising excitement. The whites of her eyes became more pronounced.

"No," he said. "Though I never asked."

"Men," she chortled. "When you boys figure out what's really worth talking about, you'll be shocked by how much time you've wasted on sports and cars."

"Are you gonna answer my question, or deliver a social commentary?" he said, playfully nudging her arm.

"We saw it on our first date."

"*This* was the movie you chose for a first date?!"

"Not really a choice. We didn't have as many options back then. We couldn't watch whatever we wanted whenever we decided to. This was playing at the Westbury Drive-In that night, so this is what we saw," she shrugged, obviously satisfied with how things turned out.

"Yeah? What'd you think?"

"I don't remember. I barely watched it. Too busy trembling in the passenger seat hoping your dad would like me."

"That's ridiculous. Dad adored you."

"Don't let the ending fool you. We started just like everyone else. You popped up a few years into us already being married. But the road was just as unclear for us as any young couple. It wasn't love at first sight or something."

Chris paused with her reflection, wishing he'd thought to ask such questions when his dad could be there to chime in. Barbara tapped his arm to pull his focus toward the screen, as Fonda and eleven others entered deliberations, signaling the real start of the movie. Despite having seen the film dozens of times between them, they were continuously enthralled.

Chris marveled at how a story could be so gripping when it was just twelve people talking in one room for an hour and a half. The beats were woven into his memory by now, but it was as compelling as it had ever been. The first vote, the switchblade driven into the table by Juror #8, the eyewitness debate — the level of tension among a dozen anonymous characters was enough skilled creation to inspire Chris. He appreciated when mastery was at work. It's what he'd always aspired to. But getting near a goal didn't make it any less of a failure. If anything, it was more brutal to have it and then have it snatched away.

The doorbell rang twice in quick succession. Chris backed out of the room without taking his eyes off the screen as Fonda began the iconic timed walk demonstration.

"Hurry up! Lee Cobb is gonna blow his top in a minute!" Barbara shouted.

Chris dashed to the door and pulled it open. A colorful bouquet caught his eye, followed by the person holding it.

"Hey," said Senada, apparently struggling to be cordial. "Look, I'm not here to bother you. I just wanted to drop these off for your mom. Can you give them to her?"

Chris watched the flowers as she extended them toward his chest, but he couldn't raise his hands to receive them. Something unidentifiable held him back. In her eyes, he saw the bravery he'd wanted for himself. To show up unexpectedly with a gift for his mother, given their circumstances, took the qualities he'd fallen in love with. And on such an understandably fraught day, Senada wasn't just on the porch because she wanted to give flowers to his mother. Ostensibly, she was likely in search of something for herself.

Chris sought a way through the impasse, but Senada pulled back the flowers before he could find one. "It's alright. I can bring them another time."

She walked away, but didn't make it ten steps before Chris couldn't bear the sight. Carrying more guilt wouldn't make his life any easier. This was a day for his mother's happiness to outshine his peace of mind.

"Senada. Wait." Chris searched for the right way to extend an olive branch. "I think she'd rather get them from you." He stepped aside, silently welcoming her inside.

Senada stood still for a moment, as if unsure the invitation was genuine. She held a skeptical eye on Chris as he closed the door behind her.

"She's in the den," he said.

Senada slid off her Toms and walked ahead of him. Chris gave her some space and forced himself to look anywhere else but at the way her legs fought against the tightness of her jeans. Anger rose within Chris, frustrated by how vulnerable he still was, and how blind he'd been to the consequences of those impulses in the past.

"Happy Mother's Day, Mrs. Mitchell," Senada exclaimed upon entering. Barbara radiated joy as soon as she heard Senada's voice, meeting her for a hug before noticing the flowers. Senada inadvertently sat in the space once occupied by Chris, who descended into the adjacent cushy lounge seat, formerly designated as his father's throne. The unspoken tension prompted him to rock slightly back and forth, coping with what he'd brought on himself.

Barbara was so wrapped up in chatting with Senada, as if they hadn't spoken in ages, that she no longer seemed to care about the home stretch of the movie. Neither woman reacted to Chris seizing the remote and pausing the movie as two jurors were discussing eyeglasses.

"These are absolutely gorgeous, Senada! My goodness!" Barbara fawned. "I need to put these in a vase. Chris, pause it."

"Already did, Mom," he grumbled, feeling regrettably juvenile.

Barbara hummed indistinctly on her way into the kitchen. Chris stared at the frozen image on the screen, but his attention was being pulled toward Senada. There was so much to say, yet so little desire to reopen that door.

"Any special instructions for this one?!" Barbara shouted unnecessarily, persuading Chris to look Senada's way in time to catch her looking back.

"Full sun!" she responded at a comical volume while keeping her gaze on Chris. They locked eyes for longer than they had in years, until Barbara's return saved them. He wondered if Senada regretted getting caught staring. Then he wondered if he'd ever stop wondering what was going on in her head.

"Do you remember this?" said Barbara.

Both heads turned toward her voice, leaving Chris puzzled over who she might be talking to, and what she might be talking about. An irrational fear set in. He wouldn't put it past his mother to ignite the unspoken dialogue on their behalf.

"12 Angry Men," Barbara continued, revealing Senada as the intended target. "You've seen it before, haven't you?"

The question yanked a grin out of Senada and, belatedly, Chris. They finally had a reasonable excuse to look at each other without apprehension.

Senada had seen the movie. Chris knew because he was there when she'd seen it. A substitute teacher had played the first half for their junior-year English class while he scarfed down a pound cake. Due to Senada's teenage struggle with unfinished things, she'd begged Chris to help her find the movie at Blockbuster so they could watch the rest. To her exhilaration, not only did Chris know where to find the movie, he also didn't need Blockbuster's help. By sundown, the pair had watched the second half in the same room the trio was watching it now.

"Yeah, I've seen it before," Senada answered.

"It's so good," said Barbara.

Senada nodded while glancing at Chris, who knew her real opinion — she didn't get the hype around the classic film. Chris had the power to reveal the truth, and Senada tacitly urged him to keep one more secret between them. Being trusted by Senada, even with a mundane detail, brought back fleeting tinges of the bond they'd shared. They were always speaking to and through each other, with and without words.

Chris spent most of the film's remaining twenty minutes keeping one eye on the TV, and the other on Senada's crossed legs. Of all the times to feel so human, Chris wished for his anger to exceed her beauty. But the time apart and the sunlight's caress of her skin rendered his hopes futile. The final horn symphony blared as Fonda departed the courthouse and the credits rolled, signaling a chance to leave without needing a reason. He was running out of time before his thoughts turned into fantasies he couldn't afford to have at all, let alone while his mother was between them.

Chris fled to the bathroom, immediately running the coldest water available into his hands and dousing it across his face. An internal clock ticked away, counting down how much time passed before his absence became strange. After assuming enough time had passed, Chris reopened the door and nearly walked into Senada.

"Shit," they said, almost in unison.

"I'm sorry," she added.

"It's okay, I —"

"I didn't realize you were in the—"

"Me too. I mean, it's fine," he stumbled. "You know what I—"

"I understand," she replied.

The exchange left Chris fumbling for what to do next. They were trapped in front of each other, yet neither seemed in a hurry to escape. Senada was too close to look past, but looking anywhere other than her eyes meant looking at a part of her that might create a different kind of awkwardness.

"Can I, uh?" she asked, sort of, while gesturing toward the bathroom he was blocking.

"Oh, yeah, of course." Chris squeezed past her, careful to keep his pelvis away from possible contact with any part of her that might recognize what brushed against it. He was already planning a cold shower, upset by how easily she created a carnal response in him. One adventurous night and twelve years later, his body still wondered about the possibilities. He didn't want to want her, and hurried to his bedroom to catch his breath amid a rush of unexpected desire.

As Senada exited the bathroom, she lingered, likely aware that Chris could see her while she fixed her hair and adjusted her jeans around her hips in a way that forced her breasts to bounce. He considered the act might've been done on purpose, knowingly disregarding how out of character such a exploit would've been for her. There was no way to know without asking, and he didn't need to know that badly. What he really needed was for her to leave so his body could negotiate with his mind on a level playing field.

Senada disappeared down the stairs and Chris overheard faint words exchanged with Barbara, followed by the front door closing. Chris paced toward the window and saw her walk, then jog, back to her house. The medicine had been disgusting but effective. He needed a reminder of how it felt to watch Senada run away.

Chris descended the stairs and played coy. "Where'd she go?"

"Said she wasn't feeling well," Barbara replied while primping the assorted stems in a tall, green vase. "She's got such an eye for beauty."

Chris nodded, for failure of words. "It was nice of her to bring them."

"Thanks for letting her," she sniped, cutting her eyes at her son while returning to the den and placing the vase on a sun-drenched windowsill.

His diplomacy hadn't been appreciated to his liking. "It's not like I was gonna tell her to leave."

"But you wanted to, didn't you?"

Chris looked away, unwilling to lie but unsure if the truth was worth telling. "The point is… I didn't," he said. "It's your day, and I knew seeing her would make you happy."

"Just me, huh?"

Barbara left the room before Chris could respond, enlightening her son to the rhetorical nature of the question.

❀

Senada was unreasonably out of breath for such a short run, propelled by anxiety as much as by oxygen. She was desperate to get out of sight.

The front door slammed shut under Senada's weight. She'd anticipated a nostalgic flood of what they used to be, but she wasn't prepared for the degree to which it would affect her.

Being close enough to touch him, to kiss him, only a few feet away from his bedroom, was more than she'd expected. The end of that hallway was where she'd often gone to feel safe, to feel seen, and to pretend to know what love felt like. She wanted to go back there, to that place, and she wanted him to come with her.

Senada wasn't used to running *away* from his house.

11

Twenty-Two Years Earlier

Chris still couldn't believe he was behind the wheel of his own car, let alone one he'd restored almost all by himself. The faint groan of the idling engine was enough to make the entire chassis vibrate. And every second in the driver's seat wrinkled his only suit even more. His mother would probably give him a hard time about it when he got home, but Senada was easy fodder for taking the blame, since she was the reason he'd attended in the first place.

Senada's body language was easy for him to read, but even a stranger would've noticed she was uncomfortable in a crimson dress short enough to expose her mid-thigh. Chris smiled wider as he watched her try to cut ties with her date. She'd predicted how the evening would play out, and it was coming to fruition. Sean had a few sips too many from someone's secret flask and was no longer worthy of her time or attention. By the third act of the evening, Senada had secured a ride home with Chris. She didn't care about being a third wheel at the end of the night, so long as she got home without having to fend off Sean's drunken advances. And her safety was worth rubbing his date the wrong way.

Allison was nice enough and easy on the eyes, so it hadn't been a wasted evening. But a bet from Senada was enough to jumpstart his ego. Once Sean had asked Senada to the Spring Dance, he unknowingly forced Chris to attend. And Allison fit the necessary criteria for a date with him: she was single and unlikely to say no.

The high school parking lot was needlessly large, and Chris looked across it like a sentry as Senada engaged with Sean, likely saying her goodbyes while he attempted to keep the party going. The intense focus responsible for four years of high honors had become a liability, as he didn't realize Allison was tugging at the passenger door. Once he lifted the pin, she heaved the door open with every petite pound she had and joined Chris.

"Sorry that took so long," Allison said with an engaging tone.

"Don't worry about it," he replied, realizing he had no idea what she was referring to.

"So… what do you want to do now?" Allison's uncertainty of his intentions was awkwardly apparent. "I don't have to be home for another couple of hours."

"Okay, uh," stammered Chris. "I have to give Senada a ride home first."

"Can't her date do that?"

"I'm not sure he should walk home, let alone give someone a ride." He gestured toward the interaction he'd been watching over. "It'll be quick. I'll drop her off and then we can do something."

Senada jogged across the parking lot in choppy steps and flung the passenger door open, startling Allison. "Hey, Allison! Love the dress! Move up so I can get in."

"Uh, sure." Allison searched around her before looking to Chris for help.

Senada was already pulling the lever as she said "I'll do it," and pushed the seat forward, contorting Allison in the process.

"Have you been drinking?" Allison asked.

"Good catch," Senada quipped as she laid across the back seat, kicked her heels off and struggled to put on the pair of Chuck Taylors she'd kept stowed there. "I want tacos. You guys feel like tacos? Allison, do you eat tacos?"

"I'm a vegetarian."

"They make vegetarian tacos. Don't they? They do. Right? Maybe. I can't remember." Senada continued to debate with herself as Allison appeared to reach her threshold with the situation. Chris's snickering probably didn't help.

"I think I'll… get a ride with one of my friends," Allison lamented, already halfway out of the car. Chris tried to quell his laughter long enough to feign resistance. "See you around, Chris."

The slam of the door snapped Senada back to the moment as they both watched Allison storm away. "And the Hail Mary falls to the turf. Incomplete pass."

"How long were you planning on using that?" he snarled back.

"Just made it up, man. Just maaaade it up."

"What if we were gonna hook up?"

"Good one," she laughed. "Best she could've given you was handy in this back seat."

"Not with you back there."

"Well, if Allison isn't prepared to fight for the back seat, she doesn't deserve the back seat," Senada griped, her slurring words making the experience even more worthwhile for Chris.

"You're just saying that because you need a ride." Without a viable comeback, she pinched his side in retaliation. He put the Nova in gear and pulled off.

They rode through the chilly night while Senada insisted they make a midnight run to their favorite Mexican restaurant. She'd eaten half of her food before making it back to their block. Once they pulled into her driveway, Senada was all smiles.

"What are you grinning about?" he asked.

"I don't wanna say," she sneered back.

"Why not?"

"Because you always make fun of me when I get sappy." He nodded in endorsement of the truth. "Fuck it, I'll say it. I'm gonna miss nights like these."

Chris took a breath, prepared to employ sarcasm and snark to take the wind out of her words. Then he changed his mind. "Why do you say that like we're never gonna do this again?"

"Because we're not," she surrendered. "High school is almost over. Things change. People change."

"That doesn't mean we have to."

"But you're leaving me." Senada turned on her puppy-dog eyes.

"It's not like I'm going far. C.W. Post is close enough to see each other whenever we want."

"Not really. You're dorming. I'm commuting to Adelphi. You won't be across the street anymore." Something seemed to catch Senada's eye. "What am I gonna do without you around all the time?"

Chris tracked where she was looking — the living room light was on. "You'll call me," he assured firmly. "And I'll come."

Senada sneered. "Will you be dressed like this when you do?"

"What's that supposed to mean?"

"Nothing," she winked. "You were pretty cute dressed like one of the Men in Black."

"Har-de-har-har. Get out of my car."

"Later," she said as she closed the door behind her. "And Chris?"

"Yeah?"

"Can you stay close?"

Chris recognized the shudder in her voice, and he responded with a single nod. Senada slowly backed away, with leftovers in one hand and her shoes in the other, and trotted up the steps. He didn't back out of the driveway until the door closed behind her.

The drive was short enough to cover the distance in reverse, backing up his driveway and into the carport. He walked through the side door and into the dark kitchen. A flick of the light switch brought his eyes to plate of chocolate chip cookies with a note: "Hope you had a great time!" He took one cookie and covered the rest before going upstairs.

As he closed the bedroom door behind him, he caught a glimpse of himself in the mirror. He took a longer look than he had before the party, imagining what it might be like to dress in such threads more often. If he was going to go where he'd hoped, it was as good a time as any to get used to wearing suits.

❀

There was no way to tiptoe through the house without drawing her mother's ire, so Senada didn't bother trying. The odor of liquor was pungent; gin had been the spirit of choice tonight. As soon as her only daughter passed the living room couch, Carrie shot out of a stupor and looked directly at her.

"Where the hell have you been?" Carrie blinked and squinted at Senada as though trying to pull her daughter into focus.

"I went to the dance, remember?" Senada deflected, sobering instantly. "I told you I was going."

"Ah… so that's why you're dressed like… that."

Senada braced for the expected, hoping to make it to her bedroom before Carrie could find the insult she was searching for.

"You're gonna end up making the same mistake as I did, walking around dressed like that."

"And there it is," sighed Senada, loud enough for only herself to hear.

"It's not like you're pretty or something! I'll bet that's what they tell you all the time! But don't you get full of yourself! You're young! And half-naked! That's all it takes for them to pretend to love you! They'll tell you whatever you wanna hear! And then they'll ignore you! You hear me?! Use you up and spit you out! Just like your piece of shit father did to me… you'll see!"

The scathing words kept coming. Years of practice conditioned Senada to find methods for tuning them out. She slipped out of the dress and tossed the shoes on the floor, quickly changing into a white T-shirt and lavender linen shorts. As soon as her head hit the pillow, she put on large studio-style headphones, shielding herself from further damage. But being berated for being herself was already enough to unsettle her. She didn't have to hear the words; she'd memorized the script.

The first act would be about Senada's provocative nature, as her mother was certain Senada had lost the virginity she'd actually held tightly to. Such an implication used to be enough to bring Senada to tears, but once its effectiveness had been reduced, her mother upped the ante with accusations around her frequent visits to the Mitchell house. Any day now, Senada was allegedly going to come back with a positive pregnancy test. According to her mother, if Chris was as smart as everyone thought he was, he'd get as far away from Senada as possible. But her mother was in peak form once she'd started blaming Senada for her father's absence. Carrie didn't seem to care about the oxymoronic rationale of her daughter drawing men in *and* pushing them away, or how Senada could be the reason a man she'd never met wasn't there. It wasn't worth fighting back anymore.

Instead, Senada wanted to focus on the music in her ears. But the right song was elusive. Her mother's voice crept between the beats, and the walls vibrated as her volume rose. Senada tossed and turned for a few minutes until she gave up and reached for the lamp on her nightstand.

❦

Chris was tired but his eyes were wide open. In the still April air and through open windows he could make out Ms. Williams's yelling more easily than usual. It was hard to hear what she was saying, but Senada had shared enough for him to guess the content. He'd never thought of himself as a protector, but Senada's mother made him wish he had special powers. There wasn't much he could do except be there for her. And it never felt like enough, no matter what Senada told him.

The volume rose gradually, but he was more concerned by how long she'd been yelling. There was no way to be sure if Senada was locked in her room again or in full presence of her mother's verbal assault. Chris sat up in bed and looked from his window to hers. It only took a minute or two for her curtains to part. A beam of white light flashed. He blinked hard to make sure he hadn't imagined it. Then it flashed again.

Chris reached toward the nightstand and turned his lamp on and off, matching the rhythm he'd just seen. Senada's light flashed once more, and he hurried out of bed. He double-checked the chain lock on the side door and ensured it was hanging free. then went to his room. An extra pillow and a spare blanket were tossed on the floor, then Chris tidied his bed. Chris found as much comfort as he could on the thick carpet. Five minutes later, his bedroom door creaked open and Senada entered, sniffling as she balanced the plate of cookies on her palm while kicking off her untied sneakers Chucks.

Unsure if Senada would want to speak or go to sleep, Chris laid still and kept his eyes partially closed. She carefully stepped over him and sat on the bed, whimpering through a couple of cookies before Chris couldn't ignore her sadness any longer.

"I don't know the right thing to say," he confessed through a whisper.

"Neither does she," Senada replied.

Senada gave up on the cookies and put the plate on the nightstand before curling into his bed. The sound of her crying nearly brought tears out of him. He stayed awake until he thought she was asleep. Just when his eyelids became heavy, she stirred.

"Chris."

"Yeah?"

"Do you think I'm pretty?"

Chris was too confused and groggy to respond right away. Senada rolled over and faced him, though she was barely visible aside from traces of moonlight along her bare arms and legs.

"I'm serious. Do you think I'm pretty?" she repeated

"Honestly, I —"

"Please don't lie to me."

"You know I wouldn't do that." He waited for an affirmation, but it didn't come. "I've never really thought about it before."

"C'mon Chris, tell me the truth. You see me more often than anyone. It's not a complicated question. When you look at me, do you see someone who's pretty?"

Senada was usually too earnest to ask trick questions, so Chris wasn't sure how to take the query. "Yeah, I think you're hot, Senada," he said with an uncertain snicker that vanished once it was met with silence. Chris wasn't ready to disclose a thought that had only crossed his mind long enough to recognize it, then push it away.

Chris cared about Senada in a way that made it hard to look at her like the Allisons of the world. His eyes worked and they were connected to his brain. Her beauty had become impossible to ignore. And Senada would've called bullshit if he'd ever tried to dance around her feelings. The only guys in the entire high school who hadn't hit on her at some point in the last four years were the ones who'd assumed Chris was already her boyfriend. But such a brittle moment wasn't the best time to confess he'd stolen the occasional glance at her crossed legs in the passenger seat of the Nova, or that he'd spent the last few of her sleepovers needing a cold shower afterwards.

"I–I don't think it's that simple."

"Of course it is." Senada sprang up and sat at the edge of the bed, her bare feet dangling above the floor. "Be a typical teenage boy for me just this once. Does the word 'pretty' scare you? Okay, would you fuck me? How's that? Is that better?"

The frantic whispering lifted Chris to his knee. He settled across from her, within arm's reach but afraid to touch her in this unrecognizable state. "Senada, what's going on? What are you really asking me?"

The question was the most honest answer he could give.

She went still for a moment before releasing a long, slow exhale. "I don't know anymore," she said. The despair in the last word signaled Chris to action, closing the space between them just in time for tears to weaken her. She sobbed into his T-shirt like it was supposed to be a secret between them, as he wrapped his arms around her.

Her walls came tumbling down, and Chris caught her before she could succumb beside the debris. It was a role he knew far too well.

12

It was an exercise in frustration and futility, but Chris couldn't resist. Since being back, if he'd sat in front of the computer, no matter what the original reason, he would inevitably land on Google search results of himself and his former company. His ego couldn't fathom building something that could fail. But knowing they were succeeding without him was akin to torture. Even more distressing, the company might've rebounded *because* of his absence. Maybe the board was right and there was something to be said for significant experience sitting at the head of the table. A healthy severance package and majority ownership stake afforded him the time to obsess over it. Either that or Chris would be left to obsess over when and how Senada might pop up next. Worrying about the company was preferable.

His woeful thoughts were interrupted by the now-familiar tune of Senada's van struggling to turn over outside his open window. He peered through the curtains and counted how many attempts it would take for the engine to start this time. It'd taken a week for two key turns to become three, but now, Senada was flirting with a fourth. Without a fix, the van didn't have much time left. He was relieved to hear the engine finally come to life.

As soon as he'd returned to the ashes of his former life on the Macbook screen, a heavy fist pounded against the front door. Eager to get out of the house, Chris had become stir crazy. There were lots of other ways to occupy his time. He'd explored most of the list, from meditation to journaling to, in a moment of unique weakness, nearly signing up for a tango class. But working on the Nova made him realize how out of shape he'd become. And that meant going to the gym with Greg had become the most prudent option.

Greg was too enthusiastic for how tired Chris was. Four hours of sleep wasn't nearly enough, but it was progress. Chris opened the door just as Greg and Senada exchanged waves while she drove past the house. Thankfully, Chris didn't have enough time to decide whether or not to wave too. She was gone before he could weigh the options.

"Hadn't seen her in a while. She looks good," said Greg, probably not intending for it to sound like a taunt, but Chris felt it anyway.

"I guess," Chris replied.

"I see you've regressed to looking like shit again," Greg asserted.

"Do you always go to the gym this early?"

"It's 7am."

"Saying it like it's normal doesn't make it normal," groaned Chris.

"You ran an entire company. Aren't you used to waking up this early?"

"I don't run a company anymore. And even when I did, my days started at seven. I didn't work out beforehand because I wasn't interested in being miserable before going to the office."

"And now you've got more time than you know what to do with." Greg looked past Chris. "Where's your mom?"

"She's been tired and not feeling well, so I told her to take a break from making the usual feast and sleep in."

"How'd she take that?" Greg said. "She's not one for sitting still."

"We'll see." Chris wondered, aware of the trait he'd inherited. "She might be elbow-deep in pancake batter by the time we get back."

"From your mouth to God's ears," Greg said as Chris closed the door behind them on the way out.

There weren't many words spoken during the short ride to the gym. There was too much on Chris's mind to pick a subject. Senada's shop flashed beside them on the way. He resisted the urge to look through the storefront, but only because Greg wouldn't have let it go unacknowledged. Spending the morning doing uncomfortable things was bad enough. Talking about uncomfortable things at the same time was a bridge too far.

"How're you holdin' up?" Greg asked while parking the car. "Now that you're a little more settled, I mean."

Chris took a hard look at the gym's entrance. "Welp, I haven't had coffee yet. Or breakfast. And now, I'm at the gym. I'm doing spectacular. You?"

"Always ready to deflect with sarcasm," Greg replied with an elbow nudge into Chris's side. "Don't ever let anyone call you inconsistent."

"I don't think they'll have time when they're done calling me incompetent, inexperienced, and inept," Chris orated.

"Sounds like you're quoting someone."

"I read it this morning."

"You read about yourself? No wonder you're in a bad mood."

They checked in at the front desk before entering the former window & door shop that'd been adapted into a modest-sized gym. Chris observed the equipment and clientele as Greg waited on the approval of his guest from a toned, blonde woman with a tight French braid. To Chris's surprise, he and Greg were at least a decade younger than everyone other than the front desk clerk. The machines and weights looked impeccable, likely because they were barely being used. A row of treadmills, however, was teeming with sexagenarians getting their steps in.

"You come here a lot, right?" inquired Chris.

"Two or three times a week, if I can."

"And you don't think you might stand out a little bit?" Chris offered as they made their way to a pair of recumbent bikes.

"I know what you're getting at. And it is very much intentional."

Chris climbed onto the bike, speechless while maintaining eye contact until Greg understood that such a statement required further explanation.

"Why would I go to some boutique gym two towns away just to be surrounded by college lacrosse players with two-percent body fat and Pilates instructors filling time between photo shoots? I don't need that kinda negative energy in my life."

They cackled and pedaled slowly enough to meet the lowest standard of a warm-up. The stress had taken a toll on Chris. It didn't take much effort to raise his pulse.

"Do you think you might be depressed?" Greg blurted, as though inviting Chris onto a train of thought already in motion.

"Way too early, man."

"I've been depressed before. Some days, I could barely get out of bed or take a shower."

"I've had my share of ripe days," Chris disclosed.

"Then I had to figure out how to handle it. The days used to feel so short when I was working eighty hours a week. Then I stopped and the world didn't. It was like life was going by faster than ever. I spent a lot of time wondering what the hell to do next."

"So that's why you dragged me here?"

"Kinda," chirped Greg. "But I know you tend to go pretty deep inside your head. It's like an ocean in there. And most things won't survive below a certain depth. I figured you could use a break."

"So, you're giving me a break… from my break?" sneered Chris.

"That was some heavy philosophical shit I just said, and you're making it sound stupid. But it's not stupid. It's brilliant."

"Call it whatever you want." Chris dismissed it before noticing the deflective tendency Greg had mentioned earlier. "I do appreciate what you're trying to do. I just don't think there's much to be done. This is my life now. I'm jobless, aimless, and alone."

"You smell that?" Greg balked and wafted something away from his nose. "There's a lot of bullshit. I can't believe you're not smelling it too."

"That's as honest as I can be."

Greg rolled his eyes nearly out of his skull. "You're not being honest. You're just not lying."

"Okay, then what the hell am I 'not lying' about?" Chris was too tired to hide the internalized frustration he'd normally suppressed.

"You're only jobless in the way that…I don't know… Bill Gates is jobless." Greg tallied his fingers like he was preparing to make multiple points. "You may not have a job, but you don't need to work. You're not exactly lining up for unemployment benefits."

"You just compared me to Bill Gates. You don't have a clue what—"

"And you're aimless like someone who doesn't want to aim because it's easier than missing the shot."

"I'm not even sure what that mea—"

"And that brings us to the real issue."

Chris stopped pedaling. "You're clearly on some kind of roll, so please… tell me what my real issue is."

"You're depressed," Greg proclaimed. "And that's a reasonable thing to feel. But then the question becomes… why?"

"That's not a question. And I know why I'm depres—," Chris interrupted himself. "I'm not depressed."

"Let's call it a rough patch then," Greg compromised. "My therapist told me that—"

"You're in therapy?"

"There it is! Deflection! That's what she talked to me about. That when we feel things we don't want to acknowledge, we force ourselves into something else. Sometimes it's work, sometimes it's sex or drugs or drinking. But you can find out a lot about your real problem if you pay attention to what you're using to avoid it."

"Even if I was trying to avoid something, how could I possibly do that when I'm surrounded by it all the time?"

"Aha! There *is* something you're avoiding!"

"That's not what I'm saying," Chris resisted.

"Exactly," sniped Greg. "Honesty is the only way out of this rut. And if you can't be honest with yourself, then at least test the waters by being honest with me. This is something all the money and free time in the world can't protect you from."

"What if I paid you?"

"Not gonna work this time, buddy," Greg retorted right away. "Because when I only heard your voice on birthdays and holidays, and it took days for you to respond to my texts, I didn't hold it against you. I understood you. I understood, better than just about anyone, what you were trying to accomplish, and I understood why you couldn't do it here. I let you make decisions that changed both of our lives, and I trusted you. Now it's your turn to repay the favor." Greg took a deep recovery breath. "Come on, let's go lift some weights."

The riot act shook Chris, while Greg transitioned to the next phase of their excursion with relative ease. It was easy for Chris to ignore the impact of his impassioned choices on others. He'd knocked down a building and left the people he cared about most to build lives from the rubble.

They continued the improvised workout, moving from one muscle group to another until they were both sufficiently fatigued. Chris's struggles with lactic acid buildup brought consistent banter out of Greg, but Chris was in too much pain to engage in the kind of small talk he'd hoped to avoid anyway.

They'd wrapped things up with a light jog as the standard 9am rush of senior citizens descended on the gym.

"Looks like a good time to get outta here. You hungry?" Greg suggested as soon as the outside air refreshed them.

"I could eat," Chris murmured, still trying to catch his breath and wait for the feeling to return to his arms.

"Are you craving anything in particular?"

As they got back in the car, Chris was only half-present, still wrestling with Greg's earlier offer of candor. Over the years since his departure, he'd taken a lot of things for granted. Greg was one of them.

"You're right," Chris muttered, unprepared for thought to become words.

"I'm right a lot. You've gotta be more specific," Greg responded as he put the key in the ignition.

Chris rested his head against the window and looked out on the mostly empty lot. "I'm not giving you credit for telling me things I already know."

"That's one of the most significant bummers of my life," jeered Greg.

"But… I'm willing to acknowledge that you may be right about how it feels to be back. I can't deny… it's been a struggle."

"Especially when you look across the street, huh?" Greg raised an eyebrow at Chris, who smiled tensely before realizing it wasn't a joke.

It'd only taken five weeks for Chris to be tired of the cycle of emotions. Avoiding the bedroom window didn't work because he could hear her van struggling to start every day. Staying home didn't work because she could be in the garden on any given day. Going out didn't work because he looked over his shoulder every ten seconds, worried he'd run into her again in their microscopic town. All in all, his daily life had become a lot more exhausting than any workout could be.

"You might be onto something. I think it's time for me to stop hiding from it."

"Hiding from what?" Greg said, already satisfied with the endorsement.

"The inevitable." It was the succinct and furtive way for Chris to profess he had no idea what would come next. But whatever it was, Chris needed it to happen soon.

13

Senada could neither afford to fix the problem, nor afford to ignore it anymore. It was bound to bite her in the ass eventually, but she wasn't ready for the moment to arrive. Prayers wouldn't save her this time. The van wouldn't start.

She'd already accepted the van wouldn't be leaving the driveway anytime soon. But the impotence of the struggling starter was like a song she'd put on repeat; a soundtrack of how far she'd fallen.

Senada folded both arms across the steering wheel in surrender, resting her head on them as if sleeping in a class she'd given up on passing. She was brought to tears from the exhaustion of fighting too many battles at once. Her body shook and writhed with every audible purge of emotion.

A vibrating sensation hummed against her thigh. Senada quickly pulled out her phone and looked at the screen long enough to recognize the un-saved number. Her follow-up doctor's appointment was the next problem to be put off. There were too many other types of pain plaguing Senada without Dr. Lawson pressing into her abdomen again. Sex was the last thing on her mind, especially since her IUD had been removed, so pain wasn't a concern in that department. Cancer wasn't worth thinking about until a medical professional said so. Pregnancy was never in the cards, though she'd sidestepped that conversation with Dr. Lawson for years. Outside of some annoying pain, the presence of a cyst or two wasn't a priority.

A figure cut into Senada's peripheral vision and knocked on the glass, startling her. It took a second for Chris to come into focus. Senada reflexively tried rolling down the automatic window before remembering a dead battery wouldn't allow that to happen. She nudged the door open for them to hear each other.

"Hey." Chris made a short greeting sound even shorter.

"Hi," she exhaled, still unsure how to process the sight of him.

"Sounded like you could use a hand." He sounded sheepish and unsure if they could speak freely.

She stepped out and opened the door for some levity. "I think my van might finally be dead and buried."

Behind her, the loud slam of the heavy door kicked her senses into high gear. She was close enough to smell the vanilla & cedarwood shower gel Chris had used since college. It was hard to ignore, spawning tactile memories of the night they'd gotten much closer. It was one of many things bombarding her senses while she wrapped her mind around how she'd ended up with her legs wrapped around his waist. Senada yanked herself back from the edge before falling completely into the memory.

"I dunno. There might still be some life left in her," Chris said plainly. "Mind if I take a look?"

"Sure," she blurted. "I mean no, I don't mind."

As he reached past her and reopened the door, Senada moved out of his way, keeping distance between them like two magnets with the same charge. Her pulse quickened at the sight of how immediately familiar he became with her most vital possession, even though he'd never been near it before. In an instant, the hatch was propped open, and Chris was exploring beneath the hood with his eyes and hands. Senada couldn't tell what he was doing but she fell right back into trusting him as though he'd never left. If there was a way to get the van started, he'd find it.

For old times' sake, Senada looked over his shoulder like she had when he first got the Nova. She used to pepper him with questions while he'd toil under the hood. The answers only mattered to him, and she wouldn't have remembered them no matter how hard she tried. Senada had enjoyed Chris's enthusiasm as he'd answered every 'what does this thing do?' that she could come up with.

"I'll be right back," he said before breaking into a jog toward his house. Senada leaned against the back of the van, her head resting against the three fading lilies as she watched him cross the street. Her inner teenager was running beside him just to remember what it felt like. She reckoned with thoughts creeping back into her consciousness like they'd never left.

Chris returned with a small canvas tool bag. "I think I know what the problem is," he said while moving intently toward where he'd last stood.

Senada recognized the battery and noted the way Chris hovered over it. He took out what appeared to be a long toothbrush, made of a substance one wouldn't want anywhere near their mouth, and rubbed it along the surface, removing a crusty white substance. He sprayed something from an aerosol can that started out as a red liquid, but calcified around whatever it touched, complete with a brief fizzing sound.

"Give it another try," Chris said in a firm tone.

Senada got behind the wheel and turned the key once more. The sputter of a resurrected engine brought a smile to her face, wider than any she'd had in a long time. "What did you do?"

"Your battery terminals are corroded. I cleared and coated them."

"Gotcha." She didn't get any of it, but the hint of smirk I garnered from Chris made the attempt worthwhile.

"The battery should alright for now, but you really need to change it soon. Before you end up stranded a lot farther from home," he said with a grin she'd longed to see. "And… you know where to find me if you need any-thing."

The last sentence was as surprising as it was genuine. Chris slammed the hood shut and walked away as calmly as he'd arrived. Senada opened her mouth to thank him, but something stole her breath. She was grateful, but that's not what she really wanted to say. And Senada was tired of saying anything else.

"Chris! Wait!"

He stopped and turned around, either oblivious or unconcerned about being in the middle of the street. A surprised look on his face was the only visible reaction she could discern.

"I need your help with something," she said ambiguously.

Senada waited for him to respond, but he offered nothing in return. She was irreversibly exposed, and it was too late to walk back the statement. Chris appeared more confused as she moved toward him in a careful hurry. She stopped a few feet away, close enough for him to be too far away to touch.

"I can make you a list of what to ask for when you take it to a shop. It won't be cheap, but it'll keep the thing running."

"I'm not talking about the car," she answered through breaths that more closely resembled hyperventilation. "Wait, well, a list would be helpful because, you know me, I wouldn't have the first clue what —"

Senada stopped talking as 'you know me' reached her ears. It wasn't news to either of them, but in the throes of feeling so alone lately, the reminder was staggering. Her bearings became impossible to find, yet she was looking at the person who'd always known how to guide her back to true north. Chris knew each 'how' and every 'why'. With him, there was no reason to pretend to be someone else. All he'd ever really see was Senada.

She struggled to decide which Senada to be — the girl he'd known so well, who could tell him everything with flippant ease, or the woman she'd become, terrified by how much she still had left to lose. This moment had occurred in her imagination, playing out in a hundred different ways, but none of them encapsulated the real thing. Chris had walked away before, and she hadn't stopped him. Now she'd stopped him before knowing if she could be honest enough to explain why. Letting him leave again, without surrendering some truth, was enough to push Senada beyond her limits.

"I miss you," she uttered.

"I miss you too," Chris replied.

The swift certainty of his delivery was a surprise. "Really? Um, okay, so listen, I have to, uh..."

Chris cocked his head slightly, as if deciphering her attempt at forming a sentence. "Senada, I don't know if this is the best time for us to —"

"There's no best time. There's no good time. There isn't enough time to wait for a good time." Senada barreled through the thought without concern for whether it made any sense. "Please, just let me get this out, because... it's been quite the journey since the last time you and I really talked. And if I don't say this now, I might lose what's left of my mind. So please... don't speak until I'm finished."

"If you don't say what?"

"Chris!"

He showed both palms in concession. "Right. Sorry."

Senada folded her arms at her chest, took a deep breath, and searched for the best route to an unknown destination.

"Remember when we were eleven, that time we went into the woods at the end of the dead-end street around the corner? Do you remember?"

Chris returned a single nod. "You tried to walk along the trunk of a downed tree. Slipped on some moss and fell."

"And broke my leg in two places." The fog started to clear up. "Do you remember what you said while we waited for the ambulance?"

Chris didn't need to answer. She knew he'd remember every word and that's why she'd mentioned it. His hardened shell was slowly cracking before her eyes. She waited, expecting him to walk away. But he didn't. In spite of how shaky he looked, he stayed.

"You told me." Senada got choked up and had to start over. "You said you weren't going anywhere. You promised to stay with me."

"I know." Chris looked into the clouds, and Senada followed his eyes, noticing how grey and overcast the morning had become.

"Well… you broke your promise. Every time I needed you, you were gone. When I got the idea for my shop and I knew you were the only one who'd get it, you were gone. When I finally got a small business loan and needed someone to celebrate with, you were gone. When I found out my mother left me a house that wasn't paid for, and I could barely keep my business afloat, I was looking for your shoulder to cry on and I couldn't find it. And when I failed at enough relationships to know that I was too broken to be loved, I looked for you, the person who always made me feel loved anyway. And you're back, and I don't recognize us."

Chris dropped his shoulders in a manner she recognized. Maybe some of her words had gotten through to him. "Things are just so… complicated between us."

"They are," Senada said with a bit of relief before swallowing a razor blade of fear and trudging forward. "But maybe it doesn't have to be that way. Maybe *we* don't have to be that way."

"I don't know what that means anymore."

It was a reasonable response. Senada hadn't considered it. What she wanted was clear, but how to get it was far from obvious.

"Maybe… we can find who we used to be." The words stumbled out of Senada's mouth and fell flat, but she tried to save them. "I don't expect it to be an overnight thing. But so much time has passed that we can't get back. I don't want to lose any more of what we could be."

"That's funny," he replied without an ounce of humor. "That's how I felt twelve years ago." He looked away. "I was tired of us not being what we could've been to each other."

A car beeped and they turned to see an old lady behind the wheel of a Lincoln attempting to go down the street. They separated and let the sedan pass between them. Once it was clear, Senada took a step towards Chris, anticipating he would return to the spot they were standing. But he didn't move.

"I want the same thing as you." Chris said.

"That's hard to see right now," she confessed.

"I promise I do." Chris paused with the irony and Senada used the silence to brace herself for disappointment. "I just don't know if I'm ready."

"That's okay, Chris. Like I said, it won't be an overnight thi—"

"No, Senada," he interrupted. "I mean… I don't know if I'll ever be ready to go back to what we were."

The finality of his words rocked Senada to the core, a reminder of how unforgiving it felt when his compassion was absent.

"So… you miss me… but you don't want me back in your life?"

"That's not what I'm saying." Chris gestured toward his house. "It's safe to assume you're going to be a part of my life in one way or another."

Resistance seethed within her. "Don't do that."

"What mistake did I make this time?" said an exasperated Chris.

Senada needed a second to ignore the subtle referendum. "Don't talk about my relationship with your mom like it's something you have to put up with. No one made you come outside. No one made you—"

Senada stopped speaking, but Chris locked onto her unfinished thought. "Don't stop. Say what you really wanna say."

"No one made you… come back," Senada sighed, already regretting the expression. "I don't know how you can throw away our friendship so easily, disappear for a decade, and then come back just to keep me away again."

"You think walking away was easy?" Chris shot back. "You can't be that blind."

"You made it look pretty easy. No phone call or text. Nothing when my mom died. Nothing when your dad died." Senada could see what the reminder did to him, and she didn't like how familiar it felt to hurt him. "What else am I supposed to think?"

Chris dropped the tool bag and took a step towards her. "Did it ever occur to you that those might be signs of how hard it was to be away from you? I had my moments too. There were times when I almost reached out to you and talked myself out of it. Times when it felt like you were a phantom limb that I could feel but couldn't see. When I reached my goal and when I had it snatched away from me. And every moment in between. Not just the rough times, the good ones too. I wanted you there for all of it."

"But I wasn't there! And you were the reason why!" she shouted.

"You weren't there! And *you* were the reason why!" he yelled back. "You rejected me! I wanted you to be a bigger part of my life than ever, and you pushed me away!"

Senada recognized they were too heated for a suburban setting and checked over each shoulder to make sure their heightened volume hadn't made someone open their curtains.

"I didn't push you away, I just couldn't let things get out of control between us," she replied, hoping to reintroduce calmness to their dialogue.

Chris picked up the bag again and moved toward the sidewalk. "I should go before I say something I don't mean."

"No," she countered.

Chris looked puzzled by her defiance. "Excuse me?"

"I want you to stay right here and tell me something you do mean." Senada petulantly crossed the street and sat on the curb, hiding a painful abdominal convulsion that followed the movement. She patted the cement slab beside her, inviting him to sit. "You can't hurt me any more than I already am. So don't spare me. Tell me the truth. Tell me our friendship wasn't worth holding onto once you realized it couldn't be more than that. Tell me our friendship wasn't real at all. That it was all a long con to get in my pants. And once you got what you wanted and things didn't go your way, you took off. That's what you're really afraid to say, isn't it?"

Senada was so incensed, nothing that came out of her mouth next would've been a surprise. But she knew it would get Chris's attention. She'd implied something neither of them believed could be true, but she didn't care. If it made him sit and talk to her, it was worth a try. She kept her back to him and waited. The sound of the tool bag clanking against the concrete signaled success. He sat beside her on the curb, resting his arms on his knees with a foot of space between them.

"The only thing I've ever been afraid to say to you is the one thing I wish I'd never said," he began, luring Senada's eyes toward his. "Everything would've been so much simpler if we were just two friends who hooked up one night and then moved on like it never happened. But that was never gonna work for us."

"Wait," Senada stepped in before Chris could lead the conversation any further from the truth. "I didn't want us to pretend it never happened."

"That's exactly what you said to me before I left."

Driven by pure instinct, she was ready to fight back. But the blur of their final argument left her unsure if she'd actually said that after all. "I just wanted to find a way for us to still be friends."

"And I couldn't pretend to still be friends."

Her heart split open and words were the only stitches she had. "But it was one night. One time. Up against years of friendship. Why did things have to change between us?"

"That wasn't my decision. Things had changed between us already," Chris said. "One night didn't start it, but one night finished it. Our bond was always genuine. I promise you that. But I couldn't go back to just being friends."

A breeze wafted between them as Senada wondered what either of them might say next.

"I thought I was doing us both a favor," he continued. "I figured it was easier than subjecting you to my heartbreak. They were my feelings to manage, and I handled it in the only way I knew how. Because I couldn't undo my real mistake. I couldn't un-say 'I love you.'"

There was something within Senada keeping her from consuming the sentiment. All she could hear was it being a mistake to love her. The idea of her mother being right all along made her retreat to the darkest corner of her mind. She was ready to defy Chris despite knowing that's not what he was saying. In death, as she did in life, her mother held a firm grip on how Senada assessed other's perceptions of her. Not even Chris was immune to it.

Senada didn't want to fight him. She wanted to fight through everything standing between them. To topple the years of separation and longing that had stolen so much time from their connection. She wanted him to show her how to be fearless with her feelings. She wanted to meet his level of honesty.

"And if I'm being honest, I knew that before the night we... you know."

"What do you mean?" she asked.

"We stopped being friends long before that limo ride." Chris took one more breath, making Senada tense. "This wasn't a long con or something. I've always wanted you to be happy. But at some point, I wondered why I would leave it up to someone else to bring you that happiness. I thought, what's so bad about being loved that way by the person who already loves you most? Everything I could've looked for in someone, I'd already found in you. And once I knew that, being just friends felt like a lie."

"But I've seen what love does to people. It ruins them. It gives them hope, and then it breaks them, and eventually... it destroys them. I couldn't risk losing what we had."

Chris stood up and grabbed the bag again, clenching it more tightly than before. "Maybe you're right. Maybe love destroys a lot of things. But it didn't destroy us. *We* did."

Senada watched him walk away, and with him, any chance of finding the courage to tell him what she was most afraid of saying. It wasn't the right time to be brave.

14

It was a chore to get a nearly fifty-year-old car to cooperate, but the same could've been said of the forty-year-old man under its hood. The thing about 'playing it cool' was, once Chris had returned to room temperature, he'd regretted remaining so composed. There was more to be said, but he was ravaged by everything he hadn't said. Although he'd been committed to hiding any remnants of heartbreak, he didn't gain the clarity that could've made him hurt less. He hadn't learned anything new. In fact, in the few days since slapping a quick fix on the van, he'd walked away with even more questions. While he hadn't lied to Senada, he hadn't been completely honest with her either.

Only a small yet bright work light, hanging from the hood, cut through the darkness of the 9pm hour. He wiped away the patches of black grease from his callused palms with a red rag before getting behind the wheel. Memories of Senada in the passenger seat barged into his mind.

Chris had grown weary of the struggle. He could admit that much. The prospect of returning to the friendship they used to have was maddening. It bordered on insulting to believe they could undo things that couldn't be undone. And if he'd had the courage, Chris would've told her every reason they shouldn't try to go back in time. Their pivotal night may have destroyed their platonic bond, but he didn't regret it. His only remorse revolved around telling Senada everything he'd felt for her when the sun came up.

The restoration was meant to help clear his mind. But after hours of work and spending a small fortune at Colvin's, he was closer to reaching his goal and further from forgetting his troubles. As irrational as he knew it was, getting the car to start would be a symbolic step. But like most symbols, it meant whatever he wanted it to mean. It didn't really change anything.

When Chris finally put the key into the ignition, an unrelenting fear overtook him: this might be as exciting as life was going to get. Far removed from the days of fundraising galas and catered business meetings, he'd become everything he'd once despised: average. It was the easiest outcome to bet on. Most people were, by definition, average. Chris had always believed there was more in store for him than suburban mediocrity. The revival of a dormant machine could've represented a step toward hope, but by morning, he was still going to be an unemployed and unattached middle-aged man.

The dreary epiphany removed any potential enthusiasm from the turn of the key. The small-block V-8 engine roared to life, pushing tremors through the idling husk behind the wheel. The rumble shook the entire chassis and poured a wave of dusty heat into the cabin. Chris laid against the headrest and closed his eyes as if enjoying an orchestra. It was all he needed before removing the key and being enveloped by a new solitude, where his steady breathing was the only sound left.

Chris exited the vehicle as more thoughts raced to take advantage of the break his mind sought. He slammed the hood and leaned against the bumper, spitting onto the innocent grass in hostility. His attention landed on the spot in the street where he'd let too many things go unasked and unspoken. But everything he wanted to know could've been encapsulated in the answer to a single question: why?

Every possible response, from the reasonable to the irrational, had gone through his mind for what felt like eons. Why did she kiss him? Why didn't she stop there? Why was he worth fucking? Why was that all he was worth? Why didn't she stop him from leaving? Why was it so easy for her to burn down their bond and then imagine a friendship could be pulled from the ashes?

There was no ideal way to have such an imperfect conversation. And Chris was no stranger to venturing through uncertainty. But the last question on his list was inevitable and internal: why did it take twelve years to be willing to ask these questions? None of them were new, but he didn't ask them back when the answers might've mattered more.

'What You Won't Do for Love' played softly from the den, welcoming Chris's reentry. The tune spurred visions of his parents dancing together to the Bobby Caldwell ballad. Barbara was relaxed on the couch with a picture frame against her chest, too enraptured by the song to notice he'd walked into the room. Chris was in no rush to interrupt. Her happiness was restorative for him, especially when she dared to spend time being more than just his mother. He envied Barbara's willingness to fall so deeply into emotions that must've also been painful.

While his days felt long, it was sobering to recognize his parents had been together for longer than he'd been alive. Chris was stressing over twelve years without someone he could've called whenever he wanted, and that paled in comparison to his mother coping with the loss of someone she'd been with for forty-five years. And his father was never coming through the door again.

Barbara opened her eyes. "Christopher, I didn't hear you come in. How's the car coming along?"

"It's running again," he said as he sat on the recliner beside the sofa. "You didn't hear it?"

Barbara looked at his shoes, then back at him. She repeated the pattern until he got the message and kicked them off his feet.

"I must've been lost in my own world," she said.

Chris pointed at the frame. "What you got there?"

Barbara lifted the frame and turned it toward Chris: a black-and-white portrait of James and Barbara's wedding day. It was a little blurry and had a slight sepia tone from aging, but it was precious in the way long marriages tended to be — flaws and all.

Chris had seen the picture countless times, the only one taken that day, from a forgotten era when people were more concerned with seeing things than being seen. Most moments didn't require a hundred photographs. His mother's regard for the old photo was a warm reminder of what it meant to value the bond between time and people.

A tear streamed down Barbara's cheek, interrupting his train of thought. Their evenings were aligned, both reliving fond memories of the same man. It wasn't the first time he'd seen his mother cry, but her recent frail state had become concerning.

"Are you going to be alright, Mom?"

"Going to be? I'm alright *now*," she giggled. "The day that I look at a photo of your father and feel nothing, then you'll know I'm not alright." She always delivered sage advice as if it were just words falling out of her mouth by chance. She sat upright on the couch to get a better look at her son.

"Did I thank you for Mother's Day?" she asked. "I can't remember. But even if I did, I'm gonna do it again. Thank you."

"I put on a movie and made popcorn," he scoffed. "What's there to thank me for?"

"Well, you did try to make me breakfast," she teased.

"And I ruined it." Chris pretended to scratch an itch on his forehead.

"I'd say it provided the humbling experience you needed to make up for it later."

Chris eyed his mother with curiosity before catching on to the implication. "It was your day. If having her there made you happier, I'll survive."

"Still… I'm sure it wasn't easy for you. But your heart was in the right place."

"Finally," he complained before noticing he'd said it aloud. Chris adjusted his posture and hoped his mother would leave the statement alone.

"Hmm," Barbara delivered ominously.

"What's that about?"

"Nothing."

"Mom."

"It's not my business," she replied. "I'm staying out of it."

Chris was playfully aghast. "Since when?"

Barbara's reluctance slowly waned. "Senada dropped off some plant food yesterday. She was… different. I thought you two might've crossed paths."

"You saw us, didn't you?" Chris asked matter-of-factly.

"Of course I did! You were standing in the middle of the street in broad daylight! Which, by the way, don't even get me started on why you felt the need to stand in the middle of the street." Barbara stopped the parental tangent, but a concerned stare remained. "You seem different, too."

Chris shrugged subtly, unsure how to get his body and emotions to sync. "I don't know. Everything around me has changed. I'm the only thing that hasn't."

"And you're fine with that?"

"Why shouldn't I be?" he defied. "Look, I apologized. And that's more than I had to do. So I can live with her popping up a few times a year for your sake, but I doubt things will never be what they were between us."

"What'd you apologize for?"

"Does it matter?"

"I don't know," she brooded. "You don't sound sorry."

"I apologized for," he began in a huff, then calmed. "I apologized for telling her how I felt about her, and wanting more, and all that shi-, uh, stuff." Chris tried to stanch the bleeding.

"Oh," Barbara mulled. "I had no idea that's what bothered her."

"Yeah, um, uh," Chris sputtered before realizing something that should've been obvious. He didn't really know what bothered her. In his haste to defend his feelings, he'd never asked. The apology was for something that had hurt *him*. But he didn't know what had actually hurt her. And now, after so much damage being done, he worried it might be too late to find out. "Dammit," he whispered.

"My goodness, Christopher. Your generation and your pride," she jabbed. "Everyone's too good for a real apology because no one's really thinking about what they've done wrong. Everyone deserves this and that, without having to compromise, because they're so amazing and no one really appreciates it. You all constantly profess your worth and never show exactly why anyone else should find you valuable." She inadvertently mocked him with every syllable. "We tried to make you kids feel a little better about yourselves, and look at how far you've taken it. You all want the love we had. The lifelong bonds that enhance every wonderful thing life can bring. The bonds that make every treacherous part of life more bearable."

"I wish it were that simple, Mom," he grumbled as he ran both hands across his face. "So much time has passed. So much has happened."

"So much had already happened to that girl. Too much. That's life. And you were by her side for a lot of it. That's love — who you want beside you while life is happening. Want my advice? Figure out what you're *really* sorry for, and then apologize for that. Because in the end, we all want a love that leaves us with nothing to be sorry for."

Barbara became flush and short of breath. Chris hurried closer to her. "Are you alright?" he worried.

"Yeah," she panted. "I think I'm just tired. I'm gonna head to bed." She stood, clutching the picture frame more tightly than ever. When she reached the doorway, she looked back at her son. "I just want you to be happy. That's all I have ever wanted for you. You know that right?"

Chris nodded, barely able to make eye contact as her words rebuilt him. She wasn't one to raise her voice. Even during his rebellious teenage phase, she'd rarely shouted. Her tenderness carried more than enough power.

"Goodnight, Christopher," she said.

"G'night, Mom."

Chris sank deeper into the chair, staring ahead at the cost of his prideful stance against Senada. For so long, he'd been too steeped in his own pain to consider the impact his absence might have. Chris had told Senada the reasons he'd left. But he'd made a myriad of assumptions about why she'd let him leave without any resistance. He'd been asking himself the wrong question all along. It wasn't about why it had been so easy for her, but whether it had been easy at all.

15

It was a pleasant change for Chris to be awakened by sunlight beaming through the window instead of by his racing thoughts. He took his time getting up before sitting at the edge of the bed and taking in an unrecognizable, energized version of himself. After laboring out of bed on so many mornings, it was jarring to want to start the day right away. He hadn't the slightest clue what he was going to do, but he was eager to do something.

He sprang to life and sat at his desk, opening his laptop and then deciding there was no need to ruin the good mood so soon. If there was anything worth knowing about his company, the next quarterly earnings call would tell him.

The man who stared back at him in the bathroom mirror was almost unrecognizable. His skin was no longer sunken and starved, the red of his eyes had finally disappeared, and he was reminded of how it appeared to be a functional human being again. He even briefly weighed the possibility of tagging along with Greg to the gym. He wasn't going to, but he was proud of letting the thought venture into his mind.

Chris had bigger plans for the day: he was ready to start the final major leg of repairs on the Nova. With the engine running again, it was almost ready for the road. He just needed to change the brakes, rims, and tires, and he'd be ready to drive without a care or clue about where he'd end up. Such an endeavor might take a day or two of sweaty, forearm-burning work, but it would be worth the effort.

With fewer things to occupy his attention, the quiet of the house became more palpable. The familiar hardwood creaked more loudly beneath his feet, but only because the sounds and smells of Barbara's usual breakfast feast were absent. His mother was as bad as him when it came to giving herself a break, but it was better late than never. The opportunity gave Chris an idea: he could return a favor to her before spending the rest of his morning with an automotive distraction disguised as a hobby.

Unwilling to accept being bad at something, Chris was ready to tackle making breakfast again. The old Chris wouldn't have tried at all unless he knew there was a chance he'd be perfect at it. But after overanalyzing every mistake he'd made over the previous twelve years, he'd come to terms with the value of well-intentioned failure. He had to start with baby steps if he was ever going to move past losing the helm of a multimillion-dollar enterprise.

With a smile wider than his cheeks could handle, Chris retrieved the weapons for his arsenal: eggs, a cylinder of biscuit dough, and a ripe avocado to take the bacon's place. He grabbed a handful of strawberries, adding some color to the plate he was creating in his head.

After a few minutes of scouring the Internet for step-by-step instructions on doing things he'd regretted never learning, he was ready. This was going to be a breakfast so delicious, his mother would assume someone had broken into her kitchen to prepare it.

Feeling adept at something again was rejuvenative. To perform well was to honor the preparation he'd done, and as he sliced avocado, cut strawberries, and enjoyed the aroma of unburned biscuits emanating from the oven, Chris was back in the element he preferred. By the time he'd poured the scrambled eggs from the pot and onto the manicured plate, he was ready to submit a photograph to a culinary publication, but decided to wake up his mother first. Chris gave the silent smoke alarm a middle finger of triumph.

Chris trotted up the stairs and down the hall to her stock, white door. The antiquated knob elicited memories of being afraid to open it, worried he might break something so delicate.

"Mom?" he said between soft knocks to no answer. He turned the knob slowly. Its ornate brass design was cool to the touch. He nudged the door open and waited for the hinges to stop squeaking before speaking again. "Mom, are you up yet?"

Of course she'd still be asleep, thought Chris, on a morning when she could've witnessed her son turning into the next Gordon Ramsay. He approached the bedside and touched her shoulder, but something felt… off.

"Mom?"

Barbara Anne Mitchell's face held a peace that Chris had never known. She laid atop the fluffy comforter that once protected him from thunderstorms. Wrapped in the same nightgown she'd worn when she'd said 'goodnight,' the framed photograph still clenched tightly in her hands. His heart wanted her to be sleeping more deeply than usual. But his mind was more honest. She was finally holding her husband's hand again.

For a moment, there was no life left in either of them. Chris crumbled to his knees, burying his head against the cotton of her nightgown. He prayed for her hand to hold his in return. The longer he hoped, the less hope he had left. Unable to hold his weight, plummeted cross-legged onto the off-white carpet. Waves of sadness crashed against the once-formidable barrier he'd created to keep himself from feeling most things. Other emotions suddenly didn't matter as much. A burning sensation tore through his chest. He surrendered to the inevitable. Barbara deserved better than an armored version of her son.

His sobbing forced his body to rock and sway against his will. Chris fought his way back to his knees and went back to her hand. Barbara's lifeless touch assured him that she was free from any pain. His other palm clutched at his chest, his heart pumping hard enough to make him wish he could trade some of his life for more of hers. He would've given back so many moments if it meant he could steal one more with his mother.

☙

Senada winced through the first sip of a hastily prepared coffee. She had plenty of time to get to the shop, but hurried through the morning routine anyway. A shower had taken two minutes instead of twenty, she hadn't bothered drying her hair, and breakfast wasn't necessary. There was an anxiety within her, but she couldn't figure out the cause or how to quell it. Too tired to be introspective, she went along for the ride.

After consecutive nights of poor rest, going straight back to bed would've been the best thing for her mental and physical well-being. But Senada was exhausted in a way sleep couldn't remedy. The easy excuse would've been to blame it on stress, but she didn't have anything new to be stressed about. Nothing was any different than it had been. And that was just the beginning of her problems.

Since their heated dialogue on the street, she hadn't seen or spoken to Chris. But she wasn't avoiding him. She'd hoped to run into him, or at the very least, initiate conversation after a suitable cooling off period, though she had no idea how long either of them needed before they could speak without barbed wire attached to every syllable. And it was even harder to tell whether the ball was in her court or his. But there was more for her to say, and less for her to lose.

The night before, Senada could've sworn she'd heard the rumble of the Nova's engine. By the time she could reach her bedroom window, the rumble was gone. It could've been her imagination, but she wanted it to be real. The Nova's revival had become a proxy for their connection. No matter how small the progress might've been, a step for the Nova created hope for them to find their way.

She'd finished the last of what she was willing to consume before pouring the rest of the coffee down the drain. As soon as she opened the front door, flashing red and white lights caught her attention. An ambulance idled in front of Chris's house. She slowly descended the steps, cautious of any sign as to why an ambulance would need to be there, and, more concerningly, why it didn't appear to be in any sort of hurry.

She reached the van, but couldn't get in until she had an answer to one of the million questions running through her mind. For every second in which nothing occurred, she became twice as worried. A mixture of impatience and concern propelled her toward the house, one pensive step at a time. As she neared the home, a police cruiser became visible, parked in front of the ambulance.

There wasn't a single sign of movement from inside or around the house. As she reached the trimmed green fescue, a man in a navy-blue uniform backed out of the front door, his hands occupied with the foot end of a stretcher. Senada covered her gaping mouth, a reflex to the sight of two paramedics guiding Mrs. Mitchell's body from the home she'd made.

Senada went from sedate to trembling as the truth took hold. Within a moment, she doubled over and sank to her knees in the dewy grass. Her heart drummed against the inside of her chest. Every sight and sound pierced deeper as the medics hoisted the stretcher into the ambulance and closed the doors. She was in a vacuum, as if the medical personnel couldn't see or hear her.

Slowly, her vision came into focus through welled tears when she noticed Chris speaking to a police officer from the doorway. Their conversation was muted as she struggled to get back to the surface of a tidal wave of grief. She wanted to run away, but couldn't figure out how. Senada remained completely still as though Chris wouldn't see her unless she moved.

After watching both vehicles leave view, Chris stood with his hands in the pockets of his sweatpants, seemingly unaware of his mother's pseudo-adopted daughter kneeling on the front lawn. Senada rose to her feet, prompting Chris to turn his head in her direction. She didn't know what she'd expected, but his expression was unlike anything she'd ever seen. There was a vacancy in his eyes, like he was unsure Senada was really fifteen feet away. He exhaled and sat down so abruptly that Senada couldn't resist vaulting toward him, concerned that he might've collapsed. By the time she realized there was no imminent danger, she'd already committed to moving toward him.

When Senada reached his side and sat on the step, she kept an uneasy posture, leaving enough space for someone else to pass between them. Despite years apart, not knowing what might be going through his mind was still rare for her. Most of the time, she could look into his eyes and immediately know what was behind them. But nothing in their history could have prepared her for such a moment. Senada was having a hard enough time identifying her own emotions, let alone which ones might be coursing through Chris.

It felt right to say something, but any word that came to mind felt akin to an intruder. There wasn't a right thing to say, but there were plenty of wrong ones. Whatever she chose could either open Chris up or cause a swift retreat. She missed being a source of support for him, but wasn't sure how to step back into such a role, and even less certain about whether her presence could still provide such comfort.

Chris began to shake as if June had become January, catching Senada's attention in time for her to witness a tear streaming down one cheek. He obscured his face with a hand, looking away without turning his back.

Senada wanted Chris to trust her again, but to get there, she had to trust her own instincts. Even if her gut was wrong, she had to make a choice and remain confident in it, for both of their sakes. Yet there she sat, unsure if she could comfort the man she loved most. Their shared sadness took the fear out of her, and she couldn't bear to stay idle. Senada had to fill the space between them.

"Chris," she sniffled, speaking with more air than sound. "You don't have to do that." Senada reached for his hand and gently lowered it to reveal his tears. "Not with me."

Senada slid toward him and carefully wrapped an arm around him, unexpectedly opening the floodgates. Restrained cries became audible weeping. She rested her head softly on his shoulder and rubbed gentle circles along his back.

In an instant, the last twelve years, and their impact, had been erased. She didn't care what had taken place before. Not anymore. The somber morning reminded Senada of the only place she wanted to be. One of the few places she knew she belonged.

16

Chris couldn't care less about the improved fit of his suit. A disingenuous display of vanity was all he could muster, tugging on the lapel as if preparing to go on stage. A performance would be necessary in an hour, so he may as well practice in the bedroom mirror. Being the center of attention wasn't something Chris preferred, but it's exactly what he'd have to endure.

His mother was gone. The last place he wanted to be was in the front row receiving platitudes from people he either barely knew or had never met while she laid ten feet away. But that was the only thing on the afternoon's docket. Barbara's greatest quality was her ability to connect with anyone from anywhere, and Chris had to deal with the fallout of such a beautiful trait.

To his surprise, Greg honked the horn twice in quick succession, rather than leaning on it, a likely acknowledgment of the solemn occasion. Chris was met by Greg's suffocating embrace at the front door. In the midst of helplessness, he shot a glance down the street. Senada's van was gone. After providing a shoulder to cry on four days earlier, she'd been absent. He didn't take it personally, but the void was difficult to ignore.

They were in the car and halfway up the block before Greg decided to break the silence. "How you holdin' up?"

"Fine," Chris said in the same way he'd rehearsed all morning. "I just want to get this day over with."

Greg heeded the unspoken request and didn't say another word for the rest of the ride to the Burnett Funeral Home. Chris searched the radio for a tune to obscure the silence, but everything sounded like noise. Once the car pulled to the curb, Chris was already planning an escape. After making sure the arrangements were in order, sending Barbara's favorite dress and pearls, and choosing a casket, he'd had more than enough of the unassuming tan-brick building.

Every detail of the lobby was maddeningly familiar from when he'd last been there, holding his mother's hand while his father's coffin rested in a viewing room. The deep maroon carpet was so thin they could feel the concrete beneath their shoes. The wood paneling on the walls was recognizable for anyone who'd lived through the eighties.

The sight of the guestbook made Chris do an abrupt about-face to avoid seeing Greg sign it. The custom was reasonable enough, but he wasn't ready to acknowledge how many Thank You cards were in his future. But such thoughts saved him from the ones awaiting him in Viewing Room Six.

Wooden double doors were the only barrier ahead. Chris stopped short of them while Greg continued without prying. Going inside was inevitable, but Chris needed some time to treat it like a choice. There'd be plenty of other opportunities to respond in a way others expected.

Chris fled to the restroom and took in his reflection once more. The suit had gone from form-fitting to suffocating. He buried his face in a palmful of running water. The tepid liquid couldn't undo the boiling sensation pulsing throughout his body.

When he left the bathroom, there was a rising compulsion to move faster, despite the uncertainty of what awaited him. As soon as he touched the viewing room door's long gold-plated handle, a hand grasped his shoulder.

"Mr. Mitchell?"

Chris wished he didn't recognize the voice, but he did, tamping down internal resistance to being called by a moniker more closely linked to his father. It was impossible to forget the funeral director, especially after seeing him each day since they'd retrieved Barbara's body from Mercy Medical Center. The tall, broad-shouldered man towered over Chris, looking more like a retired football player than a mortician.

"Thank you for your help with… all this," he replied, skipping any needless formal greeting. "I know my mother would've really appreciated it. She always talked about how wonderful my dad's service was."

"We are a family business. We know how important these moments can be for the healing process," he replied with a pastoral tone. "With that in mind, can I show you the room before your guests arrive? We want to make sure everything is to your, and her, liking."

If you say so, Chris thought as he shrugged and followed the director through the double doors.

The room resembled a church sanctuary, with a center aisle separating rows of pews on each side. At the front right corner of the space was a podium with a tiny microphone propped up by a long, thin stem. In the center was the casket, a sleek mahogany home with brass handles on all sides. Chris still hadn't reconciled that his mother was inside. As odd as the thought was, the casket didn't look like something she would've slept in. Upon closer inspection of the podium area, something more noteworthy caught his attention. A subtly beautiful floral arrangement rested on a wire metal stand beside the casket. Chris couldn't recognize a single blossom, but he didn't need to know what they were to know they were perfect for his mother. There was just one problem.

"The flowers," he said, pointing at them with palpable intensity. "Those aren't the ones you showed me."

"Um, yes, Mr. Mitchell, correct. We were informed by our usual supplier that the floral arrangements were already taken care of, so we stepped aside. They said you would understand."

"Who said I wou—"

Another large arrangement entered his peripheral vision and interrupted his words. A blue and white tapestry was in the arms of the answer to his question. Without hesitation, Senada passed Chris and placed the arrangement on the only space around the coffin that wasn't already covered by flowers. She wiped petal remnants away from her black knit midi dress, accented with a row of large black buttons down the length of the front. Senada approached both men and exchanged pleasantries with the funeral director before turning halfway toward Chris.

"I know how much Barbara loved pastels," she said with an unexpected calm. "I thought she might appreciate some of her favorite flowers in those colors." She wrapped a sympathetic hand around his forearm, rubbing it in a distinct one-two rhythm before walking past him again. Entranced, Chris watched her leave the room.

The funeral director was still awaiting Chris's approval, and he spoke to the place where Senada had just stood. "This is… exactly how she would've wanted things to be." He omitted the 'almost' from the sentence.

Chris was taught a lesson real time: there was no such thing as 'ready' for a funeral. Despite going through the exercise with his dad, too many things had changed since then for him to feel equipped for the occasion. He sat in the front row, clutching the paper program tightly until it resembled the crumpled tissue in his other fist. The room was full — Chris could sense as much — but he refused to turn around. Being watched from any angle at any moment made him remain still. In search of a viable coping mechanism, Chris found solace in staring at the casket while the ceremonial steps of the program passed by. Various scriptures and poems were read, a hymn was sung by a young woman he'd only recognized as a member of Barbara's church choir, and he counted down the itinerary until he had to deliver the eulogy.

Despite his vigilance, the moment still caught him by surprise. A soft nudge from Greg prompted Chris to stand, take a folded sheet of notebook paper from his lapel pocket, and walk carefully to the podium. The hastily scribbled words didn't make the rest of the room any easier ignore. It was hard to make out every face, but he could tell the room was at capacity. A smattering of people even lined the walls behind the back row, unable to find a seat.

Chris unfolded the paper and flattened it against the dais. He raised his chin to speak, but the microphone was uncomfortably close to his face. He pushed it away, cleared his throat, and prepared for the fight of his life. The words he'd written didn't look or feel familiar, but they were all he had.

❦

It had only taken five minutes for Senada to volunteer her seat, too anxious to stay put without the old pew shaking from her restless legs. Leaning against the rear wall was the safest option. She'd watched more of the back of Chris's head than the funeral proceedings, looking for any sign that he was pretending to be okay. Other than a few instances where he'd bowed his chin to his chest, he'd barely moved a muscle for over an hour. But it only took a glimpse of his face at the podium for every poorly hidden emotion to be revealed.

The tremor of his voice, the defiance on his face, and the way he gripped the edges of the podium; it all spoke volumes to her. While Chris fought to conform to the expectations of every pair of eyes in the room, Senada did battle with feelings he was probably better off avoiding. When he opened his mouth to speak, she clenched her jaw. With fists balled so tightly her forearms burned and her nails left marks against her palms, her knees became weaker by the second. When he struggled to look away, she blinked for him. Grief was inevitable, but she wasn't amenable to the helplessness that accompanied it. Even if she'd known how to provide solace, she couldn't. And as he struggled to speak, she struggled not to.

"My mother is… was…" he stammered and restarted. "Ever since I was a kid, she would—" The words seemed to stifle each other, like Chris couldn't decide which ones should leave his mouth first.

Senada forced herself away from the wall, unclear of her intentions, with the hope of getting Chris's attention. If successful, she trusted her instincts to make the next move. Any decision was better than indecision.

She cautiously excused herself past the row of spectators along the wall and made her way to the farthest side of the room from the podium. By the time she'd made her way to the front row, Chris was the only one who hadn't noticed her. She silently begged for his attention, hands clasped at her chest. When he made eye contact, only one thing made sense to say.

"It's okay," she mouthed.

A disheveled nod was all she got in return before Chris tried to continue. Senada ambled a few steps back to where she'd started, watching her feet to make sure not to step on someone else's. While she began charting her retreat, she realized the room was still silent. Before her interference, at least, he'd been trying to speak. She couldn't bear to watch the fruitless search through such darkness. If Chris had any hope of finding a way out, she decided he wouldn't have to do it alone. Senada hurried past the flowers, the casket, and their history to reach him.

She laid her hand gently across his, freeing him from the responsibility of holding everything, and himself, together. The simple act offered Chris the chance to be inconsolable, and he accepted. A tidal wave of sadness depleted what was left of his will. Greg was already on his feet and on his way before Senada could wave for help. Greg guided Chris back to the front row, leaving Senada alone at the lectern.

Senada remained composed as she confronted the possibilities of what to do next. She reflexively placed both hands on the podium, accidentally crumpling the paper Chris had left behind. The first few lines caught her eye, and she argued internally over whether it would be appropriate to read what Chris had intended to share. The statement looked more like a biography than a eulogy. Senada didn't know enough about Mrs. Mitchell's path through life to honor such words. But, in remembrance of her, Senada had plenty to say. Barbara had been a refuge, a stable connection to a place Senada often longed for. This was a chance to make sure everyone, including and especially Chris, knew how profound an impact she'd had.

"It's not easy to be in this room, for any of us. Barbara Mitchell meant a lot to me for more reasons than I'll ever share in such a public way. But I'll do my best to honor her."

Senada made sure Chris saw her looking at him. His expression, through the crumpled tissue dabbing at his tears, was as curious as it was grateful. Senada stayed on him for another long second before returning her attention to the room of onlookers bracing for what might follow.

"Barbara was an incredible woman. I know that's not news to any of you, but it should be said anyway. Wherever she went, a light followed. And she was not afraid to shine it. Even when darkness was easier for me to bear."

The more Senada spoke, the more she discovered what really deserved to be said. A cavalcade of memories led the way.

"I've known Mrs. Mitchell since I was ten years old. My mom moved us here, kinda suddenly. I didn't know much about why we had to move. My mom said we had to, so that's what we did. It wasn't an easy transition for me. A new town and a new school can be a lot on a kid. But thankfully, I made a few new friends. And one of the first new friends I made was Mrs. Mitchell. Before we even started unpacking boxes, she brought homemade oatmeal cookies for us. I should've known she was special when she told my mother that raisins had no place in oatmeal cookies.

"And from then on, her door was always open for me. If you needed to borrow a cup of sugar, as they say, she would've given you the whole bag. And when I mentioned I was thinking of starting my own business, she didn't doubt me at all. In fact, she was my first paying customer.

"Mrs. Mitchell knew that some people need time and care in order to grow into who they're meant to be. No matter how beautiful the flower is, it didn't start out that way. She was patient with others even when they refused to return such grace.

"My mother had some… issues… of her own. And Barbara stepped up to become the mother I didn't know I needed. A mother's love is vital to a woman when she's trying to find herself. And she knew I still had a lot of searching to do. When you've lived and loved for as long as her, you become a treasure trove of knowledge that deserves to be given to the whole world. I guess I was just lucky enough to live across the street.

"I hope I never forget the lessons she taught me. And she taught me a lot of them. But one stands out even more today: don't run away from how you feel. Stand still for a moment and see how much life is trying to show you. It's not always easy to see. But some things are too beautiful to be easy on the eyes."

There would always be more to say, but Senada was finished. Even a single added word felt trivial. She took Chris's paper and walked toward him. When she got close enough to return it, he stood and hugged her. The tender moment allowed her to crumble too. Their mourning became a shared experience as they held one another, alone yet together.

17

Twelve Years Earlier

A rented tuxedo probably shouldn't have fit so well, but Chris didn't have a frame of reference. It was all he could afford, so it had to suffice. While the ultimate mission of the evening was to stand out, every man in the room would be wearing the same outfit. Rehearsing the elevator pitch became even more important. He recited the speech repeatedly while struggling to fasten cuff links. If he punched it up any further, he wouldn't be able to remember it. But he had a long ride and a helpful partner to suggest last minute tweaks.

It was rare for anyone's fortunes to change in a single evening, but the 'An Eye for An Investor' gala was a chance for lightning to strike the same place twice in a single storm. Nearly every competent venture capitalist in the dating app space was on the guest list, and one of them held the key to unlocking Chris's budding idea.

Chris kept his tuxedo jacket in hand, for fear that wearing it too soon would leave sweat stains under each armpit before the limousine even arrived.

From the top of the stairs, Chris watched an antsy Barbara waiting with a small digital camera in her hands. He recognized her elated nature from his prom as well as his graduation ceremonies from high school and college. It wasn't far-fetched to assume Barbara had a photo album ready and waiting to chronicle the occasion. If he thought it would make a difference, Chris would've feigned embarrassment. But after nearly thirty years of being her son, he'd gotten used to it.

"My goodness. You are so handsome!" Barbara wrapped both arms as far around Chris as her diminutive frame allowed. "You should wear a tuxedo more often."

"Then he'd better buy one. Those rental fees mount up fast." Mr. Mitchell's recognizable voice bellowed into the room before he walked in with both hands in the pockets of his khaki shorts and a prominent anchor tattoo peeking out of his short-sleeved plaid blue shirt. James thought like any suburban blue-collar dad, always ready to question if something was worth the money. "C'mon, Barb. Give him a little space before you wrinkle his shirt," he jested.

"I can't help it! Look at him, Jimmy!"

Mr. Mitchell looked his son up and down. "Do you feel as ready as you look?"

"Good question." Chris aspired to his dad's degree of witty nonchalance.

James nodded and slapped his son's arm. "You're ready."

"Thanks for the cuff links, by the way."

"They're my favorite pair, so if you really wanna thank me, bring 'em back." Barbara delivered a corrective elbow to Jimmy's gut. "Right, right. Uh…just have a great night."

The doorbell rang, sparking a tense grin from Chris. Barbara's excitement quickly surpassed his enthusiasm.

"She's here!" Barbara hurried the short distance to the front door and opened it.

There was no way to prepare for the image at the doorstep. It was like the first person to ever put on glasses and realize how much they'd been missing.

Senada stepped inside as confidently as she wore the ankle-length, strapless indigo dress that barely covered her matching open-toed heels, while perfectly hugging her narrow waist and ample top. She held tightly to a black clutch as if preserving her modesty. Chris was unsure of what was making his smile so wide, but he was unable to rein it in. As she entered, he tried to verbalize a reaction, but words had never been more evasive.

"Hey," she said timidly, her attire as foreign to her as the tuxedo was to him.

"Wow, you look…" the rest of his breath refused to leave his lungs. The woman who'd worn jeans and canvas sneakers almost every day was somehow the same woman in the evening gown before him. There was no way she'd lay on the hood of the Nova to recap the night like they had as teens.

"Stunning," Barbara said as she rescued him. "He's trying to say you look stunning."

"Yeah, uh, that." It was strange to compliment his best friend for being attractive. It wasn't his first time noticing her aesthetic. Far from it. But he'd never actually told her what had been running through his mind. There was enough on his plate trying to get the app off the ground. Chris couldn't afford to open the door for Senada to become any more of a distraction than she'd already been on countless nights being the audience for his ever-evolving pitch. It might've been easier to invite someone else, but she was his biggest cheerleader. He steeled his resolve against giving Senada's figure more attention.

"I'll be damned," James said as he noticed something beyond Senada. "I think your ride's here."

"Perfect timing," Chris said as he placed a gentle hand along the small of Senada's back to usher her toward the waiting Lincoln Navigator limo.

"That is quite the ride," James quipped. "Who's paying for that? Me?" he asked with a contagious fear that spread to Barbara.

"No, Dad," laughed Chris. "The guy I told you about from that big pitch meeting."

"Martin Stoneman from Stoneman Capital," interjected Senada.

Chris withheld how impressed he was by her recollection of the event's details, hiding the pride behind a hummed assent. "He's the one who invited us."

"He's obviously not stingy with his checkbook," James said in judgment.

"I hope the wallets of these guests are just as open," Senada whispered into Chris's ear.

Barbara's eyes lit up. "Wait, don't leave yet. I need to take Senada away for a moment."

"C'mon Mom, the car is here already," her son complained.

"The car's here for *you*. What are they gonna do? Leave without you?"

James chortled. "She's gotcha there."

Both women hurried up the stairs, a confused Senada attached to Barbara's hip.

Chris gave in and leaned against the doorway. James sent a 'one sec' gesture toward the driver, who was waiting next to the passenger door by then.

"C'mon Chris," said James. He walked into the kitchen and Chris followed. His father warily looked toward the stairway, then took a tall glass bottle from the top shelf of a cabinet. "Let's take the edge off you. You're a nervous wreck."

Chris exhaled and slumped both shoulders. "Is it that obvious?"

❀

Even for a doting maternal figure, Mrs. Mitchell was particularly excited to lead Senada into her bedroom. Senada had no clue what might've gotten her so worked up, but she followed blindly to the closet.

The sliding doors separated, and Barbara parted the hangers to reveal a small jewelry box. After a few seconds of rifling through each drawer, Barbara faced Senada with one hand clenched in a fist. "You forgot something."

Terror shot through Senada. Formalwear already wasn't her forte. Mrs. Mitchell sparked panic over what could've been left out of the preparation. She'd already stressed her way through every step of getting ready.

Barbara's skeptical eye made Senada wonder if she'd revealed too much of the chest she'd been self-conscious about since developing faster than every other girl in her eighth-grade class.

"Dammit," Senada fussed as she hoisted her dress up another couple of inches, mentally preparing to repeat the action all night. "I feel like I can never get them to agree with me."

"Oh no, they're not the problem," Barbara said.

"What's the problem?!" Senada asked, already blaming Chris for inviting her to this thing.

"Relax! There's no problem," Barbara persuaded. "You look amazing. But something is missing." Barbara opened her hand and revealed a stunning pearl necklace. "Turn around."

The shock was still setting in as Senada obeyed the direction. Barbara clasped the necklace around Senada's neck, then placed her in view of a nearby mirror.

"Mrs. Mitchell, I can't take this," she pleaded. The sight of such a beautiful piece around her neck made Senada conscious of how hard she'd worked to avoid her mother on the way out the door. She didn't need Carrie's added help to feel unattractive, but her voice managed to extend through space and time. "I don't know anything about pearls. Or jewelry. I know that's probably pathetic coming from a grown woman, but—"

"Hey! Stop that! There's nothing to know. You just wear it and be as beautiful as you are," assured Barbara.

Until seeing her reflection, Senada didn't know how good it felt to see a new version of herself. It no longer felt like a metamorphosis; more like an expansion of the woman she was. And a revelation of the woman she could become. She didn't hate it.

"I dunno why he wanted me to come. I'm not the kind of person you bring to stuff like this."

"What kind of person is that?"

"The kind of person who owns pearls," she joked, though secretly hoped Barbara wouldn't laugh.

"You think too much," Barbara said. "Stop worrying about being the right person and focus on being yourself."

"Mrs. Mitchell, I'm twenty-eight years old and I still don't have the slightest clue who that is."

"Don't be so hard on yourself." Barbara tucked a few errant strands of Senada's hair behind her ears.

"Being hard on myself it the thing I do best."

"Hey," Barbara cupped Senada's face in both hands. "Just because you look like your mother, doesn't mean you *are* your mother. Understand?"

Senada eked out a nod.

"Tonight is a chance to explore who you might want to be. And your mother won't be there to stop you. The only one who could stop you, is you."

"And these shoes," Senada said, lightening the moment.

"Yeah…" Barbara took a longer look at them. "Take 'em off during the limo ride."

"Good call."

"Senada," Barbara said in a stern voice. "Let yourself have a little fun for a change."

It was the kind of statement that would've normally terrified Senada. But this time, she was excited to take Barbara's advice.

❧

The sound of both women coming back down the stairs prompted Chris to down the last of his scotch. Chris couldn't quite pin down what had changed, but something was different about Senada. She shuffled toward Chris and surprised him with a kiss on the cheek.

"What was that about?" he asked under his breath.

"I honestly don't know," she said, leaving his mind to wander aimlessly.

"Come outside, let's get a picture before you go!" Barbara dashed past everyone and out the door, firmly pointing to exactly where she wanted them to stand. "Go in front of the hydrangeas," she directed.

"The what?" asked a puzzled Chris.

"These," Senada replied confidently, tugging him by the arm to Barbara's desired spot.

"She's learning," said Barbara.

Chris held Senada around the waist for longer than necessary while Barbara fumbled with the camera. The warmth of Senada's body traveled through him as she rested a hand against his chest. Chris shot a confounded glance at her, but Senada was busy looking at the camera.

"Say cheese!" Barbara shouted as she looked through the viewfinder.

Chris stemmed his confusion and tried to match Senada's joyous expression, turning on a smile as Barbara snapped as many photos as they'd allow.

"Alright, Mom. We gotta go, I don't want us to be late. And this is starting to feel like the prom all over again."

"This is a lot better than your prom. With a much better date."

The embarrassment was almost tangible. "For the hundredth time, Mom, this is not a date." Chris turned bashfully toward Senada. "I'm really sorry, you know how my mother gets."

"I don't mind," she rebutted. "It's harmless fun."

They eventually broke free of Barbara's photo shoot and made their way to the limousine. The driver met them, but Chris graciously insisted the dapper gentleman get back behind the wheel. Chris opened the door for Senada and gracefully took her hand as she slid into the rear bench seat. He closed the door before taking a final look at the porch. James and Barbara looked back at him with unabashed pride.

"Good luck, son!" his father shouted.

Chris entered on the other side, waving at his superstitious mother holding up crossed fingers.

It didn't take long for silence to overcome the car. Chris knew he should say something, but every potential word felt more awkward to say than the last. He didn't know where to begin.

Senada reached across the leather space between them and tapped his hand. "Don't be nervous. You're gonna be great tonight."

"I'm not nervous. Are you nervous?"

"Only nervous that I won't make it through the night in these shoes," she said while taking them off. "But I'm not the one whose name was on the invitation. Tonight, my name is And Guest."

"Oh please. You'll be the most stunning person in the room by a mile. By the time we're done, they'll be more likely to remember your name than mine." Chris noticed he'd reaffirmed her physical beauty without a second thought.

"Careful. That sounded like a compliment," she sneered.

Chris looked away in embarrassment, and she yanked him out of it.

"Hey, hey. I'm kidding. Stop overthinking every little thing," she posited. "This is your night. I'll be by your side the whole time. Just tell me what you need. What can I do to support you?"

A tranquil ease showered over him. "You're already doing it." He looked forward like he was searching for something. "By the way, how's it been going with, uh… I wanna say… Victor?"

"Vincent," she shot back jovially. "Pretty good. It's still early but I like how it feels so far."

"How many dates has it been?"

"Four. Or five."

"You don't know?" Chris asked through forced laughter.

"It's not always easy to tell what constitutes a date these days."

"Not easy for *you*," he replied as he pointed both forefingers at her.

"Well, nothing about dating is easy for me," she said, the energy drained from her voice.

Chris caught a shift in the vibe and stepped up right away, inclined to make Senada feel better whenever he could. "It's not like I'm one to talk."

"Good point. In fact, why am I even here? Shouldn't this spot have been reserved for… I wanna say… Raquel?"

"Rachel," he said, fairly sure Senada knew the woman's name. "And no."

"Why not?" she mocked. "How many dates has it been?"

"We don't date, so much as one of us texts the other and we end up ordering Mexican food and having sex."

"Things must be serious if you're eating Mexican food and having sex in the same night." Senada could barely get the sentence out before doubling over with laughter. "Now that's what I call passion."

Chris resisted for a few seconds, but her cackling spread to him. Once he'd finally caught his breath, he had a rebuttal. "I don't think I could ask her to come to something serious when we aren't serious."

"Fair enough." The curiosity in her eyes was either hard to hide, or she wanted him to see it. "But why aren't you serious? You're sleeping together. Spending nights together. Sounds serious enough."

"What woman could possibly take a nearly thirty-year-old man seriously who still lives with his parents and is, technically, unemployed?"

Senada's face turned sullen. "That's an oversimplification."

"Who has the patience for nuance when it comes to dating?"

"You, I hope," Senada replied. "Since you're pitching a dating app."

"A dating app should be about keeping people from wasting each other's time. The other ones are just terrible at it because they incentivize dishonesty. My app will get people to show up as they are." Chris recognized the pitch was bleeding into conversation already. "I hate having my time wasted. Why would I want to waste someone else's?"

"Waitaminute… do you really believe dating you would be a waste of time?"

"Don't act so shocked," he chuckled. "Do you really think someone would be happy dating me?" Chris wasn't sure why he'd asked, but once he had, her answer mattered.

"Are you trying to get all the negativity out of your system before we get to the party?" wondered Senada.

"Are you trying to get out of answering my question?"

Senada tried to put scattered thoughts together. "Well, one thing I've always loved about you is how honest you are. You're never acting. You might be underestimating how valuable a trait that is to women. It's comforting to know exactly what we're getting into with a guy."

"Eighty-hour work weeks that yield little to no money while I still live with my parents and get sent off to gala nights like I'm going to the prom. I don't know, it might be a tough sell."

"Oh no," she replied, entrenched in sarcasm. "A driven man with a dream who has a supportive family. How awful."

"Well, most women don't make it sound as pleasant as you just did."

"Isn't that why you invited me?"

"That," he said, then cut his eyes smugly to avoid full disclosure. "And I knew you'd say yes."

Unfortunate as the reality was, Chris was more likely to be remembered if there was a beautiful woman on his arm. And while he could've invited Rachel, it would've been a date, which would've led to discussions that turn into relationships that end in break-ups. Chris had enough on his mind without volunteering for more problems. On what could prove to be a stressful evening, no one else provided peace of mind like Senada.

"I'll be sure not to disappoint you. Embarrass you maybe, but not disappoint you." Senada corralled the bottom of her dress and laying across the side bench seat with her feet up.

"We should be fine as long as you remember that if you aren't absolutely sure you can eat an hors d'oeuvre in one bite, better to err on the side of caution."

"That happened *one time*!" said an incredulous Senada, shooting back to an upright position on the bench.

"It happened a few times. They were just all in the same night."

"It's not my fault they didn't know how to make a crab cake in the right size."

"But it *is* your fault that you ate twelve of them."

"They were really damn good! What do you want from me?!" she screamed jubilantly as they began playfully tussling without ruining their outfits.

After a few seconds of hands incidentally making contact in places that shouldn't feel appealing to him, Chris caught a glimpse of his urges and pulled back to regain composure.

"What's wrong?" she said, sounding disappointed the fighting was over.

"Nothing." Chris didn't lie, but the statement wasn't entirely accurate. "I don't know how many nights like this I'll ever get to have. If I'm going to share it with someone, I'm glad it's with you."

The silence returned, leaving Chris in search of a new topic to discuss. But the window to do so without creating suspicion had passed. In an instant, he'd delivered the opening salvo to an uninvited reality. There was a third and invisible guest, often present and refusing to be ignored for another night.

❁

Senada wasn't prepared for how gratifying it was to hear Chris honor her presence in such a touching way. Chris usually kept compliments close to the vest. A willingness to say something like that with such certainty made his voice strike a different chord.

She'd been his biggest fan ever since first hearing the idea. Whenever he'd needed to practice his pitches or edit proposals, she was first in line to help. Senada cherished how much Chris trusted her with things he cared about, and found security in their radical honesty. They were usually open in a way that could make most romantic couples uncomfortable, but their candor strengthened their friendship.

The darkness of the Midtown tunnel swallowed the limousine, and Senada could tell Chris was getting nervous again. Whenever he was uncomfortable, he would tap a staccato rhythm into whatever he was touching. If he couldn't find something, he would tap against his own palm. Upon exiting the tunnel and entering Manhattan, his fingers were playing a full concert against the leather seat. She slid across the space and trapped his hand against the top of her thigh.

"Chris. Take a breath," she implored.

"I thought I *was* breathing," he said at a manic pace.

"Come here," she said, though he was already close to her. "Tell me the pitch again."

He hurled an exasperated look at her. "You've probably got it memorized by now!"

"I probably do." Senada gently pulled his lapel, then released it, recoiling from how flirtatious it was. "Uh, so what? Tell it to me again."

Chris inhaled, held the breath for a few seconds, then slowly exhaled. Senada was giddy at the implementation of the boxed breathing technique she'd taught him to manage anxiety.

He cleared his throat. "Technology has revolutionized the dating space, but it opened the door for one of romance's biggest obstacles."

"Chlamydia?!" Senada shouted as if answering a teacher's question.

"I hate it when you do that!"

"Don't get distracted! You've gotta stay on your toes!"

Chris fought through laughter and continued the pitch. "It opened the door for one of romance's biggest obstacles: dishonesty. People show up for dates and put on a performance. Fancy dinners and expensive excursions that don't even come close to resembling the relationships they'd have in real life."

Through erratic arm movements, Senada encouraged Chris to continue, knowing it sounded better than the last ten times she'd heard it.

"BingeMatch reduces the likelihood of deception by connecting people through variables that people are more likely to do normally and less likely to lie about: the things they love to watch on television. Users can create profiles including their favorite shows and movies, then schedule a virtual date to watch the show together. It's a fun and safe way for people to get to know each other, and takes a lot less time and hassle since that's how most of us really want to spend our Friday nights anyway."

Senada curled her lips and raised both eyebrows, hardly able to contain her excitement. "I wish I had a bag of cash so I could hurl it at your head right now."

"That's… good?"

"Of course it's good." Senada hugged him. "You're ready. I know it."

Their embrace lasted longer than she'd intended, but Senada couldn't figure out why either of them was still holding on. The hard stop of the limo's arrival — 37th Street and Park Avenue, thirty feet from their destination — gave Senada an imperative to let him go. They lingered in each other's personal space as they separated. She took a moment to discreetly compose herself, checking the dress and adjusting more comfortably in the top before the driver opened his door.

Cool night air poured into the limousine, relieving Senada's tension and allowing her to find the 'best friend' hat she'd left at home. Senada held the skirt with each hand and waited for Chris to exit so she could do the same. But he didn't move. He stared forward without acknowledging the open door.

"I can't do this," he said bluntly, staring straight ahead with a blank expression.

"What are you talkin' about?"

"I can't go in there."

"Why the hell not?!"

"I've been working on this for so long, and this is the best opportunity I'm gonna get. If I fuck this up, this company is done. My parents are sacrificing so much to keep me afloat. A second mortgage on the house. Scraping by on my dad's retirement money while I chase a damn dream. If I can't get someone to take me seriously in there, the dream is dead."

"The dream will die if you stay in here. That's a promise," she countered.

"Yes, but then I wouldn't be a failure. I'd just be a 'what if.' I can live with being a 'what if.' There's been lots of 'what ifs.' It's not so bad. I'm just gonna stay here."

Senada struggled to recognize the feeble man beside her. Chris had never seemed so small. She'd watched him chase this chance for years at a maniacal pace, without the faintest hint of a personal life. It would've been easy for Senada to find some inspirational words to get him out of the funk, but a better idea came to mind.

"Look at me, Chris," she insisted with a furrowed brow. When he didn't, she directed him by the chin. "Look. At. Me. Do you see what I'm wearing?"

She watched his pupils follow the command, but they lingered on her body in a way she wasn't prepared for. Warmth glided along her exposed skin. His tacit and unprompted approval of the dress nearly distracted her from the point she'd wanted to make.

"Now what?" Chris asked monotonously, focused on either the pearls or the deep cleavage they were resting against.

"Do you think I put all this shit on for you to bail right outside the building? This dress. These shoes. None of this is me. I'm pretending to be someone else so I can support you becoming the person you want to be. So we're going inside that building or I'm gonna make this heel disappear in a place you won't enjoy."

Chris processed the demand. Senada raised her foot to his eye level, hoping to emphasize the point by displaying the height of her heel.

"I would not enjoy that," he declared.

"You wouldn't," affirmed Senada.

Chris took another breath and stepped out onto the sidewalk, holding out an arm as if preparing to escort Senada to dinner service on the Titanic. He lifted his chin comically high and exaggerated a smile.

"Right this way, Madam," he said in a horrendous attempt at a British accent.

"Good Lord." Senada barely kept her eyes from rolling out of her head.

The Union League Club's entrance may as well have been a portal to another dimension. The institution was founded during the Civil War, and modernization had obviously not been of high priority. Every antiquated square foot was polished, pristine, and preserved. Dust didn't stand a chance in this place.

The door frames and wall amenities were handcrafted wood, and the ceramic floor tiles reflected the light of the crystal chandeliers. Despite the gigantic foyer, Chris kept Senada close while they walked, wary of even the slightest misstep breaking something neither of them could afford to replace.

Guests passed them on both sides, providing a helpful path to the nearly hidden elevator bank. Obviously, this was the norm for many of the patrons waiting beside them. Their gowns were elegant, but not brand new, and their tuxedoes were spiffier than any rental. Chris and Senada silently agreed to slow down and avoided cramming into the elevator with the first group.

As they waited for the next car to arrive, Chris sent her a contemplative look, unsure of what they were walking into, but certain about his choice of company.

"Thank you for doing this," Chris offered sincerely. "And... for making sure I do it too."

"Oh please. Don't thank me." She faced him and tidied the lapels she'd ruffled earlier, then straightened his bowtie. "I'm happy to endure sore feet and an uncomfortable dress if it gets you closer to your dream."

They were close enough for Chris to smell her perfume. He pressed his lips together to keep from breathing on her forehead, suddenly unsure if he'd remembered to brush his teeth. Once he was properly kempt, Senada rested her palms against his chest, sliding them a few inches down his jacket before pulling away one finger as a time.

"There. You're ready. Now, how do I look?" she entreated.

Chris knew how to compose an honest response to such a standard question. He'd just never used any of those words to describe Senada. As she struck a cheeky pose, he weighed how truthful he should be. Or could be. Something was shifting within him, and the night was too young to trust his balance.

Under normal circumstances, there was nothing he couldn't tell her. But he wanted to tell her something he was afraid to admit — that instead of a best friend of eighteen years, he suddenly saw someone so beautiful that if she weren't real, he wouldn't believe she existed outside of his imagination.

"You look great." he equivocated. A chime rang, saving Chris by signaling the next elevator's arrival. A new crowd had amassed by then. A cramped ride would be inevitable.

The trip was short, yet long enough for Chris to have a slowly extending physical response to Senada backing against him to make room for more occupants. The puffy dress saved him from Senada noticing it against her butt. Or she'd done a masterful job of hiding her reaction to it.

The elevator doors opened directly into the banquet hall, where nearly three hundred guests became an overwhelming spectacle. Chris and Senada were closer in age to the staff than any of the attendees. There was as much silver hair as there were tuxedos, with every man looking as if he'd just stepped off an assembly line at an 'old money' factory. The women's attire was much more diverse, with every color of the spectrum on display beside varying interpretations of the dress code. And his date shined above them all. Senada's effortless ability to stand out made her natural allure even more compelling.

Chris gently tugged her toward the bar along the nearest wall. They weaved through a dense collection of bodies to reach the bartender. Chris ordered a scotch for himself, and an apple martini for her.

"Bold of you to order for me." Senada scrunched her face at him.

"So you *don't* want an apple martini?" he retorted with a confidence he knew would madden her.

Her eyes rolled again. "Lucky guess."

"Sure. Luck," he winked.

The bartender placed their drinks on the bar and Chris slid the martini glass toward Senada. They toasted and took their first sips while maintaining eye contact. Chris tumbled into her eyes and lost track of his bearings.

"What?" she asked.

"What?" he dodged. "I can't look at you?"

"Not like that," she pressed.

"Like what?" he wondered, curious of how she might've perceived his demeanor.

As Senada nearly got out the first word of a response, Chris buckled under the weight of two heavy hands on his shoulders.

"You made it!" shouted Greg. Chris tried to match the ever-present zeal of his business partner, but nerves were getting the better of him. "What you drinkin'?" he asked, lifting Chris's arm so he could waft the scent from the top of the glass. "You sure that's strong enough? I thought by now you'd be drinkin' paint thinner. Or maybe Senada has some nail polish remover in her bag," he bantered before pivoting his attention to her. "Hey Senada."

"Nice to see you, Greg." They greeted each other with a hug before Senada held up both hands, revealing she was bag-free. "And no dice. Left the clutch in the limo."

"Good. Easier for you to double-fist these, uh…whatever they're passing around." Greg flagged down a waiter holding a cutting board-style tray and took two pieces. "It's all tiny."

"It doesn't look so bad," said Chris, taking a piece of his own.

"It looks terrible," Senada butted in, eyeing the bite more closely. "Wait. It's mini-food!"

Chris held up the piece to his nose. "Is this a slice of pizza?"

"I've got a burger," affirmed Senada.

"I've got a taco. That's what I mean! It's all tiny versions of normal food."

Chris could feel Senada's glare burrowing into the side of his skull. This was the sort of thing that would bother her a lot more than wearing high heels for the evening.

"You know what?" she asked despite chewing the burger she'd just popped into her mouth.

"I owe you?" Chris predicted.

Senada took his pizza and downed it in one bite. "You're getting me something on the way back."

"Remind me later." Chris scanned the room and tapped Greg. "We've got work to do."

"Way ahead of you," Greg said, turning toward the rest of the gathering. He wrapped an arm around Chris's shoulders and began pointing covertly around the banquet hall. "Brynn Capital is over there. We've got Amadeus Markets near the other bar. Emerson Ventures right over your shoulder. And those are just the ones I recognize from studying the guest list."

"Alright," Chris said as he searched for the confidence Senada had told him to bring. "You've been practicing the pitch, right?"

"Have *you*?" he said, as self-assured as usual.

"Let's do this," Chris declared with a single clap, making it two steps before looking back for Senada, who'd managed to find another waiter dressed like a casino dealer and holding a cutting board. She chewed one hors d'oeuvre while picking up another before she realized she was being watched. Chris stepped away from Greg and spoke softly enough for only he and Senada to hear. "You gonna be okay?"

"Of course," she mumbled through a full mouth. "Why do you ask?"

"Well, you normally only do this when you're—" he didn't finish the sentence, knowing she could do it for him.

"Don't start." Senada covered her chewing. "I wasn't the one having a panic attack in the limo fifteen minutes ago," she whispered aggressively. "Just go," she nudged. "Go mingle or network or whatever it is you're supposed to be doing."

Chris winked at Senada and fist-bumped Greg as they embarked on their effort to work the room.

❁

Bold of Senada to pull out the limo panic attack while she was staving off an episode of her own. She wasn't even hungry and wanted to avoid eating too much in such a tight dress, but the nervous energy made any food impossible to resist.

Senada took as many mini sushi rolls as she could hold from the next waiter and leaned against the bar for a more complete picture of the situation in front of her.

It was hard to tell who already knew one another versus those pretending they'd already met. She watched as Chris and Greg volleyed from one conversation to another, only interrupted by two different men of elevated age offering their company for the remainder of the evening. After pointing out the deep impression of a wedding ring on the second man's hand, she turned to the bartender and procured another martini. As a mini quiche made its way toward her, a hand landed against her arm. Senada spun as a gentle kiss landed just beside her lips.

"Oh shit, I'm sorry," an ashen Chris insisted. "That was meant for your cheek. I didn't expect you to turn around so fast."

She heard his explanation but wasn't really listening with an intent to answer. It took every neuron in her body to hide the rollercoaster of responses spinning within her. "What was that for?"

"You told me not to thank you. So I tried to be a little creative. Maybe too creative." He clenched her free hand, seemingly unfazed by how close they'd come to kissing, while Senada was still working her way through it.

"How's the… 'working the room' thing going?" she diverted.

"It's going great so far. Stoneman got a lot of word-of-mouth buzz going about the app. But I need my secret weapon."

"More whisky?" she winked. "I'm on it."

"You," he said with an air of certainty that caught her off-guard. "Come 'work the room' with me."

"What? Why?"

"I'm a man telling a bunch of people about a dating app. I think a woman's perspective might help. And by now, you know the app as well as I do."

It was difficult to pin down why she was so surprised by the request. Maybe it was because she didn't fit the room. Maybe it was because she was sweating like a hooker at mass. Maybe it was because of how sure he'd sounded when he said he needed her. Rather than trying to figure it out, Senada recalled Barbara's advice and decided to let herself enjoy the evening. She downed the rest of her martini and took Chris's waiting arm.

Entering the world of venture capital was like setting foot in an alternate universe. The surreal push-pull of every conversation fascinated Senada. People were basically asking for money without ever mentioning money. Chris zig-zagged from one interaction to the next, impressing her with how smoothly he'd rediscovered his confidence. No one would've guessed she'd talked this same man off the ledge an hour ago.

Senada found herself mimicking the habits of every trophy partner she encountered as they bounced from one interaction to the next. She stood up straighter, smiled wider, and let the hors d'oeuvre trays pass by with nothing more than a glance. New and nuanced sensations coursed through her. The higher Chris rose, the more Senada wanted to follow. He was at his best, and she wanted to make him proud, occasionally cracking a witty joke or soothing a rich man's ego; whatever might help Chris make a strong impression.

After two loops around the room, Senada realized how tightly she'd been holding Chris's arm. To her surprise, he adapted to their proximity without hesitation. Every now and then, he would look into her eyes, allowing Senada to reset and remember he was still there, still valuing her presence, and still excited to have her around.

Names and titles were hurled at her from every direction, most of which she immediately forgot. It had been a blur, conventional networking spliced with stolen glances, lingering touches, and, by the end, Senada wincing with every painful step in the heels that had finally betrayed her.

The room started to empty, allowing Senada to feel comfortable leaning on Chris, using his body to ease the discomfort of her shoes.

He leaned into her and whispered, "We can head out if you want."

His breath against the skin just beneath her ear made his words impossible to discern. "Huh?"

"I know your feet are killing you. Mine don't feel much better, to be honest. Tuxedo shoes aren't quite stilettos, but they aren't exactly a walk in the park. C'mon. Let's get outta here."

"Are you sure? If I just sit down for a little while, I might be able to —"

His unsmiling stare stopped her mid-sentence. Chris wasn't making a concession. Her comfort had become a priority. Senada didn't know how to respond because, in the most supportive way she could imagine, Chris wasn't asking for her input.

"I'm sure. I'll call the driver," he asserted.

Senada couldn't quite get a grasp on what was happening between them. Chris hadn't said anything profound, yet his words had struck a different chord all night. She couldn't put her finger on what had changed because it was still in progress.

Greg found them as they were nearing the elevator. He was already undoing his cufflinks and bowtie, dabbing sweat from his brow with a white handkerchief. "What's the verdict, big guy?" he asked. "I hope you feel as good about how this night went as I do."

"I don't think these people understand a thing about data analytics or human behavior," Chris said, almost sounding dejected.

"Did you expect something different?" laughed Greg.

"They don't need to understand the app," Senada interjected. "They just need to understand how it will make them richer."

"Sounds like you're already a natural." Greg quipped at Senada.

"You were pretty amazing tonight," Chris said.

Senada didn't recognize herself anymore, unable to conjure a response beyond bashfully looking at her own twiddling fingers.

"Uh… that's probably my cue to head out. But not before grabbing one more drink."

"Be careful," Chris said like a responsible boss.

"You first," Greg said before scampering toward the bar.

❁

Chris aided Senada in a ginger walk toward the limousine. He couldn't have asked any more of her. She galvanized his confidence in every way he'd expected, and some ways he couldn't have planned for. Over the course of a single night, she'd gone from merely attractive to someone he wanted to connect with beyond friendship. Or maybe he'd always felt this way and tonight had presented an opportunity for repressed desires to go unchecked.

She stepped inside the limo and sprawled across the long bench seat, letting out a long exhale. He slid near her legs, unbuttoning his jacket and untying his patent leather shoes.

"I can't wait to find the energy to get out of these shoes," she said into the air above her.

Chris turned his attention to her feet, cautiously removing one of her shoes, then the other. Senada lifted her head from the seat, as if making sure it was still her best friend in the limousine with her. Then she went back to relaxing, which Chris received as confirmation that he hadn't made a mistake.

"How do you think it went?" she asked, apparently unfazed by Chris rubbing the reddened areas near the bridge of her left foot.

Chris took a moment to pull his mind back to the subject she was most likely referring to. He was too occupied with providing relief to recall details right away. "It's hard to know. Sometimes you can't tell who's being honest with you and who's bullshitting you just to end the conversation."

"There's not much you can do about that," she said between pleasured hums. "How do you feel about the things you could control?"

"Like I could've done better." he hedged. "We'll see who actually takes my calls next week."

"Well, you looked like a superstar out there. I've never seen you so… you."

"You weren't too shabby yourself," he replied.

"I didn't do anything."

"You got me out of the car," he recalled.

She scoffed. "You could've done that on your own."

Chris laid her foot down on the space beside him. "No, I couldn't've. Not tonight." He rolled the window halfway down and took in the steaming breeze from riding down Park Avenue. "I've been nervous before. But not like that." He dropped the wall between them with an eye toward conveying the honesty he'd avoided for longer than he knew. "I needed you tonight. It was the biggest night of my life. And I wouldn't have gotten through it without you."

Chris lingered on Senada before looking out of the window again. It was obvious when she was reading him like a book. He could only hope she wouldn't start reading aloud. Her polished toes curled around the flesh of his thigh, and Chris realized silence could be more dangerous than words.

"Hey." Senada rolled onto her side. "What's wrong?"

Chris feigned confusion. "Nothing. Why?"

"I don't know… you seem a little off. I guess I thought you'd be sticking your head out of the sunroof and screaming to the entire city by now."

"I'm way too tired for that," he chuckled. Chris was grateful to be honest with her about one thing he was feeling, especially while his body was inundating his mind with unsolicited truth about the sight of Senada lying beside him.

"Then I guess I'll have to do it for you." She peeled herself from the leather.

"Please don't," he pleaded, knowing there was a chance she'd already made up her mind.

Senada searched across the array of unlabeled buttons, tapping each one until she got the sunroof to open a few inches. Chris wrapped both arms around her waist from behind, pulling her away from the button. She broke free of his feeble attempt at restraint, then lunged toward the button again.

"I thought you said your feet hurt!" he shouted before grabbing her a second time.

"I thought you said you were tired!" she replied amid laughter. She writhed free and turned enough to face him and grab a tuft of his shirt at the chest with one hand. "I'll twist your nipple right off. Try me."

Chris raised a eyebrow and called her bluff. She scrunched her face at him, then softened just as quickly. Her grip on his shirt loosened, then tightened again. She tugged at it harder, closing the gap between them.

They were close enough to breathe into each other's lips. Chris looked down at her hand, then back into her eyes. Thoughts of what she might be thinking turned into thoughts of how kissing her might feel. The impulse was too loud to ignore, and he slowly closed the space between them. She met him in the middle, and their lips embraced.

What began as soft kissing slowly transformed into raw passion. Years of unknown repressed desire poured out of his body and into hers. Senada wrapped her hands around his face and guided him to the bench and on top of her. His lips coursed along her neck and down her chest. Every kiss along her nearly exposed breasts brought faint moans. Chris slid the dress down and graced the air with her stiffening nipples before massaging them with his tongue.

There was little concern for the driver on the other side of the modesty panel, and little patience to wait the entire ride home. Chris watched Senada maneuver the skirt high enough to slide her black lace panties off. He reciprocated, undoing his belt as he cherished the sight of where her thighs met. Chris was more than ready and wanted her to feel the same as he plunged between her thighs, spreading her with his tongue. He engaged Senada until she could handle two fingers between her lips. Her tenseness was understandable; he felt it too.

Chris was overwhelmed by the sensations he never knew he needed from a woman he stopped being afraid to want. The slight side-to-side rocking of the limousine only made every flinch and lip-curling utterance more pleasurable.

Senada pulled Chris up to by the collar and pushed his jacket off. He cradled her face with one hand while pulling out his hardened desire with the other. Her lips remained pressed against his while her hand traveled down his stomach. Her moans lilted as she found the end of him. Senada wrapped her legs around his waist and guided his tip toward her opening.

A dam crumbled between them. With every inch Chris slid deeper, Senada wrapped around him more tightly. Their bodies were flooded with more than either of them could understand.

But they didn't need to understand it. They just needed it to happen.

18

Chris gasped for breath, a fearful sensation that shot him upright in bed. Once he was sure no one was trying to smother him, he took stock of the hazy stretch of time between the funeral and the following morning. Other than his suit jacket being on and his shoes being untied, there weren't many reliable details beyond a sturdy hangover.

A throbbing headache welcomed him. His vision sharpened against the bright morning sun beaming through the window. As his feet found the floor, Chris met the first sign of how the rest of the previous day had played out. Senada was fast asleep on the carpet a few feet away from the bed, half-covered by his comforter and still wearing the dress she'd worn at the funeral. Her remarks were his clearest memory of the service. After that, there were nothing but flashes of memories. But they were hard to differentiate from figments of his imagination.

Chris crept over her, nearly tripped over her shoes, and carefully closed the bedroom door behind him. The culprit responsible for the cranial pain was identified when he got to the kitchen. Accidentally knocking over one beer bottle created a cacophony against the other five empties, toppling them across the island like bowling pins.

"Keep it down man," Greg grunted from the living room as he brought his haggard body upright on the living room couch. "My head is killing me." He rubbed his eyes and stumbled into the kitchen. "How're you feelin'?"

"About the same as you look," Chris teased.

"Be careful tugging that thread. You ain't exactly lookin' fresh as a daisy."

Chris took the cue to assess his current state. Both men were worse for wear. His necktie was draped around the collar of a severely wrinkled shirt. Greg's shirt was a match, but his tie was nowhere to be found, and he only had on one shoe.

"Call it a draw?" Greg asked upon further reflection.

"Whatever." Chris breathed slowly and deliberately as he prepared the coffee pot. "What happened last night?"

"If you don't remember, are you sure you want me to tell you?"

"Was it that bad?"

"No," Greg snickered. "I'm just fuckin' with you."

Chris pressed both palms into the counter and tightened every muscle in his arms. "Do I seem like I'm in the mood to be fucked with right now?"

Greg cleared his throat as if the action would reboot him to an appropriate temperament. "After the burial, you were in pretty rough shape. We brought you back here. I grabbed a case of Blue Moons and you popped open the bourbon and we just hung out. Laughed a bit. Cried a bit."

Chris turned his back to Greg and observed the kitchen around him. "It's weird to be in here and know she's not coming down those stairs again."

"I know, man." Greg sat on a stool. "That might take a while to get used to."

Apprehension coursed through Chris. "I woke up and saw Senada and wasn't sure where the night went."

Greg shrugged. "I'm not the most reliable source for details; things are still a little hazy on my end. Last thing I remember, she was making sure you made it to bed without falling down the stairs."

The top of the staircase became a focal point as Chris stepped close enough to make Greg uncomfortable. "Did I say… or do… anything last night?"

"We said and did a lot of things." Greg recoiled. "Why are you whispering?"

"I just need to know if—" Chris swallowed the rest of the sentence as Senada appeared. Before she could reach the bottom of the stairs, he haphazardly pasted a smile onto his face.

"Mornin', guys." She delivered a taut grin at both men as she put on her shoes and tied her hair into a messy bun. Her face was gaunt, the way she usually looked when she hadn't slept very well, or at all.

"You want some coffee?" asked Chris. "I'm making a pot."

"Thanks, but I can't." She retrieved her purse from the dining table and headed for the side door. "I've gotta go." She walked out before either of them could respond.

The sudden curtness startled Chris and drove him to action. He removed the crumpled tie from his neck and threw it aside. Greg moved to the faucet and tossed a palmful of water on his face as Chris rounded the other side of the island and sprinted out the door.

Senada was halfway home when Chris caught up to her. She faced him before he had to resort to calling out her name.

"Hey, I just wanted to," he surrendered before rethinking. "Thank you. For yesterday. For everything you said, and for, ya know… saving my ass."

"Don't mention it. You've saved mine plenty of times." Senada pulled her gaze away, as if the words hurt to hear coming out of her mouth. "I don't know if this is the 'right' thing to ask, but… are you okay?"

Chris was grateful for her willingness to lead while he tried to find his wits. Too many emotions were flowing through him and none of them could be explained effectively. He corralled as many brain cells as he could, but nothing made sense.

"It's okay if you don't know," she consoled.

"Am I that transparent?" he said through an artificial grin.

"Only to someone who knows what to look for."

Chris became bashful before noticing Senada stayed stoic. Tired of doubting himself, he settled for the first thing that came to mind. "Would you… wanna stick around? I was gonna order some breakfast. Maybe something to help us with these hangovers."

"I'm not hungover," she confessed. "I nursed one drink all night."

"That doesn't sound like you," jabbed Chris.

Senada crossed her arms and looked away.

"Alright, well," he said with a hint of shame. "You can still have breakfast with us."

Senada checked her watch. "Maybe another time."

"Okay." He lulled in confusion over whether the interaction could be salvaged. "I'm sure I did or said something I should apologize for, so let me get it out of the way. I'm sorry."

"What makes you think you did something wrong?"

"I dunno… stress plus drinking usually equals—"

"Honesty," she accused. "That's what you're worried about, right?"

Chris didn't have the heart to acknowledge the truth.

"Have no fear," she continued. "You said a lot, like you always do when you drink too much. But nothing I didn't already know."

Chris was unclear on how much she already knew. Questioning her genuineness was new for him and he didn't enjoy it. "What about you?"

"What about me?" she asked.

"I dunno. Wondering how you're doing with… all this." By avoiding her eyes, Chris realized they were only a few feet away from the site of their last conversation in the middle of the street.

"I had a hard time sleeping." Senada coughed and winced, piquing his attention in a new way. "You and Greg were out cold. I passed the time. It was a pretty nice night, so I sat outside for a little while. Watched the stars. Read some of your mom's cookbooks."

"But you didn't go home," he attested.

"I felt like I was home." The sentiment stopped Chris in his tracks before Senada pivoted. "I could hear you, sort of, mumbling."

Chris was between clueless and helpless. "In my sleep?"

Senada nodded and continued. "I couldn't make out what you were saying. But I got worried, so I crashed on the floor."

"Why?"

"I'm not gonna answer that."

"Why not?"

"Because if you don't know why by now, it's a waste of my breath."

Silence calcified between them and putting words together was harder for Chris than it had ever been. Beneath a desire to change the subject, Chris wasn't ready for Senada to leave yet.

She checked the time again. "I really do have to get going."

"Oh… alright. Well, uh—," he stumbled.

"Let me know if you need anything, okay?"

Chris didn't know when they'd see each other again, but he had to be okay with parting ways. "Yeah, sure. Take care."

"You too."

There was so much to say, and even more he wanted to hear, but Chris only had so much to give. He needed to hold on tightly to a piece of himself.

❀

The examination room's recessed lighting emitted a faint buzz, and it was slowly driving Senada insane. After she'd checked in, endured fifteen minutes of waiting, nearly went deaf in an MRI tube, and waited another twenty minutes, all while freezing in a medical gown, Senada had become a bomb. But she didn't know what else it would take to set her off, or how big the blast would be. Senada prepared for the unknown and breathed through a dime-sized opening of her mouth.

Dr. Lawson entered, pouring cold water on Senada with confusingly lively energy. "Glad you made it. I thought we'd scheduled a follow-up for a week ago."

"Things got derailed for a little while, but I'm putting things back together." Senada talked herself out of sharing more than necessary.

"Have you been having any more of the pain we talked about?"

"Nothing I can't manage," she replied, barely listening to her own words.

"I don't doubt that. But this is about whether it's present, not whether you can handle it," Dr. Lawson challenged. "Some pain isn't meant to be managed. It's meant to be relieved."

Senada groaned at the sentiment but couldn't deny its validity. Pain was just something she'd grown accustomed to.

Dr. Lawson held up a chart and continued. "I looked at your images. Now that we have a better idea of what we're dealing with, I want to discuss your options. It's not an emergency yet, but in cases like yours, we want to nip it in the bud as soon as possible."

It was enough to mute the buzzing lights. "What's that mean? Cases like mine?"

"I mean… if this goes unaddressed for too long, it can cause more significant issues."

Senada rolled her eyes. "I already know the issues."

"We discussed some general precautions, yes. But given the location and size of these cysts, we should talk about your treatment options in greater detail."

The doctor's palpable concern abated Senada's seething annoyance.

"There's tissue along both fallopian tubes, along with the cysts on your ovaries. Typically, they would go away on their own or require medication, but these are larger than normal. If we wait too long to address them, the symptoms will worsen. More severe pain, internal bleeding, fertility iss—"

"Alright, alright, I get it," lamented Senada, unable to withstand hearing another problem. "What can I do?"

Dr. Lawson hesitated as though gauging her tone before speaking. "I recommend laparoscopic surgery. It's minimally invasive and—"

"How much would it cost?" Senada barged.

"Your insurance will cover this."

"But not all of it, right?"

"Well, no, but —"

"Then I can't afford it," Senada dismissed. "And I really can't afford to miss any time at work either. Not right now."

"How soon do you think you can schedule the procedure?"

Senada coped with a clandestine panic attack and ran through a mental checklist of bills and responsibilities. "July. Maybe late July."

"Is that the absolute earliest you can do it?"

Senada nodded, quelling the tension with measured breaths. "Unless you tell me I can get away with not doing it at all."

"I hope that's not something you're considering."

"Then that's when I can do it?!" Senada snapped, then winced in a combination of pain and embarrassment. Despite the guise of coping with stress, the news of a more severe circumstance rocked her foundation. Beyond being a failure as a daughter, a business owner, and a friend, Senada couldn't even *live* properly without something going wrong. "Sorry, Doctor."

"It's quite alright," Dr. Lawson responded with more grace than Senada's reaction deserved. "If you don't do this procedure, there are substantial risks. The cysts may grow. And if they rupture, it will become an emergency. And in rare instances, they can become cancerous."

With the last point, Dr. Lawson invited fear into the room. Maybe it was the grieving process at work, but Senada wanted to live long enough to find out how it might feel to live without so much worry. In her mother, she'd witnessed a life with no room for anything but the bad. Anguish, resentment, and joylessness hadn't just made Carrie's life worse; they'd probably shortened it. Cancer was scary enough, but nothing terrified Senada more than contracting whatever her mother couldn't defeat.

"Alright," she relented. "I'll do it. Just… can you tell me what it will entail? I won't be able to sleep tonight unless I know what to expect."

"Of course." Dr. Lawson started explaining the details of the procedure as Senada returned her focus to the ceiling. Suddenly, the buzz of the recessed lighting wasn't loud enough.

19

As though Chris didn't have enough to deal with, he was starting to feel his age. He'd heard about the perils of one's forties, but assumed much of it was hyperbole. Greg's enthusiasm for a morning run, unfortunately for Chris, wasn't contractable. After a few minutes of stretching on the living room floor, Chris would've been fine with going back to bed for another hour or two. But spending time outside of the house would likely do some good.

Grief mixed with his usual hyperawareness to create a new kind of sadness, making Chris more aware of his triggers. The vacuous house enlightened how much he'd taken for granted. The sound of Barbara shuffling around, the smell of breakfast food, her comforting eyes — it all stood out more in his mother's absence. If a run could pull Chris away from his thoughts for little while, the discomfort would be worth it.

Greg burst through the front door like a bull in a China shop, shouting Chris's name as if the house was much larger than in reality. Chris entered the kitchen just as Greg poured himself a tall glass of orange juice. Barbara might as well have been standing between them, midway through making scrambled eggs while joyfully admonishing Greg's frequent oafishness.

"Are you sure it's a good idea to do that before a run?" a wide-eyed Chris wondered aloud.

"I'll be fine." Greg downed the contents in four gulps. "I'm a machine. Let's roll."

"A wheel is a machine too. But if it was made of cheese, you wouldn't put it on your car."

"I don't know what the hell that means."

"Of course you don't," Chris hollered as they walked outside.

Hempstead Lake State Park was a vast blend of forests, bike paths, a horseback riding trail, picnic areas, and small observation beaches, but its most notable feature was the largest freshwater lake in the county. It made for a pleasant view while running through the five miles of trail, but their chances of completing the loop nosedived halfway through the first mile.

Greg hunched over a patch of dirt while the ill-advised orange juice freed itself from his stomach.

"I tried to warn you," Chris taunted from his perch atop a thick, downed tree branch a few feet away from the paved running path. "Who drinks half a carton of orange juice before a run?"

"Someone who knows," Greg heaved, "cardio is overrated."

"Is that your takeaway from this situation?" Chris surmised.

"Hey," he replied. "I only agreed to do this because I thought it would help you. So really, ipso facto, this is your fault."

Chris was no longer interested in carrying the fault for someone else's choices. He looked away, admiring the scenery to offset the sounds of regurgitation behind him. Much of the surrounding landscape was brown and dreary, but there was an occasional strand of color. A gentle breeze pulled his eyes toward the sun peeking through the mesh of tree branches above.

The heaving stopped and Greg caught his breath. "You may have been right about the juice."

"I'm sorry, can you repeat that?" Chris chided.

"Not gonna happen." Greg changed the subject. "But I'll say I'm surprised. I would've bet on you being passed out in a mixture of vodka and depression by now, not leaving me in the dust on a trail run."

"First of all, I wouldn't use beating you on a trail run as a benchmark for progress. And second… I'm just as surprised as you are."

"You're surprised you're not throwing up?"

Chris contemplated another joke before disengaging from Greg's attempt at humor. "I thought I'd have a bigger reaction by now. It's been almost a week since the burial, and I haven't cried since. I mean, it's not like I'm fighting it or something. I just… I don't feel like it. I don't feel much of anything. And I'm waiting for the real pain to rear its ugly head."

"I can't say that part shocks me." Greg finally managed to stand upright again. "Do you remember how many pitches we did before we got funded?"

"Thirty-four," Chris answered without hesitation.

"Thirty-goddamn-four. That's a lot of rejection. And I never saw you sulk or wallow or even flinch. I was a wreck, but you… nothing."

"And that's… a bad thing?"

"In business, no," said Greg. "But I don't know how helpful that tactic is in the rest of our lives. Maybe there's some value in letting things hurt for a little while."

"I don't know. I went through it with my dad. Maybe there's only room for one grief like that in someone's lifetime."

"Maybe. Either that or it was easier to manage the emotions around the pitches because there was always another pitch. But if we never got funded, if pitch thirty-four hadn't come through, then what? Rejection is easier to handle when we know another chance is coming. But when it's the last one…" Greg let a shrug complete the sentence for him.

"What does any of that have to do with why I'm not grieving?" Chris made sure his annoyance was apparent.

"You might know there's more to be felt and you're trying to keep it at bay. After the funeral, you definitely drank like a guy who didn't want to feel things." Greg chuckled, then stopped, likely reminded of his fragile constitution.

"About that night," Chris said. "Can I ask you something?"

Greg gathered himself and stood a little taller. "I'm all ears."

"I know I had a lot to drink. Senada said everything was cool, but I don't know. It sounded like maybe—." His voice dissipated, replaced by the hope that his friend would finish the implied sentence.

"Do you really think she'd lie to you?"

"I guess not."

"Then what are you worried about?" Greg bordered on condemnation, only giving Chris a few seconds before taking the response into his own hands. "If you took anything away from all this, I thought it would be that nothing should be left unsaid. What could drunk Chris possibly say that sober Chris wouldn't already want her to know?"

The notion was enough to warrant an eye roll. "I'm not in the mood for mind games right now."

"Then stop playing 'em," Greg retaliated, mimicking Chris's tone. "You're the one kinda-but-not-really asking about shit you might've said but hope you didn't. Or maybe it bothers you because you *didn't* say something."

Chris laughed off the idea. "You sound nuts."

"Do I? Remember the first time your dad let us drink a beer with him? He said you'll always get the truth out of little kids and drunks."

Chris grinned and nodded in agreement.

"You probably wished you'd said something while you were drunk so you wouldn't have to say it while sober. You probably wanted the booze to… what's the word? Absolve. You wanted the booze to absolve you."

"Alcohol can do a lot of things, but it can't absolve anyone," Chris declared, reminded of Carrie Williams and his natural protectiveness of Senada. The shame associated with inebriation morphed into worry that he may have reminded her of everything she loathed about extreme intoxication.

"You still with me, bro?" Greg butted in.

"Yeah," Chris replied. "Let's get moving."

"And no response to my point?"

Chris bottled the rising disdain for his recent choices. "Not right now."

They casually walked the trail as if they'd never planned on jogging, talking their way through many topics and, more notably, around Senada. It was time for Chris to plan his next move, and Greg was a trove of knowledge around career planning. Chris hadn't given himself a timeline to return to work, but the boredom had taken a real toll. Impending grief and an all-too-familiar setting made stagnancy even clearer. Work had once defined Chris, and unemployment reminded him of why. Money in the bank didn't make the downtime any easier to tolerate. He needed some sort of direction and a purpose.

They arrived at a parking lot full of teenagers milling around brightly colored import cars. There was a time when such a scene wouldn't interest Chris, usually avoiding such communal displays out of a deep hatred for dick-measuring contests. But in the current scene, Chris saw the potential. There wasn't much getting in the way of a teenager's attachment to things, and Chris had just as much time and even more resources. While he smiled and nodded his way through Greg's stories of the souped-up Mitsubishi Eclipse he'd driven in college, Chris thought of the last thing he'd planned to do before his mother's death. There was unquantifiable value in staying connected to a version of himself that he was actually fond of.

At the end of the trail, Greg offered a curiosity of his own. "What would you even do?"

"What do you mean?"

"What job would you do? You haven't worked for anyone but yourself in years. What does your resume even look like?"

Chris smirked bashfully. "I may need your help with that."

"Okay, that's step one," Greg laughed like he was relieved to see Chris lighten up a bit. "And then what?"

Nothing came to mind right away. The road ahead may as well have been a blank void. The only thing different about this moment than previous cycles of grief was that he had no idea what was next. He hadn't just grieved the loss of someone; he'd grieved their absence in the life he was creating.

Whether it was his father, his business, or his friendship with Senada, the real hurt had come from moving forward without them. He hadn't truly grieved his mother because he lacked the necessary criteria: he needed a path forward. But he wasn't okay with what, and who, might be waiting for him along that road.

Senada was more present than she'd been in a long time, with no signs of going away. And to move forward, he'd have to remove anything that could get in his way.

20

Senada worked with renewed fury to keep thoughts of the future at bay. Corsages and boutonnieres were built and boxed at a frenetic pace, fulfilling the flood of orders for the upcoming prom season at every local high school. Her style was unique, offering custom dye accents to match the color scheme of any couple's outfit. It was a messy process with a beautiful outcome.

Melancholic R&B music flowed throughout the work area, keeping Senada's mind in rhythm while her body defied the beat. She was too focused on dipping a carnation's edges into a petri dish of dye to notice Lex's cautious entrance.

"What's up, boss lady?" Lex said while settling into her station.

"I hate when you call me that," Senada said without taking her eyes off the flower between her fingers.

"I know." Lex picked up a petal from the floor and threw it at Senada, eliciting a grin from both women. "You've been here early for like ten days straight. Who are you, and what have you done with the real boss lady?"

The time ran out on Senada's willingness to fake humor.

Lex cleared her throat and restarted. "Seriously, though. Are you feelin' alright?" Lex asked carefully. "You've been working pretty much day and night since the funeral."

"I'm fine," Senada said. "Can you help me with Malverne's orders? I'm wrapping up Lynbrook's now."

Lex turned off the speaker and slid her stool close to Senada, who'd just closed the plastic box on another corsage before noticing a tuft of envelopes under Lex's arm.

"What are you doing?" Senada asked. "We've got work to do."

"We certainly do," Lex declared. "And we will, but I can't keep pretending all this is normal. Between the sun-up to sundown workdays and barely talking other than telling me the next thing we have to do." Lex tossed the pile of envelopes on Senada's counter. "And I know these aren't gonna make you move any slower."

Senada tossed her gloves aside and took a closer look at the red 'urgent' stamp on a large brown envelope; more confirmation of how little time she could afford to take off for a medical procedure.

"I haven't been sleeping," Senada confessed. "And I could either spend another night wandering around my house, or I could get some work done. So… here I am."

"Is there anything you wanna talk about?" Lex said in a concerned tone.

Senada pretended to consider the offer. "I think I'd rather focus on getting this work done."

After a silent beat, Lex pulled an order slip from the corkboard wall and joined Senada's efforts. The gesture implied a pact to leave the subject alone, allowing both women to get lost in the rigamarole of placing each small arrangement into its own plastic container and carrying stacks of them to the refrigerator.

A few hours went by before Lex needed a break. "Don't we have enough by now?" she panted. "I mean, do kids even go to the prom anymore?"

"You always wanna have a few extras," she replied with a grin. "Imagine you're a teenage guy trying to place one of these on your date. You're probably nervous and sweating, with no idea how delicate a corsage wristlet is. Or you're terrified of stabbing her while you're pinning it on her dress. Or you're his mother anxiously pinning one of these things on, stabbing through the stem six or seven times trying to make sure it's not too high or too low on his lapel."

"That's pretty specific," Lex chuckled. "Like you're speakin' from firsthand experience."

"Lucky for me, my date admitted to having no idea what he was doing before he could turn me into Swiss cheese. And my mother was my mother." A fond memory took Senada by surprise. "Chris put it on for me."

"Of course he did." Lex was too occupied to notice Senada's drift through time. "That should've been the first sign that you went with the wrong guy."

"If I'd known my date would abandon me, then yeah, I might've gone with Chris." Senada slowed down. "It wasn't a perfect night, but it all came together at the end."

Lex spun back around. "Am I misremembering it? Didn't your dress get ruined?"

"Yeah, but the memorable part was *how* it got ruined. Running across Long Beach and diving into the ocean is a great way to mess up a dress."

Astonishment overtook Lex's face. "That water is glacial!"

"Damn right it is. I froze my ass off and was sick for a few days, but sometimes it's about living in the moment."

"Well, my date got so drunk, he threw up on my shoes," Lex grimaced. "So my night was worth forgetting."

"You win," gloated Senada. "If your date throws up on your shoes, you have every right to hate the prom."

"But you had the amazing Chris to step in and save the day," Lex fawned with a fairy tale impression.

Senada shuddered at how often she'd relied on Chris to make her feel better. And how willingly he'd obliged for years. Their swapped post-funeral dynamic made her aware of how heavy it can be to carry someone else's peace as a duty.

"Speaking of saving the day," Senada diverted, "thanks for helping me out with the funeral arrangements. I can't afford to do too much charity work, but that was an exception. And there's no way I could've pulled it off without you."

"Stop." Lex waved off the sentiment as unnecessary to say. "How's Chris holding up?" she asked.

"It's hard to say," Senada said before having a better response. "Part of me thinks we should be in this together. Barbara was like a mother to me too. But I don't think he's ready to let me in. And I can't really blame him."

"If you asked me, he doesn't deserve you," Lex chided. "I mean, it's great that you do so much for him, with the funeral and all that. But to basically disappear from your life just because you wouldn't be with him?" Lex stopped and faced Senada. "Sorry, that came out kinda harsh."

An unfazed Senada shrugged it off. "You're not that far off. He shut me out for a really long time and missed a lot of my life. Maybe he doesn't deserve my friendship. But he doesn't deserve to carry the guilt of those years apart all by himself either. We crossed the line together. And I got scared. I knew I'd miss him, but… I didn't know how to hold onto him anymore."

"I don't want to make it sound like I don't understand complicated things. I do." Lex took a breath and tossed a handful of clipped stems into a wastebasket before taking a more earnest turn. "But if you both crossed the line, how come you weren't willing to be more than friends?"

Senada stopped pruning and paced the small alcove, calculating how much of her tongue to bite. "Sometimes it's easier to receive love from someone when you can choose how much of you they get to see."

Lost in her own wilderness, Senada sank back onto her stool and stared at the daffodils on the counter.

Lex threw her a life preserver and pivoted their attention to the music. "Ohhh I love this song!" She turned up the volume and sang, subtly coaxing

Senada to join. It took a few tugs before Senada gave in and enjoyed the tune.

They sang and danced while they worked for a couple more hours, occasionally taking turns to deal with a customer. The refrigerator filled quickly with fulfilled orders and a surplus of 'just-in-case' roses for the teens and parents who'd waited until the last minute.

The door chimed once more and interrupted Senada crooning 'So Sick' into the butt end of a floral knife as if it was a microphone.

"I'll take this one!" Lex shouted over the tune, already trotting into the customer area.

Senada was in her own world and ignoring the small bouquet she'd been crafting. When she spun around to belt the final chorus, Lex was back in the doorway and unable to hide the 'uh oh' on her face.

"Someone's here for you," she bleated.

Senada turned the volume down and collected herself, then walked past Lex. The

Chris stood at the counter, his palms resting against the edge as he observed the ornate arrangements on the wall in front of him.

Senada's shield went up at the sight of Chris leaning over the counter and observing the arrangements on the wall in front of him. She wasn't interested in picking up where they'd left off, and didn't have the time or patience for another hollow interaction with him.

Senada stepped into his vision and raised her eyebrows. "What are you doing here?"

As soon as the words left her lips, Chris's eyes darted toward the doorway, where Lex was idling. She disappeared before Senada could turn and shoo her away.

"I went by your house first, but when I saw the van was gone, I figured I might find you here." Chris sounded rehearsed. "Are you busy?"

"Kinda." Senada locked eyes with him and waited for an explanation, but he seemed to be waiting for something too. "Well?"

"Uh, this won't take long," he stammered. "I can come back later though."

"It's fine. I can spare a minute." Sooner or later, the subtext needed to become text. Senada was tired of waiting. "What's going on?"

Chris took a breath and hid both hands in his pockets. "Last time we spoke, you mentioned that, uh, that I should reach out if I needed anything."

Senada nodded and hummed an assent.

"I think I need something," he continued.

"From me?" Senada blurted, unwilling to veil her surprise.

"Sort of." Chris's compulsive finger tapping made an appearance as one hand fled his pocket and rhythmically touched the counter. "I've been sorting through some of my mom's things. I know she'd want to donate some of it someplace."

"Probably the Salvation Army." Senada pretended to guess, but she'd known Barbara's wishes for some time. "What about it?"

"That's kinda why I'm here. I haven't started yet." Chris tried to lure a chuckle out of her, but Senada wasn't going to let him off the hook with shared laughter. "I'm gonna try to push through it, but I was hoping you might be willing to help."

Senada fought off the urge to scold Chris over how much it had taken for him to ask for help. But he'd already surpassed her expectations. She'd made the offer out of politeness but never thought he would take her up on it. If this could be a small step on their journey back to a true friendship, she was eager to honor it.

Senada acknowledged the effort, placing a hand over his and putting an end to the persistent tapping.

"When do you want to start?"

"Whenever you can," Chris said, apparently unprepared for her to say yes.

"The shop's closed tomorrow. How's the afternoon?"

Chris nodded and stepped away from the counter. As sedate as he seemed, Senada knew the look on his face and remembered the last time she'd seen it. It was the face of a friend who was afraid to say too much. But the last time she'd seen it, Chris had fought through the fear and spoken anyway.

"Thanks. I'll see you tomorrow." Chris backpedaled toward the door and hit his head on a hanging planter. He clutched his scalp, displaying more embarrassment than hurt. "See you tomorrow," he repeated before leaving.

The door chime snapped Senada out of hypnosis. She was aware of her surroundings again, including the nosy coworker who'd already returned to her post in the doorway. Lex curled both lips in an obvious attempt to stifle her words while Senada stoically squeezed past her.

Senada returned to the bouquet she'd left behind and wished for a way to occupy Lex's mouth before it pulled them into an unapproved recap of what had just occurred.

"How does having the rest of the day off sound?" Senada asked while avoiding eye contact.

"Stupendous," she said, teeming with sarcasm. "But that would just give me more time to think of more questions. Probably better for you if we got this over with now."

Senada sighed. "There's nothing to avoid. You saw most of what there is to see, and I'm sure you heard every word."

"And you're okay with it?"

"Why wouldn't I be?"

"I thought he didn't deserve your friendship," Lex recalled.

"That's not all I said," Senada answered before further thought about the question raised her blood pressure. "And anyway, it's not that simple. It's a complex situation."

"And in saying that, you're acknowledging how much more complicated it might get."

"There's no simple way forward," Senada lamented.

"But you want to go forward?"

"I do," Senada confirmed.

"I hope you two have the same sense of direction."

Senada stopped evading eye contact and locked on Lex. "What good is turning him away? I told him to come to me, and he did. How would it look if I turned my back on him now?"

"I'm not saying you should turn your back on him. I'm not saying you should do anything. I don't know enough to give any real advice here."

"But?"

"But… you said it yourself. He's missed a lot. I wouldn't be shocked if you found out that one of you is living in the present while the other is stuck in the past." Lex hesitated and softened her delivery. "I hope I didn't overstep. I just… I care about you, ya know?"

Senada nodded in awareness of Lex's point. For all the concern about where Chris's head might be, it was easy to overlook how little he knew about where Senada stood. If they were going to have any chance at a future, they needed alignment around their past.

21

Chris was proud of the risk he'd taken. Instead of using Senada's vacant driveway as an excuse, he'd gone the extra mile to move the ball forward. More importantly, he'd fought the urge to set an internal goal for how the afternoon might play out. He didn't even bother assuming she'd show up. With or without Senada's help, the rest of his day committed to sorting through her closets and drawers until the matter was resolved.

The morning still required some structure. After a morning run through the park, he'd made a reasonable facsimile of a Western omelet and enjoyed two cups of coffee. There wasn't much nervousness left in his system by the time he'd returned from the nearby hardware store with more than enough cardboard boxes and packing tape to handle the endeavor.

Things hadn't been perfect since the funeral, but perfection was an unreasonable expectation. Chris was doing well enough. Granted, the definition changed from one day to the next. Once he'd accepted the impossibility of dodging every memory of his mother, he moved through the house with fewer second thoughts. But Barbara's bedroom door had remained shut. By his standard, entering that room would be a triumph.

The task at hand would keep Chris and Senada occupied, but considering their baggage, the bedroom wasn't large enough to hold much more. It had taken plenty of effort to ask for her help in the first place. It wasn't the time, and Chris wasn't in the place, to discuss things that couldn't be undone. This was a chance for them to gather whatever pieces of a friendship might still be worth holding on to. If he could do something to avoid losing Senada for a second time, he'd endure whatever arose in the process.

Back-and-forth trips between his bedroom, the den, and the kitchen had become routine. The picture frame at the bottom of the staircase hadn't slowed him down in a while. But assembling a charcuterie board to appease Senada's inevitable snacking turned the photo into a catalyst for unease. He cradled the picture like it could turn to dust and questioned if it was worth keeping on the wall.

There couldn't be a worse slate of potential outcomes. Either she'd see the photo, or she'd notice its absence. One would've been easier to explain than the other. Chris hadn't hung the photograph, but Senada undoubtedly knew it was there. If it were gone, Senada would know exactly who'd removed it, and make a reasonably educated guess as to why.

The doorbell startled him, nearly jolting the frame out of his hands. Chris had lost track of the present while weighing the impact of their past. In an instant, a different clock ticked within. Senada was comfortable enough to let herself in, and he didn't want to be holding the picture when she did. The bell rang again, and he hung the frame as quickly as he could before hurrying to the door.

Chris reached the foyer just as she entered and called out for him. Senada had a way of making his name sound special.

"There you are," she said.

Chris noticed her attire right away, noting how odd it was to wear an oversized hoodie and jeans on such a sweltering summer day. In their previous era, it was the kind of thing he would've called out. But his words had gained some weight over the years. Any comment, no matter how innocent, opened the door for misinterpretation.

"Hey," he said after an awkward delay. Chris stepped forward, assuming a hug was in order. Senada didn't mirror the action, so he stopped, just in time for her to make the same miscalculation before both of them gave up. There remained a strange gap between them that went beyond the physical.

"How're you feeling?" she asked in a soothing tone.

Being prepared for the question didn't make it any easier to answer. "I'm alright. Under the circumstances."

"Of course," said Senada. "Where do you want to start?"

The redirect was more sudden than he'd prepared for, though likely for the best. "The bedroom probably makes the most sense." He pointed an awkward finger toward the ceiling as if Senada couldn't already navigate the house with her eyes closed.

In the blind sprint of preparation for being a gracious host, Chris overlooked how comfortable Senada was with the entire home. She slid her feet out of black Toms and extended a canvas tote bag toward him. "In case the mood struck," she offered.

A closer inspection of the bag revealed a six-pack of Stellas. "I'm, uh, cutting back a bit since the whole post-funeral situation." Chris immediately regretted acknowledging the mistake.

"Oh." She seemed stunned. "I can put it in the fridge. Or take it home."

"The fridge is fine for now, I think."

Senada was on her way to the kitchen before Chris could take the bag.

"You made a board?" Senada asked as she looked over the wooden palette of cured meats and soft cheeses on the island.

"Yeah," he said with a tinge of confidence. "In case you wanted to snack on something."

"That was nice of you," she said with some apprehension.

He waited for a more joyous response while she took a closer look.

"Maybe later," she said. "If I get sidetracked, it'll slow things down."

Chris grumbled silently through the plan coming undone in a matter of minutes. "Uh, sure, no problem." He wrapped the board in clear plastic and set it aside, temporarily losing sight of his guest. After calling her name went unanswered, Chris turned the corner toward the staircase and froze. Senada was standing at the base of the stairs, straightening the last frame. Chris assumed he'd left it crooked in the haste to answer the door.

Senada faced him, holding no expression while Chris wished he could read minds. "You ready to head up?" she proposed.

Chris nodded and followed, nearly walking face first into her butt as she climbed the stairs ahead of him. As if by rote, she glanced toward Chris's open bedroom door before going away from it and down the hall.

When they reached the antique knob of the closed white door, Senada stopped and stepped aside.

"Something wrong?" he asked, watching Senada stare at her own feet for a moment.

"Nope. Just figured you should open the door."

"Oh. Right." Chris reached around her. Senada pressed into the wall, as though avoiding contact between his arm and her waist. He had questions, but none of them were worth asking yet. Instead, he turned the knob, nudged the door open.

The stillness restrained him. A full life had occupied the modest room, and somehow, parsing through her things and giving them away was supposed to 'honor' her. It was a harsh contrast that Chris had no interest in trying to understand. At least not yet. But it was an effective kick-in-the-ass. This act was bigger than the baggage either of them brought into it.

❁

Senada was slowly losing trust in her senses. After spending two hours trying to decide which outfit best conveyed 'don't read into this,' Senada felt foolish. Waffling over the right way to show she didn't care was as ironic as it was a waste of time. And once the air of Barbara's bedroom struck her, such bullshit mattered even less. Senada focused on the reason they were there, and why they were facing it together.

Chris didn't make the other dynamics easy to ignore. But she wasn't sure if it was intentional, or if she was reading too deeply into every gesture. The charcuterie board displayed the considerate friend she'd missed, but it was hard to know if he'd received her beer offering the same way. And a severely crooked picture frame couldn't have been left that way by chance. Was it to make sure she noticed it, or was it haphazardly returned to where it belonged because he knew she'd notice if it was gone? Love makes some things mean more, but sex blurs the meaning of those things. And yet an abundance of love is what gave sex the chance to ruin everything.

"I guess I don't know where to begin after all," Chris sighed, interrupting her thoughts.

"How about you start with the nightstands, and I'll start with the closet?" she posited. "Do you know what she wanted to donate?"

"Anything someone might need, maybe?" he pondered, clearly unaware of how unhelpful his answer was.

Senada had been a consistent recipient of Barbara's philanthropic spirit. She was comfortable with at least one guess. "She'd have loved to give her dresses and jewelry to people who might not have any. I'll start there."

She waited for a response and watched Chris rub the back of his neck and struggle to act. Senada took the lead and slid open the heavy shutter doors. Her jaw dropped at how full the closet was. So many sweaters and modest dresses, accompanied by a tall rack of shoes. Before the overwhelm could take an even stronger hold, she grabbed the closest item she could reach.

"For you," he said over her shoulder. Senada turned and saw a newly assembled cardboard box resting at her feet. Chris walked to the other side of the bed with a matching box of his own.

Senada opted to remove items from hangers and neatly fold each article of clothing before placing it in the box. When she wasn't immersed in the repetitive activity, she occasionally stole looks at Chris, but only if it seemed safe enough for her attention to go unnoticed.

The first break in the action was caused by Chris struggling to open the nightstand drawer on Mr. Mitchell's side of the bed. The loud jostling shook a ceramic lamp until the compartment opened with a harsh metal grinding noise.

"Sorry," Chris atoned. "I don't think this drawer's been opened since my dad died. Crazy, right?" He sounded immensely uncomfortable, a state of mind she'd gotten used to unraveling with well-chosen words.

"Eh, I don't know. I get it," she countered. "Hard to look back. Hard to let go." The thought escaped before Senada could restrain its ambiguity. "That's just a guess though."

Senada watched more closely as Chris exhumed one of Mr. Mitchell's many wristwatches, a silver-plated edition meant to look more expensive than it was. Chris held it in both hands like a newborn. The sight of his enjoyment made her display a little of her own. Chris brought the time-piece to his ear.

"Still ticking?" she asked.

Chris shook his head and lowered the watch.

Senada searched for something beyond silence. "Maybe you can find a shop that can get it working again."

He looked at the watch for another moment. "Maybe." Chris shook off the disappointment, much to Senada's satisfaction, and slid the defunct time-piece onto his wrist.

The dense silence made Senada long for a playlist. The only sounds were their feet compressing the thick carpet with every step. Listening to music had been one of their favorite ways to pass the time, back when such a prac-tice required burning CDs on her computer and blasting them from a radio in the back seat of Chris's archaic vehicle. She doubted their capacity for such nostalgia and talked herself out of pressing play.

"How's the Nova comin' along?" she spat out before finding a reason not to. "I haven't heard it in a while."

"That's because I haven't touched it in a while," he repented. "With every-thing going on, it hasn't felt like the best way to spend my time."

A braver Senada would've said it might be the best way to spend his time, reconnecting with things that made him…him. But she only mustered an understated nod before returning to the closet. She thought his eyes were lingering on her back for a few seconds, but she'd lost touch with what was real versus what was just in her head.

"Can you put on one of your playlists?" he asked.

Senada turned halfway around, prepared to share pleasure and shock at how aligned their thoughts were, but Chris was focused on a stack of white envelopes and papers, sifting through them one at a time like he was slowly dealing from a deck of cards. The request wasn't as big a deal to him.

"Sure." Senada answered. "In the mood for anything in particular?"

He shrugged and sat on his mother's side of the bed, only a few feet away from Senada. "Shuffle?"

"There's no telling where that could take us," she snickered.

"Sounds good," he replied, leaving Senada to wonder if he'd really heard what she said. She pressed play and returned to folding clothes before the first song faded in.

Music filled the space around and between them, keeping their heads bouncing and feet tapping in rhythm with Senada's eclectic tastes of R&B, country, hip-hop, and EDM. Chris had long embraced her affinity for any sound that moved her soul. Occasionally, she'd even catch him miming the lyrics to one of her more obscure choices.

Over the next hour and a half, they hadn't spoken much but a lot was said. The stacks of boxes were growing, slowly but surely. Once they'd run out of space to navigate the room without the risk of tripping, Chris started taking the boxes downstairs.

The closet was nearly empty, save for the small jewelry box on the shelf at eye level. It was exactly the way Senada had remembered it from the day Barbara pulled her aside before the gala. Senada pulled open each tiny compartment, pinching the delicate decorative knobs with an abundant fear of breaking them.

The first slot held numerous pairs of earrings, all set in yellow gold, featuring stones of various colors. The next slot housed a series of rings in assorted styles, some appearing much older than others. The bottom compartment was deeper and filled with necklaces. One strand wasn't tangled up in the others. Senada held up the pearl necklace she'd had the honor of wearing for one night.

Every pearl was as vibrant as the day she'd first seen the necklace in Mrs. Mitchell's hand. She lifted it to eye level and was transported back to that moment. Senada never thought she deserved such affectionate gestures, but Barbara had always seen something in Senada that wasn't apparent to anyone else.

Senada held the pearls up to her neck and turned toward the nearest mirror, but her hoodie was in the way. She quickly pulled it off, revealing a simple white top veiling a black bra, then returned the pearls to her neck. Lost in how the necklace looked on her after twelve years, she hadn't noticed Chris in the reflection behind her.

Senada panicked and hid the necklace behind her back. "Oh, uh, shit. I didn't see you come in." She scrambled for an explanation before accepting she'd been caught like a burglar with their hand still in the safe. "How long were you standing there?"

"Long enough," he said with monotonous calm.

Senada couldn't feign innocence. Chris looked confused, but she couldn't assume which aspect puzzled him most. Either she'd define the moment, or he'd define it for her.

"It brought back some memories," she said while revealing the necklace, "and I kinda got… caught up in them."

Chris took a long look at the necklace. "Ahh. I get it." He raised one corner of his mouth and moved on, returning to a tall dresser on the other side of the room.

Senada couldn't discern how he'd read the moment, but she wasn't okay with the mystery. "That's it?"

"Hmm?" he said without looking up from the box he was filling.

Senada lunged for her phone and turned off the music. "That's all you have to say?"

Chris held up outstretched arms. "What do you want me to say?"

"I don't know. This is just the kinda thing you would call me out for." The enduring silence left Senada wondering why she was having such a strong reaction.

"This isn't some sort of game, Senada." Chris walked around to the foot of the bed. "I don't have anything to say about it."

Senada switched to an accusatory tone. "Would you say something if you did?"

Chris sat on the bed, just out of her reach. "What is this? What are you doing?"

Senada put the pearls down on Barbara's nightstand as if they were poisonous. Unsure where to stand, she settled on leaning against the wall across from Chris.

"What is this?" she asked, pleading for sincerity from someone she'd never had to beg for it before.

"What is wh—"

"This! Why are we here? Why am I here, in this room?"

"I wanted your help," said Chris.

"Bullshit," she scoffed.

"That's not bullshit!"

"Was I the only one you could've asked? Was Greg busy?"

"I didn't ask him." Chris looked down at his hands with dejection. "I didn't want to ask him."

"And I'm sure that's not a coincidence."

"On that, you're right," he capitulated. "But that doesn't make it bullshit."

"What was the plan?" she said with rising indignation. "You asked me to come over, under the guise of helping you with something you didn't really need my help with. But you *knew* I wouldn't say no." Senada paced the small area between them. "Then what? You'd put some meat and cheese on a cutting board, make me notice the photo on the stairs, then go through this funhouse of memories until I'd be happy to hop into a time machine with you?"

Chris's eyes widened in astonishment. "You sound nuts right now."

"Do I?!" she shouted back amid nervous laughter. "Tell me I'm wrong!"

"You're wrong," he said with an eerie calm. Chris could never resist a back-and-forth with Senada. Such a languid response gave her pause.

"Well?" she said, still waiting for him to inevitably match her fervor.

"I made the charcuterie board because I had a feeling this process might make you a bit anxious. It's been a long time, and I was still banking on you being a nervous snacker."

Senada nodded at the sense he made. "Okay."

"The picture was crooked because of me, but only because I was rushing when I put it back on the wall. I thought it might make you uncomfortable so I considered taking it down, but then I got worried that if it weren't there, it might cause an issue. Go figure."

Regret tapped on Senada's shoulder as she braced for more. Chris stood up and exhaled through flaring nostrils.

"And I asked for your help because… you lost her too. It's been so long since I knew, without a doubt, that we were on the same page. And feeling the same things. I thought doing this together might be a chance for us to feel a little less… I dunno… apart."

Chris sat beside the box on the other side of the bed. Senada was catatonic, desperate for the right words to find their way out.

"You really thought I'd use a ploy to get closer to you?" he challenged. "And not just any ploy. This?" he pointed around the room at the boxes and open drawers and closets, then at the pearls on the nightstand. "Or that?"

Senada was surprised by how resolute he was. No yelling. No anger. Only a firm, grounded presence. Such a reserved response made it hard to determine how wrong a turn she'd taken. It would've been easier on her if he was shouting her down or cursing her out. At least then, she'd be able to tell when he'd stopped being angry. This version of Chris was more difficult to decipher.

"We haven't been a part of each other's lives for a long time. I wasn't sure where your head might be with things between us, and I didn't want this to get... confusing for you."

"For me?" Chris stood again. "How could I possibly be confused? You made yourself very clear a long time ago. No, *you're* the one who's confused. I may have crossed the line with you once, but that didn't suddenly make caring about you a crime. I haven't done anything today that I hadn't done before we ever took things too far. But you can spend the night in my room just like old times and I'm supposed to shrug that off like it didn't mean anything more to you right? Or commandeering the flowers for the funeral without saying a word to me. Is that just something a friend would do?"

"Yes!" Senada exclaimed as she deleted half the distance between them.

"Then how are you allowed to go back to being my friend with no issues whatsoever," he yelled back, "but I try to show you I still care, and you hold it against me?!"

Chris finally delivered on the anger she'd expected. She took another step towards him, ready to hear what was really on his mind. But he took a step of his own, away from her.

"What is there to care about now that didn't make you pick up the phone sometime in the last decade, Chris?! Don't blame me for you running away from your mistake!"

"My mistake?! It's only my mistake now?!"

"Hey, I'm not the one who was so naïve to take one night of fucking and turn it into love!"

Senada knew how to say something solely to hurt a person she was supposed to care about. She'd learned from the best, and now her greatest fear had been realized — she'd become her mother. The words tore through Chris, turning him into someone she'd never met. Pieces of him crashed at her feet, and she searched for a way to put them back together. "Chris, I didn't mean that the way it soun—"

Sadness emanated in the form of a chilling sensation in her chest, pushing against her lungs and making it hard to breathe. She moved toward him, unsure if hugging him could undo some of the damage, but he diligently stepped around her.

"You can let yourself out," he said as he walked to the door. Senada sat in the space beside where he'd been sitting.

"Chris," she said, hoping to appeal to some part of him that might still remember where her heart resided.

Chris turned around and revealed welling tears in his eyes. "You know the last thing my mother said to me?"

Senada shook her head, unwilling to burden him with more of her words.

"She told me to make sure I apologized for what I was really sorry for. I thought it was nonsense," he said. "But I get it now."

Senada gave up on the possibility of reaching him, instead sitting in the wretched feeling she could only blame herself for.

"I'm not sorry for falling in love with you." Chris struggled to bring his eyes to hers. "I'm sorry I took so long to realize it. That's where I went wrong. But falling in love with you… could never be a mistake."

Tears found their way out of Senada's eyes, but he was already out of the room. She took one more look at the pearls, splayed across the nightstand, until Chris slammed his bedroom door, rattling the walls with agony.

After one more glance at his bedroom door, she went down the stairs and stopped at the photo again. Senada moved the frame, leaving it crooked, the way she'd found it.

22

Gratitude should've been hard to feel after a fight, but it came more naturally than Chris had expected. It had only taken one afternoon to break every dam of emotion he'd built, but it allowed the real grief to pour through the cracks. This was the turning point he needed, and he had Senada to thank.

He wasn't proud of spending the last six days binge drinking, volleying between crying and fits of rage, and loafing on the couch until his own odor reminded him to shower. On day seven, Chris poured the last few drops of his stock of Dewar's into a coffee mug and downed it in one gulp as he ignored yet another phone call from Greg. The text message that followed got the same treatment. Chris didn't want to talk to anyone, no matter what they might've wanted to say. Rather than deal with the real possibility of Greg showing up unannounced, Chris made a mental note to respond before the day was done.

A thud on the front door pushed Chris to the brink, banging against the inside of his head. He shuffled to the door and opened it in time to see a delivery truck pull away. A large box sat on the porch, labeled from Colvin Motor Parts. Chris put the mug aside and braced to lift a box he knew would be densely packed with brand new rotors he'd ordered back when he still had the will to restore the Nova. Every step on the soft grass was met with a groan as Chris lugged the box to the carport and dropped it beside the car, flinching at the loud metallic clank against the concrete.

His train of thought was interrupted by the sound of Senada's van struggling to kick over. Chris rolled his eyes at how the issue could still be lingering after his advice, but it was no longer his concern. When the engine finally started, it signaled him to hurry back inside and avoid Senada driving past the haggard remnants of the man she'd burned down a week ago. To his surprise, there was still enough pride left to hide the ashes.

The sudden jog back inside created a disagreeable bubbling sensation in his stomach. Chris stumbled into the bathroom and hovered over the toilet until dry heaves gave way to brown liquid and bile flooding into the bowl. He retched and writhed until there was nothing left but sore abs and exhaustion. The cool linoleum awaited him as he sat on the floor and looked forward and backward, taking in every decision that had landed him there. Once he trusted his legs to support him, Chris stood and caught his reflection in the mirror.

The man who stared back was hard to recognize. Worse, he looked like someone Chris didn't want to know. Patchy facial hair and crusty eyes depressed him further. A heavy sigh forced rancid breath into his nostrils. The entire portrait made him morbidly grateful his mother couldn't see it. Guilt was ruthlessly tearing into him. This wasn't the way to honor her memory, or everything she'd done for him. Chris was still getting a handle on failing himself, but willfully failing his mother, whether she could see it or not, was a bridge too far.

Amid anger at himself, there was anger at Senada. The sound of her voice calling him naïve was tattooed onto his brain. The idea of colluding around his mother's final wishes was unconscionable. It had taken a long time to cope with his love going unanswered. But taunting him for falling in love at all felt unnecessarily cruel, even as punishment for twelve years apart.

The phone rang again, triggering Chris to anger. But this time, the number was unknown. He cautiously accepted the call.

"Hello?"

"Hi, I'm calling to speak with Christopher Mitchell." A woman with the tone of a bill collector was on the other end, much to Chris's confusion.

"What can I do for you?"

"Is this Chris Mitchell, CEO of —"

"What do you want?" He wasn't in the mood to be reminded of his former title.

"My name is Miriam Hendricks. I'm a VP with a new consulting firm. I'd like to discuss a promising opportunity with you."

Chris tried to process what he'd just heard, one word at a time, through the throbbing in his skull.

"Mr. Mitchell? Are you still there?"

"Yeah, uh, what is this about?"

"We got your number from one of our investment managers. Gregory Harris. He said he's worked with you before. We're looking to recruit people who know what it takes to make something out of nothing, and from what I've heard and read about you, I think you'd be an excellent fit. We'd love to bring you out to our offices, have you meet the team, and see if you'd be interested in joining our firm."

"Your offices?"

"Yes. In Palo Alto."

Chris caught sight of his reflection again, unsure how to revert back to his old internal settings. "Listen, as much as I appreciate the offer, this isn't quite the best time for me."

"Would you prefer I call back at a better time?" she posited.

"That would be great," he said between disgusting belches.

"Not a problem. When would be a good ti—"

Chris hung up the phone and hunched over the toilet bowl again. False alarm, but he was fine with ending the call anyway. There was nothing else worth listening to.

Chris couldn't imagine feeling any worse, and he wasn't interested in finding out what it might take to fall further. Best case scenario, his rock bottom was the bathroom floor. To pick himself back up, Chris needed a reminder of how much control he could still wield over his life. But first, he needed to drink some water.

❉

Senada didn't take many lunch breaks, but when she did, they weren't usually so unfulfilling. The spoon had as much of her attention as the cheap wonton soup she stirred with it. Her sweet-and-sour chicken was already cold, and her can of Diet Coke was likely flat and room temperature.

The mere mention of her mother, on a normal day, would be enough to drag her mood through the dirt. But witnessing the qualities she'd loathed since childhood come alive in herself, especially with someone she cared about so much, was enough to justify the deep depression she'd endured all week.

Lex spun toward Senada with a mouthful of beef and broccoli obstructing her speech. "You gotta eat something. We need to fuel up to get through today. Parade prep is crazy enough without doing it through starvation."

Senada cringed at the sight of Lex's half-chewed food. "Please swallow. Then speak."

Lex rushed through ingestion. "Between the decorations and the floats and all the flowers the kids are gonna want to put in their hair, the parade is gonna be a lot to manage. And at the rate you've been going, I'm worried you might fall over from exhaustion if you don't fuel up. I'm tough but I can't pull off Fourth of July prep without you."

"Relax. It'll get done," scowled Senada. "I just need... I don't fuckin' know," she sighed.

"Give yourself a break," Lex reassured. "It couldn't have gone *that* bad."

"Trust me. It did."

"I've heard the details ten times by now," Lex said before consuming another spoonful and mumbling, "and I can't think of anything you broke that can't be fixed. You just need to talk to him."

"Good plan," Senada said while raising a sarcastic pair of thumbs. She pushed her lunch away. "I cannot believe I said that shit to him. I made a complete ass of myself worrying about keeping things light and simple. And I ended up making them even more complicated."

Lex looked in the air like she'd just had an idea. "Call it… an understandable misunderstanding."

"Why the hell would I call it that?"

"I just mean the lines between friendship and relationship can be a little blurry sometimes. Think about it: how much really changed the day after you two slept together that wasn't already the case before?"

"A lot," Senada said, already prepared to deride whatever Lex might say next.

"You're telling me I'm wrong?"

"No. I'm letting you finish your point. *Then* I'm gonna tell you you're wrong."

"I'm not buying it. You had no idea that the same guy who would leave the door unlocked for you, keep snacks by the bed for you, and sleep on his own floor for—"

The door chime cut into Lex's speech, saving both of them from whatever misguided point she was headed toward. Senada wiped her hands and went to the front.

Frank had excellent timing. Just when Senada was in search of a distraction, the landlord reminded her how important it was to be specific when making requests of the universe.

"Hey Frank," Senada said with fabricated politeness, already bracing for a contentious interaction.

"We need to talk." Frank's Brooklyn accent was impossible to miss, but he still leaned into it harder than necessary. "I've been really patient with you for the last few months, letting you pay as you get it. But I can't keep this up forever."

"I know, Frank, I know." Senada hoped to appeal to his patriarchal senses, as she was around the same age as his daughter. "And you've been so patient with me while I keep my head above water. Can't you bear with me for a little while longer?"

Frank huffed and rolled his eyes. "How long is a little while longer?"

Senada hesitated, holding eye contact as they played rental chicken. "September?"

"July."

"How about August?"

Frank sighed. "Alright. August."

"August 15th!"

"Don't push it, Senada," Frank said bluntly on his way to the door.

"Worth a shot, right?" Senada was good at feigning satisfaction when she had to.

"Yeah, yeah," he said before the door chime drowned out his exit.

Once the door closed, Senada descended to an even lower place while returning to the station and burying her head against her crossed forearms. She wriggled away from Lex's attempt to console her with a gentle touch. Instead, she stood, pushed her food into the trash, and put on her gloves, leaving Lex in a daze as she got right back to work.

"Do you need to talk about it?" offered Lex.

"No." A tidal wave of stress bore down on Senada, and if she sat, she didn't trust her ability to stand up again. An array of red, white, and blue blossoms was spread across the cutting board and Senada pulled the pruning shears. A few clipped stems in, she realized Lex was still lording over her. "Are you gonna watch me or are you gonna help me?"

Lex obeyed silently and joined the fray, while Senada blindly charged ahead, creating one themed arrangement after another. Beads of sweat formed on her forehead and her hands cramped under the strain of a non-stop hour of work.

Lex looked at the clock and stepped in. "It's closing time."

"Thanks, Lex. You can go home," Senada said while steadily clipping multiple stems at a time.

"So can you," Lex said with an air of worry.

"I'm gonna stick around a little longer. Get a jump on things for tomorrow. Ya know, between the parade, and wedding season, and the weather being so nice, and—" Senada abruptly went silent and froze. Lex gasped, covering her open mouth with both hands.

Senada looked at a thin line of blood dripping down her left forearm, following the trail to a fresh wound caused by an errant snip delivered at a frenetic pace. Lex scurried to the bathroom and came back with paper towels in time for the searing pain to set in.

"Get the first aid kit," Senada requested between short breaths.

"Oh shit, that's right!" Lex rushed to the front counter and back again in seconds. "Are you okay? Should I call 9-1-1?"

"I'm fine, Lex. Trust me, I'm —" Senada's voice gave out from a different kind of pain. Tears were falling onto the gauze before she could pretend not to cry. Her walls didn't just crumble; they were ripped from their foundation as she wept over wounds much deeper than the one in her arm. The landlord's riot act was the cherry on top of a sundae no one should ever have to eat.

Senada had always thought she was prepared to be alone. But after losing her biological mother, her real mother, her best friend for the second time, and possibly her business, the sense of loneliness was no longer defined by her creative interpretation. There was nothing left to lose except her mind.

Lex embraced Senada, guiding her toward a stool. They took turns applying pressure until Senada declared herself ready for the cut to be cleaned. Once the bleeding stopped, they were relieved to see it wasn't as deep as they'd feared. Lex poured rubbing alcohol on a wet paper towel and counted to three before pressing it into Senada's arm, causing her to squeal, curse, and groan through the reverberating burn.

"I know you're my boss. But I'm not asking you again," Lex said halfway through wrapping a bandage around Senada's arm. "Go home. Please."

Senada nodded reluctantly.

"Thank you," Lex said with enormous relief. "I'll shut things down here."

Senada took her time throwing her bag over her uninjured arm before walking out the back door. Behind the wheel of the van, she declined the prayer ritual, certain there was no way something else could go wrong. But the streak of off-base instincts continued; the van wouldn't start. Or even crank. A turn of the key yielded nothing.

There weren't any tears left to cry. She sank her forehead into the center of the steering wheel and closed her eyes. There was a tap on the window, pulling her out of the voluntary coma.

"Go home, Senada!" Lex shouted through the window glass, adding wild arm gestures for greater effect.

"I'm trying," Senada whimpered.

Lex opened the door and Senada sat back, repeatedly banging her ponytail against the headrest.

"Come on. I'll give you a ride home," said Lex, already stepping away as if the request had been accepted.

Senada blew a hard breath into the van's metal ceiling. "I think I'm gonna walk."

"You're kidding," Lex chuckled. "How far is that?"

"Not far enough."

❀

Chris kept a close eye on the setting sun, using it as a running timer for how much longer he could work on the Nova without artificial light. Seized brakes required a lot of elbow grease and even more hammering. He sat beside the front wheel well, in an awkward enough position to ensure back pain by morning, and pounded away and the old, rusted rotor. It was a battle of wills, and Chris had faith that he was about to be the victor.

Between short bouts of swinging a steel mallet resembling a miniature sledgehammer, Chris took bottle-cap sized sips from a water bottle he kept near three other empties. The row of plastic charted his efforts toward hydration after such a rough morning. It might be a while before his stomach would trust a drop of alcohol again.

After another ten minutes of effort, five minutes of deciding it wasn't going to happen, and then another ten minutes of stubborn banging, Chris finally got the rotor off the wheel hub.

"Fuck yeah!" he rejoiced, basking before acknowledging he'd have to repeat the process on the passenger side. He stood and gulped the remaining water, collected the empties, and brought them into the kitchen so he could bring another batch outside. Carrying five bottled waters at once meant kicking the door open, but he stumbled down the steep step and dropped one. It rolled ahead and toward the car, but was stopped by a black canvas sneaker.

Senada picked up the water bottle, holding it closely at her waist as Chris took in the surprise.

"Remember that list you mentioned? Of the things I need to get for the van?" Senada waited for a confirmation that wasn't coming. "Can I have it?"

Chris expelled a grunting breath. "What are you doing here?"

"I just told you," she snarled. "My van is dead. I need to fix it. So if you can take a break from being mad at me for like five minutes, I'd really appreciate that list."

"Is this some kinda joke? Go to Pep Boys or something. Google it. You didn't need to come here." Chris put the bottles on the car's hood and extended an open palm toward her for the last one.

Senada held it more tightly. "Chris, don't do this."

He reached for the bottle, but she pulled it away just in time to make him grab air. "Do what?" he groaned.

"I made a bad judgment call. I've done it before. Come on, I've done it *with you* before." She helplessly opened her arms, revealing a blood-soaked bandage that Chris forced himself not to acknowledge. "Don't punish me like this."

"I'm not punishing you," he said, casting her plea aside like a nuisance. "Be an adult. Walk into a shop and ask someone to take a look at it."

"Be an adult? Seriously? You know what I need, you know you can help, and you're gonna leave me to deal with it on my own?"

"Keep the water," he said with a chilling curtness before returning to his work, crouching and putting a shiny silver rotor on the wheel hub. Senada could stand there and watch, but he wasn't obligated to acknowledge her.

"I guess I can't be surprised you're doing it again," she asserted, standing over him. He looked up at her teary eyes against the backdrop of a cloud pattern draped in a mix of orange and blue. "This is obviously your thing." Senada stormed off, hurling the water bottle across the yard on her way down the driveway.

"What's that supposed to mean?!" he boomed while struggling to his feet.

She turned around at the end of the driveway. "You heard me! This is what you do! You don't get what you want from me, and then you leave me to figure things out on my own!"

Chris charged toward her, but stopped a few feet away, avoiding getting too close. "What the fuck are you talkin' about?!"

"Don't play dumb!" she shouted.

Senada suddenly buckled at midsection. The sight distracted Chris from his anger. but she persisted like it was nothing.

"This is exactly what you did when you left," she continued. "You didn't get what you wanted, and you took off."

"That's not why I left, and you know it."

"Oh yeah? So if I would've said 'Sure Chris, let's do this. Let's be together.' You still would've left?"

"I had to go," he replied calmly.

Senada waited an excruciating amount of time before asking another question. "And you would've stayed gone without visiting for more than a weekend at a time? You still wouldn't have called me, or texted me, or checked on me? That's how you would've treated me if I'd let our friendship become more than that?"

Chris looked away, too ashamed to give her the satisfaction of confirming how right she was.

"I thought so." Senada walked a few feet before turning around, dropping her bag, and standing squarely in front of Chris. "Why wasn't I enough?"

His eyes returned to hers. "What?"

"Why wasn't I enough? Why wasn't I — your best friend, the person you claimed to love and trust more than anyone — why wasn't I enough? Just like this?"

"Don't be ridic—."

"And don't call me ridiculous," she interrupted. "You wanted me to love you back. Well… I did, didn't I? Look at what we used to have. Look at who we used to be to each other. I loved you, Chris. Just not in the way you wanted. You wanted something else. You had to have more than that from me. Why wasn't my kind of love, the kind I could actually give you… why wasn't it enough?"

The surrender in her eyes blunted the frustration Chris felt. He knew how hard it was to ask such a question. Countless variations of the same question had plagued him over the years. And he owed it to both of them to be fearlessly honest.

"It wasn't enough for me because it's not enough for you," he said, easing the words out of the smallest possible opening he could speak through and still be heard.

Senada's puzzled face was expected, yet Chris was unprepared to elaborate.

"You deserve more. I wanted to give you more than that."

"You don't get to decide what I deserve."

"I'm doing it anyway."

"Fine," she chuckled nervously. "But that doesn't make it the truth."

"It does to me."

"What about me? What about the things I think I deserve?"

Chris reflected on the last few weeks, and how tired he'd become of giving in to the whims of the world. Senada was going to have to react to him for a change. "Honestly, when it comes to this, I don't care what you think you deserve."

"You don't care what I think?"

"Not when it comes to this."

"I think I know what I deserve better than you do," she delivered with a raised eyebrow.

"I don't care," he defied.

Her nervous giggles morphed into staunch resistance. "Okay, since I'm having one of the worst days of my life, and I could use a laugh, I'll entertain this bag of bullshit." She stepped closer to him and folded her arms. "What makes *you* so sure about what *I* deserve?"

"I know you," he stated without a moment of hesitation.

"You don't know me." Senada shook her head and faced the dwindling sunlight. "Not the way you used to."

"I know enough," he asserted, reminiscent of their past bond.

"Uh huh," mocked Senada.

"I know that you snack so much because you have to keep your mouth busy when you're nervous or you might smoke a cigarette again." Chris took a step towards Senada, though she still wouldn't face him. "I know that… you got the strawberry-shaped scar on your knee from when we ran away from Danielle Mathison's house party when her parents came home early. We ran through a dried-up ravine near the parkway, and you fell." Chris smiled at the evolving grin on her face. "I know your passion for flowers was sparked by us watching that Kurosawa movie with my parents."

"Dreams," she said through the corner of her mouth, her eyes shimmering against the sunlight.

"Yeah," he remembered. "That's the one."

"I may not know everything about you anymore, but I know everything about how you became you. And I did change after we slept together. I got selfish. Because I knew there was no way someone else could come along and see everything I saw. They'd never know the things I know, or the ways I know them. I couldn't bear to watch someone know you less and pretend to love you more. Because you deserve something real, not some… I don't know. Not some façade of love. You deserve someone who loves all of you."

A tear fell from Senada's eye and onto her shirt. Chris had finally opened his soul, and a lightness coursed through his body, but he still wasn't ready to be her comfort again. As much as it stung, he couldn't bring himself to wipe her tears this time. He retrieved his phone from his pocket and tapped the keyboard at a steady pace. Ten seconds later, a chime filled the air between them.

Senada checked her phone. "What's this?"

"The list of what you need to fix the van, and where to get it." Chris turned and walked back up the driveway.

"That was fast," she replied in shock.

"I might've… typed it right after I got the van started for you," he admitted. "I was waiting on you to ask. I figured you'd let me know if you needed me. That's *your* thing." Chris turned enough to show her a smile before he couldn't hold it any longer. He stopped at the front bumper of the Nova and touched the hood with his fingers. "You were right."

"I'm right a lot," she chuckled through tears. "Can you be more specific?"

"I abandoned you. The 'why' doesn't matter." Chris found the boldness to face her, and she responded in kind. "Maybe you were right about other things too. But you weren't wrong for not loving me back. And we may never be the way we were. But wherever we go from here, I won't make you feel that way again."

Their raw openness was familiar, though over the years, he'd grown accustomed to keeping a round in the chamber. But the war was ending; holding back didn't serve him anymore. He returned to the rotor, occupied with a

C-clamp and a ratchet, and waited to hear her walk away. Beneath the manifold, he peeked at the street, expecting her sneakers to cross his view.

"Thank you, Chris."

The cue pulled him up from the well. Chris bumped his head on the edge as he sat up. He hissed in pain, rubbing the back of his skull.

"Sorry," she jeered. "I was just saying… thanks." She held up the list on her phone. "For this and," she delayed, "for everything else you said."

Chris regarded the sentence with a single nod while taking another look at the bandage, then back at her face. The day had exhausted him, and there was more to be done before his night could end. There wasn't much fight left in him.

"Are you close to getting her road-ready?" she asked humbly.

"Close enough," he replied.

Senada lingered in the corner of his eye for another few seconds, then slowly turned and walked the rest of the way home. For once, watching her leave brought him a sense of peace. It might've been fleeting, but it was better than nothing.

23

L ex drove her mid-sized sedan in a way that people probably assumed Chris would drive his muscle car. The idea of Lex behind the wheel of something with as much power as the Nova terrified Senada, but the thought was a vital distraction from grabbing both armrests and hanging on for dear life as they sped down Sunrise Highway.

Senada jostled from side to side as the Altima did the same, changing lanes and speeds with unexpected ferocity. It was unkind to the burdening pain in her abdomen, but Senada breathed through it. Music probably would've helped, but cycling through satellite radio stations didn't feel safe until there was an abrupt halt at a red light.

"How much farther is this place, uh, Calvin's?" Lex asked with a dash of agitation.

"Colvin's," Senada responded as she checked her phone's map to be certain. "It's in Merrick, so we should be there in a few minutes."

"Seems odd to send you three towns away for things that you probably could've picked up sometime in the last five miles."

Senada threw up both hands and shook her head. "This is where he goes. He says they're the best. And since he's forgotten more about cars than I'll ever know, I should probably take his word for it."

"So you get all the stuff on that list, and then what? How much longer am I going to be vacuuming dirt and petals out of my car before this van is fixed?"

"It's a holiday weekend; there won't be much to deliver for a little while. The parade runs right outside the shop."

Beneath the sarcasm, Senada knew it was a fair question. In the eighteen hours since receiving the list, she'd barely thought of anything else except the conversation that led to Chris sending it. While his unwavering candor wasn't expected, her spirit welcomed it. She'd spent the rest of that night in bed and staring at the ceiling, wondering why their exchange had left her so hollow. Something was missing, as though the conversation ended before she was ready. And in spite of misreading his prior intentions, Senada was tempered by his resilient willingness to give her something she'd asked for.

She'd forgotten how to see his actions without reading more into them, and it frustrated her to no end. Chris wasn't the only one who'd been permanently changed by their impulsive night together; he was just the first to admit it.

"Does he expect you to fix it yourself? You needed help calling a tow truck this morning," Lex teased with guttural laughter.

Senada caught the infection of Lex's humor, and appreciated her partner's commitment to getting a laugh, especially during a difficult time. "I'll cross that bridge when I get to it. This list is so long, it probably costs a fortune. I doubt I'll be coming home with all of it today."

Lex hit the gas and snapped Senada into the headrest again. They went through a series of green lights until a sharp right turn, then parked near the entrance of the store. Senada took another look at the list.

Lex loomed across the center console. "Do you even know what you're looking at?"

"Of course I do! There's a battery, a starter, an alternator, and a, um." Senada waned at the sight of what became a foreign language. "I know those three."

"That's three more than I would've guessed." Lex nudged an elbow into Senada's shoulder. "I guess we'll have to take our chances."

They walked into an environment teeming with the trappings of masculine hobbies. Senada couldn't identify anything in the store except the spray paint, and only because it was easily recognizable. She scanned the scene and signage until she got a warm indicator of where to find help.

"Welcome, ma'am! Lonnie here! What can I do for ya?" asked a man with a prominent grey beard and glasses. He rolled up his sleeves a little more as both women neared the counter.

"Hi, I have a list of things I'm supposed to get for my van. Some of it I recognize, but I'll need some help with the rest. I need something called a rotor, a cap, fuses, and uh," Senada squinted and looked more closely.

Lonnie cleared his throat loudly. "Mind if I take a look at it?" he said with a fatherly grin.

Senada slid the phone across the counter and analyzed his expression as he perused.

"What's the make and model?" he asked.

"That I *do* know," Senada poked at her own incompetence. "Ford E-250. Oh, uh, 2012 is the year."

Lonnie hesitated for a beat, then removed his glasses and slid the phone back to Senada. "2012 Ford Econoline van?"

"That's right."

"Are you sure?" Lex whispered in her ear.

"Shut up," she retorted under her breath before reverting back to Lonnie. "Is that a problem?"

"Not at all," he said. "Russ! Get up here!"

Russ shuffled to the counter beside Lonnie and smiled politely at both women. "Whaddya need, Lon?"

"Remember the stack of boxes?"

"The call-ahead order?" asked Russ.

"Yeah," Lonnie confirmed. "She's here."

Senada cycled her attention between the two men, waiting for something to clear up their ominous exchange.

"Okay no problem," said Russ. "Give us a few minutes and we'll get you loaded up. Where'd you park?"

"Right out front," Lex interjected.

"Wait, hold on. How much is all this gonna cost? I might not be able to get everything on the list today."

"It's been taken care of," Lonnie beamed as Russ stepped away with a printed sheet of paper.

Senada's sprinting thoughts were spliced with Lex's giggling, which was slowly getting louder. "I don't understand. I never paid for anything. I've never even been here before."

"Sweet Jesus, Senada," Lex said through laughter. "You really need to get some sleep."

Unlike Lex's humor, Senada's confusion was not contagious. Lonnie winked and shrugged as Senada caught up to what the others already knew. Lonnie tore a fresh receipt from the printer and handed it to Senada.

"They'll bring the boxes out to your car," Lonnie assured. "And do us a favor. Tell Chris we said hello."

Senada looked at the receipt, and the amount made her jaw drop. She ran a hand through her hair and bellowed from deep in her diaphragm.

"What's the problem?" asked Lex.

"I'll never be able to pay this back," said Senada.

"I have a sneaking suspicion he's not gonna bill you," Lex jeered as she led the way out of the store. Senada struggled to grasp the gesture, unwilling to consider there wasn't a deeper intent behind it.

24

Checking his physique in the mirror had become a new routine for Chris. So was calling it a 'physique', which, upon further post-shower reflection, didn't quite feel like an apt descriptor. Chalked up to the bereavement process, he'd been more aware of his own mortality than ever. Loss was a reminder of how temporary things could be. He'd found a helpful respite in a routine of morning jogs and workouts, and its impact was showing. He didn't look the way he did in his twenties, but neither did most people his age.

A shrinking midsection made it easier to disregard how much Korean barbecue he and Greg were about to consume. Once in the passenger seat of Greg's SUV with an arm draped out of the open window, Chris refused to let anything bother him except the oppressive heat. A breeze was enough to bring a smile to his face, and the slightly mended relationship with Senada was a bonus. He braced to find out how she may have received the gesture with Colvin's, but his heart was in the right place.

"I can't wait for you to drive *me* around for a change," Greg complained cheekily as he parked.

"The car is older than we are. It takes time," said Chris. "Can you go another few days without being a passenger princess?"

"I can't make any promises."

Greg barged into the restaurant as if it were Chris's house, stunning the hostess with jokes and quips before Chris had a chance to request a table for two. It probably would've caused a scene if the place was more crowded, but barbecue wasn't the first choice for most professionals in the middle of a workday.

"I gotta admit, I was glad to get your message," Greg said as they settled in at the grill table. "But I wish you picked someplace that didn't expect us to cook *and* pay."

"It'll force us to slow down while we inhale red meat by the pound," Chris said as he browsed the menu. "You'll thank me later."

Greg gawked back at him. "Where does Mister 'Filet mignon, medium rare' get off talking down red meat consumption?" Chris nodded at the accurate admonishment while Greg went on. "You stopped being stressed out for a couple of days and changed already."

"Would you rather I endorse two men in their forties shoveling fried food into their gullets with reckless abandon?"

"Yes!" Greg hawed.

Greg got his wish. The concept of such a restaurant was fertile ground for overconsumption. Getting caught up in conversation made it difficult to keep an eye on portions. Before they could blink, they'd eaten themselves into motionlessness. Chris was already preparing to dodge every mirror in his home. During a lull in the action, Greg took their dialogue beyond small talk.

"Have you heard from Miriam yet?" Greg asked with a remarkable lack of subtlety.

Chris started and stopped a response as he stifled miniature belches. "A couple of times."

"They must really want you."

Chris put down a forkful of beef and squinted at Greg. "You would know, right? You gave them my number."

"They asked for a recommendation, and I gave them one," Greg defended. "You've been gettin' all stir crazy. I figured a job opportunity might do you some good."

Chris shook his head. "I doubt there's much of an opportunity in it. I'm available and affordable," he bemoaned.

"What are they offering?"

"I haven't heard it."

"That sounds like a conviction without a trial," Greg replied before taking a big gulp of lemonade and recoiling at its tartness.

"What's to hear? There's not much they could offer me that I don't already have."

"Now you're talkin' like a real rich guy."

"I'm not rich. I just stopped letting money define my happiness," Chris pronounced as if it was odd to employ another style of logic.

"I'm surprised you can find a way to eat with your head so far up your own ass," Greg chirped with a self-satisfied expression.

"I heard it that time," Chris chuckled. "But I'm not gonna pretend that my priorities haven't changed lately."

"Hey, I'm not knocking it," said Greg. "Just be honest about it."

Chris leaned back and looked around as if someone might notice his search for a way to avoid truth without lying. "Right now, I think I need to tie up loose ends."

"What loose ends?"

"I'm not sure," Chris said as his jaw tightened like a defense mechanism. "Well, I'm not *entirely* sure. Things just feel so… unsettled."

"That's understandable, man. Losing your mother, blindsided like that. Give yourself a break while you find your footing."

After three months of despair around losing his job, his company, and moving back to his hometown, it wasn't far-fetched to presume a new job might be just what he needed to turn things around. Especially a role that would take him out of town again. Without close family, there was even less reason to ever come back.

But in the aftermath of Barbara's passing and a riot act from Senada, Chris stopped being so sure about running away.

Money hadn't defined happiness for him, but the way he'd made it was a major component. As a CEO, he was relied upon and trusted to create positive outcomes that would benefit others. In his role, Chris had more than a job and a company; he had a purpose.

"Hey, can I ask you something?" Chris wasn't quite sure where his thought was headed. "When we first got funded, why didn't you come with me?"

"I told you. I couldn't," Greg replied, more focused on laying fresh strips of raw beef across the hot grates.

"Yeah, I know. But why couldn't you?" Chris pressed. "You were single, no kids, fresh out of Columbia Business. It was the opportunity of our lives, and you stayed here. Why?"

Greg swallowed the bite he'd been chewing and cleansed his palate with another sip. "Don't get me wrong. I had a great ride with you, running and gunning through V.C. meetings and all that. And I couldn't've been happier when we finally hit our mark. But… that was the opportunity of *your* life. Not mine."

It became evident that, in his escape, Senada wasn't the only one Chris had left behind. "I don't think I've ever told you this, but I'm sorry."

Greg pushed a breath through his nostrils and tilted his head to one side, then the other. "For what?"

"Putting you in that position."

"What position?" Greg huffed, then smiled. "I'm at cool with how things played out. And you took care of me on the back end. There are no regrets on this side of the table."

Chris couldn't express how unbelievable it sounded for him to be blameless in such a circumstance. Greg caught on and put the fork down to clear the fog between them.

"If this was just about money, I would've been in the aisle seat right next to you on that flight," Greg reflected. "But the life I really wanted was right here. I supported you because I wanted you to be as happy with your life as I was with mine."

"I thought I was," Chris replied with a healthy dose of introspection. "I thought I was doing exactly what I was meant to do. But the more I got used to being back here, the more I realized I was searching for something that success couldn't help me find." Chris watched a burning strip of beef on the grates. "Twelve years is a long time to waste chasing something that never would've really made me happy. I kept going, thinking it would. Thinking that one day, being out there would justify leaving here. I went across the country to find something I'd left behind. And now… I don't know if I can get it back."

Greg took the seared meat off the grill and held it in front of his mouth. "If it can be done, I'm pretty sure you'll figure out a way." Greg popped the smoking beef into his mouth and immediately realized it wasn't ready to be ingested, waving a futile hand in front of his open mouth before finally being able to chew.

Chris reached across the table and turned off the grill. "That's it. I'm cutting you off," Chris gloated.

Greg caught his breath. "Good call. Might've done some long-term damage that time."

There was nothing left on Chris's docket for the day. But something still ate at him, begging for more of his attention. He checked the time. "I need to get back," he said, already sliding out of the booth.

"Time is money, huh?"

"Not anymore."

"You really don't care about money, do you?" Greg speculated as he groaned his way out of the booth.

"Nope." Chris sensed a trap.

"Great." Greg wrapped an arm around his friend. "So, lunch is on you then?"

25

The best thing about the local Fourth of July celebration was how alive the streets of Rockville Centre became. From face painting stations to a puppy parade, from high school marching bands to the bagpipe band of the volunteer fire department, it was a blissful day for the town to flood the streets. The small neighborhood became a true community, reminding Senada of how much there was to celebrate.

The bright and sunny carnival atmosphere became a temporary shield from the storms traveling through Senada. The van finally had what it needed, which should've brought relief, but the boxes still sat in its trunk while she considered the ramifications of asking for more of Chris's help.

Accepting support, especially from him, should've been easy. He was there for Senada more than anyone throughout an adolescence of needing all the relief she could get. But such a sizable purchase struck her as the action of a man who wanted something out of her. Senada was tired of questioning what was genuine about Chris.

The enormous smiles of every little girl outside of the shop were undoubtedly real. Lex did her best to organize them into a line in front of the Symbol of Symphony table as Senada laid a handmade floral tiara on each kid's head. Every child's exuberant laughter lifted Senada's spirits. She watched them pose and fawn over every piece — woven crowns of lavender, camellias, and daisies.

Even Lex got into the spirit, going the extra mile of dyeing her hair red and blue. Senada tapped into her inner child and had her face decorated with stars and glitter. Whatever awaited Senada on July 5th — bills, rent, surgery — wasn't allowed inside until then. The most important debt she owed was to herself. No amount of struggle would get in the way of joy.

"I don't think I've ever seen you so excited," Lex said as Senada finished cheesing for a camera with twin sisters wearing nearly identical wreaths atop their blonde hair.

"Thank you!" the girls said in unison as they galloped away, warming Senada's heart even more.

"It's a beautiful day," Senada responded while waving to the children.

"I love it too, heat and all," Lex panted, wiping her brow and taking a long sip of iced tea. "But I'm waiting for the fireworks. That's my favorite part."

Senada grimaced at the mention. "Absolutely not."

"You don't like fireworks?! What kinda suburban girl are you?"

"I love fireworks!" Senada countered. "What I don't love is being packed like sardines with the entire town on a patch of grass too small to host a football game. It'd be nice to enjoy the show and have some personal space at the same time."

"In this heat, I can't argue with your logic," Lex said. "But for this occasion, I'll push through it."

Senada would've laughed, but a sudden distraction took away the ability. Through the many bodies passing in every direction, Chris emerged across the street in a way that made Senada wonder if he was a mirage. Real or not, it only took a second for her to realize how happy the sight made her. Until his eyes found hers, Senada hadn't realized she'd been staring. Chris crossed the street, weaving through a group of war veterans from the local VFW contingent. A few feet before reaching the table, he was halted by a dachshund and its owner, both clad in matching American flag attire. Senada raised her eyebrows at Chris and offered a tender grin, which he reciprocated.

"What a day, huh?" he said.

Senada put her hands in the pockets of her cut jean shorts, occupying them before they could do a 'should we hug or not' dance again. "I gotta admit I'm a little surprised to see you."

"Why's that?" he asked, appearing puzzled by something she thought would be obvious.

"You always hated the parade. You avoid large crowds even more than I do." Senada forced a harder laugh than the statement warranted, hoping to ease the bluntness.

"I wouldn't miss a puppy parade," he winked. "The rest of this, I'll admit, I could do without." Chris waved at Lex, who waved back without breaking her inquisitive stare. Senada spun her head and glared back at Lex until specific direction was conveyed.

"Oh, uh, I'm gonna grab some more… lavender," Lex spouted before scooting through the shop's entrance.

"Thanks," Senada said melodramatically, then turned back to Chris. "You missed the parade of puppies. I hope the wiener dog was enough to scratch that itch."

They shared a moment of awkward restrained laughter.

Senada pursued a thought before she could talk herself out of it. "I've been meaning to thank you for the van stuff."

He raised one corner of his mouth. "Happy to help."

"Can you make me a step-by-step of how to put that stuff on my van? That would be helpful too," she added. "I opened the hood and didn't know where to start."

"Did you really open the hood?" he skepticized.

"Of course not," she blurted. Senada stepped outside herself, able to see how easily they fell back into a banter that would cause confusion. She wasn't flirting with him. Or she wasn't doing it on purpose. But Chris had a way of making her feel safe enough to have any emotion, even if she wasn't always brave enough to verbally express it.

"I think I can help with that," he replied with subdued calm.

"I'd really appreciate it." Senada assessed his body language for any sign worth decoding, following Chris's eyes as he looked at the happenings around them. "People are about to head over to see the fireworks. When's the last time you saw those?"

"I can't remember," mourned Chris. "Maybe when I was ten."

Senada wasn't surprised he hadn't seen them in a long time. But she hadn't expected the question to affect him so deeply. "You should stick around. I hear it's pretty amazing to watch."

"You've never seen them?"

"I've heard them from our block. Sometimes, if I was lucky, I could make out the tops of some of the bigger flashes through the tall trees."

She could tell he was calculating. "But you've never seen them?"

"Only the ones on TV," she quipped.

Chris hummed in deep thought. Senada grew impatient waiting for him to disclose where his mind had run off to.

"What? What is it?" she asked.

"I have an idea. Probably. Maybe." He scanned the surrounding area as if looking for a solution. "Can you meet me in the Home Goods parking lot?"

"The one on Main?" Senada knew what her response would be, but stalled long enough to feign making up her mind. "I think so. I just need to clean this up once people clear out. Fifteen minutes?"

"See you there." He turned and walked down the block, weaving seamlessly through throngs of people who were dwarfed by his presence in her eyes. Senada walked inside the shop as Lex appeared to be aware of her decision, already turning off lights around the showroom.

"We've gotta shut down before the fireworks start," Lex declared. "I'm hoping to get a better spot than last year."

"I'm not going to the fireworks. I think."

"You aren't sure if you're going to the fireworks?"

"I just made plans with Chris, believe it or not," Senada confessed. "But I'm not sure if they involve fireworks."

"I'd put my money on fireworks," winked Lex.

"Please stop."

"I'll stop if you help so we can get going," Lex implored.

Senada joined the effort. They brought the table inside and cleared the remaining tiaras. There was one intact crown left, and Senada decided it was meant for her head. It felt foolish to derive glee from such a silly thing. But she recalled the day's mantra: nothing was getting in the way of joy. Senada placed the floral piece on her head.

The soles of Senada's 'special occasion' white Chucks barely touched the sidewalk as she glided down Village Avenue. The normally bustling area was barren, likely due to most residents being at Pette and Barasch Fields to watch the show. Everything — from the coffee shop to the Mexican restaurant to the crafts store — was either empty or closed. The only sign of life was a veterinary hospital, and its tabby housecat sitting on a windowsill watching with a judgmental eye as Senada passed.

Senada slowed her gait to something she assumed was a normal pace. There wasn't plausible reason to be so excited for an unknown scenario, yet she couldn't help herself. It was undoubtedly a good thing that she and Chris would have a chance to redefine their friendship, particularly after everything they'd been through since his return. As Home Goods appeared ahead, some clarity appeared with it.

Chris leaned against the front bumper of the Nova, clad in a hooded top he hadn't worn earlier. They locked eyes and he welcomed Senada toward the symbol of many ambitious nights. The sight of the revived car was surreal, particularly after becoming used to its presence in the driveway over the time since she'd last rode shotgun. A smile didn't wait for permission to appear on Senada's face, and it grew wider with every forward step.

"Surprise," he said with a reserved yet vibrant ego.

Senada folded her arms and lifted her chin, admittedly impressed by the accomplishment.

"You finally got her moving," she exclaimed before walking around the car like she wasn't already familiar with every inch. When she arrived at the front again, she lingered near a familiar spot on the hood. "May I?"

"Of course," he gleamed.

Senada hopped onto the hood, and the warmth of the idling engine tinged the skin of her thighs. She sat cross-legged and soaked in the darkening sky, remembering every time she'd had that vantage point.

In the sudden thrust back through time, things made more sense. Chris, and so much of what he'd ever done, made Senada feel safe, untouched by a world that otherwise refused to let her have peace. Plenty of good came with feeling secure, but it also reminded Senada of things she'd rather forget. The epiphany made her fearful side want to run home and barricade itself in the bedroom, while the safest parts of her wanted to sit on that hood until she'd forgotten how to flee.

"What's with the hoodie?" she pivoted, desperate to distract from her racing thoughts. "It's like ninety-five degrees."

"It's for where we're going." His cryptic tone added intrigue. "Get in."

Senada hopped off the hood and heaved open the passenger door, which let out a loud, grinding screech. But she was unfazed, excited to descend into the passenger seat.

"That door hasn't gotten much use lately," he said as he closed the door for her. "Nothing a little WD-40 won't fix."

Senada looked for every familiar detail she could find. She turned dials and pressed buttons until Chris entered with a recognizable scowl that brought her much delight.

"Are you finished?" he asked.

"Not even close," she said. "I've got a lot of lost time to make up for." The words held one meaning when she'd thought of them, and another when they left her lips. Senada cleared her throat and tucked her antsy hands between her thighs. "I'm done now."

Senada observed the way he put his arm behind her seat and backed out of the parking space. The rumble of the powerful engine made her body tremble in a way she'd missed. The transition from reverse to drive, followed by Chris hitting the gas, jolted her bones as they sped away. She took off her sneakers and socks and rested her bare feet on the dashboard, just like she used to. The breeze nearly took her flower crown away, but she caught it in time. The sudden motion made her jealous of the flowers, and she loosened her ponytail so her hair could get lost in the breeze too.

The air felt different, doing more than just touching her skin or pushing strands of hair away from her face. Senada became a part of the breeze, moving in and out and around with the freedom she'd longed for. While she'd been busy fighting Chris at every turn, unwilling to let him care for her, she'd been blind to an unsettling truth; she liked being cared for by him. Her mother had programmed a natural defiance against depending on a man, but Chris was more than just a man to her.

As Chris focused on the road, Senada was enraptured by him, sliding a hand up his arm and along the back of his neck, as if it were a sentient limb she had no control over. Chris reacted to the gesture before she did, slowly showing a bewildered expression. Senada gasped and pulled back, reminded of her role in how things had become so fractured between them. She took her feet off the dashboard and returned to a normal seated position.

The problem had been misinterpreted from the start. Trusting Chris's intentions wasn't the only issue. Senada had lost trust in her own actions, and what might've been driving them. Comfort made her relinquish control to the boldest part of her spirit, a place that didn't care about whatever boundaries they'd set.

The Nova came to a stop, giving Senada the chance to focus on anything outside the car. They were in an open field, with a housing project on one side, and a lake surrounded by overgrown plant life on the other. Ahead was a softball field, barely visible amid the decreasing daylight. "Where are we?"

Chris turned off the engine. "A park."

"I can see that," she said before jabbing him in the side. "But what are we doing here?"

"I'm not sure yet." Chris reached blindly into the back seat, pulled out a dark green mound of fabric, and handed it to her. "But you're gonna wanna put this on."

Senada unfurled the mound and revealed a hoodie with C.W. Post University on the front in faded yellow lettering. A hazy memory became clearer by the second. It was what she'd wear to bed in his dorm room when she needed to get away from home for a night or two. "No fuckin' way!"

Chris relayed a gratified nod. "Found it while I was unpacking."

"This was the only thing protecting me from that frigid air conditioner your roommate had."

"It was way too strong for a room that small," Chris laughed heartily.

"Exactly." The hoodie begat another question. "But tonight is like an oven. Why would I wanna put this on?"

"Because tonight, it'll be the only thing protecting you from the vicious mosquitos waiting for us out there. The lake is full of 'em."

They got out and took their assigned seats on the hood, atop a beach towel to blunt the engine's remaining heat. Chris laid against the windshield and folded his arms behind his head. She laid beside him, with a foot between their bodies, ecstatically donning a sweatshirt big enough to conceal her shorts and half of her thighs.

"I'm still not sure why we're risking being eaten alive by mosqui—" A loud boom in the distance, followed by two more in quick succession, stopped Senada's speech. Both heads turned toward the source as bright sparks of white light lit up the sky above the trees. It wasn't as visible as it might've been from the crowded fields a mile away, but it was perfect enough for them.

"How did you know we'd see it from here?" she thought aloud.

"I didn't," he replied, still stunned by the colors and shapes cast across the sky. "I took a guess."

"What if you were wrong?" she wondered.

Chris brushed off the query. "I hadn't thought that far ahead."

Somehow, his willing uncertainty removed her doubt. From the moment they'd slept together, she'd regarded him as a force trying to dictate how she bloomed. But he'd actually been taking chances all along, with the sole aim of making her happy.

On the night of the gala, they'd both taken a risk. But she retreated, leaving him to put out the fire they'd started together. Chris abandoned her, but only after she'd done the same to him. It didn't excuse his absence. But as Senada laid beside him on the Nova again, more enthralled with him than any fireworks display, his decision had never made more sense.

A vibrant blast of white twinkling light flashed, jumpstarting Senada's senses and shaking her entire body for a split-second.

"Scared?" he teased.

"No." She slid closer to him and landed a petty jab against his mid-section, forcing one of his arms down. Senada stayed close and his arm ended up wrapped around her. Chris was warmer than the night air. Senada nestled against him and laid a hand on his chest. It was too late to pull away without an explanation, and she couldn't provide one. The proximity of their bodies conjured thoughts of how far apart their lives had been for too long.

"You okay?" he asked, a reasonable question that made her take stock of the scene. To an unbiased observer, there wasn't much to interpret. But neither of them could claim neutrality.

"You know I want back what we had," she said in the spaces between staccato pops and flashes. "But if I'm honest, I don't know how we're going to do it."

After a long pause, Chris answered, "Neither do I." She focused on the way her hand rose and fell with his heightened breathing. "I figure… we can take it slow. Make up for lost time, right?"

"I like the sound of—" Her words were snatched as a wave of abdominal pain forced Senada into contortion. She reflexively pushed him away.

"What?" Chris sat up with a look of intense worry. "What happened?"

Senada respired and waited for the pain to subside. "Nothing. I'm fine."

"Are you kidding me?" Chris raised both hands as if wanting to touch her but unsure where or how he might be able to provide comfort. "Talk to me. What's goin' on?"

Once the pain had dissipated, she cautiously laid back down and tugged at Chris to return to their prior position. Much to her relief, he obeyed the directive, despite obvious reticence.

"If I promise to tell you later," Senada appealed, "can we stay in this moment right now?"

Senada could tell he didn't want to agree, but Chris holding her more tenderly and returning his attention to the fireworks were enough of an answer for her.

The booming sounds and twinkling lights awakened her, one cell at a time. She couldn't get comfortable, and it wasn't because half of her body was resting on hard glass while the other was against unforgiving metal. Her roots were growing too big for her pot. It was time to try someplace new. And while Chris was far from a novelty, Senada only had one night of evidence to understand who she might become with him. Twelve years ago, the prospect scared Senada. But beneath sparkling night sky, ignoring the urge again was much more terrifying.

Senada sat up and leaned into Chris. The multi-colored lights spread across his skin, and the occasional flash revealed his hesitant eyes. Chris was taking too long to join her in the world she'd made for them in her mind. Senada couldn't wait any longer. Her hand led the way again, gently moving his head by the cheek and allowing their lips to reconnect.

They got lost under the lights and sounds, in rediscovery of each other. A small, short peck slowly turned to impassioned kisses. Their hands weaved around each other and pulled them closer, removing the air between their bodies. Senada crawled onto him and straddled his lap, giving in to the intensity of every mutual movement. In fleeting moments of analysis, she felt an understandable confusion in his touch.

Senada didn't have all, or any, of the answers. But she knew what she needed to know: nothing was in the way of her joy.

26

Twelve Years Earlier

Senada was running out of time, and she knew it. One-word text responses and pretending to be busy had gotten her through a week of confusion after the gala. But Chris would only buy those excuses for so long, assuming he'd been blind and naïve enough to believe them in the first place. He'd probably want to discuss what happened, but any conversation would be one-sided. Senada had no idea what to say to her reflection, let alone to him.

Sitting in front of her vanity, Senada took turns looking at herself and looking at the photos of them lining the mirror. She'd thrown away years of something beautiful, stable, and predictable for one amazing night she wanted to undo. Being Chris's best friend was easy, natural, and steady. And most importantly, she knew how to do it. But they'd crossed into unfamiliar territory, and she was more afraid than ever of outcomes she could neither anticipate nor control.

Whenever Senada thought she'd made a proper assessment of the circumstances, minutes later, she'd convinced herself of an opposing rationale. A sudden sexual impulse could've been the culprit, but Senada knew it was more than that. Something about Chris had shifted in her consciousness. Hindsight made her reconsider everything she'd ever known about their bond.

"Senada!" Carrie yelled from the other side of the bedroom door.

Before Senada could respond, her mother pushed against the door, likely too inebriated to realize it was locked. Senada pushed away from the vanity and cautiously approached the door, unlocking it slowly in case her mother risked falling into the room.

Senada spoke through a narrow opening. "Yeah, Mom?"

"What'd you do with my, uh, my..." Carrie slurred.

It had become difficult to look at her for longer than a few seconds at a time. Her yellow eyes and jaundiced skin were even harder to handle than the frequent bouts of confusion Carrie suffered. Senada didn't enjoy who her mother had become, but at least in the past, she was easier to look at. Years of alcohol abuse and cirrhosis turned her into another species of someone who was already hard to see as human.

"What did I do with what, Mom?" Senada sighed.

"Don't get smart with me!"

"I'm not getting—" Senada opened the door fully open. "I don't know what you're asking for."

Carrie looked at Senada as though she suddenly didn't recognize her daughter, squinting more closely like a stranger had broken in. Senada was familiar with the mannerism, and knew the best thing to do was stand still and be quiet until her mother caught up to reality again. Something caught her attention and she shoved her daughter out of the doorway to enter the room.

"What the hell is that?" Carrie rambled while pointing at a teak box filled with potting soil, a gift from Mrs. Mitchell so she could start planting her own flowers.

"It's a planter, Mom," Senada replied, bracing for whatever judgment was sure to follow.

"Looks like a box of dirt," Carrie suspected. "Why you bringing boxes of dirt into my house?"

Explanations were futile, but Senada couldn't help it. "There are marigold seeds in it."

"Marry what?"

"Marigold. It's a flower."

"Looks like dirt," Carrie resisted.

"They're not showing yet."

"Hmph." It was the sound of her mother running out of mean comments.

The doorbell song couldn't have come at a better time. Senada walked diligently toward the front door, careful not to move too quickly for fear of inciting her mother. Senada walked out onto the porch and nearly stepped into Chris's chest before realizing he was there.

"Hey stranger," he said with a hint of a smile.

"Oh, uh, hey." Senada was already dreading things he hadn't said yet.

"Good to see you too," he said joylessly. "What's been up with you?"

"I've just…"

"Who is it?!" Carrie shouted from behind Senada. She stumbled into the doorway and leaned against the frame. "Oh, of course. Christopher."

"Hi, Miss Williams," Chris droned in a way that would normally make Senada snicker because he sounded like the teacher in Ferris Bueller. But the depression had become impossible to hide.

Senada closed the door behind her before Carrie found a reason to intrude any further. She tugged at Chris's arm, signaling for him to sit on the steps beside her. "I've just had a lot going on," she continued.

"I assumed as much when I hadn't heard from you all week." Chris paused as if waiting for Senada to fill him in. "Anyway, I came by because I've got some news that's too good for text."

Senada couldn't match his excitement, but she wanted to.

"I don't know what we did right at the gala, but whatever it was, it worked," he said with growing elation. "We've got VC meetings set up all over the city, and even a few on the west coast! If we play this right, we're talkin' major moves. Getting a real office space, hiring engineers, hiring salespeople, assembling a board." Chris sighed like a masseuse had finally hit the right spot. "Can you believe it?"

The moment warranted celebration, but she didn't have much left to give. Senada had already surrendered more of herself to him than she'd ever imagined she would. "That's incredible, Chris. I'm really happy for you."

"Are you sure?" He was understandably puzzled by her bland response.

Rather than be honest with him, Senada took the easy route and got defensive. "What's that supposed to mean?"

"I don't know. You seemed so excited about this stuff at the gala, and now…" He stopped and Senada battled to keep her chin up. "I know things kinda took a turn with us. And I just wanted to… I dunno… talk about it. This is new for me. I'm not sure what to do next."

"Nothing," she cut through without hesitation. "We don't do anything."

"Um, alright," he replied, unprepared for such a callous delivery. "I'm not sure what you mean."

Intensity rose but Senada kept it at bay. "I mean… we had a great time. We had some fun, and things went too far. It happens. There's no need to make it more than that."

Senada was sprinting down a foggy road and leaving Chris in the dust. As much as her heart was breaking, it would've been worse to slow down and take in his emotions as well. The man who'd kept her from shattering countless times was showing cracks. She volleyed between competing impulses to push him away and pull him closer. Holding onto him had never been in doubt before, but after allowing him inside so much more than her body, new questions surrounded her. In a single night, everything she'd known had been torn asunder and tossed aside. Things between them had changed irreparably, and Senada wasn't ready to adapt.

❀

Catching his breath was hard enough, but doing it without showing the hurt was beyond Chris's skillset. He hadn't known what to expect when they'd parted ways at the end of the limousine ride. And with each passing day of uncharacteristic silence and notable absence, he'd grown more fearful. But he hadn't anticipated Senada minimizing the connection with such ease.

"Okay," he said, pacifying himself amid a search for better words. "I'm not really sure what to say."

"What do you wanna say?" Senada was frigid and plain, as though barring him from a protected area.

There was no path toward an honest answer without consequences that weren't worth the trouble. Chris had no impressions of them falling madly in love or anything. But he wasn't prepared for sex to pull them apart. Beside her, he'd become cliche naïve geek who'd misread the prom queen being nice to him. A complete rejection would've been easier, but Senada was doing something much worse. She was telling him it all meant nothing.

He knew what he really wanted to say, but love got in the way. Chris settled for something predictable. If she was willing to erase the night from their shared history, Chris hoped she would at least answer one question for him.

"Do you regret it?"

"It shouldn't have happened," she muttered.

"That doesn't really answer my question."

"Yes, it does."

"I don't think so."

"Well, I can't do anything about what you think," she shot back. "But I'm not changing my answer just because you don't understand it."

"Alright, alright," he cowered. "So, what happens now?"

"I told you. Nothing. I thought we could just move on, but it sounds like that's not gonna happen."

Her dismissive approach was hard for Chris to fathom. "Do you really think I could move on from something like that without any sort of hesitation?"

"I don't think you could do anything," she replied. "This is what I'm asking you to do."

"But… we're best friends. Why would you want me to do that?"

"Because that's what I'm doing!" she shouted back like anger was impossible to restrain. "We are friends. But friends don't do what we did. So we've got two choices: pretend it never happened or pretend we're not friends. I know which one I'd rather do. Do you?"

As unbelievable as the choices were, Chris recognized what she was doing. He'd been privy to her dating life since high school and this was standard operating procedure. If someone got too close, they wouldn't be around much longer. With her, you either lived on the edge, or you got pushed off of it. And if Senada would force the same options on Chris as any other guy she'd encountered, then the choice had already been made for him.

"Are you sure you really wanna do this?" he pleaded.

"I don't see another way out of this," she replied.

"Alright." Chris stood at a measured pace and walked down the steps.

"Chris," said Senada. "Wh-what are you doing?"

He turned around and looked up at her. "I'm not going to pretend I didn't feel something. And you'll never convince either of us that you didn't feel something too. If that means we can't be friends anymore, then I'll have to live with that. But I won't lie. To you or for you."

Chris walked down her driveway and back home, unwilling to turn back for fear of what he might see. And by the time he reached his door, he was afraid of a life without her. If they'd really been friends, he could've turned around, apologized, and put the pieces back together. But Senada was right. Whether referring to a week ago or a minute ago, real friends wouldn't do what they'd just done.

27

The engine kicked over with ease and settled into a low hum, eliciting a smile from Senada as she listened from her bedroom window above the driveway. While she enjoyed much-needed sleep, Chris had gotten up two hours earlier and she'd just found out why. Through half-opened eyes, she wondered what else might be on his mind beyond fixing the van.

The night had been a blur of released passion and repressed desire. For the last twelve hours, they'd worn nothing but each other, save for Senada wearing a bedsheet toga while they'd watched a movie, and Chris putting pants on to answer the door when their late-night cheesesteak craving had arrived. The sandwiches required reheating when a sudden greater urge for kitchen sex got in the way.

Deep calm coursed through her as she stared at the ceiling, recalling every kiss and touch, her body awakening for more of what their connection provided. But she stayed tethered to the present, fighting a sense of déjà vu and assuring herself that the experience had little in common with twelve years ago.

Chris had guided her through emotional exhaustion and rejuvenated her spirit through physical passion. While the relief would likely fade, there was optimism for the inevitable questions around what should come next.

Senada slid out of bed, noting the chilly combined sensations of sweat-soaked sheets and a breeze pouring into the open window. She stepped on the C.W. Post hoodie that he'd taken off in one swift motion before devoting attention to her breasts. The memory was enough to harden her nipples against the fabric. The hoodie was long enough to make underwear invisible, and it put one less thing between Chris and another round. Desiring more of a man right away was a sensation she still needed to adjust to.

The experience hadn't been without its moments of timidness. But Chris took his time in considerate exploration of her apprehensions as well as her body. When she'd tried to ignore her hesitation or brush off her fears, Chris wouldn't let her off that easily. They'd talked through much of it, eager to express all the ways they felt, what they were enjoying, and why. They'd spent the night going back and forth between making love and *making* love. Senada drafted off his confidence, while slowly finding her own.

She nearly danced her way into the kitchen and brewed a larger pot of coffee than usual, mindful of all the ways she had to move to avoid discomfort. The growing bouts of pain were enough to garner frequent looks of concern from Chris, and she'd internally rehearsed a way to tell him what was going on. What was less clear was why she'd been afraid to mention it sooner. It was like she could only feel fearless with her body when it was capable of performing in a way that could satisfy him. Senada struggled more with how he might perceive her naked soul than her naked body.

As much as they already knew about each other, they'd been ships passing in the night for some of life's critical moments. They weren't seventeen or twenty-eight anymore. Not only was Senada unaware of what he might currently want for the future, but until her recent slate of doctor's appointments, she hadn't put much thought into her own future either. Senada was content with riding their current wave until it reached the beach.

Senada's feet were connected to the floor in a new way as she reached the front door and stuck her head out, cautious of being naked from the waist down. Below her, Chris had just closed the van's hood and was wiping grease from his hands with a rag, a sight that warmed her grateful heart.

"Do you want some coffee?!" she shouted down to him.

"Sounds good," he answered while gathering his tools. "I'll be up in a sec."

"Black, two sugars?" She didn't have to ask, but wanted to show off her memory. He obliged her with a grin and a nod, then went back inside.

Chris was in the kitchen and washing his hands by the time Senada tipped a second spoonful of sugar into the mug. There was something about the attention he paid to getting every speck of dirt away from his cuticles, and the way the effort made his forearms flex, that she thoroughly enjoyed. She shook her head quickly as if a fly had flown across her face, when really, she was snapping herself out of an erotic spell. She placed both mugs on the white round kitchen table, shoving the pile of mail to the side.

"Your van is officially fixed," Chris said as he focused on drying his hands with a handful of paper towels.

"I really can't thank you enough."

"Then it's a good thing you don't have to thank me at all." The sentiment meant more to her than he realized. "Shit, this is good," he remarked after two sips of fresh coffee.

"It's just Colombian coffee," she giggled. "What do you normally drink?"

"Not this," he said as he brought the mug to his lips again.

She prepared a cup for herself and watched from the corner of her eye as Chris sat at the table and peeked at the envelopes. A severe reaction would give the mail more significance. She ignored it, but Chris didn't.

"You'd tell me if you needed help… right?"

"Help with what?"

Chris held up two envelopes with one hand, both with 'Due Immediately' stamped in red on them.

"Oh," she said despite having no alibi, "those are nothing."

He nodded slowly. "And you'd tell me if you *wanted* help, right?"

Her stern glare made Chris stand down, but knowing him, it would only buy Senada a day or two. Receiving his support at Colvin's was hard enough to stomach. And while the entire Internet knew he could afford to pay every bill with his couch cushion money, the balance paled in comparison to what it would cost Senada to let him 'save' her.

"I won't push it," he conceded. "But you know where I am."

Senada was thankful for something else grabbing his attention. He left the mug on the table and moved toward the window. With so many plants around, the sun had a hard time getting through most windows, but the kitchen windowsill held four small pots beneath a wave of sunlight. They were organized by color: red, orange, yellow, and violet.

"What are these?" he wondered.

"Bellis perennis." She paused to enjoy his confusion. "Daisies."

"I like the colors." Chris was too focused on the flowers to notice a smile wide enough to make Senada's cheeks burn. "Why are they doing that?"

It was Senada's turn to be confused as she approached. "Doing what?"

"Bending like that." He pointed at a slight curve in their stems, careful to avoid touching them. "Are they dying?"

"Quite the opposite." Senada wrapped an arm around his waist, eager to bring Chris into the world she'd created while he'd been away. "It's called a heliotropism." She spun the pots, turning each bloom away from the light and toward Chris. "Some plants seek out a stimulus. In this case, they're looking for the sun."

Astonishment cascaded across his face. "How long does something like that take?"

"Come back tomorrow and you won't be able to tell that I spun the pots."

"Is that an invitation?" he charmed.

"Maybe," she teased, adding a kiss to his cheek that turned into multiple kisses on his lips. "Alright, alright. Don't get me started again."

"Why not?" Chris pulled her in and kissed her neck. "The shop's closed."

"Can we at least eat something first?"

"Need to refuel already?"

"Let's call it that," she said, playfully nudging him away. "I'm hungry."

"What do you have in mind?"

After some brief exchanges about their wildly divergent food desires, they opted for the most sensible option for two people who wanted very different meals: the diner.

Like most restaurants of its kind on Long Island, the Golden Reef Diner was a staple of its community. It was the go-to destination for everyone, occupied by different demographics at various times of the day. In the afternoon, it was a haven for housewives and stay-at-home moms fresh out of yoga class and on the hunt for healthy food served in inflated proportions. Once the sun went down, it was the home of date night for teenagers who'd just left the movie theatre down the block and couldn't afford any of the several restaurants they'd passed on the way. But by the time Chris and Senada walked in, there was a sea of septuagenarians enjoying an array of breakfast options and bottomless coffee.

They entered arm-in-arm, staying close without having to discuss whether they should hold hands. A cushioned booth near the window allowed them to face each other with enough space to prevent more canoodling, and thus, more distraction from the many things Senada had in mind. Ice water was promptly poured into their glasses, signaling a chance to open some lines of candor.

"Can I tell you something?" she asked, intentionally making eye contact.

Chris stopped mid-sip of water. "Of course."

Senada moved her glass toward the window and rested both forearms on the table. "The last time we were this close, I wasn't open with you about where my head was. And I don't want us to skip our past or our friendship to dive into something that might become even more complicated."

"Okay," he said with some trepidation. "Can you catch me up?"

Senada picked up a napkin and began folding and unfolding it to occupy her nervous hands. "I don't want a repeat of what happened before." She watched him become unsettled by the reminder. "And I'm not placing blame or anything. I pushed you away and I'll own my role in how things turned out. But if we're gonna do this, whatever this is, we can't pretend we're in our twenties anymore. A lot has changed."

"I agree. And I want us to know each other the way we did before."

Relief poured over Senada. "I'd like that." A strange silence fell over the booth, then Senada giggled like a child. "I don't know where to begin. I haven't had to break the ice with you since we were ten years old."

Chris laughed heartily. "I imagine asking to join me and my dad while we threw a football around was a little easier than this."

Senada had a ready-made response. "I didn't know how much there was to be afraid of yet."

"What are you afraid of now?"

"The same things I was afraid of twelve years ago." Senada's giggles waned as she realized he wasn't entirely aware of what she meant. "You know how things were with my mother."

Chris was reliably consistent in response to Carrie's introduction to any conversation, keeping a steady eye as if hoping to soothe Senada with stability and strength.

"Are you ready to order?" The waiter apparated next to the table with a notepad in hand.

"Can you give us a few more minutes?" asked Chris. The waiter nodded and stepped away, and Chris returned to Senada. "Go ahead."

His protectiveness of Senada's vulnerability nearly disrupted her train of thought. "My mom… made it hard to really understand how love was supposed to work."

"Your mother had a serious problem, Senada. That's not on you," he consoled.

"That's not what I'm saying. I mean, yeah but…just let me get this out." She reached across the table and wrapped both hands around his. His calloused knuckles were balanced by her weathered palms. "You know how you're afraid of heights?"

Chris huffed and shook his head. "I'm not afraid of heights."

"Sure," she mocked.

"I'm not, but go ahead."

"You told me all about the time you got woozy on the 48th floor of a Manhattan high-rise!" she screeched. "My point is… the way you felt then is the way I felt after the gala. Sure, you know that you're inside and safe and everyone is fine. But none of that is enough to make you any less scared.

"Knowing that I was in that moment with you, as safe as I could've been, didn't make me any less scared. It should have, but it didn't. My mother made me so afraid of what love meant, and how people used it to manipulate each other to get what they really wanted. Especially boys… men. I heard that over and over until she didn't need to keep saying it for me to keep hearing it. And after that night, after what went down in the limo, you became a man to me."

Senada froze at the awkward phrasing. They exchanged humored glances, then laughed together.

"You know what I mean. You stopped being… Chris," she continued. "You became someone who might use me, or take things from me, or throw me away. And I can manage that with other guys, but you… you know me. You know everything about me. No one is more equipped to destroy me than you. And once we crossed that line and got even closer, I was afraid to keep you there. Not just afraid. Paralyzed."

Chris held her hands a little tighter. "But you know me, Senada. I would never use you, and there's nothing I could want from you that you haven't already given me ten times over. That's the only thing that kept fear from eating me alive."

Senada looked up from their interlaced fingers. "You were afraid?"

"You thought you were the only one who was scared?" he asked, toeing a line between incredulity and empathy. "Jesus Christ, I barely slept that night. Or that entire week. I thought you regretted it. Or that you didn't enjoy it. Or I hurt you. I didn't want you to think I'd planned for any of that to happen. I didn't want to be like any other man to you, because you've never been like any other woman to me."

They shared a few impromptu meditative breaths. The waiter saw a window to return, and they quickly ordered whatever came to mind since neither had spent a second looking at the menu — a bacon cheeseburger for him, and a tall stack of buttermilk pancakes for her. The waiter's departure gave the green light to continue their conversation.

"That's what scared us twelve years ago," Chris resumed. "What are you afraid of now?"

"It's funny in a fucked up kinda way… my mother spent so much energy making me afraid of love. And by the time someone came along and showed it to me, it was too late. She made me think real love didn't exist, but I spent most of my life watching your parents have it. And when it never came into my life, I started to think I just didn't deserve it. And once I'd accepted that, I pretended I didn't want it at all. I focused on myself and my business, and having a life that made me forget whatever I might've been missing out on. Then, you came back and—"

"And you remembered what was missing?" said Chris, finishing for her.

Senada was in awe of how Chris could understand something that was still confusing for her. "You get it."

Chris stepped in and took the lead. "Do you remember that first morning we saw each other again? When we talked in the kitchen?"

"How could I forget?" she replied, then thought further. "You weren't in the best mood."

"I was pissed," he corrected. "But not at you."

"At your mom?"

"She took the brunt of it," he said in a regretful manner. "But it wasn't about her. It was about me. I was mad at myself."

"Why?"

"Because I missed you. And I didn't want to."

"I know the feeling." Senada held his hands more tightly and smiled slowly. "Imagine if she was here to see this."

"She would have a field day," snickered Chris. "We'd never hear the end of it."

They shared a somber moment of reflection. Senada didn't need to say what she was thinking about him. But she did have to share something else on her mind about Mrs. Mitchell.

"She treated me so much better than I deserved, she acknowledged. "I never got to ask her what she saw in me."

"I think she saw a little bit of herself."

"She told you that?" wondered Senada.

"Just my guess," Chris admitted. "She wasn't shy about calling you the daughter she never had."

Senada sat with the new information. There'd been two shining examples of what type of woman she could be — her mother and his mother — and they couldn't have been more different. The women shared two common traits: they were mothers, and they weren't quite Senada's mother. The only lesson to learn from a comparison was how unpredictable motherhood could be.

Maybe some women were meant for it and others weren't, but Senada wasn't bold enough to sacrifice a child's well-being and happiness to find out which category she belonged in. A spurt of pain signaled Senada's body had been listening. She writhed and grimaced in the booth, pressing a palm against the table's edge in an effort to abate the discomfort.

"Alright, Senada. I need you to tell me what's going on," Chris urged. "I've already let it go for too long."

It wasn't the best time for Senada to dive deeper into the inadequacy plaguing her. But if Senada was going to be honest with Chris about how she used to feel, then she might as well be up front about what was happening in the present.

"I'm having some health… I dunno what to call them. Issues? Concerns?"

"What kind of health concerns?" His bluntness would've been harsh if she didn't know him so well.

"Hey," she jumped in before his thoughts got too far in front of both of them. "I'm okay. There are cysts on my ovaries. I go under the knife in two weeks to have them removed. I'm told it's a common procedure. They were caught before any real damage could be done."

Chris sighed in reluctant acceptance. "What caused them?"

"It could be lots of things, but if I started listing them, you'd either get more confused or more scared." She hoped to lighten the mood a bit. "And I can tell when you're scared."

"Are they cancerous?" he said, refusing her attempt at levity.

"No."

"Can they come back?"

"Yes."

"What do you have to do to keep that from happening?" he asked, already taking out his phone to either take notes or Google something.

"Would you like to have Dr. Lawson's number? You can cut out the middleman," she jested.

"That's not funny," he said.

"If you knew what I knew, you'd be laughing too."

Like a saving grace, the waiter returned with their food. Senada beamed at the sight of her pancakes, but eyed Chris's fries with the same level of zeal.

"Is this the kind of food you should be eating?"

"I regret telling you already," Senada flared.

"Okay, okay, I'll stop." he acquiesced.

They paused the conversation to enjoy their first meal together in years. It took her back to the ways their bond had been built in the first place, and Senada was content knowing her health circumstances wouldn't keep them from enjoying a moment they'd waited so long to share.

❁

Chris kept a close eye on his fries in case Senada still couldn't be trusted around his side dishes. But she stayed focused on her syrup-smothered pancakes instead of grabbing at any small bite she could reach. Senada could make a meal out of the Sweet'N Low packets if left to her own anxious compulsions.

The tables had been turned. He was the nervous one. Unlike Senada, worry made Chris eat less. His appetite had taken a hit upon hearing of her health status, but he forced down half the burger before slowing the pace. There were more questions, but he wasn't interested in adding more weight on her shoulders. Chris had to trust her to be open with him.

His cellphone vibrated on the table, putting a hold on the list of questions he was compiling. The area code told him enough about who and what to expect on the other end.

"Chris Mitchell," he greeted.

"Hello again! Miriam here."

Chris nodded away from the table to signal he didn't want to disturb Senada, to which she offered a concerned smile. Business Chris was a stranger to her, and he was already crafting an explanation for his absence, no matter how brief.

He walked into the foyer and stood aside, allowing other patrons to pass unobstructed. "What can I do for you, Miriam? I'm a little busy right now."

"I wanted to touch base since you never called me back," she said with a mysterious confidence.

"I thought you might take that as a response."

"I take it as someone who's making a decision based on his past instead of his future."

"That's bold of you." He feigned annoyance but enjoyed having his ego massaged. "Are you a fortune teller? Are you about to tell me my future?"

"If you come to our offices and take a look at our offer, you very well might be looking at your future. But let's be honest: if you *really* wanted to say no, why haven't you said it yet?"

"I hung up on you," he asserted.

"And you answered this call," she countered.

Chris couldn't formulate a good enough response to a solid point. It was hard to know why they might be interested in propping up his return to the workforce. But there was little harm in finding out. Opportunities didn't come around often, especially after a well-documented failure.

"Judging from your silence, my senses tell me you're considering a visit," said Miriam.

Chris peered back at the table and caught Senada munching on one of his fries. "I don't need to visit. If the offer isn't up to my standard, having a nice fountain and a corner office won't move the needle for me."

"Shall I send over our proposal?"

Chris kept watching as Senada was midway through another handful of fries and looking out of the window, apparently lost in thought. Senada was especially beautiful when she thought no one was looking. It reminded him of how he'd ended up back in position to have his heart broken again.

With Senada's omnipresent fear and doubt, their relationship making it through the week, let alone a lifetime, wasn't guaranteed. Chris could string Miriam's firm along, maybe use their offer as leverage to get better ones, and ensure a soft landing spot down the road, in case Senada decided she was right twelve years ago.

"Send it," he said quickly before hanging up and returning to the table.

"I thought I had more fries than this," he said smugly as he slid back onto the seat.

"I don't know what you're talking about." She squinted at Chris, teasing him while inhaling another bite. "Everything okay?" she asked while gesturing toward his cellphone.

"Yeah, it was nothing. Another headhunter."

The remaining half of his burger had become even less appealing since taking the call. Chris needed things to be clearer, and normalcy was the best way to know where their bond might be headed. If they were going to try their hand at a real relationship, he needed to explore the basics.

"Hey, I've got an idea," he began. "What do you think about us going on a date?"

"Well, we had sex a few times last night, so a date does feel like a natural next step," she cackled.

Chris grinned before attempting earnestness again. "Seriously though. Maybe if we stopped being so precious with every part of our relationship, we could manage our fear a little better."

"Did the headhunter give you this idea?"

Chris was so comfortable going back and forth with Senada, he almost told the entire truth. "Sort of, yeah."

Senada took a more serious turn. "Okay, let's do it. I've got a lot of work to do over the next couple of weeks, getting ready to be out of commission for a bit. Maybe after that?"

"Sounds good. I'll take care of everything."

They may have rushed things physically, but if they were going to make it, Chris couldn't rush her heart. Prematurely challenging her intentions for the future would only blow up in his face again. But he needed to know, even if things weren't perfect between them, that he wouldn't be in this alone.

28

Time apart from Chris couldn't have come at a better time. Between frequent surges of pain and the mounting stress of an inconvenient vacation from the shop, there wasn't enough bandwidth for Senada to consider his insecurities along with her own. She couldn't blame him for her status, but his comfort had to take a back seat for a little while.

The few days after a holiday weekend offered a good opportunity to reassess the shop's workload and plan for larger events in the fall. It also provided the best chance for her to take off for a week or two. Far be it from Senada to understand why so many people got married, but most of them jumped the broom in September and October.

Senada sat at her workstation, which was covered with a calendar, invoices, bills, and receipts instead of the usual petals, stems, and water.

Lex was beside her and inspecting the next few weeks of her future. Her audible breathing portrayed an impending panic attack. "I don't know if I can do this."

"Relax," Senada said without looking up from the station. "You'll be fine. I promise."

"You sound really sure considering you haven't taken a day off in the entire time I've known you."

"I sound sure because I *am* sure." Senada put down the pen and rested supportive hands around Lex's shoulders. "And I know you'll figure this out, because you're so scared of fuckin' it up."

Lex cocked her head. "I'm not sure that makes any sense."

Senada replayed the sentence in her mind. "Just go with it."

Lex took another deep breath. "Gimme the rundown one more time."

"I've explained it six times already!" Senada shouted through guttural laughter. "We'll be closed to all same-day deliveries. The nursery has moved up our usual monthly order, so we can pick it up tomorrow, and be stocked for the entire time I'm gone. And if anything comes up at all, my phone will be right next to me."

"Okay. I think I've got it." Lex stared ahead as though trying to retain the information more effectively. "Sort of."

Senada knew exactly how Lex felt, albeit under different circumstances. An irrational fear of her own was barraging her senses. A man was planning a date and all she had to do was show up. Every romcom she'd ever seen said this was supposed to be a good thing. But her fight-or-flight response was already waiting for a cab to the airport.

The necessary details of their Friday night plans were slowly being doled out, one text at a time. Each message concerned her more than the last. A date was a wonderful idea. Though it soon became clear they had conflicting definitions of what constituted a date.

Once she'd been informed of a dress code, her antennae went up. Formal attire was a step in the wrong direction for distinguishing this edition of their bond from the one they'd sabotaged. Any excitement she could've had from planning an outfit was countered by thoughts of the last time she'd worn a fancy dress and heels in his presence. And while her outfit wouldn't quite be black-tie formal, it would be close enough to trigger some significant and unfortunate memories.

"At least Chris gave you one less thing to worry about," Lex said.

A mildly distracted Senada wondered if Lex was reading her mind. "Huh?"

"Since he fixed the van." Lex kept a probing stare on her. "You okay?"

"Yeah, just thinking about the procedure."

Lex rested a consoling hand on Senada's healed forearm. "I'm sure everything will be fine. You'll be back in this seat and driving us both crazy again before you know it."

Senada teetered between lively and modest. "It's not the procedure I'm afraid of." She pushed away from the desk and faced Lex. "Have you ever thought about having kids?"

Lex became more discombobulated than Senada had ever seen, displaying the whites of her eyes. "This is starting to feel like Thanksgiving dinner with my parents. Can we talk about something lighter? Politics maybe?"

"Seriously though," Senada said despite steady chuckling. "Have you?"

"Sure, I've *thought* about it. But that's not unique, is it? Haven't you?"

"No," Senada blunted, then eased off the conviction. "Well, I hadn't."

"Damn. Chris has really done a number on you."

"It's not him. He doesn't even know about it. This popped up before we reconnected." It was as good a time as any for the thought to come out. "The surgery… it's got my wheels turning on what could've been. What kind of mom I might've been if I had a real one, ya know?"

"I don't want to overstep, but I feel like our imaginary HR department would've fired the absolute shit out of us a long time ago, so I'll just ask: what's stopping you from finding out?"

"I couldn't put a kid through some Faustian experiment like that."

"A what?"

Senada vigorously shook her head. "Nothing. Don't worry about it. I'm just a little unhinged this week."

"Steady mind-blowing sex will do that," Lex taunted.

"It's not mind—," Senada stopped, then rerouted. "It's not steady." While lying about the quality of the experience would've been more prudent, she recalled an orgasm so powerful, Chris had to help her walk to the bathroom afterward.

Senada couldn't call the sex steady, even after a round in the shower when they were supposed to be catching their breath, and another that interrupted an attempt at watching a movie. In both instances, they were voracious enough to abandon pursuit of a condom that was only a room away. They'd had a lot of sex, but in a short amount of time.

The recollection took Senada down a rabbit hole of wondering why that aspect was so easy for them, yet the idea of a fancy date terrified her. Perhaps sex was the easiest way for her to be fully present. Or maybe it wasn't that complicated; they were great at sex and ill-equipped for much else.

Senada couldn't bear how warped her idea of connection might become if trusting Chris with her body meant restraining the parts of her spirit that desperately wanted to feel freedom.

29

The balance of Chris's debt to Greg had significantly increased. With his former colleague's help, Chris got a dinner reservation at a steakhouse known for its fantastic rendition of Senada's favorite dish: macaroni and cheese. It was the final cog in his plan for a wonderful evening.

The shower could've been scalding hot or freezing cold. In his nervous haste, Chris had barely noticed the water, nor the amount of shampoo he'd used before his eyes burned from excess lather running down his scalp. He moved in rhythm to a song being composed in his head while shaving the stubble from his face. A navy-blue suit, eggshell white dress shirt, blue paisley necktie and brown shoes fit better than he could've planned. Everything was coming together for an introduction to how their relationship could look if they stopped being afraid.

At present, Chris's primary fear was how late he'd been running all afternoon. Looking over Miriam's extensive proposal had cost him more time than anticipated. He wasn't ready to respond, but the offer was certainly worth more than ignoring it and blocking her number.

A mid-six-figure salary was beyond the budget of an upstart firm, but analyzing their books wasn't in the job description. Add stock options, a corporate car, and a pre-approved apartment lease agreement upon signing, and the offer should've been worth a cross-country flight. But Miriam was probably a few months too late.

As he put the finishing touches on his hair and double-checked the smoothness of his shave job, his cellphone nearly vibrated off the bathroom sink. He put the call on speaker and returned to his reflection. "Yeah?"

"Hello again, Mr. Mitchell," said Miriam.

"Make it quick. I'm already running late for something important."

"Just wanted to see if you had a chance to check out our offer," she inquired.

"I did." Chris was half-paying attention as he assessed the look of his jacket, unsure whether to button it or keep it open. He chose an unbuttoned look, then regretted the necktie and took it off. "I have to admit, this is all very surprising."

After one more look at the clock, he walked out of the bathroom, continuing the conversation on the way toward the bedroom to retrieve his wallet and keys.

"I told you we were serious," she said with swagger. "Are you?"

"I just need a little bit more time," he said while descending the stairs, glancing at the final frame as if it were an unconscious habit. "But I'm giving serious consideration to your offer."

"What offer?"

"Oh shit." Chris stopped and stared at Senada standing in the open doorway. His gaze traveled down her body and back to her face. A pair of black heels led up to an onyx spaghetti-strapped dress emphasizing every immaculate aspect of her frame. But Senada didn't look nearly as happy to see him as he was to see her outfit choice.

"Uh, I'm gonna have to call you back," Chris said into the speaker before hastily ending the call.

The customary warmth of her presence was undone by an arctic display.

"I got tired of waiting. I figured I'd come to you," she said with a pleasant ease that he knew was temporary. "And I guess I've gotten a little too comfortable walking into your house."

Senada didn't sound angry. It might've been easier if she did. Instead, she found a way to weep without shedding a tear. It was the same way she'd sounded in the message she'd left for him after learning he'd gone to San Franscisco without saying goodbye. It was the most painful thing he'd ever heard.

"Who are you gonna have to call back?" she accused. "The headhunter?"

Chris opened his mouth, but nothing came out, no matter how hard he searched for words.

"If this was some simple thing, you'd have told me, wouldn't you? So I can assume this must be pretty complicated. Right?" Senada's jaw tightened, and her hands became more active as her tone intensified. "Are you gonna answer me? Or pretend you weren't saying exactly what I just heard? Hmm?

"Senada," he begged.

"Do I have the wrong idea? Is it not what it looks like? Which cliché do you want to go with before our first fight as a *real* couple?"

The implied air quotes surrounding her last two words gutted Chris. After everything she'd told him, convincing her to see the bigger picture of his rationale would've been futile. "It's not what you think."

"Not my favorite cliché but okay, we'll go with that one if you want." Chris braced for the familiar experience of Senada's wit being weaponized. "In order for it to not be what I'm thinking, I should probably share what I'm thinking, and then let you sort it out from there. How's that?"

Chris put his hands in his pockets and leaned against the wall, preparing for the storm he should've seen coming.

"I'm thinking… you made a bet and didn't have the money to cover the loss. You wanted things with us to move at the pace you wanted, but just in case this went south, you hedged that bet with an opportunity to run away again if I didn't fall into your lap. Does that sound about right?"

"It's not like that at all," Chris sighed.

"But you know that's how this looks, because we've both seen this movie before." Senada walked into the nearby kitchen and targeted a cabinet, removing a bottle of Scotch and pouring some into the first glass she could reach in the drying rack. She downed the contents, then poured another while the first still burned. "Why wouldn't you just tell me you were thinking about going back?"

"I wasn't really thinking about it, I just—" he stopped prematurely.

Chris wasn't lying, but he wasn't being honest. He'd waited too long to disclose the truth. Now every word would sound like deception to her ears. But misleading her any further would only make his deepest fears come to fruition.

"I wanted to hear their offer, just to see where things might go. I kept putting them off because… I wanted to know where things were headed with us before I committed to anything."

"Why would you put them off if you weren't considering their offer?" Senada took a small sip. "You're being pretty thoughtful about a decision you weren't thinking of making."

"It's not that simple, Senada. Give me some credit for not being a complete asshole."

"That's asking for a whole lot right now."

"Okay, can we slow down for a second?" he said, hoping to cut through to Senada's truer self instead of engaging with the defensive version she was subjecting him to.

"Are you sure that's a good idea? If things move any slower, I might lose you to the other side of the country. Again!" she shouted.

"Again?!" Chris's shame subsided as she reminded him of why he'd been so afraid in the first place. "You didn't *lose* me to the other side of the country. You *gave* me to the other side of —"

"Oh, don't do that. That was years ago, and we'd gotten past it. That was the whole point of all this," she said, pointing to both of their outfits. "To start over. And now look at us. Going down the exact same road. Should we skip the dinner and jump straight to sex?" Senada slid out of her heels.

"Please stop," he groaned, desperate to rein in the unpredictable route of the conflict.

"You'd rather we have the fancy dinner first?" Senada put the shoes back on without losing eye contact. "I really hope the food is normal-sized this time."

"Can we sit down and—"

"I don't want to sit down!" Senada pulled back and exhaled slowly, holding her midsection in the way he'd become most concerned about. "I want to have dinner."

"I'm not worried about dinner right now," Chris said helplessly.

"I am." Senada snapped back to a bizarre serenity, speaking casually while putting the glass down and corking the bottle. "You made plans. We've been thinking about dinner all week. I'm starving. I want to have dinner."

"I'd rather not sit through an uncomfortable meal with you right now," he countered.

"Why not? We're in this for the long haul, right? We've got a lot of meals left. I'm sure some of them will be a little uncomfortable." She moved toward the door.

"Please, just wait a minute."

"I don't want to wait a minute. I don't want to talk about this anymore. I don't want to think about this anymore. I just want to have dinner."

"We have to talk about this!"

"No we don't!"

Senada pulled the door open enough for the hinge to squeak before Chris stepped past her and pushed it shut.

"Get out of my way," she demanded in a low voice.

Chris was at a loss. It was hard enough to predict what Senada wanted. Getting her to do something she didn't want to do was useless, even if it was in their best interest. Chris stepped away from the door and raised his hands in surrender.

"Alright, I give up," he said. "But I'm not going to dinner with you like this."

Chris watched a switch flip in Senada. Her gaze softened and she took off her shoes again. He wasn't sure how to interpret the shift, but it looked like she'd given up on fighting. The woman before him was no longer someone he recognized.

❀

Senada meandered back to the kitchen island and pressed both hands against the surface, wishing she had the power to shove it through the floor. There was an unspoken responsibility being hoisted onto her shoulders, and it didn't seem fair. Chris held Senada in high regard, a status she'd neither asked for nor thought she deserved.

"Why would you give me so much power over your life?" she asked. "Why would you let anyone's feelings swing your life in one way or another?"

"Some people's feelings are worth that much," he answered.

"Not mine." Her melancholic delivery echoed against every surface in the kitchen, resonating in her soul as much as it ever could in his ears.

"You always say shit like that, and I never understood it. What is so terrible about someone thinking you're special?"

"Because they're wrong!" The sudden yell startled Chris. The island became the only thing holding her up as she succumbed to tears. "They're fuckin' wrong. You were wrong. Your mother was wrong. Everyone's been wrong except my mother…and me. We've always known what I'm good for. You and me…we're good at the easy stuff because I'm made for the easy stuff."

"I don't know what that means. What easy stuff?"

Senada couldn't figure out how to put words to a feeling she'd felt for so long but never thought would be worth sharing with anyone, especially Chris. She faced him and, for once, did the first thing that came to mind without giving a second thought to how Chris might perceive it.

Senada pulled the spaghetti straps off her shoulders and let the dress slide down her figure. It crumpled at her feet, and her pride fell beside it.

Chris took a step back in abject shock. Senada moved toward him in nothing but a simple black thong and got close enough to force his eyes onto her body.

Senada had a million things calling out to her more sensible nature, but none of them could get her attention. The chilly central air and the sensation of tears rolling off her cheeks and onto her breasts were the only sensations breaking through her armor.

"Look at me, Chris," she whimpered. "All of me."

She'd never seen a man so unwilling to look at a naked woman before. What she thought would be a look of desire was actually a look of fear, like he'd picked up the shame she'd just dropped.

"This is the easy stuff. This is the one thing we can do without all the other bullshit," she said. "Nothing else can touch us unless we stop touching each other."

Senada stepped away from the dress as though it were molten skin, unsure whether she was becoming more of herself or leaving herself behind. Every reservation and restraint disappeared. In a tragically ironic way, it spoke to her trust in him.

"You couldn't have this," she asserted, close enough to touch him. "And you left."

"That's not—"

"But this is what it'll take to make you stay… right?" Senada tried to put his hand on her, but he resisted. "You don't wanna touch me?"

"Not like this, Senada. What the hell are you doing?"

She sniffled through her words. "You wanted me to try to hold onto you, right? This is the only way I know how to do it."

"That's ridiculous. Just talk to me. What is going on with you right now? You're scaring me," he replied, sliding both hands away from her and pinning them behind his back.

Senada stepped into him, opened his jacket and pressed her breasts against his chest. The fabric warmed her immediately as she brought both of her hands to his face.

"Senada, please stop."

"You don't want me?" She glided one hand down his body and pulled him close enough to feel his restrained dick throbbing against her. "I don't believe you," she breathed into his ear.

"I want you," Chris said, nudging her hips away with both hands. "*You*, Senada. Not whoever this is."

The statement struck her like an anchor word, breaking a hypnotic state. She instantly became aware of herself, more naked than she actually was, and cautiously stepped back as Chris gently pushed her away.

"Oh my God," she mouthed, barely audible.

Senada covered her breasts as much as she could with one arm and scurried back to her dress. It wouldn't conform to her one-handed attempts to unfurl it, making the panic even worse. Knowing Chris was watching made it harder to find her way out of the distress. She rushed to the door, but he stopped her, either because he didn't want her to leave or because he cared about the possibility of their neighbors seeing a naked Senada running down the street.

She reversed course and ran up the steps, shutting the bathroom door behind her before realizing where she was. Uncontrollable sobbing began, with tears pouring into her palms as she leaned against the door and slid to the floor in despair.

❁

Chris stood, in shock, at the base of the steps. He couldn't grasp what he might've done to turn the friend he'd fallen in love with into the woman who'd barricaded herself in the bathroom. A complete stranger was on the other side of the door.

Every step of his ascent was deliberate and careful. Chris wasn't sure how Senada might receive an attempt to communicate. It was a relief to hear her crying; she was still conscious and aware. He removed his jacket and draped it over the banister, giving more time to decide on his next move.

With someone he didn't know as well, it wouldn't have taken as much thought. But with her, Chris could plot the ten steps that might follow any decision he made.

Reaching for the doorknob was the most natural choice, but Carrie used to do that whenever Senada retreated to her room to escape further abuse. Knocking made sense, but he could feel her body pressing against the door. The vibration might jostle memories of her mother stomping through their hallway in a drunken tirade. Ignoring her would've been the most daring option, and would likely do more damage to whatever trust she still had in him. Chris didn't' want to give Senada any more reasons to question his willingness to stay by her side.

Chris laid a hand against the wood and held an ear close to a small gap in the door jamb. "Can you talk to me? Please?" he whispered, unsure if she'd even heard him over the sound of her tears. After ten seconds without a response, he asked again. Still no answer. Just more sobbing.

Silence didn't feel like the right response. He looked down the hall at the doorway to his bedroom. When she'd been at her lowest, his room had been a dependable sanctuary. And most of the time, silence was the only solace Chris could provide. It had worked before, and this time, it was the safest option at his disposal. And being the safest choice meant it was the best choice.

"That's okay. You don't have to talk," he whispered. He knelt near the door and sat with his back against it. Through the hollow slab, Chris felt Senada's body relying on his. "I'll be here when you're ready."

It wasn't up to Chris to decide if it was the right thing to say, but he knew the best place to be — wherever Senada needed him most.

30

Senada could maintain composure with dirt on her hands, but gripping the rim of a toilet was far beyond her scope of practice. A wave of intense nausea lifted her out of a deep slumber and away from the linoleum. It wasn't quite the way she'd preferred to be greeted by the morning sun. After making a spectacle of herself to an unprecedented degree, the scotch-and-bile-filled porcelain bowl was a more appealing sight than anything she'd find in a mirror.

Rolled-up bath towels had supported her head and hips while she'd spent the night in the fetal position, hurtling between sobbing and sleeping. Senada would've spent the rest of her life in that bathroom rather than open the door and face Chris.

Embarrassing herself in front of him wasn't a new phenomenon. Since they'd been kids, she'd done it countless times. But a nervous breakdown was uncharted territory for both of them. And following it up by stripping to her underwear and throwing herself at him was a far cry from anything she'd been capable of before. Adding insult to injury, he'd rejected her. It shouldn't have been the most hurtful part, but her ego was more bruised than any part of her body had been from a prolonged stay on a tile floor.

The grind of Chris's teeth and occasional snoring were the only noticeable signs that he'd been on the other side of the door. As best she could tell, he'd been there all night. Whatever he might've expected from the night before, it was safe to assume he was more surprised than her.

When she wasn't heaving with all her strength, Senada could still feel Chris pushing her away. The rejection dwelled beneath her skin, stinging all the more because of the source. Explaining herself was hard enough before her clothes came off. Getting him to understand the urges, fears, doubts, and delusions that transformed her from an insecure girlfriend to an amateur seductress would be no small feat. But Chris had still kept his promise — he'd never left her side.

Once she'd concluded there was nothing left to give, Senada flushed the toilet. Hours of retching left her feeling like she'd done an intense ab workout. A faint cough induced soreness. She rose to the sink and ran water through her palms until it was cold enough to offer relief to her face and rinse out her mouth. A heavy exhale wafted into her nose and prompted a search for mouthwash in the cabinets.

A capful of blue Listerine provided a burning sensation to her mouth, inadvertently blunting the impact of her reflection. Her hair was tossed on one side and matted on the other. The little bit of makeup Senada had applied was streaked across every part of her face that the water hadn't touched. One strap of her dress was still on her shoulder, a hint of how she'd probably looked from Chris's perspective the night before. Senada pulled up the other strap and turned away from the mirror, unable to take another second of her reflection before summoning the will to open the door.

Senada pulled the knob carefully, half-expecting Chris to collapse into the bathroom. But the only sign of his presence was a throw pillow on the floor, usually reserved for the den couch. She peeked out and looked both ways for signs of traffic. The coast was clear enough to tiptoe down the stairs. Her heels had been neatly placed beside the front door. Halfway toward them, Chris appeared, and things suddenly became audible.

He stood in front of the stove with his back to her, still dressed for the date they'd never had. Sneaking past him would've been impossible, but Senada would've given anything for an invisibility cloak. The only choices she had were to make herself known or stand on the other side of the island until Chris turned around and noticed her rundown presence.

Before she could make up her mind, Chris turned around. The look on his face was hard to identify, so she looked anywhere else. Both sleeves were rolled up to the elbow and he held a saucer with two slices of dry toast. He cleared his throat subtly. "Good morning."

"Morning." Her embarrassment was too great for a two-word greeting.

Chris placed the saucer on the island. "Uh, I heard you. I mean, I could hear that weren't feeling well, so I, uh, made you some toast." He stepped aside to reveal a simmering pot on the stove. "And some plain white rice. Two things even I couldn't mess up." He put forth a shy grin and she did her best to mimic it.

Senada slid onto a stool, careful to make sure her dress was secure. "Thanks," she said in meek acceptance. He returned a quick nod and swung his attention to the rice. Senada's couldn't decipher what any of this meant, or why he wasn't pissed or upset or even mildly annoyed.

The toast looked good, for toast, but it still turned her stomach. She fought off a dry heave that tried to make its way out. Her body was rejecting something. Senada retraced her steps, parsing through hazy memories of details she'd heard from Dr. Lawson; vague comments about side effects that didn't connect the dots. There was no shooting pain. It had been, she realized, the longest span without doubling over in a long time.

Senada retrieved her phone, intending to call Lawson's office, but seeing the date sent her in an entirely different direction. A monthly event was missing from her schedule. Her eyes darted toward Chris, who'd just turned around with a bowl full of steaming rice and set it in front of her. In an instant, Senada leapt out of her skin and could see her own gobsmacked expression as though the bathroom mirror had followed her to the kitchen. They made eye contact for a split second, long enough for Senada to put the pieces together.

There had been more than one window of opportunity, during their marathon of sleepless sex weeks earlier, for her greatest fear to become a possibility. But it couldn't be. Senada had been beyond careful, bordering on acutely paranoid, of such a risk. Even when her IUD was still in place, she'd always insisted on condoms. Though if last night reminded her of anything, it's that, when it came to Chris, her more rational self wasn't always behind the wheel. Memories of their fireworks, and two unprotected connections, made Senada tremor from head to toe.

An appetite rushed back into her body. The first slice of toast was halfway down her throat before Chris noticed she was eating. While still chewing, she started on the second.

"You might wanna slow down," he warned.

Senada had less than zero interest in his opinion. The angst-driven snacking had never been more prevalent or more necessary. Nausea had taken a back seat to something with the potential to make her ill in a manner that couldn't be remedied by regurgitation. She pulled the hot bowl closer and nearly put her face into the rice before Chris could hand her a spoon. The heat of the first bite seared her tongue, forcing her to slow down.

"Senada." Chris wrapped his fingers around her free hand and looked into her eyes. "Take a minute to breathe." Senada exhaled through pursed lips and glared at him, unhappy with how right he was. "You're scaring me."

It no longer mattered that Senada wasn't ready to talk. She had something to talk about, and it couldn't wait. The only obstacle was a lack of confirmation for her paranoia. There wasn't much sense in pulling both of them to that place, twelve hours after the biggest fight they'd ever had, just for it to be a false alarm. The chances weren't zero, but they were slim. A delayed reaction to the pint of scotch she'd inhaled could just as easily be the culprit. She was sick in the morning, but that didn't mean it was morning sickness, especially after only a few weeks since they'd had raw sex.

Senada sought out an organic way to leave without subjecting both of them to another fraught conversation. And telling Chris that she needed to get to the pharmacy as soon as possible wasn't going to help.

"Are you ready,to talk to me?" he asked tenderly.

Even the simplest reaction had become complicated. "I don't know what I could say to excuse my behavior last night."

"Is that what you think I'm asking for?"

Senada could tell she'd never win this guessing game.

"I don't want an excuse for it. I don't think it needs an excuse." Chris wiped his hands with a towel, then leaned over the island. "I hurt you. I understand that. I let my ego and fear put things in jeopardy between us, and I understand if you don't trust me right now. But… if something about what I did made you respond like *that*, then I never want to do it again. I'll shut down the job offer Monday morning and never fly west of the Mississippi if I can prevent another night like that."

Finishing with an attempt at lightheartedness was a missed mark, but Senada couldn't fault him for trying. He had no idea how much he didn't know. Neither did she.

"I want you to be able to trust me again," he added.

"Chris," she sighed, exasperated. "I wish I didn't trust you. This would be so much easier to handle if I didn't trust you. I'm used to not trusting guys." Senada calmed enough to remember why she'd been hesitant to eat, and nudged the bowl away. "I don't know how to trust myself with you anymore."

Chris appeared primed to respond, then withdrew. "I don't think I know what you mean."

"That's okay," she relented. "I don't even know where to —"

Fatefully, the hum of his cellphone undercut Senada again. The familiar vibration offered her a perfect excuse to leave. But Chris didn't move or react to it; his unblinking stare remained on her.

"You're not gonna answer it?" she asked, irked by his blatant kowtowing.

"It can wait."

"You don't have to prove a point to me," she assured. An imminent conflict presented a chance for an emergency exit. "Answer it."

"No," he resisted.

"Fine. I'll do it." Senada grabbed his phone and held it overhead in anticipation of resistance. His bluff had been called, but Chris didn't respond. Senada answered without breaking eye contact. "Hello, Califor—"

"This is an automated message from Calverton National Cemetery, contacting you with regard—" Senada yanked the phone away from her ear as if she'd heard classified intelligence.

"It's Calverton," she said nearly as robotically as she'd heard it.

Chris tightened up, like confusion had replaced whatever he'd been feeling. Senada handed over the phone at the same time as he reached for it, then tried to read his face while he listened intently.

A few seconds passed, then he pressed a button, then thirty more seconds went by while Senada heard nothing but her own pumping heart. At the end of the call, Chris lowered his chin at the same rate as the phone.

"Mom's grave marker is finished," he said.

Senada's original plan evaporated. Last night's events had transformed her into a blank slate, less capable of understanding her own state of mind, let alone his. This news tethered Senada to a role she was more comfortable with. And running from Chris felt too much like leaving him behind at a time of need.

"Are you alright?" she asked tenderly.

Chris returned to indistinct cleaning. "I'm fine. It's just a formality."

"I'd call it a little more than a formality, Chris." Senada stopped short of sharing how significant it might be for both of them. "Do you want to go?"

"Go where?" Chris was frustratingly aloof, but Senada no longer trusted her intuition enough to challenge his sincerity.

"To see your mom," she said, unsure why he hadn't predicted her response.

"It hasn't crossed my mind," he shrugged.

"Let it cross your mind."

Senada festered along a disparate chain of thought. With so much going on in their lives, separately and together, it was hard to fathom how much time had already passed since Barbara's passing. After the brief interment ceremony set in a staging area far from wherever her plot would be, Senada hadn't given any more thought to returning than Chris had. As sterile as his reaction was, it didn't surprise her.

She couldn't wait much longer. "What do you think now?"

"There's no rush." Chris capitulated in a way that incensed Senada. "I'm not saying I won't ever go out there again." He alternated pointing at each of them a few times. "But I think this exact moment might not be the best time for a distraction."

"Did you just call your mother a distraction?"

"You know what I mean," he barked before blindly tossing the rag on the counter behind him.

"No, I don't," she asserted. Senada still wanted to get out of his house, but instead of finding something to run away from, she'd found something to run toward. She hoped that if Carrie could have such an impact from beyond the grave, maybe Barbara possessed a similar ability. "I wanna go."

Puzzlement peeked through his exhaustion. "You're being serious."

"I am," she murmured. "I want to see her."

Chris took a closer look into Senada's eyes as though waiting for her to crack. "Weren't you just having an intimate conversation with a toilet?"

"Yes," she said with abrupt confidence. Senada stood a little taller and held eye contact in spite of the pooling sensation brewing inside her belly.

After a heavy nasal breath, Chris nodded. "Alright. I'll go change."

"Of course." Senada looked down and remembered her own attire. "I should probably change too. Meet you outside in fifteen minutes?"

While Senada had gotten a reluctant Chris to agree to the trip, she hadn't planned on him being mute for the entire hour and a half of the trip. With every passing exit sign on the Long Island Expressway, his mood sank deeper. Upon reaching Exit 68, there was still enough time ahead of them and tension between him that she couldn't rule out the possibility of the Nova being turned around before reaching their destination.

She swayed between confidence in the decision to make the trek, and unease about convincing him to go. But Senada had her own reasons for the coercion. Holding a 'just in case' plastic bag at her side for the whole ride didn't damper the trip. She was too distracted to be sick.

Outside of a tiny administration building, Senada sat in the parked Nova and watched Chris stand at a kiosk near the entrance that resembled an ATM. When he returned, a transparent ache came with him. She intuitively rubbed the back of his neck as they inched along the cemetery's narrow, winding pathways, passing large fields full of white marble headstones, set in manicured rows. The afternoon sun peeked through the surrounding trees and into the cabin as they parked at the edge of Section 20.

Chris may as well have been a statue, staring into the sun, seemingly immune to discomfort. Senada committed to following his lead. Her influence might've gotten them there, but his mother was the reason they'd come so far. If they were ever going to leave the car, then he'd have to take the lead.

A battle was underway, but Senada couldn't tell which side was winning. His forearms clenched and relaxed as he squeezed the bottom of the steering wheel in a pulsating manner. Without warning, Chris sprung out of the car like he was escaping something. Senada hurried out to join him. He stopped at the threshold where the pavement ended and Kentucky bluegrass began.

"3-4-2-0," he murmured as they looked out on a sea of flat bronze markers, each belonging to the spouse of an American serviceperson. "It might be a long walk."

Senada laced her fingers between his and squeezed. The first step would likely be the hardest, and she wanted them to take it together.

Senada read every grave marker she could without slowing Chris down. With such densely packed graves, it was impossible to reach one without walking across others. The least she could do was acknowledge their names. She held as tightly to the sentiment as she did to Chris's hand.

Every carefully crafted plate was a person who'd been loved and lost. The presence of death didn't make Senada uncomfortable, but cemeteries had a way of reminding her how alive she wasn't. Life could end at any moment, yet she'd wasted immeasurable time on the mundane. The things that mattered most shouldn't be left to wait. As Senada pondered what to say upon reaching Barbara's resting place, Chris stalled.

"What's wrong?" she checked.

Chris pointed toward the grass at their feet. "This is it."

There had already been many iterations of what awaited then, but Senada was still hesitant to look, aware of the difference between an array of random names and 'Barbara Mitchell' cast in bronze. The title of 'Beloved Wife and Mother' could never encapsulate everything she'd represented. Senada rested her free hand across her sore abdomen as Barbara's latter title reverberated throughout her body in an unforeseen way.

"I'll give you some space," she offered, already stepping away before being tugged back.

"For what?" he wondered.

"In case you, ya know, wanted some time alone with her."

Chris took a cynical look at the hundreds of yards of open field surrounding them. "What am I supposed to do?"

A few responses milled through her head, but offering them didn't feel appropriate. "I don't know. I'm sure you'll figure something out."

Eager to put some distance between Chris and her inner monologue, Senada stepped away. A not-so-gentle breeze obstructed anything he might've said from reaching her ears. Every nervous mannerism in his arsenal was on display, from fingers tapping against his palms, to pacing in short bursts, to curling his lips when there was a lot to say and few words available.

A clearing beneath an oak tree served as an appropriate observation deck. It was hard to disconnect a cemetery from what it symbolized for so many veterans and their loved ones. Given how much its occupants had endured, any doubts surrounding a future with Chris felt trivial by comparison. The love in this place had endured the kinds of uncertain separation that a decade on opposite sides of the country couldn't possibly compare to.

Small bouquets and single stems decorated some of the grave markers. The ritual had always confused her. Why honor the fallen, she wondered, by leaving something else to perish on top of them? But she'd made most of her living from flowers dying for the sake of décor. The paradox was one of many she'd learned to live with.

Too lost in thought, Senada hadn't noticed Chris was already halfway back to her. He appeared weathered yet resolved.

"We can go," he said, walking past her without slowing down.

"Okay." Senada wrapped an arm around his back as they ventured toward the Nova. They made it twenty yards before a wave of nausea compelled her to stop.

"You alright?" he said fearfully. "Should I run and get the bag?"

Senada took a few breaths to decide what an honest response was. "I'm alright," she replied. A surge of distress had brought a moment of clarity. "Would you mind if I —," she gestured toward Barbara's grave, hoping he would save her from finishing the question.

Chris reassured her with an understanding nod. "Of course."

The soft ground succumbed beneath every step away from him. When she was close enough to recognize Barbara's nameplate again, she looked back.

Chris leaned against the front of the Nova, his arms folded and his eyes pointed toward the ground. Even from a distance, she detected concern.

She didn't know how to be cared for without putting up a fight, yet Chris had fought back to care for her anyway. He didn't deserve to live in darkness, but that was all she really knew. If she couldn't shed some light, they'd never find their way out.

Despite standing over the bronze marker, it felt distant. Senada sat on the heels of her sneakers and sank her knees into the dense lawn. She picked each errant blade of grass away from its surface until none remained. The bronze rectangle was difficult to look at. Barbara carried a lot of weight, whether she was looking into Senada's eyes, or the harsh sun shined on her name. Senada couldn't prove it, but in this place, Mrs. Mitchell was incredibly present.

"Ya know, until just now, I didn't realize that you usually started our conversations. You always knew how to get me to talk. Hopefully you can help me with that one more time.

"You raised such an incredible man," she said, boomeranging a look at Chris and back. "Sometimes I want to knock on his skull to make sure his brain is still in it, but I always want to hug him afterward. But you did say that when it was right, it was a little of this, a little of that, and a lot of love.

"Chris is fearless in a way I don't understand. It's one of the things I love most about him. I can't bear to think of how much life I've missed out on just from being scared all the time. At this point, I probably stick with fear just because it's the easiest feeling to reach. And it's familiar.

"I look in the mirror and I see a trainwreck. But he sees… something better than that. I have no idea what. Even when he says he loves me, it's hard to believe. I don't see what he sees. How can it be true if I can't see it? I know, I know. That's what faith is.

"And if what my body is telling me is true, I'm really gonna need some of that faith you were always talking about. Because I already have no idea what I'm doing. Add a baby to the mix, and I'll become my mother. And the only thing she taught me was how love shouldn't feel."

Senada shifted her weight and sat on the grass, careful to keep her back to Chris in case sadness got the better of her.

"Chris would make one helluva a dad though. Like, khaki-shorts-and-corny-jokes kinda dad. I don't ever want to hold him back from the life he deserves. I feel like I already did that once. And I have no idea who I'm supposed to be. Maybe that's why I let him go to San Franscisco without putting up much of a fight."

The breeze intensified, pulling strands of hair into her face. Removing them allowed a hand to cross her nose and, with it, the aroma of Chris's shower gel. Senada let out a broad smile and a faint hum. It was the same thing she'd smelled after he fixed her van the first time. The peaceful moment allowed her to recognize a signal, like her body was coming into focus. If Senada was ever going to see herself in a way she'd never imagined, Chris was who she wanted by her side.

"How do you know you'd make a good mom? I guess I always thought it was something you'd known in your soul from the very beginning, like some sort of intuition I never had. What even is a mom? My mother was pure chaos, but you were peaceful. She was aggressive, but you were always so composed, even when I wasn't. The two of you couldn't have been more different, yet you both got to be called 'Mom.'

"I dunno, I think I might be rambling now. You never let me talk for this long." Senada giggled under her breath, self-conscious about laughter in that setting. "I don't even know what I'm asking for. Maybe you could give me some sort of sign that I'm not doing a beautiful thing badly, some reminder that things only become different when—"

Senada looked toward Chris again, but he was gone. She assumed he'd still be sitting there, patrolling the area, but he was nowhere to be found. Panic heightened, along with concern over what could've made him leave and where he might've gone without the car. She walked, then ran, toward the

Nova. There was no sign of him, but something stirred on the other side of the car. Senada stepped around the bumper and found him crouching in front of a colorful bush with vibrant lavender flowers. Leave it to Chris to find the only other color amid miles of greenery.

"What are you doing?" she wondered, pretending her fear of abandonment hadn't made her sprint fifty yards.

"Hey," he said with a mix of surprise and intrigue. "Check this out."

Senada knelt beside him for a closer look.

"Lilacs. Right?" he asked like a student hoping for a good grade.

His unexpected enthusiasm brought a tingling sensation throughout her body. "Yup. Syringa." There was tenderness in the way he touched the delicate flowers. "They're supposed to represent remembrance and love."

"You have these in your shop."

She was in shock. He wasn't asking. He knew. "Yup. Next to the counter."

"I remember." Chris sounded pleased with himself.

"Odd choice for a military cemetery though," she posited as she looked at the various shades of green around them. "They really stand out here."

"I dunno." He observed the lilacs more closely. "Maybe that's the point. To remind us of why these places exist. It's not just a place for tears and sadness. There's room for some good things too."

She looked toward the bronze marker she'd left behind, more certain than ever that Barbara had heard Senada's every word.

31

Seven Years Earlier

Since she was a little girl, Senada enjoyed the feeling of cold soil on her hands. No matter how often her mother yelled at her for playing in the dirt, she'd always found her way back to it. It drove her teachers crazy when she questioned how the thing we relied on to foster life and sustenance was also the thing we rebuked. Don't track dirt into the house. Don't ruin your clean clothes. An otherwise well-behaved child, Senada had to be reminded that dirt belonged outside. She discovered that if she couldn't bring dirt inside, it meant she must've belonged outside.

Barbara was the first person to not only accept Senada's temptation to play in the dirt, but to also connect the compulsion to a source. Senada liked feeling responsible for care and consideration. She knew all-too-well how damaging it was when someone couldn't be trusted.

A yard of her own was no longer enough. After extensive research, intense effort, and a small business loan, Senada turned her fully bloomed passion into a budding business. Symbol of Symphony Floral Shop became a welcome distraction from the things crumbling inside her.

Growing up under Carrie's roof made Senada suspect that some people didn't deserve love. Senada used to blame an unknown and absent father, until she got to know her mother. Maturity and time helped Senada land on the verdict she'd learned to live with: the Mitchells were family, while others were just related to her by blood.

Visiting Mrs. Mitchell was a blessing and a curse. As the only real matriarch Senada had ever known, Barbara's calming and steadfast presence was invaluable. She also made it painfully evident that Carrie's treatment of her daughter was a daily decision.

There weren't many ways to show gratitude that Barbara would actually accept. Tending to her precious garden was the best way Senada could find. With caring for James amid his failing health, Mrs. Mitchell rarely had the chance to maintain domestic tasks. And although Senada wasn't much of a cook or a cleaner, a little gardening was within her capabilities. Passing the car in the driveway, and the troubling memories attached to it, were a small price to pay.

"I should've known I'd see you here eventually."

The surprising comment reined in the memories before they could do any more damage. She stood up from the shallow holes in front of her, with a shovel in hand, and welcomed some company. "Hey, Mrs. Mitchell."

Barbara grinned through the screen before stepping outside.

"Sorry, I thought—"

"You thought," Barbara interrupted, "I would be at the hospice, and you could tend to my flowerbed in secret." Barbara approached and observed the trays of new plants set beside the row of holes. "And I see you're adding begonias."

"I figured I'd surprise you with something that had a bit more texture," Senada stammered, "to balance out the bright colors."

"Is that so?" Barbara pulled a patio chair and sat beside Senada.

"I should've asked you. I can make it like it was." Senada knelt down, already prepared to fill in the holes and return the begonias.

"Stop talking to me like you're in trouble or something!" Barbara laughed from her diaphragm. "And thank you for taking care of my garden."

"Happy to help."

"Is that the only reason you're here?"

"Not much more to it," Senada replied without making eye contact.

"Uh-huh," Barbara doubted. "The azaleas are coming in nicely."

"Last week's storm was good to them," Senada said rapidly, happy to pivot to small talk about the weather.

"Some flowers need storms in order to become what they're meant to be." Barbara picked up the reddest of the bunch. "You know you don't have to sneak over here, right? It's not like you were ever any good at it anyway."

"I know," Senada began. "You've been going through so much with Mr. Mitchell, I just didn't want to disturb you with my bullsh--, uh, problems."

"What bullshit?" Barbara emphasized the entire word.

"The usual." Senada could still hear every word she wasn't saying. "Why does everyone take everything so seriously?"

"We *all* know how much you hate that," Barbara teased.

"We went on three dates and had a pretty good time. Why complicate it by trying to," Senada lifted her hands and made air quotes, "take things to the next level."

"I haven't been on the dating scene in ages. What do you kids call the next level nowadays?"

"A relationship," Senada clarified.

"Someone wants to commit to you. How tragic."

"It *is* tragic," she contested. "And you know why? Because it's a shitty deal. What's so great about liking someone so much, you'll deny yourself the experience of anyone else? All so you can spend your time with one person and, what, fall in love? Then it becomes an even worse deal that'll only end with regret and resentment. Why sacrifice any of myself just to have someone else around for a little while?"

Barbara delivered a slow nod of assessment. "Good question."

"Shit, I'm sorry." Senada scrambled to pull back her abrasive stance against long-term connection. "I wasn't talkin' about you, Mrs. Mitchell."

"No, no, I hear you."

"Level with me for a second," Senada pressed. "You never once thought about what your life could've been if you never got married?"

"I thought about it all the time."

"Exactly. But back then, what else were you gonna do?" Senada caught her own tone again. "With all due respect."

"Oh, you misheard me. Marrying Jimmy wasn't my only option." Barbara leaned back in the chair and took a deep nasal breath. "I wanted to open a bakery."

"I had no idea." Senada stopped tilling. "Chris never told me that."

"Oh yeah. I had plenty of money saved up and a location in mind. Right in the heart of the market district."

Senada sat back and took off her gloves. "Why didn't you open it?"

"Because I only cared about one person loving my pastries. So I married him." Barbara rose from the seat. "Whatever I might've sacrificed, pales in comparison to the life I've had with that man."

A distinct pause was followed by stifled cries. Senada rose and gave Barbara a comforting embrace. "I'm sorry. I didn't mean for my question to upset you."

"It's not you." Barbara freed herself from an unintended smothering. "It's Jimmy. He doesn't have much time left. I guess I'm finally seeing what the end of our story looks like. And hearing you talk about this, about struggling to see the point of love…makes me wish I'd said more to him while he could still hear me. After all these years, you'd think we wouldn't have much left to say to each other."

Senada looked over Barbara's shoulder and toward the classic car in the driveway. Even though an obvious double entendre may not have been Barbara's intent, her words had that effect.

Barbara composed herself. "Do you want some tea?"

"Uh, sure," said a puzzled Senada. "Are you going to be okay?"

"Me? Yeah of course. Not my first time crying over this." Barbara moved toward the side door. "Hopefully, it won't be my last."

"I don't understand. You *want* to cry?"

"No. But I like knowing it can still make me cry. It means I'm not finished caring." The screen door squeaked as Barbara ambled through, unaware of the questions she'd left in her wake.

"Mrs. Mitchell! Wait!"

Barbara turned around in the doorway. "What is it, hon?"

Regret had been Senada's greatest nemesis and her most consistent companion. She hoped to avoid the mistakes that might keep her life from becoming better than it was. But fear either pulled Senada into a bad decision or paralyzed her with indecision.

"Why didn't you open the bakery anyway? After you got married?"

"I did." Barbara pointed a thumb over her own shoulder. "It's called The Mitchell Kitchen. You've been one of my most loyal customers."

"The service is top-notch," Senada bantered. "But wouldn't it have been great to have that space?"

"That space didn't miss out on anything," Barbara reflected. "It became a stationery shop. That's where I got all the 'Thank You' cards after my baby shower. Then it was, um, a frozen yogurt place. Then a locksmith. Then it was vacant for a while."

"I wonder whatever happened to it," she mocked.

"Well, now it's where I get my flowers."

Barbara delivered a huge smile and disappeared inside, leaving Senada with a valuable lesson about a lot more than love. Dreams don't go away. They may change, but if they're real, they won't disappear.

32

Chris took two water bottles from the refrigerator, knowing there was a greater than zero chance of Greg being sprawled across the front lawn. A triangular sweat stain on the back of his heather grey T-shirt and the sweat burning in his eyes were poignant reminders of how much energy they'd exerted during a trail run.

To Greg's credit, he was relatively conscious and moving, albeit on all fours, when Chris returned with hydration. Chris rolled a plastic bottle toward his wheezing friend, then sat on the front step.

"There's something really wrong with you man," Greg mumbled between coughs.

"Catch your breath before you start complaining," Chris mocked elatedly.

Greg coughed twice more. "This was supposed to be a light jog."

"I said it would be a jog. I never said anything about light."

"Semantics!" Greg hollered as if it took the last of his strength. He rolled onto his back and opened the water bottle. "Don't take your stress out on me."

"You could've stayed home." Chris raised an eyebrow as soon as Greg shot him a shocked look.

"You need me," Greg chuckled. "How else would you know if you're working hard enough?"

"That explains so much," Chris checked the time. "You can stay on the lawn but I've gotta get ready. I have to leave in an hour."

"Don't tell me Senada's the reason we were running so fast." Greg scooted across the grass avoiding an imaginary attack. "Is she why I'm slowly moving toward the light?"

"If she knew you were the one who gave my name to that firm, she'd come out here and finish you off." Chris walked inside and left the door open, knowing Greg was bound to follow after hearing that. Sure enough, the weary man was on his feet in an instant and right behind Chris once they entered the kitchen.

"Hey, I was just tryin' to help," Greg said. "I figured a job offer might be a good kick in the ass for you. I didn't think you'd drag it out like this."

Chris leaned against the island while Greg moved to the sink and poured the remaining water over his head for relief.

"You thought I'd take a job on the other side of the country for the second time without thinking about it first?"

"Of course not," Greg blustered. "I just didn't think it would take you so long to turn it down."

Once he'd put a few pieces together, Chris landed on a noteworthy discovery. "That sounds like you did it to prove a point."

Greg pretended to make up his mind. "Correct."

Chris opened his mouth to speak, then stopped, clenched his jaw, then started again. "Are you fuckin' kid—"

"No, I'm not kidding." Greg declared.

Chris had a right to be furious. And he wanted to be. But his blood pressure wouldn't rise, no matter how hard he tried to manufacture outrage. Though newfound calm didn't make up for a major unknown. "Why?"

Greg took a heaving breath and two big gulps of a second water bottle from the fridge. "You were the only one who couldn't seem to figure out the obvious. There's only so many reasons a man with a few million dollars would move back in with his mother, remember? I figured if you got offered a chance to start over, you'd either see the real reason you came back here or come to grips with why you left in the first place. Win win."

An abundance of witty retorts ran through Chris's mind, but nothing properly represented what he was thinking. Seeing how his potential departure had broken down Senada was more than enough for him to understand why he'd left without a real goodbye. He'd been accusing her of running from what they could've been, while he'd run from everything they already were.

If the long ride home from Calverton had shown him anything, it's that however much he knew about Senada's inner compass, it paled in comparison to how much she wasn't telling him. They technically hadn't resolved their fight, and yet it felt like there was no argument to be had.

"I might've learned the lesson you were aiming for." Chris squeezed the now-empty water bottle in his hand for the satisfying crunch. "But I don't know if I can undo the damage I caused while learning it."

"Look man, I'm no expert on this stuff—," Greg started.

"And in spite of that fact, you're gonna power through the ensuing statement," Chris lamented.

"We're not living in the same dating landscape as we were back when we were pitching the app all over town," Greg continued as if Chris had never insulted him. "People will block you on all platforms if you don't communicate for 24 hours. You two didn't talk for the better part of twelve years. The fact that you even have a chance to fuck this up bodes pretty well for the odds of fixing it."

"I'll be damned." Chris wanted to mock Greg, but the sentiment was unexpectedly astute. "You might be on to something."

"If I talk long enough, I usually stumble onto something."

"Do me a favor and stumble outta my house," Chris said as the two men shook hands and then hugged. "I've gotta take a shower."

Chris pulled away but Greg kept a firm grip on his hand. "On the off-chance I'm wrong, and things don't work out…stick around. It's been good to have you back."

The touching moment was enough to blunt their customary sarcasm.

"Don't worry man," Chris said. "If things don't work out this time, I'm just gonna keep trying."

❖

For a change of pace, Senada decided to be grateful for a trip to a hospital. The impending procedure was enough to warrant a heart attack, but there was no use in stressing out about it. The relative upside was she'd get an answer for the biggest question of the prior 48 hours. While she'd normally be peeved by pre-surgery food and coffee restrictions, Senada didn't need either one. She was wide awake, and, in spite of searing nervousness, her appetite was nearly non-existent.

Senada had never been under general anesthesia, but she'd hoped it would bring about good sleep. The ceiling of her bathroom got most of last night's attention, out of worry about what might happen if she'd strayed too far from the toilet. Any food she'd consumed found its way back out within an hour. Water was the only thing she could trust. During a lull in the action, she'd read every word on a pregnancy test box, yet it remained sealed. Cold feet decided it was best to outsource the job to Dr. Lawson rather than add another significant worry to an already extensive list. Waking up consisted of peeling herself off the floor and gathering the few things she might need to get through the only predictable part of the harrowing day ahead.

At least a detailed copy of the itinerary made it easier to plot out every possible opportunity for distress. The pre-surgical procedure would be simple enough: a few jabs in the arm, including a blood test that might change a few lives. But recovering from general anesthesia for a few hours would be quite the undertaking. Noise-cancelling headphones, a sleep mask, and a meticulously assembled playlist were imperative. Once every necessary item had been haphazardly shoved into a canvas tote, Senada looked out of her bedroom window and across the street, just in time for a clear visual of Chris rushing to the Nova.

The engine's rumble reached her ears before he'd even closed the door, conjuring visions of being picked up for school almost every morning since their junior year had begun. It would've made more sense to be waiting in the driveway when he pulled up, but then she'd miss the view from her favorite vantage point.

When she reached the front door, Chris met her and took the tote bag from her hand. "How're you feeling?" he panted as she walked past.

Before she could answer, Chris was beside her, both hands on one of hers, in an overreactive state that brought a smile to her face. He opened the passenger door and guided Senada into the seat. When he got behind the wheel, a persistent side eye was already burrowing into his temple.

"What?" he wondered.

"What's your deal right now?" Senada covered her curving lips with a hand, careful not to giggle too noticeably.

"What's my deal with what?"

"You're acting strange," she accused.

"I am not." Chris backed out of the driveway and the five-minute drive began.

"You walked me down the steps and opened the door for me."

Chris petulantly scoffed at the implication. "I'm being, uh, caring. Being a, ya know, a gentleman."

"Bullshit," she chafed. "I'm not having open-heart surgery, Chris. It's a routine procedure." At a red light, Chris clutched the steering wheel. Senada rubbed his forearm until his grip relaxed a little. "I'll be fine. I promise."

"That's not really a promise you can make," he exhaled.

Senada was humored by his level of concern, a welcome distraction from the anxiety she was barely quelling. Checking on Chris was a way for her to crawl out of life's quicksand.

"Alright," he relented. "How about a compromise?"

"What do you have in mind?"

"I'm going to tell you that I'll back off, and we'll both pretend I'm telling the truth."

With uncertainty around what it would look like to restore their bond, especially after potentially Earth-shattering news, a mutually silly moment had come at the right time. "Deal."

They parked in the vast lot of South Nassau Hospital and, to Senada's surprise, Chris allowed her to carry the tote bag, walk through the facility's sliding doors, travel up to the Women's Center, and register without hovering at every turn. After a brief wait, a nurse called Senada's name.

"I'll be here when you come out," Chris said, unaware of how far removed he sounded from his restless body language.

"Hey, keep it together," she teased. "Between the surgery and the recovery, I might not be coming home until tomorrow." His gaze lowered for a split second, and Senada immediately supported his cheek with her palm. They locked eyes and shared a kiss of recalibration. "I'll call you as soon as I get back to my phone. I can make that promise."

Senada winked and Chris nodded as she followed the nurse through a pair of heavy automated double doors that clunked to a close behind her. As if the sound were a signal, her smile eroded. Analytically placing one foot in front of the other was the only way to keep her breathing from becoming too shallow. The nurse led Senada into an examination room and gave the green light to change into a hospital gown and sit on the gynecological chair. Her shaky legs were relieved.

The next twenty minutes played out as designated by the itinerary. The blood test started an internal countdown until her mother's ghost would burst into the room and admonish Senada's carelessness while basking in being right all along. Until then, Senada had to endure an ultrasound before the procedure could begin. Dr. Lawson's arrival butted it on Senada wondering how it might feel to be rendered unconscious. A chance to stop thinking for a couple of hours sounded therapeutic, but she couldn't rule out the many other thoughts that might come along for the ride — questions around being mom, foreclosure proceedings on the shop when she couldn't afford a child and a dream, and how Chris might react to the news.

Every thread took her into increasingly implausible scenarios, from learning she was having triplets to finding out she'd been under anesthesia for the last five months, and Chris had never actually come back.

Dr. Lawson barged in on Senada's psychotic break, wearing a stony, expressionless face while scanning a series of papers.

"Well," Dr. Lawson said without looking up from the clipboard.

"Well, what? Is something wrong?" Senada asked out of formality, already convinced of the outcome. She was pregnant and she knew it. "Just tell me, Doc."

Dr. Lawson sat on a rolling stool and wheeled the ultrasound toward the chair. "Tell you what?"

Senada hesitated, straining to get words out. "I, uh, just... the way you were looking at the... and you said 'well' like something was...'"

"Are you feeling okay, Senada?" the doctor queried.

"Definitely not," she admitted instantly.

Dr. Lawson squeezed gel on the transducer and lifted Senada's gown without missing a beat. "What's on your mind?"

Senada watched Dr. Lawson's every nuanced movement as the cool gel was diligently smeared across her abdomen with a guiding hand. She wondered if the doctor was playing coy until she could find the best way to deliver the news. "Alright, everything looks good."

Senada's trust issues had stopped being picky. "Good, as in…?"

"Oh, sorry," the doctor whiffed. "I mean there's nothing preventing us from moving forward. The anesthesiologist should be with you shortly to talk through the procedure in more detail and make sure you know exactly what to expect." Dr. Lawson moved toward the door.

"Wait," Senada interrupted. "That's all you found in there?" she asked like her body was a foreign land being discovered for the first time.

"Yes." The question was enough to turn Dr. Lawson around and bring her back to the stool. "You seem surprised."

Senada's windpipe was already tightening, and now words were choking her. "I thought… maybe…" Senada reset and restarted. "I've just been so sick lately and barely able to keep anything down and I couldn't remember my last period. I thought I might be—"

The silence allowed Dr. Lawson to get caught up to her patient's implication. "You thought you were pregnant?"

Senada could only nod.

Dr. Lawson inquired further. "Were you hoping to conceive?"

The nuanced amendment was enough to beckon tears from Senada's eyes. She couldn't wipe them away fast enough to stem the tide of sadness before another wave was on its way.

"I don't know," she whimpered. "It feels like that's the sort of thing I should know. I mean, I should be sure about something like that. Right?" Senada looked up at the fluorescent lighting. "What's wrong with me?"

Dr. Lawson slid closer to Senada. "I've been on this side of that question for a long time. Long enough to tell you, with one hundred percent certainty, that there is nothing 'wrong' with you." Dr. Lawson stood returned to the door. "If you want, we can continue this discussion after the surgery. Until then, give yourself a break, okay?"

Senada nodded, unsure what more there could be to discuss, but grateful to have talked about it at all. Telling Chris how close they'd come to forming a trio would be difficult enough. A dress rehearsal was helpful. In the meantime, she was relieved to have an answer without having to ask an even more difficult question. Fear and doubt had pummeled them enough. Senada wasn't sure how much more they could take.

33

According to Chris's logic, it was permissible to deceive Senada, so long as it might bring her some peace of mind. And lying was even easier because she'd already seen right through him. There was absolutely no way he was going to be calm until she called to be picked up. The best-case scenario was already under way.

After extensive trips to the mall and grocery store, Chris lugged multiple shopping bags through Senada's front door. He even called in the calvary, which sped down the block and pulled into the driveway just in time.

Lex hopped out of the shop's van. "I cannot wait to hear how you came up with this plan!" Lex shouted while greeting him with a hug. "It's from one of those 90s movies she loves, isn't it?"

The notion made Chris hesitate and wonder if he'd subliminally plagiarized his ruse from someplace else. "If you help me, I'll tell you whatever you want," he compromised. "I need to turn this place into something that will bring Senada nothing but good vibes and peace. And since you spend every day with her in a place she created, I figured you might have the answers I'm looking for."

Lex took a prideful look at Chris's exasperated face. "You've made a wise decision coming to me with this."

"I hope so," he exhaled.

"Let's do this!" Lex exclaimed, punctuated by a hearty slap on his shoulder in playful condescension.

The next two hours were a hastily coordinated activity. While a typical man might've found it overwhelming to try and make a woman feel better without an instruction manual, Chris had a wealth of resources at his disposal, and years of experience by Senada's side during low moments. He knew her favorite bath bomb, the scents she preferred to keep nearby when she was seeking comfort, and the fabrics she most enjoyed against her skin. He'd combed every aisle of Bath & Body Works until he'd found cucumber melon lotion and a candle advertised to smell like biscuits and gravy. And while he wasn't equipped to cook any of her favorite foods, he'd purchased enough extra ground beef, roasted chicken, and potatoes in various forms to make up for the mistakes he was likely to make. There were enough sweet chili Doritos and sweet tea to put her right back in the hospital if her portions went unregulated. Though alcohol was against her recovery plan, Chris procured a six-pack of Stellas just so she'd see them in the refrigerator and know he hadn't forgotten.

All of his instincts told him this would be impossible to pull off without Lex. It didn't take long for Senada's colleague to reward his intuition. Seconds after he'd considered placing rose petals on the floor leading to the bathtub, Lex talked him out of it, citing Senada's deep hatred of the gesture. In her eyes, purposefully stepping on the remains of flowers was the antithesis of romance.

In what felt like an instant, Lex had transformed Senada's living room into an abundance of every color conceivable by the human eye. Nearly every smooth surface was covered with flowers that Lex informed him were daffodils, asters, dahlias, magnolias, and something called ranunculus, a name he Googled for fear she'd made it up to mess with him.

After stocking the freezer with Senada's favorite mint chocolate chip ice cream, Chris caught a glimpse of the kitchen windowsill, and the four small blooms facing where the morning sun had been. To punctuate the endeavor, he spun each pot until the bloom faced him.

Lex's voice entered the kitchen before she did. "We're all set!"

"Are you sure?" he worried.

"Would you be able to tell if something was missing?" she taunted.

"Touché," he chuckled. "I can't thank you enough, Lex. Seriously."

"Damn right you can't," she winked. "Senada's gonna love this so much."

"I hope so." Chris wished he was more confident in the future outcome.

"I'm gonna clear out the trays and take the van back to the shop." Lex said on her way out of the house, leaving Chris with his fears. He walked nearly every square foot once more, admiring the risk he'd taken. On his way past the bathroom, he discovered one more plastic bag had been left behind. It would've been tragic to forget dinner candles.

They were small, round containers filled with wax and a short wick, but something about them captivated Senada whenever they'd made a late-night jaunt to their favorite Mexican restaurant. Since the establishment no longer existed, Chris called every restaurant in the area until he'd found one willing to sell him the candles, albeit at a significant markup.

The surprise was worth holding back for as long as possible, and the medicine cabinet was the most viable hiding spot. Chris stacked the candles on the bottom shelf until he ran out of room. After a bit of rearranging, the shelf above had enough room for the rest of them, but a pink-and-white box put an abrupt end to the effort. He dropped the remaining candles in the dry sink and took a closer look without touching it: a pregnancy test.

Immense confusion clouded his vision, and he tried to amass the pieces of the past few days. The intense nausea, the noticeable fatigue, and the uncharacteristic mood swing stood out in a different way. But he couldn't imagine Senada would keep something so significant from him. Their recent conflict had been rough, but it didn't seem to warrant withholding something of this magnitude. Though it shed some light on the intensely out-of-character response she'd had in his home.

The box was still sealed. Senada had either taken a different test and already disposed of it, or she hadn't taken one yet. In either instance, a house remodeled into a botanical garden wouldn't stand a chance of easing what might be going through her mind. The mere likelihood could've been enough to send her off the deep end. Chris couldn't fathom how much it must've taken for Senada to hold back something like this.

He closed the cabinet delicately while cursing aloud and kicking himself for putting Senada's worst fear into view. Add on the concern over being abandoned again, and Senada might've felt more alone than ever. He held himself responsible for so many of her worries. Retrospectively, the floral gesture seemed trite.

There was a lot to say. But first, there was a lot to hear from her. The first step would likely prove to be the most difficult: he needed Senada to talk to him. And if there was any chance of receiving her clearest perspective, Chris had to remove every reason for her to retreat. An even bolder idea came to mind. Under these new circumstances, it was a risk worth taking.

Chris sprinted out of the front door and ran down the stairs up to the hood of the reversing van. He slapped it with both hands, startling Lex. Chris reached the driver's side door as she rolled down the window.

"What the hell are you doin'?!" she shouted.

"I need one more thing from the shop." Chris gasped for air as Lex waited for clarity. "I need the mail."

34

Although she'd never gotten high, Senada imagined anesthesia recovery to be a fair equivalent to the experience. She was sleepy enough to be barely awake, yet awake enough to be unable to sleep. The nurse could've told her a week had passed since the surgery, and Senada would've believed it without a second thought. When lucidity returned, her cellphone screen confirmed only a day had passed since she'd entered the double doors.

Her senses pinged in a new way as the recovery room's dim lighting eased her waning numbness. Dr. Lawson even sounded different when she re-entered and greeted her recovering patient.

"How are you feeling?" asked Dr. Lawson, more chipper than Senada was prepared to accommodate.

"Like I got hit in the stomach with a baseball bat," she replied. Bluntness served as a sign of progress.

"That's normal. But you can breathe a little easier. The procedure was successful." Dr. Lawson handed Senada a grip of papers. "Here's your recovery guide. We'll schedule a follow-up appointment in a couple of weeks, but you need to take it easy until then."

"Got it." Now that her body was on a path to normalcy, Senada split her attention between the stress of being away from the shop and the potential strain of her relationship with Chris. But domestic problems were a nuisance she literally couldn't afford to bother with. The landlord, the nursery, and her customers wouldn't give a shit about a doctor's orders. "Can I go?"

"Not so fast," the doctor insisted. "Do you have any questions?"

Senada held up the papers. "It's all in here, right?"

Dr. Lawson tucked the charts beneath an arm and sat beside the bed. "Maybe not. You had a few other concerns before the surgery."

The last thing Senada wanted was a reminder of everything she'd said and thought over the last few days. If there was a type of anesthesia that could induce amnesia, she would've taken a double dose. "Can we save that conversation for the follow-up?"

"Sure," the doctor replied with obvious reluctance.

"Is there anything else?" Senada strained to sit up. "I need to call my ride."

"You're good to go, but unless I'm mistaken, your ride's been in the waiting room all morning. Smooth-shaven, brown-eyed guy with a few grey strands who was asking about you to everyone in scrubs that he could find?"

His ability to warm her heart was as pleasant as it was embarrassing. "That sounds like him."

"We'll talk soon, Senada," Dr. Lawson said as she neared the door. "Take care of yourself."

Under a nurse's guidance, Senada was wheeled through the heavy double doors and into Chris's care. He couldn't decide whether to trust the nurse to get Senada to the entrance or take over the effort. Chris sprinted to retrieve the car as soon as the outside air touched their skin. Senada waited patiently as he pulled up in the Nova, a standout vehicle among the modest sedans and minivans idling outside. He was back to being his old overbearing self, but this time, his consideration was welcomed and necessary. Along with exhaustion and stress, moving didn't feel too good. The sooner Senada could get in bed, the better. If Chris could facilitate the transition more quickly, she would happily embrace his helicopter parent approach.

It didn't require full consciousness for Senada to notice something was different about him. Chris held her hand with a care she hadn't experienced before. He stared at the road with heightened alertness, and at the red lights, he checked on her while pretending to look elsewhere. His eyes explored more deeply into hers. Answers would've been nice, but she wasn't in the headspace to ask questions. Some things didn't need to be understood.

But his mind was obviously someplace else, and withholding thoughts and feelings was not what they needed. At the final red light, Senada succumbed to curiosity. "What's on your mind?" she asked while rubbing his arm.

Chris departed momentarily, to a place she couldn't find. "I want you to be okay."

"I am," she reassured. "Everything went fine. No more cysts."

"Are you sure everything is fine?" he said with an ominous tonal shift.

Senada backtracked, reminded of the whirlwind they'd endured a week ago. It would be understandable for Chris to have a hard time moving past it, especially since they hadn't really talked about it before the cemetery trip. The surgery had gotten in their way, allowing them to go through the motions in mutually assured distraction.

"I know we've got a lot to talk about. And it should've happened sooner." Senada was so caught up in finding the right way to address her uncanny behavior, she hadn't noticed they were already in her driveway. She clutched Chris's arm before he could get out of the car. "Wait."

"What is it?"

"We should talk about this before I go inside. Because once I go inside, I need to focus on recovering. I don't want things to be up in the air between us. After the way I acted that night, if you wanna walk away, I'll understand.

But I need to say my piece and clear things up. And you can make up your mind from there."

Senada waited for a response, but Chris offered little beyond a slightly open mouth and a blank stare.

"Alright, listen. When I found out about the job offer, I panicked. It was scary enough to let you leave when I was the one who'd pushed you away. But we were finally on the same page. And the thought of you leaving again made me go…let's call it…temporarily insane." Senada kept rambling, figuring Chris would step in at some point. But she couldn't handle the quiet. Silence wasn't a good sign. "And I know I blame a lot of things on my mother, but for once, something wasn't her fault. To be completely honest, I think it has to do with—"

Chris raised both hands like she'd pointed a gun at him. "Wait, hold on."

"I'm serious, I really think—"

"Senada, please just stop while I—" He delayed, then started again. "What are you talkin' about right now?"

Senada took a resetting breath. Her thoughts were clear, and she needed to get them across. "The night of our date, I know I was completely out of my mind. There's no excuse for it. I'm not even gonna try to make one up. All I can say is it'll never happen again."

"Wait, wait, wait." Chris stared at the steering wheel. "*That's* what you wanted to talk to me about?"

"Well… yeah. It was a pretty big deal, and we never really talked about it."

"I don't care about that!"

"I do!" Senada shouted back, startled by the echo inside the Nova. "We keep talkin' about trusting each other and not being afraid to talk like we used to. That means we should talk about it."

"But I don't understand." Chris closed his eyes and rubbed his temples, navigating the pivot in their discussion. "I thought that *was* you being fearless."

Senada repositioned herself, prompting a gritty moan. "I don't understand what you're saying."

"I kept something major from you. And I should've told you right away, but the truth is… I'm the one who was afraid. Your reaction was strange. And it was one of the more fearless things I've ever seen you do. Would you really take off all your clothes and confront me about what I really wanted if you were afraid?"

Senada had been so accustomed to her impulses being wrong, she hadn't considered such an action could ever be assessed another way. Her intuition was rarely an ally.

"I guess I never really thought about it that way." Senada looked at her lap in a half-assed effort to conceal her smirk. "Wait," she wondered, "then what did you think I wanted to talk about?"

Chris regressed and Senada braced for a confession. "I thought you wanted to talk about possibly being…pregnant," he said, cowering before Senada could locate the right reaction.

Her anxiety went into overdrive. "How did you know about that?" She couldn't wait another second for an explanation. "How?!"

"I found the test in your bathroom," he confessed.

Senada was more furious than her fragile state could contain. "What the hell were you doing looking through my bathroom?!"

"Okay, now *that*, I actually have an explanation for."

"I'll bet you do." Senada got out of the Nova as fast as she could, with little thought to the intense pain resonating throughout her torso. Chris got out and ran around the car to reach her.

"Don't touch me!" she hissed before his hand could touch her arm. Senada held tightly to the railing and lumbered up the stairs.

"Alright. But can you listen to me for a second?" he appealed.

"I'm not in the mood for more bullshit. We're talkin' about trying to find trust again, and you're sneaking through my shit while I'm in the fuckin' hospital?!"

"It wasn't like that at all," he insisted. "Please just slow down before you hurt yourself."

"I don't need your help!"

"Wait. Before you open the door, can we—"

"No!" Senada shouted as she pushed open the door.

The scent lifted her soul from her body. It was a deeper aroma than flowers could provide on their own. Vibrant colors glinted against her pupils with the help of the morning sun. Senada was moving but didn't know how. She floated from one corner of the living room to another, appreciating every petal and every blossom, every stem and every leaf.

The more she moved, the more flowers she recognized, throughout the living room and kitchen and hallway and bedroom. The atmosphere flooded her spirit with all the reasons she'd opened a shop in the first place. The escape she'd created had found its way into her home; a feat she'd never thought possible.

She turned to Chris, who was still standing in the doorway. "You did this?"

Chris nodded and added a cautious smile.

"How did you…?" she asked, pretending the answer mattered. Reminded of her health, she slowly moved toward Chris, who hurried to meet her for a careful embrace. His comforting arms gave her permission to feel a lot more than gratitude. Years of withheld tears poured out of her eyes and onto his shoulder.

"I couldn't think of the right flower to represent how I feel about you, about us, about what I want for our future," he said. "I spent a lot of time on Google, and even with Lex's help, I couldn't make up my mind. So… I got every flower I could find."

"Chris…it's beautiful." Senada pulled back enough to look at his face.

With a solemn hand, Chris moved strands of hair away from her face. "I know I didn't find out the right way, but if the test comes back positive—"

"It won't," she interrupted, shaking her head in a way that more closely resembled a shudder. "I'm not pregnant." Chris's body tightened in an instant. "Are you disappointed?"

Chris brought both of her hands to his chest. "What?"

"We never talked about it before, but if you were hoping to, ya know, be a dad," she said, wandering aimlessly through an emotional wilderness, in desperate need of water. "I just didn't want you to be disappointed."

Chris kissed her lips, then her forehead. "I could never be disappointed with you." They embraced again, then he pulled back. "Wait. Are *you* disappointed?"

Senada turned away and weaved through the plants to sit on the couch. "I don't know."

Chris sat next to her, accurately sensing that more was on the way.

"I've spent my entire life assuming the worst thing I could do was be a mom. But then… for the few days I thought I might become one, I stopped being so afraid of it. And now, knowing I'm not pregnant, the idea of motherhood feels different. I mean, I know what I'm used to feeling, but now, that feels foreign to me. I wish I could give you a clear answer, but I can't." She clutched his hand, unwilling to look up. "Is that alright?"

"Senada, I'm not going anywhere. Not again." He wrapped a hand around hers. "I'll follow you wherever you go. And no matter who or what you decide to be, I'll love you every step of the way."

"One day, I'm going to believe I deserve you," she sniffled.

"I'm willing to wait," he jested before receiving Senada's grin followed by playful fist in the gut.

35

While Senada's recovery period didn't quite count as a vacation, they'd treated it like one. Atop the priority list were pain management and rest. Beyond that, they'd completed a pact to watch TV shows that only one of them had never gotten around to indulging. Much to her delight, Chris pored through every season of *Homeland*, while he watched anxiously as Senada enjoyed *The Wire*.

Per her orders, Chris had been restricted to one attempt at a cooked meal per day, frozen pizzas notwithstanding, before she could make them order in. Most importantly, Chris had become a personal assistant whose primary responsibility was to keep Senada from calling Lex at the top of every hour.

With only one day left before her return to the shop, Chris was eager to make the most of it, which meant waiting on a Sunday afternoon in a crowded Friday's to satisfy her craving for their signature Jack Daniel's sauce. When asked what she'd like to have with it, Senada simply shrugged and raised both arms. It was the best laugh he'd had in days.

The safest bet was to give her a panel of options, so he got every entrée that came with the sauce, assuming anything extra would become leftovers. The server returned with two full plastic bags of steak, ribs, chicken and salmon, with multiple side dishes for them to enjoy. The smell of macaroni and cheese, mashed potatoes, and seasoned fries emanated from the foil containers and filled the Nova with a delicious scent blend.

Driving along Sunrise Highway, Chris was struck by how far they'd come in a life that still seemed short. Others might look back on over a decade apart and assume it was valuable time that had been wasted. But there was so much more for them to experience together. If only he could get her to relax long enough to enjoy it. Most of their laughter had been muted by concerns around the shop and the perils of her finances. He'd already maxed out Senada's threshold for moral support. She'd resorted to brushing it off as symbolic and useless.

Chris kept trying, even when she wasn't willing to receive it. A greasy meal teeming with saturated fat could only do so much, but at least he knew she'd enjoy it.

The botanical garden in Senada's living room thrived, due in no small part to it reminding her of work. It wasn't as lucrative as selling to customers, but it created space for Senada to feel more like herself.

Chris walked in on her violating the doctor's orders, sitting at the kitchen table amid scattered papers. More notably, the phone was at her ear and tears were in her eyes.

He sprang into action, placing the bags on the counter before rushing to comfort Senada without knowing the cause of her distress. She didn't react to his arrival, focused instead on whoever was on the other end of the call.

"Alright," she said, barely getting the word out. "Thanks for letting me know." Senada hung up and slid the phone away as if she'd discovered it was radioactive.

"What's goin' on?"

"Can you sit down for a minute?" she asked, her eyes firmly shut.

Chris obliged and sat on the opposite end of table. A hand covered most of her face as she rubbed her forehead hard enough for the tiny veins in her hands to bulge.

"Right after you left, I got this weird call from my landlord."

Chris cleared his throat and bleated, "Weird how?"

"He thanked me. Which is an odd thing to do to someone who's almost two months behind on their rent." Senada spoke like the lead detective in a whodunit film, laying out who'd committed the crime and how they'd almost gotten away with it. "But when I reminded him of that fact, he informed me that not only am I not behind, but I am, in fact, paid out for the remainder of my lease."

Chris took in her harsh stare but remained unflappable. "Okay."

"Then another weird thing happened. I called the nursery to put in my order for August and make sure they'd received a payment for June. Apparently, they'd received payments for June *and* July, and there's a credited balance to cover me through Christmas."

He listened while meticulously crafting an argument, in anticipation of Senada's inevitable demand for one. But she wasn't done.

"I started to get a little worried that Lex had maybe misplaced a decimal point and tapped out the little money I had left. But I applied a little pressure, and eventually she copped to it."

"Copped to what?" he bluffed.

"Chris…"

"Hey," Chris reached across the table, moving the useless papers to the side to hold her hand. "Look at me."

She obliged, appearing more annoyed than relieved. "You can't do this."

"You can't stop me," he said, mildly amused.

"I mean I can't *let* you do this for me."

"I don't think I was clear." Chris shifted from a jovial romantic to the serious businessman he'd once been. "I didn't handle it this way because I was afraid to ask for your permission. I never intended to ask for your permission. Because, and this will probably be the only context that I'll ever say this: I don't care what you want."

The gesture was grand, and her reaction was understandable. But Senada had provided him with things that were more valuable than any amount of money. She'd reintroduced him to the parts of himself that he'd forgotten to pay attention to. Parts that he'd forgotten were valuable. And she was the part he cared about most. Taking care of Senada was akin to breathing, less of a decision and more of a necessary act.

"How can I claim to love you and just stand by while you're stressed out over something I know I can help with?" he asked rhetorically. "You've known all along that I could help. But you weren't going to ask."

Senada sat back, clearly wishing he was wrong while knowing he was right. "You know how much I hate it when people try to take care of me."

"I know," he replied. "And I'm not taking care of you. I'm making it easier for you to take care of yourself. If paying a few bills allows you to enjoy the thing you're most passionate about, then that's an easy choice to make. Because if you're doing what you love, then you're being the person I love."

Senada sank her head into her hands and let tears run down her cheeks. He moved to console her, but she waved him off, clarifying that she wasn't ready to be comforted.

There wasn't much left to say. Chris resumed what he'd planned on doing before things had taken a somber turn. He prepared plates for them, careful to include a little of every option, and brought them to the coffee table. As he scoured the cabinets for glassware, Senada embraced him from behind and soaked the back of his T-shirt with her tears. Her rushed breathing intuitively slowed his pulse. Senada was as safe with Chris as she'd always been. It was a vital truth, and he was willing to remind her of it, every day, if that's what it took.

EPILOGUE

Five Years Later

No matter how many seasons Senada spent kneeling in its soil, the garden would always belong to Barbara. And while the flower choices had changed over the years, Senada had no interest in redefining the precious space. Impatiens were still present, in various shades of red, white, deep purple, and bright orange.

Due to Chris's urging, Senada contributed some character of her own. The aesthetic became more balanced with the inclusion of green ferns and hostas, and bleeding hearts brought a unique bloom style to the palette. Senada's inherited responsibility was to maintain the garden's integrity as if Mrs. Mitchell was still over her shoulder and assessing her progress.

The honk of an unfamiliar horn pulled Senada from the side of the house and into the driveway. A sleek, silver minivan pulled up. Chris looked a lot more enthusiastic to be behind the wheel than Senada ever would've expected.

"Didn't you say we'd get a minivan over your dead body?" she shouted with a beaming smile.

"Today is not a day for bringing up old comments!" Chris replied.

"You said it yesterday," she bantered as they met in front of the new car and kissed.

"This car is proof that today is about the future," he stated.

"You think we needed more proof?" she lamented.

"Speaking of things we said in the past," Chris started, "I thought you were going to take it easy today."

Senada pretended to be reminded of her original plan as she looked down at her dirty apron. "I guess my nerves got the better of me."

Chris placed a hand on her hip, tying a finger around a beltloop of her jeans. "Give yourself a break. This is all new for us. There's no right way to handle the stress."

"Tell me again that we can do this," she sighed.

"We can do this, Senada. Trust me," he chimed. "Do you think I would've sold the Nova and bought this thing if I wasn't sure we could do this?"

"It's not like you gave it up never to be seen again. Greg is here every other day showing it off like he's the one who restored it."

"We agreed on him having full custody, but I still get supervised visits," he joked. "You wouldn't get it."

"You're absolutely right." Senada rolled her eyes and nudged him away. "I have no interest in getting that."

From the corner of her eye, her old home stood out. Despite selling it three years earlier, she'd been programmed to look in that direction like it was where she was supposed to go at the end of every day. On more than one occasion, she'd parked the shop's brand-new van in the wrong driveway. In one instance, she'd made it halfway up the steps before realizing her key wouldn't work.

Senada looked up the block instead, soothed by Chris's steady hand rubbing her lower back. She checked her watch, then checked it again to make sure she'd seen it right the first time. "What time do you have?"

"I'm sure it's the same time on my watch as it is on yours." Chris pulled her closer, likely sensing how badly she needed a distraction.

"I think I'm going to wait in the garden," she said, pulling away. "Let me know when they get here."

Chris grabbed her arm and guided her back to his side. "You're not gonna be any less anxious in the garden. Especially when you're pretending to pass the time. Let's just hang out right here for a little while."

Senada checked her watch one more time. "They're late."

"I know, honey." Adding a pet name was egregious, especially one she hated so much. But it was a solid diversion attempt. Chris brought out the big guns.

"You know what I really want right now," she opined, "Doritos."

"Shocking."

"Or maybe some Combos. Do they still make those?"

"Senada."

"Fine," she ceded with a furrowed brow.

Despite her resistance, Chris had been right all along. Nothing could distract from what awaited them. His certainty was annoying, and in the year of buildup to this day, she'd expressed that opinion often. But in truth, his indestructible stillness provided the balance Senada desperately needed.

What she hadn't expressed was how peaceful she'd been. With every passing day, Chris reminded her how beautiful it was to know that a day could start and end without any concern about whether she'd do something that might risk their connection. No matter how unpredictable the world might be, their relationship had become a lighthouse amid the storms.

A corporate black sedan turned onto the block. It rolled slowly enough down the street for Senada to make out the sound of tire treads peeling away from the pavement. She held Chris's arm and sensed the nerves he'd worked so hard to hide for her sake.

The car pulled to the curb and two women, one brunette and one redhead, in dark pantsuits were inside. Their warm smiles allowed Senada to finally relax a little. One brunette woman stepped out and approached the couple. The other woman opened the rear passenger door, but she didn't get out.

"Good to see you again, Mr. and Mrs. Mitchell. Today's the big day."

Senada smiled and sensed her husband doing the same. "You've done this before right?"

"A few times, yes."

"If you could provide any tips on how to handle it, I'd really appreciate it."

The woman looked at the car, then back at Senada. "Just… take your time."

Senada nodded pensively as the brunette signaled the redhead.

A pair of tiny white sneakers peeked out beneath the open car door and landed on the curb. A stiff breeze swept away a mop of messy blonde hair, revealing a pair of gripping blue eyes on a little girl half Senada's height. The redhead guided her across the lawn by the hand.

Senada clasped her hands together and looked at Chris, who was already wiping tears as they walked across the lawn to meet them halfway.

"Mr. and Mrs. Mitchell," one woman said, "I'd like you to meet… Hayley."

Senada knelt in front of the little girl, supported by Chris standing over her shoulder. "Hi Hayley," she said. The name was the most beautiful sound Senada had ever heard leave her lips. "My name is Senada, and his name is Chris."

"Hi Hayley." Chris waved and did his best to reach her eye level.

Hayley stepped forward timidly, clutching a plushy dolphin in one hand, and picking at her lip with the other. "Hi," she said through nibbles on a fingertip.

Senada looked more closely at the four-year-old, recognizing the blossoms on her sky-blue shirt. "Do you like flowers?"

Hayley nodded in two big up-and-down motions.

"Do you know what flowers those are?" she asked while pointing at Hayley's shirt.

Hayley looked down at the shirt, then shook her head.

"They're called sunflowers. And they're really pretty. I have some. Do you want to see them?"

Hayley looked up at the redhead and received a nod of approval, then slowly stepped toward Senada's open hand. Hayley looked at it for a few seconds, then up at Senada, then Chris, then back at the hand.

Without warning, Senada discovered how long she could hold her breath. Just when she thought she might faint, Senada felt the clasp of Hayley's tiny saliva-soaked fingers.

"Ready?" asked Senada. Hayley nodded and Senada led the way toward the garden. Chris followed, close enough to make sure Senada knew he was right behind her.

With every tiny step, Senada walked toward a life she'd never thought possible, beside the only man she'd dare to live it with.

LOST

IN

THE

SUN

AUTHOR'S NOTE

In the life of a fiction writer, one of the more frequent questions and assumptions I encounter is how much, if any, of my work is autobiographical. As you might expect, my consistent response, "None," receives either skepticism or disappointment.

A dear friend recently reminded me of one of the best Author's Notes I've ever read, from John Green's *The Fault in Our Stars*, in which he writes, "Neither novels nor their readers benefit from attempts to divine whether any facts hide inside a story."

In the same way some things are valuable because they are temporary, I believe some stories are impactful because they are fiction. Any truth you might seek from my stories, I promise, lies within you.

Life is a complex entity, and I write about love through the perspective of a broken man, using pieces of my most honest self to tell a story about what I've learned from being brave enough to love, and fallible enough to lose. I hope you can use some of my pieces to better understand your own.

STORY PLAYLIST

Music is an integral part of my writing process for every story, but for *Lost In The Sun*, it was even more important. I thought it might be fun and insightful to open a window into my process and give readers the chance to explore the creative space I occupied for this tale.

Embers – James Arthur

Catching Feelings – Annie Tracy feat. Leon Thomas

Diamonds in Teal – Lucky Daye

Why – Sasha Keable

Sexual Love – Maeta

Forévà – Tayc

Damage – H.E.R.

Never Knew – Kenny Lattimore

Hell With – Ni/Co

DFMU – Ella Mai

ACKNOWLEDGMENTS

This book was a different and much more difficult experience than my first, which made my supporting cast even more valuable. Their consistent and impactful presence was vital to my personal peace, a key component of my creative process.

To my son, you have been my true north for sixteen years and counting. One day, I hope the sacrifices I've made will make sense to you, and you create a life throughout which you won't have to take the same risks as your dad. I want you to take risks beyond my wildest imagination. Don't be like your father when you grow up. Be yourself. I promise you won't regret it.

To Megan, thank you for being such an incredible and insightful editor, blending your talent with my vision, and slowing down the freight train that I often become. This book is in your hands, which means I kept my promise.

To Heather, thank you for being a thoughtful and considerate creative and human being. Your ability to turn my words into images that encapsulate my stories is unmatched. I am already excited to finish my next book, so I can slide in your DMs and ask you to make another cover for me. Keelah Se'lai.

To the amazing women of my Saturday Writing Group, thank you for being a beautiful and timely respite for longer than any of us probably could've predicted. Our creative space is valuable beyond what even my words can express. I am honored to be at the helm, and I appreciate each and every one of you.

To Megan's Thursday Writing Group, thank you for the abundance of feedback, insight, and laughter. Even on the days when it was hard to put one word in front of the other, your efforts and support pushed me through.

To Chuy, your work ethic and balanced approach to life is a continuous inspiration to me, someone who works himself into the ground until my spirit breaks. Thank you for reminding me not to take myself or anything else too seriously. And thanks for introducing me to new gadgets. I never thought I would become a pen snob, but then you showed me the Ridge Pen. My first drafts will never be written with anything else.

To Kelli, your persistently engaging and moving playlists manage to pull my attention away from (almost) anything. Thank you for keeping me aligned with my ideal creative energy, relying on nothing more than my scattered thoughts to curate music that blocks out the noise within me.

And to my readers, thank you for joining me as I explore the questions of life and love that resonate most within my soul. Not only do I hope you've enjoyed this story, but I hope you've taken something from it that's worth carrying into the life and love you experience long after you close this book.

JARED GLENN is an author and editor from Long Island, New York. He has written for every medium, from screenwriting and theatre to poetry and essays. In addition to his award-winning debut novel, *Left Unsaid*, other works include *The Repass*, a stage play which was featured in the Bishop Arts Theatre Center's 1619 Project Play Festival, *Baldwin/Kennedy*, a stage play, and The Absence of Light, a nonfiction essay series about the various bonds between art and love.

Connect with Jared —

IG & Threads: @write.and.fear.nothing
TikTok: @writeandfearnothing
Substack: The Absence of Light